BRANDED

SAFFRON A. KENT

FOREVER
NEW YORK BOSTON

Copyright © 2025 by Saffron A. Kent

Cover design by Daniela Medina
Cover images © Shutterstock
Cover copyright © 2025 by Hachette Book Group, Inc.

Forever
Hachette Book Group
1290 Avenue of the Americas, New York, NY 10104
read-forever.com
@readforeverpub

First edition: October 2025

Forever is an imprint of Grand Central Publishing. The Forever name and logo are registered trademarks of Hachette Book Group, Inc.

The publisher is not responsible for websites (or their content) that are not owned by the publisher.

The Hachette Speakers Bureau provides a wide range of authors for speaking events. To find out more, go to hachettespeakersbureau.com or email HachetteSpeakers@hbgusa.com.

Forever books may be purchased in bulk for business, educational, or promotional use. For information, please contact your local bookseller or the Hachette Book Group Special Markets Department at special.markets@hbgusa.com.

Print book interior design by Marie Mundaca

Library of Congress Cataloging-in-Publication Data
Names: Kent, Saffron A. author
Title: Branded / Saffron A. Kent.
Description: First edition. | New York : Forever, 2025.
Identifiers: LCCN 2025021655 | ISBN 9781538775448 trade paperback | ISBN 9781538775455 ebook
Subjects: LCGFT: Romance fiction | Novels
Classification: LCC PS3611.E67458 B73 2025 | DDC 813/.6—dc23/eng/20250506
LC record available at https://lccn.loc.gov/2025021655

ISBNs: 9781538775448 (trade paperback); 9781538775455 (ebook)

Printed in the United States of America

CCR

10 9 8 7 6 5 4 3

BRANDED

To everyone who craves adventure and dreams about getting swept off their feet by a rugged (and bossy) cowboy. To my husband, who swept me off my feet the first time we met; and my Adora, my dream come true.

CONTENT WARNING

The contents of this dark romance book may be triggering to some readers. It contains explicit sexual content and a morally gray hero. Here is a complete list of trigger warnings:

False identities
Stalking/obsession
Revenge/retribution
Abduction
Drugging
Blackmail/coercion
Forced marriage
Violence
Bondage
Knife play
Gunplay
Dubious consent
Nonconsent
Off-the-page domestic abuse set in the past
Off-the-page murder set in the past
Parental grief

PROLOGUE

IN HIS LETTER, he told me to wear something white.

It sounded like an innocent enough request, something to help him recognize me when he saw me for the first time. But now that I'm here, standing at the door of the café, it feels like…

I'm a lamb being led to slaughter.

I know. I *know* I'm painting a pretty dramatic picture. And I'm not someone who gives in to drama at all. In fact, I try to stay away from it as much as I can. But this has to be the most dramatic thing I've ever done.

By *this*, I mean going to meet a man that I've only ever talked to in letters.

Actually, no. That's not what I'm doing. I'm not going to meet *some man* that I've been talking to in letters for the past six months.

I'm going to meet a man who up until last Friday called Montana State Prison his home.

So, basically, I've come to this café, wearing a white dress with a delicate lace overlay and a swishy skirt, to meet a convicted felon that I've only ever talked to using the prison pen pal system.

Well, *ex*-felon, since he got out on parole last week.

In any case, I'm stupid, aren't I? This is stupid. More than that, this is *dangerous*.

So what if it's broad daylight and the café, from what I can see through the glass door, looks fairly busy? He was the one who picked this place and told me to meet him here. Maybe there's a reason for that. Maybe he's got his friend watching, ready to pounce on me when I go to the bathroom. Maybe there's a secret hallway in this establishment that he can drag me into as I'm coming out of the restroom.

Except...it doesn't feel dangerous. Just terrifying.

So despite myself, I push open the door and step inside.

For the first few seconds, my vision seems blurry. All I can make out is fuzzy colors and shapes, but slowly things become clear. I see red leather seats and wooden walls. I see people, tons of them. Almost all of the tables are occupied, and there's a long line of customers at the counter, ordering and waiting for their coffee.

Witnesses. It should be a relief.

But how on earth am I going to find him in a churning sea of broad shoulders and tall bodies, most of them wearing Stetsons? Maybe if I was taller than my five-foot-two frame or wearing heels rather than these stupid schoolgirl Mary Janes, I'd be...

Oh, but wait a second.

I don't need to worry about finding him because I think that *he* found *me.*

See, there's a man.

In the center of all the chaos.

Still and unmoving.

He has a trucker's cap on, black with an intricate *R* in white. Even though he's sitting down and there's no way for me to know, I can tell he's the tallest man in here. At least he's certainly the broadest, given how his shoulders span and block the top of his high-backed chair and almost all of the potted fern behind him.

And I think, I *think*, it's him.

Even though he looks...wrong. He looks nothing like what I imagined.

I never thought he'd be this large, busting out of his black T-shirt. Or that his skin would be so tan that you'd guess he'd been living under the open, free sky rather than inside a concrete block and barred windows. I definitely never thought his face would look that… merciless.

The upper part of his face is hidden, courtesy of the cap, but whatever I can see makes me think that like his body, his face is also a study of superlatives. Like that stubbled jaw of his quite possibly is the most angular jaw I've ever seen. And his lips, dusky rose, may be the fullest set of lips that I've ever come across.

It's laughable to call him beautiful, given how aggressively masculine everything about him is, but that's what he is. Beautiful. Ruggedly so. Like the mountain range that you can see wherever you go in Montana.

Before I can really question my thoughts, I'm walking toward him.

While my footsteps are drowned by the din of the crowd, I can hear my heartbeats clearly. There's a stampede in my chest, wild heart, wilder beats, and strangely, I think he can sense it from afar.

I'm sure he's watching me walk over.

Again, I don't know how I know this because his eyes are hidden by the cap he's wearing, but I do. I can feel their gaze, all heavy and charged, through the space. The intensity only growing the closer I get to him.

Until it feels like a calloused hand sliding over my skin. As soon as I reach him, he looks up and that hand tightens.

No, that phantom grip around my neck turns hot.

Branding me.

Much like his pitch-black stare.

For some reason, I gave him blue eyes in my head. Probably because of the ranch he said he grew up on, and when I think of a ranch, I think of blue skies and vast lands.

So, no, he does not look like the man from my dreams at all.

And yet, *yet*, somehow, he feels so familiar too. I don't know how to explain it, but I feel it. God, I'm losing my mind, aren't I? Shaking my head slightly, I begin, "You're…" I grab the back of the chair I'm standing by and steady myself so I can continue. "Are you…Bo? Bo P-Porter?"

Something flickers through his face.

Or so I think.

It comes and goes so quickly that I can't be sure. But I think it was in response to my question, my voice. It makes me feel stupid— and relieved—because what if he isn't the man I'm supposed to meet at all? I probably should've thought of that before I walked over.

Maybe that's why my belly has been churning and I'm hearing alarm bells in my head.

"I, ah, I'm sorry." I clear my throat. "I'm supposed to meet a Bo Porter here, and uh"—I dig my nails farther into the chair as his charcoal eyes turn even more intense—"but maybe you're not—"

"Peyton."

I think I break my nail at that.

At *his* voice.

If my voice caused a reaction in him—and I'm not saying that it did—his voice makes my knees go weak. It's all deep and scratchy. Like along with keeping him locked away, someone locked up his voice too. And this is the first time he's spoken in the eight years since he got put away.

I try not to dwell too much on that. Or the fact that once again, his voice is nothing like I'd imagined. I imagined it to be deep but not bottomless deep, and I imagined it to be rough but not so gravelly rough. The more important point is that he is the right man after all.

He is my Bo.

Well, not *my* Bo, but still.

The confirmation doesn't put me as much at ease as I'd hoped. Not only because of these conflicting feelings that I have about him but also because he said *Peyton*.

I throw him a jerky nod. "Y-yeah. Yes. Peyton. I'm...Peyton."

I give him a shaky smile to make it look convincing before quickly looking away and taking a seat at the table. But then my gaze lands on something, and my heart that was already pounding in my chest speeds up even more. There's a teapot and a cup sitting in front of me, presumably for the person he was waiting for: me.

Along with a muffin.

More than the tea, that muffin does it for me.

It makes my pounding heart squeeze and my voice go wobbly. "Is that...? That's tea." I don't wait for him to reply before saying, "And that's...that's a strawberry crumb muffin. It is, isn't it?" I swallow thickly, still staring at it. "It's so hard to find. It's... I told you that."

Finally, I look up.

Only to find he's gone rigid. Which, if I'm being honest, isn't all that different from how he's been all this time, spine straight, shoulders back, his eyes alert. But now I notice the muscle in his cheek beating like a heart.

Almost like my heart.

I'm not sure what it means, though.

I'm not sure what *any* of this means, him ordering me tea because I told him I like it better than coffee and that if I can find a strawberry crumb muffin at a café, then that's the only thing I'll eat because they usually have the apple crumb but very rarely the strawberry crumb.

Except that my heart is racing and there's a mad rush in my veins.

"In my letters. I told you what I like to order and...and you..." I fist my hands in my lap. "How did you know I'd even show up?"

Because I never said yes.

Three weeks ago, he sent me a letter saying that he was getting out and that he'd like to meet me here. But I never replied. I didn't know what to say when seeing each other wasn't ever in the cards. I mean, he's the man I met through the prison pen pal system.

Prison.

Our lives were separated by metal bars, and up until this morning, I had all the plans of never having them merge. Of forgetting about him and being smart. Like I always am about everything.

But here I am.

"I didn't," he says back, his gaze just as steady and analyzing as ever.

Fuck, his voice.

It's a truth serum. Has to be. Because words spill out of me without my own volition. "I'm sorry about that. For not writing back. I just... I got scared."

"Not enough."

"What?"

"To stay away."

Again, I can't read his tone.

I can't read him, period. But maybe I'm not supposed to. Not yet.

Even though we've known each other on paper, this is our first meeting. So maybe it's supposed to go like this. Maybe he's supposed to be all aloof and dark, wrong-looking—no, just *different* than what I'd imagined—and make me shiver and shake.

Maybe his dark and not-blue eyes are supposed to feel like a branding iron.

"I wanted to see you," I say. "I couldn't..."

His voice goes even lower, if that's possible. "You couldn't what?"

My belly trembles in response. "Stop myself."

And in turn, the muscle in his cheek jumps.

Clearing my throat, I continue, "I hated the idea of you just sitting here, waiting for me to show up and I...I couldn't take that. Not after everything we've shared and—"

"Get up."

"What?"

"Get up," he repeats on a deep growl. "And leave."

I draw back. "I-I'm sorry. Did I—"

He leans forward a little, his eyes fiery.

It happened in an instant, too, the charcoal going up in flames. As if there's a fire inside of him and it's raging.

God, he looks so intimidating like this.

That's what it is, isn't it?

That's why he looks so wrong and different and whatnot.

It's the fact that he appears threatening, sitting here, with his large and muscular body and a brutally beautiful face. All this time that I talked to him in letters, he never felt dangerous. Even though I knew the man I was corresponding with was a convicted felon, I never once felt afraid.

I do now.

"Get the fuck up and go."

I flinch. "But I don't understand."

"You don't need to."

My hands begin to tremble. "I—"

"This was a mistake."

This time, I go still. "Mistake?"

His nostrils flare, his face cruel. "Yeah. So what you need to do is listen to me and leave." He growls again when I don't move, "Now."

"Is it…" I twist my fists in my lap as my cheeks burn and burn and *burn*. But not enough to stop me from asking, "Did you picture someone d-different? Than me."

Because if I was picturing him in my head all this time, he was probably picturing me too. While *I* found him different from my imagination, he probably found me different too.

And *different*, when it comes to me, is the code word for *lacking*.

Guys usually don't find me or my body very appealing. A body made of pasty flesh and jiggly curves. A body less than perfect.

So maybe I *should* listen to him and leave.

But again, instead of doing the smart thing, I sit there and let him peruse me. At my question, his burning stare moves to my blond hair, which is in a braid that falls to my waist. A few loose tendrils caress the base of my throat where I can feel my pulse fluttering under his gaze. He takes in my trembling chest, the wide square neck of the dress he asked me to wear exposing more than I'd like.

He stays there for a bit before coming back up to my face.

But when it's over, his perusal, it feels like it went too fast. Like he was taking me in only to dismiss me more than to study me.

"Yes."

So there it is then. His only answer harsh and curt.

Like me, he *had* pictured someone different.

Except he still made my heart race with both ecstasy and apprehension. While I probably repelled him.

So, at long last, after six months and within two minutes of meeting the man I dream about every night, I force myself to be smart and do as he says.

I get up, the scrape of the chair dragging against the floor sounding louder than the noises of this crowded café.

Feeling weak and dejected—completely opposite of what I felt when I walked in—I walk out.

And promise—God, I promise—to forget about Bo Porter.

PART I

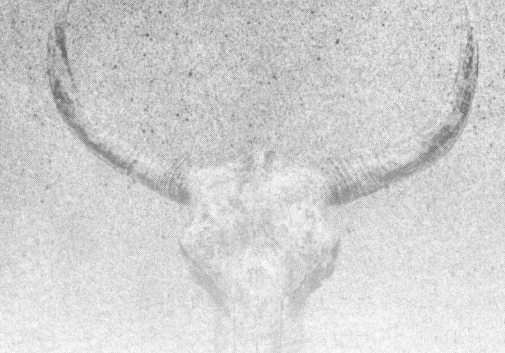

CHAPTER ONE

To: Bo Porter
From: Peyton Turner

Dear Mr. Porter,

I hope this letter finds you well.

My name is Peyton Turner and I'm a freshman at Montana State University. I'm writing to you because we're covering reformation in the prison system as a part of our sociology class and for my final assignment, I'm supposed to write an analysis paper. My professor has encouraged me to interview an inmate and use the information to construct my argument. I'm telling you this up front because I want you to know that I may use parts of our letters to write my final commentary, and I don't know how you'd feel about that. So if you'd rather not do this with me, I won't blame you.

This is my first time using the prison pen pal system so I'm not an expert, but from what I understand, most people enter into this looking for a connection, a friend, maybe; someone to talk to. And I want you to know that even though this is part of an assignment, I can be your friend for a little while.

In fact, how about to get the ball rolling I tell you a secret?

Or rather something embarrassing about myself.

So this assignment? It's not a regular assignment. As in, I'm doing this for extra credit. Because I just got my midterm grades and they're bad. They're so bad that I'm failing and my professor provided me with this option as a last-ditch effort.

So there.

Can I tell you another secret?

Or again, simply a fact. This time, non-embarrassing, though.

My professor gave me a list of inmates in the pen pal program and I chose you specifically because in your profile you mentioned that you liked to read. So I figured we'd have something in common.

So what's your favorite book?

For me, it will have to be Wuthering Heights *by Emily Brontë. The rocky moors; the hero in love and driven by revenge.*

Have you read it?

I read somewhere that the library at Montana State Prison is in need of a major overhaul. That makes me sad, because reading should be as accessible as breathing, in my opinion.

In any case, I hope I hear from you but if not, that's okay too.

Hope you have a great week!

Until next time (hopefully),

Peyton

PS: Okay, I have one more thing to confess and I've been thinking about it and I just didn't know—still don't—how to bring it up except to just bring it up so: I googled you. Well, I googled all the names on the list my professor gave me but still. For full disclosure: I typed your name in the search bar, clicked on the first article that came up. It was just a short piece in the Post. *I didn't cyberstalk you, and I won't. I understand what an absolute violation of privacy it is and just because you are where you are, doesn't mean that I can poke around in your life. But I... I don't know how to put it delicately, but I just wanted to make sure that you were, for the lack of a better word, safe. Or rather your crime was (as safe as any crime can be). I realize that I could've just asked you but then… I mean, it just makes good sense to be careful, right? Not to say you're a bad person, or that the crime you were found guilty of defines you. It doesn't.*

Oh gosh. I'm not making much sense, am I?

Forget what I already said. All I'm trying to say is that I was doing my due diligence and I'm sorry I violated your privacy.

———

To: Peyton Turner
From: Bo Porter

Peyton,

I can't remember the last time I received a letter.

Or sat down and wrote one.

And now that I am, it makes me feel like I'm back in school or something but anyway.

First, you don't need to address me as Mr. Porter. That makes me feel a little too old and if I had to choose between being back in the classroom and lying on my deathbed, I'd rather be passing notes during lessons.

Second, what kind of a moronic professor encourages their student to make contact with a convict?

But then again, you don't sound real smart either if you think a drug bust is safe. Just because it doesn't sound as awful as aggravated assault or attempted murder doesn't mean you want to meet a junkie in a dark alley.

Or maybe you do.

I've got no idea what college kids are up to these days.

I will say though that whatever you're up to doesn't seem to be all that good for you, seeing as you're failing and your last-ditch effort—as you called it—is asking for help from a convict that you stupidly think is safe.

Bo

———

To: Bo Porter
From: Peyton Turner

Dear Mr. Porter,

Did you call me and my professor stupid?

It looked like you did but I'm still giving you a chance to rectify your mistake before I go ahead and call you rude.

Or worse, an asshole.

Because I believe in reserving judgment and second chances. I believe in reformation (what a coincidence, given I'm writing a paper on that). Which means just because someone is stuck behind metal bars on a drug charge doesn't automatically mean he's a rude asshole.

Even though that rude asshole also implied that somehow I'm the one making wrong life choices because I failed one class.

For your information, I happen to be a straight-A student and this is the first time I've gotten anything less than an A-minus. Not that it's any of your business.

I can't believe I was all broken up about violating your privacy. Clearly, I wasted my apology.

A piece of advice: If writing letters makes you think you're in school, then maybe you shouldn't sign up for the pen pal service.

I'll find someone else for my assignment.

Have a good life.

Sincerely,
Ms. Turner
(Yeah, that's right. It's Ms. Turner to you.)

———

To: Bo Porter
From: Peyton Turner

Dear Mr. Porter,

Maybe there's something in the water at Montana State Prison.

Or maybe all of your fellow inmates are as rude as you because after weeks of writing letters to them, I have yet to receive a single response.

My best friend, in a moment of pure hilarity, pointed out that maybe it's you. You're keeping them from writing back to me because you're a jerk. But I'm not that full of myself to think you'd go to such lengths to mess with me.

But that's not the point.

The point is that, unfortunately, I'm stuck with you.

Look, I'm not going to beg but I'm also not going to let you keep me from getting a passing grade either. I tried to get my professor to change my assignment but apparently, he's had it with me so I need to write this paper if I want to pass. So I'm willing to start over. But I need an apology from you in order to do so.

An apology, in case you didn't know because I don't think you would, is a regretful acknowledgment of an offense or failure.

It's only fair.

Until next time,

Ms. Turner

To: Peyton Turner
From: Bo Porter

Peyton,

I didn't think I'd hear from you again.

But I guess there's something to be said about desperate times, desperate measures.

Now, your best friend, she sounds smart. What grade did she get? I bet she managed to scrape a passing grade.

Maybe I did keep them from writing back to you. But maybe I did it because I was doing you a favor. Because from what I remember, most guys in the pen pal program have at least been charged with one count of assault and robbery. Doesn't sound very safe to make your cut. So then instead of demanding my regretful acknowledgment of an offense—thanks for the definition, by the way—you should be acknowledging your gratitude.

In any case, I'm not good at issuing apologies.

But since you're unfortunately stuck with me, the least I can do is admit that I was a jerk to you and vow that I won't be one in the future.

How's that?

And if we're doing this, you need to know that I don't like repeating myself. So how about you stop calling me Mr. Porter and we can get this show on the road because I'm sure as hell not calling you Ms. Turner.

Bo

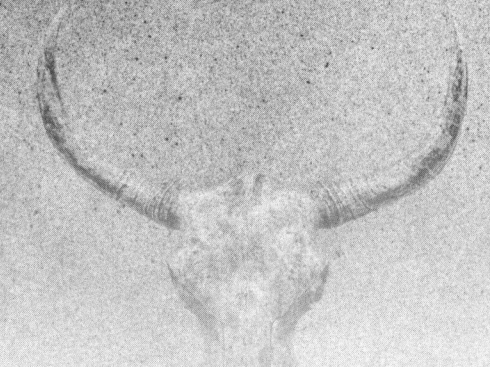

CHAPTER TWO

I'M NOT PEYTON TURNER.

I'm only pretending to be her.

This isn't the first time, though. I've been doing it ever since she and I were both five. It started out as a fun trick with both of us dressing up like Ariel for Halloween one year and having people confuse us as twins and graduated to me going to her cello lessons because she hated the cello and I loved it, or attending detention at school in her stead so I had a place to go when things at home became too much to bear.

We're not, though.

Twins, I mean.

We're not even sisters.

Just best friends that somehow look very similar to each other.

We both have the same shade of golden blond hair and blue eyes. We are the same height, and growing up, we had the same build too. If we kept our heads down and didn't make too much eye contact with the other person, we could usually fool them into thinking we were the other.

But then around the age of seventeen or so, things changed.

Puberty that I thought had passed me by caught up to me, making my body bloom differently than hers. It made my hips become rounder and my thighs all pudgy. My boobs went from a B cup to a full D, and my belly developed rolls. But Peyton remained as svelte and slender as ever.

So these days I pretend to be her in other ways.

I fool her boyfriends on the phone for fun because our voices are still freakishly similar and because pretend-flirting is the only kind of flirting I'll let myself do and she knows that; I take her big brother's calls when she isn't in the mood to hear him lecture her about her low grades and partying. And sometimes when guys call me or send me their dick pics because somehow I always attract creeps, Peyton is the one to fend them off because I have zero experience with them. Oh, and I also do her extra-credit assignments—which I think are kinda fun—that include writing letters to inmates in prison. Or just one inmate.

She in turn goes shopping with me, and she did my hair and makeup today before I went to see said inmate. Nothing crazy, though; I wouldn't let her, but still.

"Are you seriously not going to tell me what happened today?"

That's her.

Peyton. The *real* Peyton Turner.

Cross-legged and with a determined look on her face, she sits in the middle of my bed among her scattered clothes and an open suitcase. Usually when she has that look, it's very hard to deter her from the path she's chosen.

But I still try.

I hold a bikini in each hand and wave them at her. "Which one?"

She keeps her focus on me, though. "Seriously?"

"Yes." I nod and wave the bikinis again. "If you don't tell me which bikini you want, there's a very high chance that I'll pack the wrong one and then you'll be the one regretting it. Because you're the one who has to wear them."

She gives me a look before asking again, "Tell me what happened at the café today."

There's a pinch in my chest that I ignore and forge ahead. "Fine. The red one it is."

I throw the other one aside—the one that I definitely know she'd pick; we've been friends forever, so I know what she likes— and I make a show of folding the little strings on the red one before reaching out to dump it in her suitcase. As expected, she gasps and scoots over to me on her knees, then snatches the bikini away.

"Are you insane?" she exclaims, putting her hands on her hips. "The red one makes me look like a lobster."

I purse my lips in response, trying to hold back a chuckle.

Narrowing her eyes, she extends one hand, palm up. "Give me the gold one."

I dutifully hand it to her, still trying to control my mirth.

She shakes her head as she grumbles and dumps the bikini on top of the neatly folded clothes in her luggage. "I'm going on a vacation with my boyfriend and even if I plan to break up with him when I get back, I still want to look my best. It's the Bahamas, okay? Who knows when I'll get the chance again to go to the Bahamas and get away from here?"

Yes, she is going on a vacation; and yes, she plans to break up with Ben.

I don't blame her; he's kind of an asshole who thinks the whole world revolves around him and his father's ranch. I told her to break up with him the first time I talked to him on the phone. But she kept it going because she needed a date to the New Year's party a few months ago, and because she knew it pissed off her brother.

Peyton has a difficult relationship with her brother, with her whole family, actually.

Well, the truth is that she hates her family. And she has reasons. Reasons I fully understand because I have a difficult relationship with my family too.

"Told you to make your choice," I say in a singsong voice.

Her response is to poke her tongue out at me.

I chuckle, and together we finish packing for tomorrow. She leaves early morning, and gosh, I'm going to miss her. She asked me to go with her now that our finals are over and the summer is upon us. But I refused. I didn't want to be the third wheel, even though their relationship is going to expire soon. Plus, this summer I was planning on doing something that I've been wanting to do for a long time now. Usually I always have extra classes or extra shifts at the library or whatever job I'm working, but this year I told myself that I'd put on my big-girl panties and do it.

Plus, I also wanted to…write to him.

I wanted to be here so I could get his letter every Friday and write him back that very day. So it gets to him in time on Tuesday. But then he said he was getting out early and asked to meet me and…

My heart twists.

It twists and twists until I think my heart is becoming a tight and throbbing fist rather than just an organ.

I try to ignore the pain in my chest because tonight was supposed to be all about spending time together, watching movies and eating popcorn and ice cream and anything else with too much salt or sugar in it. But I guess I've been doing a poor job of it because as soon as we zip up her suitcase and put it aside, Peyton grabs my hand, pulls me to sit on the bed beside her, and gives me a grave look. "Okay, on a scale of 1 to 10, just tell me, how bad was it? With 1 being excruciatingly bad. The worst ever."

I meet her gaze and sigh in defeat. "Minus 394."

She opens her mouth before closing it and frowning. "Very random. Is that—"

"Bad," I explain. "That's bad, Pey. It's less than 1. It's less than 0 even. It's a negative integer."

She rolls her eyes. "You know how much I hate geometry, Riri. Why would you put me through that?"

Riri.

That's my name, or the shortened version of it.

My actual name is Reverie.

Reverie Bell.

"It's algebra. You… Never mind." I shake my head. "It was bad. Really bad; that's it."

She narrows her eyes. "What did he do?"

I open and close my fists in my lap. "Nothing. He did nothing. It's just…"

"It's just what?"

This time when I close my fists, I do it hard. I do it in a way that my nails, even though they're short and blunt, dig into my skin and make it sting. "It's just that I don't think he was expecting me. Or rather someone like me."

Peyton's spine straightens and her eyes grow angry. "What is that supposed to mean?"

Crap.

I shouldn't have said that. Definitely not to Peyton.

Peyton and I, we're more sisters to each other than best friends. We grew up together, see. In Black Rock, Montana.

Peyton's family owns a ranch called Wildfire—the second-biggest ranch in Montana—and my family worked for her. My mom was her nanny and my father was one of the ranch hands. Growing up, we were inseparable. We went to the same schools; we played together, studied together, spent all our time together. And when she and her mother moved away from Black Rock to Bozeman, my mom and I went with them.

Peyton and I have gone through everything together: difficult families that are more absorbed in their own affairs than us; school and classes; periods and teenage hormones; boyfriend drama—hers, not mine; and now college. While I excel inside a classroom, Peyton is more outgoing. She loves to party and live large, and I try to do everything I can to live as small as possible. I'm the rule-follower, and Peyton is a rebel. Despite our differences, though, we're two peas in a pod. I love her to pieces and would do anything for her.

Just as she'd do anything for me.

Including pranking boys who would call me fat in high school and teaching them a lesson.

"You know what," I say, trying to put her at ease, "just forget it."

She turns to face me, her features still set in anger. "Did he say something to you? Did he say something *rude* to you? Because I swear to God, I'm going to—"

I grab her arms and stop her. "Look, it doesn't matter, okay? It doesn't… He probably was expecting someone else. Someone who, I don't know, looked different than me." She takes a breath to say something, but I keep speaking: "Which is fine. I don't care. I'm happy with the way I look, with the way I am. I just don't need people to remind me and… I guess that's what threw me today."

That and the fact that I let myself do it.

I let myself go on an adventure. When I'm not the kind of girl who ever does that. I'm smart. I'm practical. I'm very, *very* careful. And there's a reason for that.

A very good reason.

But I ignored all of that, and for the first time in my life, I let myself go. I let myself be reckless. Like any other college freshman, I let myself flirt with boys—and not just pretend-flirting on the phone by impersonating my best friend. Granted, I was flirting with a convicted felon via letters while using my best friend's name, but still.

I just… I wanted to live for once.

And yes, part of the appeal was that I thought I'd never meet him in person, so this was a safe way to do something totally crazy. While the other part—the bigger part—was that I couldn't control myself.

Something about him, about his words, spoke to me.

There was some magic in them that I still haven't figured out. Or rather now that I've met him, I think it was fire. Hot, burning fire that I couldn't help but want to touch, want to be branded with; I don't know. All I know is that once I started writing to him, I didn't want to stop.

But of course that was stupid.

All of it was stupid, and honestly, I'm glad that it's over now. I can go back to my old life with classes, my job at the library, my other summer plans.

"You know you're gorgeous, right?" Peyton goes, breaking my thoughts.

God, I love her.

I also know that she's my best friend and she wears rose-colored glasses when it comes to me.

The truth is that I'm not gorgeous. I'm far from it. I'm too short and rounded. My ass and thighs are too big but my waist is too small, making it impossible to find pants and skirts that fit. Actually, I can hardly find shirts that fit, either, with my too big and too disproportionate chest. So I always end up with baggy jeans and a loose sweatshirt, clothes that I hate but are necessary. Not to mention, my nose is too small, and my eyes are too big. My chin is too jutting out, and my lips are too swollen. I have too much hair that I can never hope to tame, so I always just braid it, and my skin is too pasty and pale.

I'm either too much or not enough.

But it's fine.

It's not a big deal.

Do I sometimes wish I looked different? Of course. Everyone does. We all have things about ourselves that we'd change. Mine just happens to be my body. Peyton would never agree with me, but that's okay. That's the testament of her loyalty, so I give her a fond smile. "I know."

"And he's an asshole for making you feel anything less," she adds.

I swallow, my heart clenching. "I know that too."

Peyton studies my features, her brow furrowing in concern. "I mean it, Riri. You're beautiful. You're amazing and I love you. And if that convicted criminal *asshole* can't see that, then it's his loss, okay? He doesn't get to make you feel this way."

That, I completely agree with.

He absolutely does not.

If I really think about it, I don't even *know* him. All we did was write some letters to each other over the course of a few months. And maybe there were thirty-seven letters in total, and *maybe* I shared things that I've never really shared with anyone. But that doesn't mean I actually know him. I can sit here and write out a list of things I don't know about him. I mean, I hadn't even seen him until this morning, and five minutes in his presence was enough to let me know that I never wanted to see him again.

So Peyton is right; he doesn't get to make me feel this way.

This time my reply is filled with conviction. "I definitely know that."

She bites her lip before saying, "Although, I can't help but think it's my fault."

"What? Why?"

She sighs. "Because I encouraged you. Right from the start. Because when you came to me and said that you were exchanging letters with a felon who, by the way"—she raises her hand—"you started writing to because of me and my stupid grades, I didn't stop you. I didn't caution you like you always caution me. I didn't say, 'Think, Riri. He could be an asshole. He's in prison, for God's sake.' No, I said, 'Go ahead, Riri; live a little. Flirt it up. Be bad.' Because I said it would be good for you to actually act your age for once and not live like an old woman just because of"—her eyes go big—"you know *who.*"

I do know who. And again, it's a testament to her loyalty that she wouldn't say exactly who because I don't like to talk about her.

My mother, specifically.

She is right; I do live like an old woman—all cautious with no adventures—because of my mom. Because of all the choices she made in her life and how it affected her. And by extension, me.

Peyton was also right when she said she was the one who encouraged me when I came to her and told her that my letters had somehow become so much more than a mere assignment. In fact, when I told her that he wanted to meet me and that I wasn't sure about it, it was she who said I had to do it.

I *had* to or I'd regret it.

But I don't blame her, no way. What happened to me today was not her fault. She was being a good friend like always. A friend who wants more for me than what I allow myself.

"Hey"—I turn to face her fully now as well—"are you crazy? It's not your fault."

"But—"

"No." I cut her off again. "Absolutely not. I've always done your assignments and I will always do your assignments. In fact, I probably should've done them all in the first place rather than letting you try to handle some yourself." She rolls her eyes, but I continue, "So if we really think about it, it's *my* fault. Because if I had done your assignments like always, you wouldn't have been failing your midterms and you wouldn't have needed to do the extra work."

She shakes her head. "But I should've stopped you. I should've said something."

"You couldn't have stopped me," I tell her.

"But—"

"No, Pey, you couldn't have. No one could have. I *wanted* to do it. I *wanted* to write to him. And I may have been scared in the beginning but I wanted to go see him. *God*, I wanted that so much. I…" I swallow thickly. "I may have told myself that I wouldn't go, that I was still making up my mind, but I knew, deep down, that there was no way I wouldn't go see him today. There was *no way* I could be anywhere other than at that café at eleven."

I know that now.

I knew it the moment I walked in and found him sitting there with his trucker's cap on and his eyes pinned to the door. That's how he found me so quickly, wasn't it? Because he was watching the door.

He was *waiting* for me.

He even ordered my favorite things. I want to be so angry at him—and I am—but every time I think of that tea and that muffin, it makes something clench in my belly. It makes my heart even achier. How could he be such a complete jerk but then do such a thoughtful thing? No, actually, he turned into a jerk after he saw me.

Gosh, he must've been so disappointed.

So utterly disappointed that the girl he's been corresponding with for the past six months turned out to be nothing like he imagined. Turned out to be so lacking.

"I really want to punch him," Peyton says, once again pulling me out of my thoughts.

I swing my eyes over to hers. "I know."

"Stupid fucking cowboy."

Despite myself, my heart picks up speed.

And at such a silly thing too.

Yes, he's a cowboy.

He has a ranch. I'm not sure where or what it's called, but I know there's a creek running through the middle of his land and he misses it. He didn't tell me that in so many words, but the way he talked about it made me think he did. Which again goes to show that I didn't even know him.

Not really.

In any case, it's not really a special thing, being a cowboy. This is Montana; this is cowboy country. Every other guy who lives here is a cowboy. I grew up with them; and to be honest, my—and Peyton's— experience hasn't been really great. I mean, my dad is a cowboy and her dad, too, and neither of them is a paragon of virtue or anything. In fact, they're downright evil. So again, he's not really special, and there's no need for me to go all shaky and weird.

Liar.

You know you have never seen a cowboy like him.

Even though he wasn't really in his element and hadn't even been a cowboy for eight years, I could still picture him out on the field, working the land, that big bronzed body of his weathering the sun. I could picture him wrangling a horse and roping cattle with those burly muscles. I bet he could tame a wild horse with only a look from his fiery dark eyes. Or he could stop a stampede with only the sound of his deep, rough voice.

But that's neither here nor there as I answer Peyton. "Yup."

"Of course he is," Peyton concludes. "I knew I hated cowboys for a reason."

Yeah. So again, all of this was really stupid, getting tangled up with a cowboy who also happens to be a felon. Which means I really need to stop thinking about him and move on with my life.

And that's why I declare, "Movie time! Let's stop talking about him and get our night started, shall we?"

She still watches me with a careful gaze. "Are you sure you don't want to come with me? Just to take your mind off of things."

"I'm sure."

"But are you, though?" she insists. "It's the Bahamas."

I chuckle. "I know, but I am. I'm just going to spend my time relaxing and maybe picking up some shifts at the library."

And doing that thing I always wanted to do.

"Ugh. Fine." Her shoulders sag. "I love you; you know that, don't you?"

My smile is a little wobbly. "I know. I love you too."

"You're amazing and gorgeous and beautiful," she says with a pointed stare. "Don't let anyone make you feel any less, okay?"

I nod. "Yeah."

She's right. Not about the being gorgeous part but about the part that no one gets to make me feel any less. Least of all a man named Bo Porter that I've only known for six months.

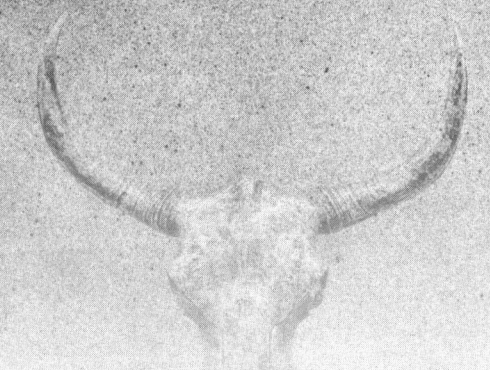

CHAPTER THREE

To: Bo Porter
From: Peyton Turner

Dear Bo,
You're right.
You're so not good at making apologies because that was a shitty one. And normally, I'd tell you to go away, but you already know I'm desperate and stuck so I'll accept it.

By the way, you also don't know that you should probably say please when you want people to do something for you. As it is, notice how I granted you your wish and addressed you by your first name up top. And since you're so unfamiliar with the proper etiquette, allow me to also tell you your response to this should be thank you.

As for my best friend, yes, she's smart and she's also none of your business.

Also, if—hypothetically—you did keep your fellow inmates from writing to me because you thought you were keeping me safe, let me tell you that you don't need to worry about me. I can take care of myself.

Anyway, please be advised that I'll be sending you a list of questions for the assignment with my next letter.

Until next time,

Peyton

PS: Look how I granted you another one of your wishes down here too.

To: Peyton Turner
From: Bo Porter

Peyton,

Thank you.

For granting me my wishes. And for that lesson in etiquette. I especially liked the one where you taught me to say please. Must've skipped school the day they taught us that. But then again, you already know I don't like school. Or reading for that matter. I know you thought that was something we had in common but sorry to disappoint you.

Reading's not something I did in my previous life. I could blame growing up on a ranch for that, but it was all me. I'd take mucking the stalls or mending fences over sitting still any day. Not a good thing when you're trapped behind bars with a bunch of guys who have more testosterone running through their veins than blood and have a history of a short fuse. Reading keeps you busy and from creating havoc. So it's more of a necessity than a hobby.

Anyway, thanks for the heads-up. I will be sitting on the edge of my seat for all your questions.

Bo

PS: So how'd I do? Am I polite enough for you?

To: Bo Porter
From: Peyton Turner

Dear Bo,
    So you're a cowboy.
    You never mentioned that on your profile but I should've known. All signs were there. You guys tend to be a little abrasive. I guess all that mucking and mending is injurious to good manners. I grew up with cowboys. Well, until we moved away to the city when I was eleven, but I know cowboys. In fact, if I had known that you were a cowboy, I probably never would've sent you a letter.
    But we already know I'm stuck with you so it's neither here nor there.
    So tell me about your ranch.
    Do you miss it? What's the thing you miss the most?
    I miss where I grew up too. Even though a ranch means cowboys and they aren't my cup of tea, I still miss the land. All that space, the rolling plains and the woods. The fact that I could get lost when and if I wanted to. I could walk and walk for miles and never see another soul. I could sit in my favorite spot and read for hours and no one would come bother me. I miss reading in my favorite spot. I guess that's the thing I miss the most.
    I'd go back if I could.
    But it's okay. I'm happy here too. I have my school, my books, my job. My life is good and safe, careful. Like I always wanted it to be. A little unadventurous but at least there are no cowboys. Or rather, the only cowboy that I have to deal with comes on a folded piece of paper, tucked inside a white envelope.
    Without further ado, please find the list of questions on the next page. I'm trying to write about the prison education system and I'm going to be honest, I absolutely hate sociology. And so even though I don't like you very much and don't care if you find my questions

annoying, I'm sorry for such a long list. I almost fell asleep writing it so I totally do not envy you for having to answer them.

Until next time,

Peyton

PS: Surprisingly, you're getting there. For an asshole cowboy, you're a fast learner.

To: Peyton Turner
From: Bo Porter

Peyton,

Who is he?

I'm guessing he's a cowboy. The one who made you live a careful life. Isn't that what you called it? A careful, unadventurous life. So who is it? An ex-boyfriend, your daddy?

Did he hurt you? What'd he do?

Because in my experience when a girl plays it safe, it always has to do with a man in her life. Is that why you can't go back to your ranch? Because of that asshole?

As for mine, I miss it, yeah, but not a favorite spot—although if I could call something my favorite spot it would be the creek running on the north end of the property—or something similar. I miss the real things, the everyday things. The dirt that gets on your boots, your clothes, under your nails; the smell of hay and leather; the splinters that get into your hands when you're mending fences no matter how good you glove up. The wind in my hair when Rebel, my thoroughbred, gallops through the fields, his shifting sleek muscles between my legs.

But it doesn't matter. I'm exactly where I'm supposed to be, behind bars and away from everything I'd ever known.

Anyway, I answered all your questions. They were annoying but you'll be happy to know I managed to stay awake through them. At the risk of sounding full of myself, I do think you'll scrape a passing grade this time around.

Bo

PS: Maybe all I needed was someone to teach me. And for a little college girl, you're a good teacher.

That was it.

That was the moment. When he asked me about my careful life. About who hurt me.

That was when something shifted inside of me. Of course, I didn't know it back then, but I know it now. That was the very first night when his words wouldn't let me sleep. I tossed and turned until I gave up and sat down at my desk to write him a response. To tell him things about me that I don't usually tell anyone.

Let alone a stranger I didn't like.

But he so casually asked me about it when most people don't care. I don't want them to, either, because I don't want to talk about it, but the fact that he could gauge things, read between the lines from miles and miles away, made me feel like he deserved an answer.

Not to mention, it was a good thing he was a stranger because the stakes were low and I was safe.

He made me feel *safe*.

So crazy but no less true.

And I realized today at the café that he had always done that before, made me feel safe, because at the time, he was doing the exact opposite. He was scaring me.

Which is why I'm doing this, I *think*.

Roaming the streets in the middle of the night when I should be in bed like the good girl I always claim myself to be. My roommate and best friend is passed out on our couch, but instead of going to bed myself, I'm just outside the café where we met, and I'm turning the corner to go to a motel two blocks down.

Because that's where *he* is.

Or at least that's where I saw him go earlier today.

I never told Peyton this because I knew she would've hunted him down and given him a piece of her mind, but when he demanded that I leave, I did, but I didn't go too far. I barely made it outside before I had to find my balance and catch my breath. Everything happened so suddenly, so unexpectedly, that my whole body was shaking. So there I was, leaning against the brick wall just outside the café, trying to find my bearings and willing this deep ache to stop, when I saw him leave.

Something possessed me to follow him, and I did.

To this very motel I saw him disappear into.

To this very motel I'm walking into now. Because I'm angry, okay?

I'm angry at him for behaving the way he did. For taking away my sense of safety. No man, not one *single* man, in my life has ever made me feel the way he did, all safe and cozy. Like I could tell him anything and he'd listen. And then he took it away like it didn't matter. Like none of the things we shared mattered. And maybe they didn't, not to him.

Maybe he just wanted someone to kill time with while he was stuck on the inside. Maybe it was all fun and games until he saw me and cast me aside because I didn't meet his expectations. But he isn't getting off that easy. Not until I tell him exactly what I think about him.

Stupid asshole criminal *cowboy*.

The guy at the reception desk greets me with a smile that I'm not sure I return with equal enthusiasm. "Hi, I'm here to see Bo Porter. Can you tell me what room he's in?"

"Sure, give me a second." I watch him type things into his computer before he shakes his head. "Uh, Bo Porter, you said?" I nod and he shares, "We don't have any Bo Porter currently booked in."

"Are you sure?"

He keeps looking at the computer screen. "Yes. No Bo Porter. Are you sure you got the name right?"

I don't know why, but his seemingly friendly and normal question makes something move in my belly. Something uncomfortable and heavy.

"Uh, I think so," I say, swallowing. "I met him at the café just two blocks down this morning, and…" *I stalked him and saw him enter this building*, my brain finishes for me. "Are you absolutely sure?"

"Yup," he says, watching me.

Again, there is nothing in his gaze that should scare me or make me feel not at ease. But I am scared, and I'm not at ease. I shift on my feet, my hands getting clammy. "So no tall guy wearing a trucker's cap with a fancy *R* on it?"

I see recognition go through his features as soon as I say it, but he responds, "No, I don't think so."

"You're lying," I say, surprising him.

Surprising myself.

I'm not confrontational. At all.

But this, I need to know.

"I don't…" He takes a breath. "Is there anything else I can help you with?"

"Tell me his name."

It seemed like the most important question to ask. For obvious reasons and for reasons I don't understand yet.

His eyes widen a little bit, but he says, "I don't know what you're talking about."

"You do know," I insist. "You're lying."

"I'm—"

"Look"—I lean over the desk a little and his eyes go even wider—"I understand you may not be allowed to give out this information. Believe me, I do. I understand. But I need you to do this for me, okay? I need you to tell me. I need you to…" I swallow thickly, my emotions sitting right in the center of my throat. "You don't know me but I'm very smart. I am. And I'm telling this to you so you know how stupid I've been. So, see, I've been writing letters to this man, right? For the past six months and I knew it was a bad idea. I knew it was crazy and insane and… And then he told me he wanted to meet me and so I went, right? But then he…"

I take a deep breath here, clutching the edge of the desk, trying to get myself under control. I wasn't planning on dumping the entire story on him, and in a way that makes so little sense. I was just… I wanted him to understand that I need to know.

It's imperative that I know.

I open my mouth to apologize, but the guy, looking really spooked and confused, blurts out, "Grayson."

"What?"

He glances over to the computer for a second before coming back to me. "Arsenal Grayson." I watch him going for the phone by the computer. "I could just give him a call and tell him you're here and…"

He says something else, but I miss it.

I miss it because I rush out of there. Even if I had stayed back there, I know I couldn't have heard him over the loud, *loud* pounding of my heart. The loud fucking rush of blood in my veins.

Grayson. Did he say Grayson?

He said *Grayson*, didn't he?

I need to get away from this place. I so fucking need to get away from here. I need to *run*.

So that's what I do. I start running as soon as I hit the pavement, my footsteps even louder than my heart now. My breaths exploding out of my chest, my skin sweaty and prickly and tight. So tight that it feels like I will burst out of my own body.

But it's fine.

It's fine because if I keep running, if I get as far away as I can from the motel, from where *he* is, I'll be okay. I'll be *alive*.

Oh God.

Oh God, I can't believe…

I can't *believe* this is happening. This is…

But he's Bo. He's *my* Bo.

He can't be a Grayson. He can't be… There has to be a mistake. He's not a Grayson. And he is *absolutely not* the same Grayson as the Graysons of the Rawhide ranch in Black Rock.

Because that would mean…

I don't know what that would mean. All I know is that if I don't get away, he'll kill me. He'll kill me because I'm from Wildfire ranch. It doesn't even matter that I'm not a Turner. He'll kill me simply because of my association, because the Graysons have vowed to kill every single one of us.

But again, I don't get it. I *don't*…

Then, in the next breath, all my thoughts explode and I burst out of my skin anyway because I hear him. I hear his footsteps. They're loud and thudding. *Pounding.* So much so that the ground shakes beneath them and I lose my balance.

And then I can't run anymore because he's on me.

His arm is locked around my waist like a shackle, and my back is pressed against his chest. The chest that I dreamed about a million times over the last six months and the one that I saw at the café today. The burly and broad and *oh my God, so fucking hard* chest that is leaving bruises on my body right now.

I open my mouth to scream, but something else entirely comes out. A ragged whisper, a plea: "Please, don't hurt me."

And then his big and rough hand closes over my mouth, and all hope for me is lost.

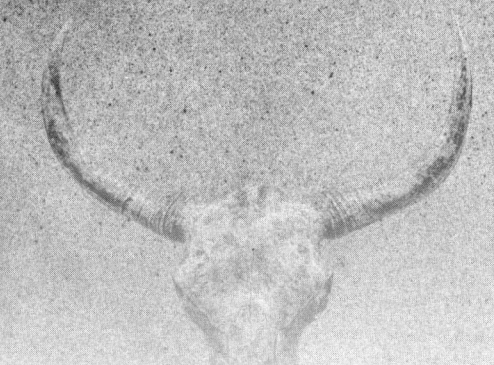

CHAPTER FOUR

To: Bo Porter
From: Peyton Turner

Dear Bo,
    It's 2:11AM and I can't sleep.
    I keep thinking about your letter. About what you asked. It was so surreal. I can't believe you noticed. *People usually don't. Not that I want them to but still.*
    I don't really talk about it or even think about it all that much. Because it's not going to change anything, but it's my mother. She's never been a good judge of character when it comes to men.
    Or rather just one man, my daddy.
    He isn't a nice man; he liked talking with his fists more than his words, and growing up, I watched my mother take the brunt of it. She also took the brunt of his infidelity, as well as his lack of attendance in my life. He'd come and go as he pleased, without a care for anyone. My mother, though, always waited for him. Always turned the other cheek, always treated him like he was the only man for her. I never understood why, except she'd say that she loved him, and you didn't choose the people you loved.

So I told myself that I'd never be put in a position like this: to fall in love with a cruel man.

I'd always be careful and smart; wary and cautious. Even if it meant leading a simple life. A life without adventure or twists and turns. Meaning no nights out, no partying, no going away to exotic places on spring break. Definitely no boyfriends. Honestly though, my best friend dates enough for the both of us and just by watching her I don't think I'm missing anything. But anyway, it's just me and my school and my job at the library. It's not the most exciting life but it's peaceful. It's exactly what I never had and what I wanted.

In fact, writing letters to an asshole cowboy behind bars is probably the most exciting thing I've ever done in my life. And good thing I did because your answers were really helpful. It pains me to say it because your ego's just going to grow bigger, but I do think I may be able to score a passing grade. Who knew that an asshole cowboy could teach a little college girl something? Although, I will say I'm not little.

If I didn't hate you so much, I'd ask you to teach me how to ride too. Because in my non-adventurous life, I've never ridden a horse before. But you know, I've seen people do it and read about it a lot so how different could it be?

Until next time,

Peyton

PS: I'm sending you another list of questions that are just as annoying as the last but only because I think I like you now.

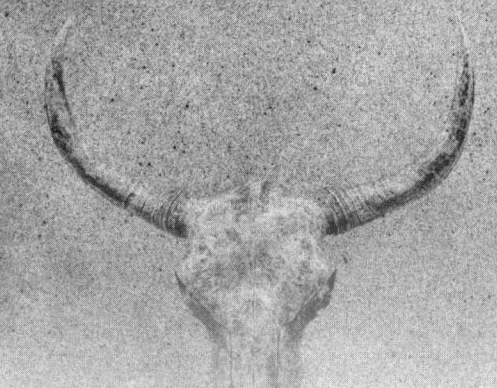

CHAPTER FIVE

I CAN'T SEE.

My hands are tied. My feet are tied too.

I'm lying on my side, and there's a throbbing pain in my shoulder. I'm trying to think why. I'm trying to think where I am. Then I try to move. My hands, my legs, my shoulder, *anything* that I can think of. Which is when I realize I'm in a box.

No, wait. I think…I think I'm somewhere else. Somewhere much scarier. Much, *much*. Because this thing that I'm in is moving. It's jostling me. Jolting and bumping and… Holy God, I'm in a car.

I'm in a *trunk*.

I'm blindfolded and all tied up in the trunk of a car, and I'm being *taken* somewhere. Oh, my *fucking God*! I'm being kidnapped. By Bo.

No, by a Grayson.

I am, aren't I? He's kidnapping me. He is… I can't breathe. I *can't*…

This isn't real. This isn't…*happening*. This has to be a mistake. This has to be…

I'm wheezing and thrashing and hitting my feet, my shoulder, my palms against the walls in an attempt to break free. Even through my mad panic, I know it's foolish, that I'll never be able to get free. Still, I keep doing it and doing it and *fucking doing it*. Until it becomes my downfall and drains out whatever energy I had.

And I slip away.

There's a head on the wall.

A bear's head. It has the meanest yellow eyes I've ever seen. I'm trying to determine if it's real; it can't be, right? I mean…

Wait.

Wait a second.

I can *see*. I can fucking see!

As soon as my brain registers that, I knife up into a sitting position and frantically look around. Instead of a car or whatever vehicle the box was in, I'm out of the box and in a room now. A room with walls made of dark wood and decorated with animals' heads. There's not one, not two, but *three* bears' heads surrounding me.

Three.

In addition to a pair of antlers. What the…?

The room is sparsely occupied, so there isn't much to see except a chest of drawers to my left, made of the same dark wood as the walls and the floor, and a nightstand. Again, dark and wooden. Oppressive. And then there's the bed that I'm currently sitting in.

I look down at myself, and the first thing I notice is the burns. Rope burns around my wrists. All red and angry. My dress from yesterday—somehow, I know enough time has passed that it's tomorrow—is all dirty and streaked with dirt and grease. A sheet covers my lap, dark like the rest of the decor and stark against the backdrop of my white dress. The sheet is scratchy, as if it hasn't been used in a while, but it's warm. Meaning somehow *I'm* the first person to end its disuse, and I've been doing that for possibly a few hours now.

Oh my God, what is this place?

What the fuck is this place, and what am I doing here? *What…*

I spring out of the bed, but as soon as my bare feet hit the hardwood floor, I realize how weak I am. How shaky and jittery, and how the entire room spins. I'm going to throw up. I *am*. I feel the bile rising. But somehow, *some way*, I manage to drag in a breath and keep the contents of my stomach in.

When I get my bearings back, my eyes zero in on the door right in front of me.

And I run.

I don't think about it. I don't think about what I'm going to find on the other side of it. All I know is that I need to get to it. I need to turn that silver knob, open the door, and get out of here. I need out, out, *out* of this oppressive room where I can't seem to catch my breath. And I'm there. I'm *right there*, my arm stretched out, fingers within touching distance of the knob, when it happens.

When something flies through the air—I feel it pass by me in a whoosh, making the hair on the back of my neck stand up in a sudden chill—and thunks itself into the door.

A knife.

A pocketknife with a black handle and a sharp and glittery blade. It's barely an inch away from my head, and the thought of that gap closing, and that blade lodging itself somewhere else other than the solid wood, makes me clench my eyes shut. It makes my heart pound so loudly that it could've been knocking at the door that the knife—and me—is stuck to right now. But no amount of mayhem in my body could've prevented that voice from reaching me.

That rough and deep, unused-as-the-sheet-over-my-body, voice.

"Wouldn't do that if I were you."

Crazily, my initial thought is that this is probably the *very first* time he's spoken since we met in the café. Like he said his last words to me and then didn't speak up at all until now. Why that would matter, why that would even enter my brain, I don't know. All I know is that he's here. He's *behind* me, and he just threw a knife at me.

He threw. A knife at me.

A knife.

Oh God, oh God; *oh God, what is happening?* What is this? What is…

"You run, I'll catch you," he goes on, raising goose bumps up and down my body. "Be a waste of both our times."

I should turn around now. Instead of standing stuck to the door, staring at the knife that could've killed me, I should face him. I should show some strength. Even through the mind-numbing fear, I know that.

But I can't move.

I'm *shaking* like a leaf, but I cannot make myself move.

Not even when I hear him take in a deep breath, as if sighing with impatience, followed by rustling in the background. Then, "We're in the middle of nowhere. There's not a lot of places that you can run to. Plus, I don't really think you can run at all. The drug I gave you takes a while to wear off, and until it does, you're gonna be disoriented and wobbly. So your best option is to stay here, get some rest."

Drug.

He *drugged* me? He… *Oh my God.* In a flash, I whirl around and there he is.

Or at least, there his *naked* back is.

He's standing at the chest of drawers, and his back is turned. There's a towel wrapped around his narrow waist, but other than that, he isn't wearing much of anything. I glance to the side where I see another door, ajar and with steam wafting out of it, telling me that he was in there, probably taking a shower. I was so occupied with everything else that I failed to notice there was a bathroom in here as well.

But I'm noticing now.

His hair's wet, all dark and dripping drops of water. I watch them sluice their way down his thick, muscular neck before getting lost in the expanse of his back. And expanse is right because it's huge. It's muscular with dense, fanned-out shoulder blades and the sleek, tapering line of his spine.

I was right when I said he reminded me of the mountains I see through my window every day. Unwavering and strong, made of thick, burly muscles. They make him look like a fighter who could crush anyone with his fists. An outlaw, a criminal who snatches people off the streets.

Who snatched *me*.

I feel the bile rising up again, but I push it down because I'm not finished perusing his back. Because scary strong muscles aren't the only thing that needs my attention; there's something else on his back that needs to be studied. Up by his left shoulder blade, specifically.

A letter.

It's the first letter of my name. An *R*; but most importantly, it's a brand. Like the one you see on animals, on cattle. Put there by a hot, scalding iron; and *oh my God*, it's insane. Why does he have a letter branded on his back?

A second later, my thoughts disintegrate because he drops his towel—the only thing that was covering him—and I clench my eyes shut again. I clench them and *clench them* so hard that I start to feel dizzy again. My knees start to shake, and my stomach feels queasy. I don't know if—

"You can open your eyes now," he says.

And they pop open.

The first thing I notice is that he's covered. He has on a shirt *and* pants. I can't tell very many details about them, other than they're dark-colored, because my focus is on other things.

Like his face.

I know I saw him only yesterday, but I'm looking at him like I'm seeing him for the first time. And maybe I am because a day ago I thought he was the man of my dreams, but today I know he's from my nightmares.

I know there hasn't been any mistake at all. No matter how badly I want it to be, I know this isn't a mix-up. I *know* he isn't Bo Porter. He's a Grayson.

His eyes are as dark as they were yesterday, but now I can picture them glittering in the night, as if they belong to a wild animal, a predator evolved to see in the pitch-black. His jaw is still as stubbled as yesterday—maybe more so—but today I think the growth could be as sharp as the blade still inches away from my face. His cheekbones are high and peaked just like they were at the café, but today they look like dangerous cliffs that you could fall off of and plunge to your death.

God, he's a death trap, isn't he?

His entire body. His face.

But nothing—not even the pain of death—could diminish one thing about his beauty. If anything, now that I know who he is, it all makes sense. Why I felt so afraid. Why he looked so threatening. Why his beauty felt heartbreaking. Because it is.

But what was he doing at the café? How did he know to be there? How did he know to order those things for me, that I only told Bo about? How...

"How do you feel?" he asks, leaning against the dresser now.

My tongue is sticking to the roof of my mouth, but somehow I unglue it. Pressing myself to the door, I say, "You...you d-drugged me?"

He roves those predator eyes over my face. "Had to."

I dig my nails into the door. "H-had to?"

"Couldn't have you screaming when I put you in the trunk of my car."

His words cause a massive shiver to go through my body, making the rope burns on my wrists tingle. I have to drag in a shaky breath so I can keep talking: "What...what is this place?"

His eyes are boring into mine, his features blank. "A hunting cabin."

"Did you"—I take in another shaky breath—"k-kill them?"

"Kill who?"

"These animals," I answer, not taking my eyes off him. "The heads. Did you…"

No expression passes over his face at my question. "Most o' them."

For this next question, instead of the door wood, I dig my nails into my thighs. "Did you…kill…" I close my eyes for a second. "Did you kill him? Did you k-kill Bo?"

Again, nothing flickers through his features. They are cool and aloof as he replies, "No."

A breath escapes me.

Probably the first one since I came to that's not been broken or choppy.

I open my fists and press my sweaty palms to my thighs. "So then, he's…okay? You didn't… You didn't hurt him? You didn't—"

"There's no Bo," he says, cutting me off.

Since we started this conversation face-to-face, this is the only time his features have changed. There's an expression lurking there that I can't name for sure, but it looks akin to…irritation, with lines around his mouth and his eyes clenched tight.

"What?" I breathe out.

His jaw clenches for a second. "The man you're getting so bent out of shape about doesn't exist." Then, "Or rather, he does but he doesn't care that you do. So you should probably save your concern."

"What? What does that m-mean?"

"It means he sold you out."

I go back to holding on to the door, my nails digging into the wood. As if bracing for something, something big and life-changing, as he speaks. "Bo Porter, the guy you think is your little boyfriend and who you thought would be a safe choice because of his drug bust, is a fuckin' junkie. It's hard to score coke when you're on the inside. Can't do it without some serious help. He knew I could provide him that help. Usually I don't like to give people like him the time of day, but fortunately for him, he came into possession of something that he knew I'd want."

My legs are sliding against each other, sweaty and sticky. My palms are slipping along the door, but somehow I hold myself up and parrot, "Something you'd want."

He dips his chin. "Your letter."

"My..."

"The very first one." Then, with his jaw pulsing, he goes on, "So you see, you really wouldn't wanna meet a junkie in a back alley. Because he'll sell you out for a bag of coke while you're standin' there with your pretty little mouth open and your eyes wide in shock, ready to pass out at the betrayal."

That's what I look like right now, I think.

He just described me.

He forgot to mention, though, how I'm shaking right now. How my sweaty limbs are about to buckle under the pressure of what he just revealed. How I'm about to all but collapse. And not just from the betrayal but from something else I just now realized.

It was always there, in the back of my mind, hovering. I refused to acknowledge it. I refused to think about it because I wanted to be smart. I didn't want to be like my mother, who fell in love with a man who was wrong for her. But I can't deny it anymore.

I love Bo.

I'm in love with Bo Porter.

I'm not sure when it happened, but it did. Somewhere along the last six months, the stranger who made me feel safe right from the beginning somehow became the very first man I fell in love with.

"So it's been..." I blink and breathe. "You?"

His dark eyes go back and forth between mine. "Me."

I blink and I breathe again. Then, "This w-whole time?"

Something moves across his face again, but I'm too dizzy to puzzle over what. "Since the beginning."

This is when I break.

Or my mind does, because all the thoughts, all the feelings, all the emotions I'm capable of come to the surface and run rampant. They run from one part of my brain to the other. They run through my veins and fill the corners of my body, making me feel so heavy, so, *so* heavy. So achy. So riddled with *pain*.

God, it's so much pain that I have to let go of the door and press both my hands on my belly. I have to clench my thighs, tighten my muscles so I can withstand it. Withstand the truth.

That there's no Bo. There never was. The man I fell in love with doesn't exist. Or he does but everything about him was a lie. I fell in love with a lie. An illusion.

My first love wasn't a love at all; it was a betrayal.

But I don't… I still don't get it.

"Why would you want *my* le…"

My subconscious catches up before my brain does, and my words trail off. He would want my letters. Because he thinks Peyton was writing them.

He thinks I'm Peyton.

He didn't kidnap me because I'm *associated* with the Turners. No, he kidnapped me because he thinks I *am* a Turner. He thinks I'm his enemy. He thinks I'm something to kill and destroy.

Because that's what the Graysons and the Turners have been doing to each other.

Everyone in town, in the whole state of Montana, knows about the two feuding families of Black Rock. They've been warring with each other over land for years, for decades. The feud doesn't involve just trivial disagreements. It doesn't even stop at ambushes in the middle of the night—cutting fences and stealing cattle. Setting fire to timber and destroying equipment isn't enough for them. It involves making people disappear; spying, shady dealings, and blackmail. Their enmity was the reason why we left Black Rock in the first place; it wasn't safe for us to stay there anymore.

Because one night, the Graysons brought years' worth of fighting to our home.

I know I should be afraid, and Jesus Christ, I am—I am *shaking*—but I can't help noticing the irony. We've both been pretending to be other people. We've both been lying to each other. The only difference is that he did it out of malice, the depths of which I've yet to find out, while my lie was innocent.

Tell him.

Tell him now.

I open my mouth to do just that, but something else comes out: "So you...you pretended to be"—I can't say it; I can't say the name of the guy I've foolishly been in love with—"him a-and wrote me letters because you wanted to, what, fool me?"

"More like get you to trust me, but fool you works too."

I press myself harder into the door, my shoulder blades digging into the wood. "So you could...bring me here?"

He studies me for a beat, as if looking for something, but I don't know what. I don't have anything to give him.

I'm not even the right girl.

"Not exactly," he says finally, shifting on his feet.

"What?"

"Bringing you here wasn't the plan."

"The p-plan?"

"All straight As, right? Except sociology." His jaw pulses. "Thought you were smart. Followin' me back to my motel though, not so much."

My eyes are wide. "You...you knew?"

"I'm an ex-con," he says, his gaze steady and his features neutral except, once again, there's a hint of irritation. "You don't tail an ex-con, especially when you've got zero skills to make out your own tail." At my confusion, he goes on, "You picked up a couple of guys on your way over. I took care of them later."

My heart races. "Did you... Does that mean you killed them?"

He gives me a flat look. "No, just knocked 'em out. Can't kill people in daylight."

I shake my head. "I'm…I can't…"

"Thought you would have smartened up when you left but"—his jaw pulses again—"you had to come find me, didn't you? I was a little shocked when the front desk guy called, said a girl came lookin' for me. So no, it wasn't the plan to drug you and bring you here. But I couldn't take the chance of you runnin' back to your family and tellin' them about me either."

Family.

He means the Turners. I need to tell him. I need to tell him I'm not the girl he thinks I am. But once again, something else comes out: "I won't say anything."

He doesn't dignify that with a response.

"I won't," I insist, clawing my nails at the door. "If you let me go right now, I'll…I'll forget about it all. I'll forget about the letters. About the kidnapping. About whatever you did. About e-everything. You just need to let me go. You just—"

"No," he says.

Definitively. Decisively.

Like that concludes all discussion. Like he can keep me here. Like he has *a right* to keep me here.

"You can't do this," I say, my voice pitching high. "You can't keep me here. You can't—"

"I can."

"They'll be looking for me," I blurt out. "My family. They'll be… You have to let me go. You have to l-let me go to my family."

Lie. Lie. Lie.

All lies, but I have to say something, *anything* to make him let me go.

"And I will," he says, all calm-like. "In my own time."

"But this is…" I shake my head. "My f-friends. My—"

"You've got no friends," he reminds me, his dark eyes glittering. "Your only friend left for the Bahamas for the summer. You've got no job, no classes. Your mother's tourin' Europe like she always does and your father and your brother's in Black Rock. I took care of your phone and you've got no one. No one is lookin' for you. No one will miss you. The only person who'd wonder about you if your letter didn't arrive like clockwork on Tuesday is standin' right here."

He's right. No one will miss me. I have no friends. No classes, no job. The only person I thought I had is right in front of me.

"Are you g-going to kill me?" I ask then.

He lets a beat pass by before replying, "No."

"So then why—"

"You're no use to me dead."

"Use me for what? What are you going to use me for?"

This time he stays silent the longest, scrutinizing me as he stands there with his feet shoulder width apart, his spine straight. His hands are fisted at his sides, and his gaze is as steady as ever. And even though he's all the way across the room from me, it still feels like he's right by my side.

Right where I am.

It feels like I can smell him, his dangerous musk. Like I can hear his heart beat, a threatening drumbeat. It feels like he's sucking in all the air, leaving nothing for me. Choking me without laying a finger on me.

Finally, dragging a long breath, he answers: "Revenge."

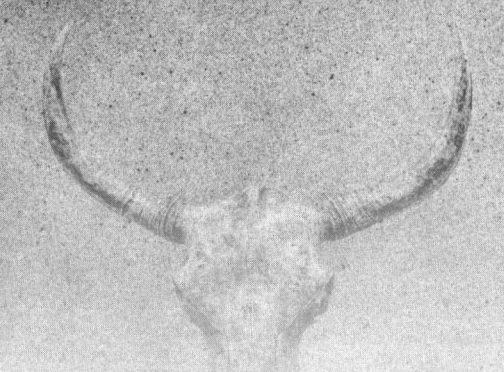

CHAPTER SIX

To: Peyton Turner
From: Bo Porter

So your mother was an idiot to fall for a man like your father. And now you're letting them both win by living the life of a ninety-year-old.

Did I get that right?

Bo

———

To: Bo Porter
From: Peyton Turner

Dear Bo,

I do not live the life of a ninety-year-old!

I don't go out and party and get drunk like the rest of my classmates because it's the responsible thing to do. In fact, it's the opposite of living the life of a ninety-year-old. Because at least, I don't puke my guts out and look like I'm on my deathbed while walking to my class. Along with doing a stumbling walk of shame the following *morning because the guy I've chosen to sleep with turns out to be a freaking slob who pees in the sink because he's too hungover to look for the bathroom.*

Is that a clear enough picture for you?

Another thing: I'm not letting him win either. Again, I'm doing the opposite of it. I'm getting even by being smart. Getting even or revenge isn't about making the other person pay. It's about living a good life and not letting them affect you. It's about not letting them take a piece of you.

Because they've already taken enough.

Peyton

To: Peyton Turner
From: Bo Porter

Peyton,

That's pretty, what you said about revenge.

Bet you read that in a book. Because that's all you seem to do. By your own admission, you don't really do anything other than read. You lived on a ranch but you've never ridden a horse. You miss the place you grew up in but you won't go back to it. Because you don't really go anywhere. You don't see anything or meet anyone.

You live a careful life. A safe life. A life where you hide out from everything that could touch you all because you don't want to make the same mistakes your mother did. So your solution is to not make any mistakes at all.

That's neither revenge or being smart.

That's being a coward.

So I don't think you're the one I should be seeking advice from, do you?

Bo

———

To: Bo Porter
From: Peyton Turner

Dear Bo,

I could be really angry right now.

I could be calling you names and you'll deserve them. You know you'll deserve them.

But I won't. Because I think something happened to you, didn't it? Something big. Something bad. Something that's made you angry. So angry that you're lashing out at me even though I'm not the one you're angry at.

And yes, I did read about revenge in a book. It was a very good book too. It's called Wuthering Heights and you already know it's my favorite book. You remind me of Heathcliff but instead of rocky moors and an estate, you have a ranch and dusty cowboy boots. You should read it. And then you should think about letting go of some of that anger.

Also, in my first letter I told you that even though this is an assignment, I can be your friend so consider this my official application.

To be your friend.

Peyton

PS: You are an asshole, just so you know. And if you were in front of me, I'd punch you.

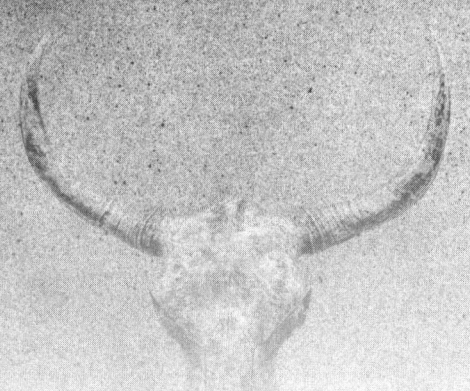

CHAPTER SEVEN

WHEN I WAKE up the next day, I know exactly where I am.

In a hunting cabin.

His hunting cabin.

The man who's been lying to me for six months. He's been playing me for *six whole months* just so he could lure me out. And when I found out his real name, he brought me here. For revenge. Because something happened to him, didn't it? Something *bad*. I thought it had happened to Bo. But there is no Bo; there's only him.

The sound of crinkling paper alerts me that I'm not alone, and gasping, I sit up in the bed.

Unlike yesterday, he's in the room with me. He sits in a chair in the corner, facing the bed. There's a small table in front of him with a brown paper bag that he was staring at, but as soon as I sit up, his attention shifts to me. His black eyes lock with mine and my breaths hasten.

He looks…rough.

Or rather rough*ened*.

I don't know what else to call it, but his hair's all rumpled, sticking out in places as if he's been running his fingers through it all night. His stubble seems mussed up as well, thicker than yesterday, darker, and the eyes through which he's watching me seem red-rimmed and slightly sunken. With the way he's sitting there, legs sprawled, leaned over, his elbows on his thighs, it feels like he spent the night in the same position.

Like he never went to sleep.

My thoughts break when he straightens up, his face a blank mask, and sits back. "Good, you're awake."

I think I'm still getting used to his voice, all deeply timbred and gravelly, because for the first few seconds after he speaks, I find myself getting lost in his drawling, low-pitched syllables, thinking about the letters, trying to *hear* the words he wrote.

God, you're an idiot, Riri. A massive idiot.

"There's breakfast," he continues with a tip of his jaw.

Clutching the sheet to my chest, I glance to where he pointed, and sure enough, there's a plate of eggs, bacon, and toast on the nightstand, along with a glass of juice. But what my eyes snag and catch on is the muffin that sits by the toast. It's my favorite, the one he also ordered at the café. The strawberry crumble.

My heart clenches so hard in my chest that I have to consciously make an effort to not curl into a ball. To not rock and scream, trying to bust the door down with my fists like I did last night after he left me locked up in the room until eventually I passed out only to wake up now. I want to demand that he take it back, everything he said yesterday. Everything he revealed. I want him to tell me that he was lying. That all his letters were true and this is a bad joke.

A nightmarish joke.

I want him to tell me that he's my Bo. He's the man I fell in love with and didn't even realize it until I found out he doesn't exist.

"Eat it," he keeps going, his voice all business, breaking into my furious thoughts. "Freshen up, and then we need to leave."

At this, I go on alert. My pain and heartbreak take a back seat as fear takes over.

"Leave where?" I ask, my voice sounding too high for first thing in the morning.

"For town."

I shift on the bed, clutching the sheet tighter. "What town? W-Where are we?"

I know he said we're in the middle of nowhere, but it has to be *somewhere*. It has to be…

"You don't need to worry about that," he says and just like that dismisses me.

He stands up and heads to the door.

With slowly escalating breaths, I watch his long legs eating up the distance to the door like he can't get out of here fast enough. Like his life depends on being away from here, from *me*. The girl he kidnapped and is now *holding* against her will. And that makes me so mad, so *fucking* mad, that I throw the sheets aside and jump out of bed.

Not only that, but in a blind rage, I pick up the glass of juice and throw it at him. I watch it sail through the air, splashing the liquid everywhere before it hits.

Not him, though.

He gets a few drops of juice on him, but other than that he's safe. The glass, unfortunately, hits the door, probably the same spot as the knife, before shattering into countless pieces that rain down on the floor. The thwack makes me flinch, but I'm not deterred. I stand with my fists tight, my chest trembling.

Slowly, he turns around to face me.

He glances down at the broken pieces of glass along with puddles of liquid before his eyes come back up to me. And that roughened look, the one that made me think he probably didn't sleep at all, is gone. His eyes are alert now. His thickly stubbled jaw is firmly set, and even though the rest of his features are as blank as ever, I can still sense the thrum of intensity just beneath the surface.

It makes me waver a little bit. That lurking threat, but fuck that. *Fuck* being afraid.

Fuck cowering. I'm so angry right now. So, *so* angry. And it's not just him toying with me; it's also the fact that this is happening in the first place. That somehow this is my life right now. *Somehow,* after doing everything right, after being cautious and careful and playing by all the rules, I still ended up here.

I *still* ended up like my mother, falling for the wrong man.

I lift my chin up. "Tell me where we're going."

Because I'm going to fix it.

I'm going to get myself out of here. I'm going to save myself. Unlike my mother. *And* I'm going to save my best friend too. Because he doesn't want me, does he? His entire plan—whatever the fuck it is—hinges on Peyton, but he isn't going to get her.

I won't let him.

He takes me in, my raised chin, my heaving chest. My fisted hands and my battle stance.

Good.

Let him see I'm not some doormat who's going to lie down and let him walk all over me. I'm not a little college girl who'll let him do anything he wants just because he's a big, bad *criminal* cowboy.

Once he's finished with his perusal, I see his chest moving with a long breath as he shifts and leans against the door. He crosses his arms as if he's hunkering down, settling in for the long haul. Then, "No."

I clench my fists harder. "So then, I'm not going anywhere with you."

"I think you are."

"No, I'm *not*. Not until you tell me exactly where we're going and why we're going there."

Again, he takes his time responding.

He takes in my cheeks that must be flushed right now; the pulse fluttering in the base of my throat; my hair probably in disarray and all sleep-mussed. And something in his gaze changes. I don't know what it is, but it darkens and glitters as he challenges, "Or what?"

"Or I'll…"

I trail off, trying to think of an appropriate response, but he takes advantage of my pause and says, "Scream?"

"You—"

"There's no one around to hear you. Middle of nowhere, remember?"

"I—"

Cocking his head to the side, he keeps going: "And didn't you already do that last night?" I open my mouth to retort, but he gets there before me. "Not sure it did anything except give me a headache, so I'd save my breath."

"Oh, I'll take the headache," I say, glaring at him. "Maybe this time if I scream loud enough, I can make your head explode."

His eyes glitter with a light I don't understand but that gets my heart racing. "Or maybe I can gag you again. And if that doesn't take care of the problem, I can always give you the tranq. I don't want to, but I will."

My heart thuds. "The tranq?"

"The sedative," he explains. "Also known as xylazine."

I frown, my mind racing, and then it dawns on me. "That's… You gave me a *horse* tranquilizer?"

His eyes glitter again. "Yeah."

"But that's…that's dangerous. That's so… It's found in illegal substances," I say, my voice squeaky.

"I'm aware."

"You could've *overdosed* me."

Something like arrogance flickers through his face before he says, "Haven't been a cowboy in eight years, but I know my tranq doses. Besides, it was for your own safety."

"Safety?" I repeat, my voice even squeakier.

"Yeah, more than screamin' inside my trunk, couldn't have you movin' around and hitting somethin', hurtin' yourself in the process."

"But you can't just… I could've been *allergic*."

"You seem fine to me, but"—he looks me up and down—"I could always check you for rashes."

"You—"

"Now, if there's nothing else, how about you eat your breakfast before it gets cold and then get ready to go." He jerks his chin at me. "You've got thirty minutes."

God.

Oh my *God*.

Glaring at him, I snap, "I'm not eating your stupid breakfast."

"You probably should."

"What makes you think I'll eat anything after what you just told me?"

"Probably because you skipped dinner last night and must be hungry."

My stomach growls as if awakened by his words, and if that light in his eyes is any indication, I know, *I know*, he hears it. But I ignore it. "No, thank you. I won't touch the food you give me with a ten-foot pole." I don't know what makes me say it, but I add, "Plus, I don't eat bacon."

That gives him pause. "What?"

"I'm a vegetarian," I inform him or, rather, lie.

He looks at me for a second. "You're a vegetarian."

"Yes." Then, "It's funny that it never came up before. You know, when you were lying to me and pretending to be *my Bo* for six whole months." I notice his jaw clench at this, but I keep going: "I think killing animals for food is disgusting. Killing animals for *sport*"—I make it a point to look around the room and at all the animal heads— "is disgusting. *You* are disgusting."

Again, he looks at me for a second or two, his jaw tight. Then, with a deep breath, he says, "Fine, I'll get you some grass to munch on the way."

"I'm not going anywhere with you," I snap, barely resisting the urge to stomp my foot. "Not until you answer my questions."

"Why, do you think you could stop it if you knew where we're goin' and what's gonna happen to you when we get there?"

What's going to happen to me…

Okay, okay.

Don't panic.

Do not panic.

I breathe through my nose, fill my lungs and my body with air and determination. I squeeze my eyes shut. "Look, this is insane, okay? This is *absolutely fucking insane.* This is… You can't keep me here. You can't… You can't kidnap people. This is not normal. None of this is normal. This is…" I open my eyes and let him see my frustration. "I don't know why you want revenge. I don't know what they did but they did something, didn't they? This isn't just some family feud. This isn't about Grayson-Turner rivalry. I know it. I knew it back then when we were…" I take a deep breath because my belly is clenching in pain. "When we were writing to each other. You never…said anything but I knew. And I'm sorry, okay? I'm *sorry.* I'm sorry that bad things happened to you. I'm sorry they did what they did. But it has nothing to do with me. *Nothing.* So please let me go. This is… This is not fair. I don't deserve this. And"—I shake my head—"whatever it is you're planning, it's not going to bring you peace. I know you think it's all bullshit, that I read it in books or whatever, but it's the truth. Revenge is not the way. Revenge is not the answer. It's not—"

"You done?"

My breaths are choppy and so fast, it feels like I will pass out. "Just please, okay? Don't do this. Don't—"

"Eat your breakfast or don't. You got thirty minutes," he says, unfolding his arms and pushing away from the door, once again ready to put this behind him.

And I just…

Lose it.

I completely lose it, but this time as I scream, I go for the plate. I pick up the breakfast he left for me and throw it at him. I don't even know where it lands, but the sound tells me that the plate also shatters like the glass. I'm busy picking up the fork that's lying on the nightstand and clutching it in my hand like the knife.

And I launch myself at him, fork poised to stab, but before I can take even two steps toward my target, he gets to me himself. He grabs me around the waist, picks me off the ground, spins me around, and plasters my back to his chest. All in one fluid, scary move. And now I'm standing here, trapped in his grip, his muscular arm like a steel band around my belly.

Very easily, like child's play, he divests me of the fork and throws it aside. Even through my heavy breathing, I hear it clatter to the floor pathetically. And then, *oh God, then*, he wraps his fingers around my neck and squeezes.

Not hard, not soft, just firm, and all my noisy breaths stop.

I go still. I'm not even shaking. I'm petrified, turned into stone.

Even so, I can feel him behind me.

Like a dark predator, his chest moving, breathing, sliding across my spine; his heat—God, he's so hot, almost burning up—making me sweat; his scent making me dizzy. And his hands on me, large and rough, threatening. This is what I imagine being in the clutches of a wolf or a panther would feel like.

Helpless and afraid.

So, *so* afraid.

But I don't think my skin is supposed to break out in goose bumps or that my nerves should feel electric like they do now. I don't think I should be opening my mouth to breathe him in more or feel a quickening in my belly when I do.

I'm sick, aren't I? So twisted for feeling this way.

He lowers his face, his stubble, sharp and razor-like, sliding along my cheek as he says, "You done throwin' tantrums?"

I swallow.

He flexes his grip around my throat, making me squeak. "You done or not? Say yes or no."

I clench my eyes shut. "Y-yes."

"Good," he says, flexing his fingers around my throat again. "Now, I want you to listen to me, okay? You listenin'?"

"Yes."

His chest moves with another breath. "First, there's glass everywhere, yeah? Your fuckin' temper tantrum made a mess. So after this, when I tell you to stay put on the bed until I clean it up, you're going to."

My eyes pop open. "What?"

"Is that clear?"

"Y-you…" I lick my dry lips. "You want me to stay put on the bed because there's g-glass everywhere?"

"Yeah," he rasps, nodding, causing his stubble to sting my skin and making me bite my lip. "You gonna do that for me?"

"Why?"

"Because you could hurt yourself."

"Like in the…in the trunk? Before."

"Yes," he says, and that quickening in my belly increases.

Why would he care? What does it matter to him if I get hurt?

God, this is *crazy*.

I somehow manage to jerk out a nod. "Yes. I-I'll stay p-put."

"Good," he praises again, and something about that makes me feel all strange in my body again. But I can't focus on it, because he continues. "Now, I've got very little patience left," he says, and I swallow again. He grazes his thumb over my pulse as he continues, "But I'm gonna tell you a story, okay, and I want you to listen carefully. Gonna do that for me too?"

My fingers dig into my bare thighs, but I nod again. "Yes."

"Good, very good," he murmurs, and I drag my nails across my thighs. "There's a man in Black Rock. We call him the Quiet Mustang. Because he's got trouble talking. When he was young, he was in a car accident. We've got no proof but Turners were behind it."

My eyes are wide. "T-Turners?"

"Yeah," he says, his voice low. "They rigged the truck and caused the crash, killed everyone inside. Except the boy. He went through the window and hit his head against a tree. He lay there, bleeding for hours, before someone found him. The doctors said he hit his head so hard that all the words got knocked out and he'll probably never speak again."

I keep dragging my nails on my thighs. "Is that… Is that why you're d-doing this?"

His chest shudders with something very similar to a chuckle. "No. We took care of it a long time ago. Set fire to their timber and blew up their equipment."

"You…" I swallow again and his thumb strums my vein. "That's a-arson."

"Yeah," he says, shifting his jaw and grazing his sharp stubble along my skin. "And in this case, you guys started it first."

I shake my head. "But I don't—"

"But that's not the point," he goes on, his warm breath wafting over my skin. "The point of the story is that what they say is true. When one of your senses is gone, the others work overtime. He doesn't talk much but he can see fine. They say he can see in the dark. He can shoot in the dark too and he never misses."

Another chill racks my body and his grip on me tightens. It feels both suffocating and like the only thing keeping me from falling apart right now.

"The *point* is," he says, his voice even lower and his heat almost making me melt, "that right now, your brother's at a livestock auction with my brother. Probably bidding for the same shit my brother's bidding on. Because you Turners aren't all that smart when it comes to actual cattle ranching. But when he leaves to go back to your ranch, that man, who's already got an axe to grind with your family, is gonna be waitin' for him a mile up the road. With a sniper rifle. And the only thing that'll stop him from pullin' that trigger and exacting his own revenge is you doin' exactly what I tell you to do."

My breaths are so fast and loud that it's a surprise I can hear him. But I do.

I hear him clearly.

"Do you understand what I'm sayin' to you?" He squeezes my neck once again, making me flinch. "If you aren't in my car in the next thirty minutes, all quiet and cooperative and ready to go where I'm takin' you, your brother's gonna die. You already know I'm not gonna kill you, don't you, but I never said anything about not killin' other people when it comes to you."

———

"Get out," he commands.

We're in his car—the one he put me in the trunk of—and after driving for about forty-five minutes, we're in a town called Broken Ridge. I've heard of it. It's midway between Bozeman and Black Rock. I've never been here before, but it looks like any other town. A wide, busy street with pedestrians and parked cars and trucks. A feed store, a general store, a pharmacy. I also see a couple of coffee shops, a bank, an ATM. There is nothing here to give me a clue as to why he brought me here.

Or what he's going to do with me.

I want to ask him, but I know he won't tell me. I also know there's every chance that if I do ask him, he may get angry and really do what he said he would. He may kill my best friend's brother. I know Peyton hates her family, but I'm sure she doesn't want them to be killed.

And isn't this my fault?

This whole situation.

I'm the one who acted stupid, who was fooled. He may be looking for payback, but I'm the one who made it easy for him, who kept writing him letters, who went looking for him. So it's my fault. I can't let anyone be killed over it. So I have to do what he says.

But I turn to him and ask, "What did you do?"

Even though we're only a few feet apart, I can't really see his eyes. They're covered by the low brim of the trucker's cap he had on the first time I saw him. I study the intricate *R* on it. I think about the *R* branded on his shoulder blade. About how he doesn't even know that the letter he has on his body is the first letter of my name.

I wonder if there's some cruel poetry in that, some cosmic sign that this was going to happen. That we were going to meet this way.

Waving silly thoughts away, I prod: "To get put away. What was your crime?"

I know Bo was caught in a drug bust, but he's not Bo, is he? So what did he do, then?

His jaw moves back and forth, and even though it's light out, the car seems to grow dark inside as I watch his soft mouth move and say the most heinous things: "Aggravated assault and attempted murder in the first degree."

"You t-tried," I say, stuttering over my words, "to kill someone?"

He dips his chin, but I still can't see his eyes. "That's what they charged me with. But that wasn't my real crime."

"What…what was your real crime?"

I see his jaw pulse once again. "I failed to finish what they started."

"What?"

"But I'm gonna fix it now."

Before I can ask what he means by that, he reaches his arm back and grabs something from the back seat. It's the same paper bag he was staring at this morning. He sets it between us and, finally, tips his hat up enough so I can see his eyes.

They're dark as always. But now they have a stillness to them that I haven't seen from him before. Like his eyes aren't simply dark; they hold a darkness that goes beyond just the color.

Then, "I'm gonna take their daughter to the courthouse in a white dress I bought her and make her mine. Because death alone isn't enough for the family who took everything from me. I'm gonna take everything from them and it starts with you."

CHAPTER EIGHT

THE WHITE DRESS he bought me is beautiful.

It's made of delicate lace and embroidered flowers. It's held up by two fragile spaghetti straps, and the silky fabric molds around my large breasts and flares around my big hips, hitting me just above the knees.

As I look myself up and down in the bathroom mirror, I realize I'd never pick out this dress, which would probably be doing myself a disservice. Because it's stunning. Not only due to the intricate needlework on the lace, but also because instead of hiding things like all my other clothes do, like the dress I wore to meet him did, this dress highlights them. My pillowy breasts, my small waist, and my rounded hips that give me an hourglass figure.

It's like he knows me more than I know myself. He knows how to turn what I think are my flaws into something beautiful.

Even though my hair's all over the place, messy and unkempt, and my blue eyes are terrified, I do think I look pretty in the white dress.

At the courthouse.

Somehow in my perusal of this town from the car, I missed the big white building with the big white pillars. I missed the lettering on the front that said, "Broken Ridge County Clerk of District Court."

I missed it, and now here I am, gripping the sink tightly because my knees are about to give out. I'm either about to hit my head on the ceramic on my way down, or I'm going to puke all over myself. Either way, I'm ultimately going to die.

Or at least, that's what it feels like.

Like my life's about to end. And it is, isn't it?

It took me a bit to understand what he meant back in his car. I couldn't put two and two together. Not until we got inside the building, and he told me to go change in the bathroom, pointing toward the brown paper bag I was clutching to my chest like a shield. That's when it hit me. What he meant by the white dress in a brown bag, the courthouse, the daughter.

But I'm *not* the daughter.

I'm not even a Turner. I'm useless to him. I'm not the one he wants in a white dress. He shouldn't be forcing me to mar—

Don't say it. Don't say that word.

I straighten up from the sink and exhale shakily, deciding something.

I'm going to tell him the truth.

That's the only way. He needs to know I'm not Peyton, and forcing me to do what he wants me to do isn't going to get him what he wants. He's wasting his time with me. He's wasting his…shooter friend's time as well. Killing Brecken Turner over me, the daughter of the nanny and a ranch hand, isn't going to get him his revenge.

I'm the wrong girl.

As I walk to the door, I know there's every chance that once I tell him, he may kill me and Peyton's brother anyway before going after the real Peyton, but it's a chance I have to take. Somehow I get to the door and manage to open it, and there he is. All towering and broad-shouldered, a figure to be reckoned with, standing at the end of the hallway leading to the restrooms, waiting for me.

But he's not standing alone; he's got someone with him.

A cop.

Right there. *Right* by his side. And they're absorbed in a conversation. So much so that they haven't yet noticed me. Not even when I start walking toward them.

Slowly.

One foot in front of the other.

The cop—the sheriff—is the one talking while my kidnapper remains silent. He has his arms folded across his chest as he listens, and to most, he may appear bored and aloof. But somehow I know he's not. He's annoyed. If that pulse in his jaw is anything to go by. How strange that I somehow know him, too, even though we only met two days ago.

Finally, his focus shifts, his dark eyes home in on me, and I stumble slightly with the force of his stare.

It's powerful and heavy. Thick and hot.

His eyes move. They go from the top of my head to my feet, all in one go, in a hurry. As if he doesn't want to miss anything. But once he's done that, taken me in as a whole, he goes slowly. He stares at me deliberately. He spends a lot of time on my neck, the base of my throat, and I wonder if he's thinking about his fingers wrapped around it from this morning.

Before he moves on to my chest, which is trembling with my racing breaths.

He watches me breathe for a long time, as if he's trying to learn how to do it himself. As if he's forgotten how to take the air in, and maybe he has because I haven't seen his chest move even once all this time. And when I'm just about to reach him, his gaze drops down to my thighs. I don't know what he sees down there except meaty flesh, but whatever it is, it makes him unfold his arms and finally turn to me.

It makes him fist his hands by his sides.

At last, my walk down the hallway ends, and I come to a stop a few feet away from him. I don't have to wonder if every girl who takes a walk down the aisle feels what I'm feeling in this moment.

Or if every guy who waits for her at the end feels what *he's* feeling. I already know they don't.

I already know that a girl isn't supposed to feel this intense rage and a man isn't supposed to do this for revenge.

Intense rage at the fact that he made me, *forced me*, to wear a white dress, while he himself is dressed in all black like this is his funeral. Like his life is ending rather than mine. And then he has the audacity to look at me like that. To stare at me in a way that made my skin all heated. That branded me. Without my permission.

He has the *audacity* to imprint himself on my body without my consent.

Just when his tightly clenched jaw moves and he opens his mouth to say something, I turn toward the sheriff and blurt out, "Help."

My sudden plea shocks the sheriff.

It shocks me too. I didn't know I was going to do that until I did. And now that I have, I can't go back. I have to take a chance, especially when it's right there. Only a couple of feet away. Turning to him completely, I grab the sheriff's arm as if it's my lifeline, and *Jesus Christ*, it may very well be. "I need help. You need to help me. I've been kidnapped. H-he kidnapped me. This…this man, he kidnapped me."

The sheriff's frown thickens as his eyes jerk over to him behind me, and I grab his sleeve in urgency. "No, look at me. Look at me!" My frantic voice brings the sheriff's attention back to me, even though he still looks confused. "Whatever he told you, it's a lie, okay? I don't know what you were t-talking about but he's lying. He's a liar. He just got out of prison. He's on parole and you need to… You need to arrest him, call his parole officer."

When it looks like the sheriff's going to say something, I dig my nails into his arm and keep going, my voice even louder than before: "Two days ago in Bozeman. H-he drugged me, okay? And then h-he put me in the trunk of his car. Look"—I show him the marks on my wrists—"he tied me up. With ropes. I have evidence. And then he brought me here. He said he…"

"Come with me."

This is from the sheriff.

Even though I'm hyperventilating and dizzy, I can still make out the concern on his face and also in his tone. And it's so relieving, this reaction, that I almost burst into tears. I almost crumple down to the floor.

I don't, though.

I hold on to the sheriff—Cooper, his nameplate says—even harder. "Please, I want to go home. Just…"

"Let's go," he says and begins walking.

And since I still haven't let go of his arm and my fingers have a death grip on his sleeve, I go with him. The corridor we're making our way through is crowded. It has people coming and going, men with uniforms everywhere. This has to be the safest place or the second-most-safe place other than the police station, right? There's cops all over. I mean, they can stop him, can't they? Sheriff Cooper, even though shorter and stockier in build, can stop him and that shooter friend of his.

On that thought, Sheriff Cooper stops at a door and enters.

It's an unoccupied office; the space is dominated by a giant desk, and the room holds a few other things I have no hope of paying attention to. I also do not have any hope of keeping it together and not jumping practically a mile when Sheriff Cooper abruptly stops, spins around, and thunders, "What the fuck?" He stabs his finger over my shoulder and keeps going: "I thought you had it under control."

I go still at his words.

I watch Sheriff Cooper's mouth open and his angry face contorting as he continues, "What, you've got nothing to say? She almost got us caught back there." Leaning forward, he warns, "You got any idea the favors I had to call in to get your fucking license?"

He shakes his head. "Should've said no the moment you called. I knew this whole Grayson-Turner bullshit would land me in a world of trouble one day." He stabs his finger again. "You listen to me, Arsen, if this comes back to me, I'm gonna lose my badge. Hell, I'm gonna lose my life and I ain't fucking dying for no one, you hear me? Not even for a Grayson. No matter how much goddamn money you throw at me."

As soon as the sheriff finishes, a click echoes in the room.

It's the office door closing and it's mostly soft, especially after the tirade by the sheriff. Still, it serves as a wake-up call. It's not as if I hadn't been able to figure it out; I was slow figuring things out in the car, but this I got the moment the sheriff opened his mouth. But now that the door's been closed, and I'm trapped inside with not one but two people, *two people* who mean me harm, my body is catching up, and I slowly turn around.

His presence hits me like a sucker punch.

He stands by the door, almost covering it, blocking the only way out of this room with his large body. And this time, I don't have to wonder about his eyes being hidden by his cap. They're fully visible, and if the eyes are the window to the soul, his soul must be pitch-black. Again, in a way that goes beyond the color and into the depths of a bottomless pit.

A *fiery* pit.

I follow his stare and find that it's glued to my hand. My fingers that are still clutching the sheriff's sleeve, and as soon as I realize that, I jerk away. And as if my fingers on the sheriff's arm were holding his stare hostage, his eyes snap away as well and come back to me.

"You..." I breathe out, my teeth chattering and chills running up and down my back. "He's w-with...you. He's... I should've known—"

"You shut the fuck up," Sheriff Cooper snaps at me, making me jump, and this time, he's the one who grabs my arm and does it so painfully that I gasp. "One more word outta your mouth and I'm gonna—"

His words are swallowed up then.

No, actually I think his words are being crushed right in his throat. By the very hand that was wrapped around *my* throat only a few hours ago. I was so terrified back then, but now I realize I probably shouldn't have been. Because the grip he had on me was not even close to the grip he has on the sheriff.

"Let go," he growls.

"Y-you motherfucking—"

"Now," he growls again, cutting off the sheriff's words.

Sheriff Cooper's chest is shaking. "Are you off y-your—"

I notice his knuckles going pale from the force with which he's choking him. "Hands off her now or I'll kill you right here for touching my wife."

"She ain't..." the sheriff squeaks, trying to dislodge his hand. "Y-your wife...y-yet."

In response, he increases the pressure even more. Then, in the same low tone, "Papers."

The sheriff's eyes go even bigger, and he sputters, "Y-you... c-can't—"

"Won't say it again."

Still, the sheriff resists. But only for a few seconds before he reaches his hand back, scrambling to search for the papers on the desk. He clutches them in his shaking hand and offers them to the man he called Arsen. Without taking his hand off the sheriff's throat, he commands, "Pen."

The sheriff lets the papers go, and they fall limply onto the desk. He searches frantically for the pen. A few moments later, he has it in his hand and holds it out as well. Without taking his hand off Sheriff Cooper's neck, he takes the pen before flicking his eyes down to the papers.

And then I watch him sign his name in clear, concise letters.

In a handwriting so familiar that I see it in my dreams. He has a habit of pressing his writing instrument so firmly onto the page that I can feel the indentations of the letters with my fingers. In weaker moments, I've gotten up in the middle of the night and stroked the pages with my eyes closed, trying to make out the words he wrote me. I know if I tried, I could feel them now too.

Like braille.

No, knowing him, it's a brand on that paper, his name.

Arsenal Grayson.

Arsen, like the sheriff called him. Like setting fire to the timber on purpose.

When he's done branding his name, he lifts his eyes to me. They're still dark and fiery, and I know I should look away, but I can't. It's like watching a train wreck. It's like *being* in a train wreck.

I hear the rustle of papers on the desk. Then, "Your turn."

Tell him. Fucking tell him. Tell him you're not who he thinks you are.

But something else comes out entirely. "H-He's not… He can't breathe."

"Sign the papers," he says, ignoring me.

"You're going to k-kill him."

"Sign the fuckin' papers."

"You have to let him go."

His eyes bore into mine as he decrees, "I will. When you sign the papers."

"What?"

"You want him to live," he says, his jaw pulsing, and in the periphery, I notice and hear the sheriff squeaking. "You sign on the dotted line."

I jerk my eyes away from him and take in the sheriff. He's all red now, the veins standing on his temples, his eyes bloody. He's still trying to dislodge Arsen's hand, and for a second all I can think is that it feels so weird calling him that. Arsen instead of Bo, the name I've called him in my head for six months.

Quickly, I pull myself together and turn to him. "You can't do that. You can't—"

"I'm not the one doin' it," he tells me, his features somehow both aloof and intense.

The sheriff makes a choking sound and I flinch. "This is *insane*. This is not—"

"Sign the papers."

I shake my head, pleading, "Don't do this. Please don't do this."

"*Sign...*" he begins slowly, "the papers, or he dies, Peyton."

I cringe.

I open my mouth to tell him the truth. I'm not the one he wants. But for some reason, I can't say it. I can't *say* the words. I don't know why. They could be my out. They could free me. But my mouth stays shut, and then the moment's gone.

Keeping his gaze locked with mine, he leans closer. "If you don't sign your name in ink, I'll *make* you sign it in his blood. You know what I did, don't you? You know who I am, what I'm capable of. So if you don't want me to scratch the *attempted* from the attempted murder, you pick up that pen and write your name on the dotted line. Because either way, you're leavin' here as my wife."

His wife.

I leave my body then and watch myself from above. I watch myself reach for the pen, my fingers trembling. I watch myself sign my name on the dotted line like he asked me to. It's not my best handwriting. In fact, it looks nothing like my usual handwriting. My letters appear shaky and haphazard, unreadable really, but I don't think it matters. All that matters is that I did it.

I did what he told me to do, and now I'm his *wife*.

I slam back into my body, but before I can gather my senses, he turns back to the sheriff. He whips his knife out of his pocket and plunges it into the man's arm.

Just like that.

No warning; no fanfare.

And then he muffles the sheriff's howl with the same hand that held the knife and says, "You're right. If this comes back to you, you'll lose more than your badge. So you're gonna follow the plan, yeah? You'll make a copy of this and give one to me. Then you'll go file the original and tell County to hurry the fuck up and put the certificate in the mail to me. You understand that, right?" Sheriff Cooper jerks out a nod, and Arsen continues, "Good. That's very good. But we forgot the most important part, didn't we?"

The sheriff's eyes bug out even more than before, and he looks confused, so Arsen sighs and says, "You'll keep your mouth shut about all this." He pauses to whip the knife out of the man's arm, and this time, the sheriff puts his own hand over his mouth to muffle his scream. "Because if I find out you've talked, I will"—he wipes the blood on the sheriff's uniform—"slit your throat while you're sleepin' beside your wife and she won't know anything about it until she wakes up the next morning with your blood soaking the sheets and your dead eyes staring up at the ceiling. Am I clear?"

Sheriff Cooper's eyes are terrified as he jerks out a nod.

Then, Arsenal pockets the freshly cleaned knife as he finishes, "And the next time you put your hands on my wife will be the *last* time you put your hands on anything. I'll cut them off your body and shove them down your throat."

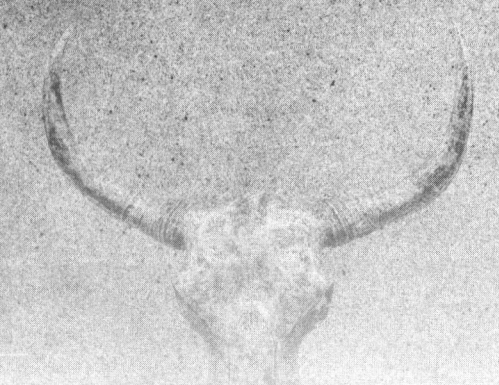

CHAPTER NINE

To: Peyton Turner
From: Bo Porter

Peyton,

I read the book.

I hated every minute of it and thought it was crap.

But more than that, I didn't get from it what you wanted me to get, and I remain as angry and rude as ever. In any case, reading your favorite book even though I hate reading in general was the only thing I could come up with to show you that I acknowledge being an asshole to you in my last letter.

As for your offer of friendship, I'm not sure it's very smart. For a smart college girl, you should know better than to be friends with a convicted criminal. Or maybe it's pity.

Is it?

Bo

To: Bo Porter
From: Peyton Turner

Dear Bo,

I think I taught you well.

It was the perfect apology: reading my favorite book and being tortured through it. I don't think anyone has ever done that before. But come on, don't keep me in suspense. What did you get from it?

And for a criminal asshole cowboy, you should know better than to accuse me of pity. My offer of friendship was genuine. Although, it's not on the table anymore. Because believe it or not, we're there already.

We are friends.

Until next time,

Peyton

To: Peyton Turner
From: Bo Porter

Peyton,

It wasn't revenge that destroyed Heathcliff's life but love.

If he hadn't fallen for Catherine, he wouldn't have suffered and made others suffer. Whether for his pain or amusement. Revenge gave him a purpose; love destroyed his life.

So I'm not the kind of a friend you want in your life but I guess that ship's sailed.

Bo

CHAPTER TEN

The Dark Stallion

EIGHT YEARS AGO, I wanted to kill Hank Turner but failed.

They dragged me away before I could see the light go out of his eyes and charged me with attempted murder.

They were wrong.

I *am* a murderer.

I couldn't kill him, but I *did* kill that night. And spending eight years behind bars isn't enough for that. No amount of punishment is enough or is ever going to be enough for breaking the promise I made. But maybe if I avenge that night, I can begin to atone for it.

Although what I'm doing right now isn't atoning.

Drinking cheap whiskey at a titty bar while getting a lap dance. I'd been to a few titty bars before I got put away, and strippers have never really been my thing. Something about their asses in every drunk asshole's face seems to put me off.

I don't like to share.

If my woman's ass was anywhere near another man, he'd be going home without a face.

But I'm a man, and a man has certain needs. After being locked up for eight years with only my fist for company, those needs have, shall we say, *grown*. I've been trying to avoid them ever since I got out almost a week ago, but I can't.

Not tonight.

Especially not tonight.

So I had to look up the nearest strip club on the GPS and drive down here. Even though I don't think it's working. The girl on my lap is pretty good. She knows when to bear down and just when to pull back. Plus, she smells great. A little cloying for my taste, but overall it looks like she puts effort into keeping things classy. If anyone could give me what I need tonight, it'd be her.

But so far, it isn't happening. If anything, my need has grown further, and I'm getting pissed off at no relief.

"Just so you know, I can do a lot more than this, cowboy," the woman in my lap whispers into my ear.

"How do you know I'm a cowboy?"

Still twisting over my lap, she takes me in. My cap first, followed by my face and then the rest of me. I know when a girl likes what she sees, and this one likes it a whole lot. I'd be lying if I said I've never taken advantage of looks thrown my way.

I have.

Before everything. Before my life changed.

"Big and strong body that can only come from backbreaking work," she begins, "rough and scraped-up hands because you use them from sunup to sundown probably mucking the stalls or mending fences; sprawled thighs as if you're sitting on a horse, not a chair. And I know it's dark and I can't really tell, but I bet you've got a killer tan from working outside all day." She runs her eyes over me again and concludes, "A cowboy through and through."

She's right.

About some things.

My body *is* big and strong, and I do have a killer tan. It's just that it's from working out in the prison exercise yard and sometimes using inmates as my personal punching bags when my anger at things got bad, not from working the fields. And I do use my hands, but to stab motherfuckers who touch things that belong to me. And no, I haven't ridden a horse in eight years, but I remember how to because it's a thing you never forget.

But all I say is, "So you meet a lot of cowboys, then?"

"It's Montana. Every schmuck who comes through this door's a cowboy." Then, shrugging, she adds, "Or wants to be one."

At this, a low chuckle escapes me because she's right. For some reason, everyone wants to be a cowboy. But my father used to say there's a difference between playing a cowboy and actually being one.

I don't remember a lot about him because he died when I was twelve, but I do remember him saying this to my older brother: There are men who want to wear a Stetson and play at being wild, and then there are men who don't need no hat to be wild. They're born with a wild heart and a wilder soul. So they got no choice but to be on the back of a horse, riding into the wind and the sunset. I always knew he was telling the truth, but I never knew how much until I got put away.

Trapped inside a cinder block with no wind or sunset.

I deserved it, though.

"But tell you what," she goes, pulling me away from my thoughts and inching closer.

"What?"

"Only real cowboys know how to ride."

Another chuckle. "Is that so?"

"And it's your lucky day because I'm a cowgirl myself," she says, smirking and writhing her hips with a renewed enthusiasm, probably to show off her skills. "So what do you say, cowboy, want a ride?"

I take her in again.

Dark hair piled on top of her head with tendrils falling all over her made-up face; lithe and toned body; tanned skin; skimpy linge-rie. She's a walking, talking wet dream, but unfortunately for me, not my dream.

Not only because most of my dreams have turned into night-mares filled with blood and fire and explosions. But also because, for the past six months, the few dreams that haven't turned into nightmares are filled with letters in white envelopes and books and sociology and Heathcliff and Catherine.

"What's your name?" I ask, my fingers fisted around the whis-key tumbler.

"Elektra."

"Elektra," I repeat.

"Yeah"—she keeps smiling as she takes her hand off the back of my chair and brings it to my face—"so how about—"

I grab her wrist just as she's about to make contact. And I will admit I do it tightly. So much so that she stops moving and frowns in confusion. Not her fault; despite the gathering anger in my gut, I've been a perfect gentleman so far. I haven't groped her. I haven't leered at her. I haven't crossed lines or boundaries. So I get why she's confused.

But the thing is that I'm pissed.

I have no intention of taking it out on her; I'm an asshole but not one of those assholes. I just don't like to be touched the way she was going to. I also don't like to be lied to. Ironic, I know, but I did mention I was an asshole.

"Tell you what," I begin, putting my whiskey down and flexing my fingers around her wrist, "I'll give you a thousand dollars if you tell me your real name."

"What?"

"Because it isn't your real name, is it?"

"That's—"

"Unless your mama actually wanted you to grow up and give lap dances for a living."

She grinds her teeth for a few seconds before saying, "Here I thought you were different."

"You got that by just grindin' in my lap for ten minutes?"

"You're just like the rest of 'em," she spits out.

I hum. "I'm an asshole, yes; but I'm a different kind of asshole."

She twists her hand in my grip. "I don't think so."

Still keeping a hold on her wrist, I shift in my seat and reach for my back pocket to get out my wallet. As soon as she sees it, her struggles halt. "Look around, look at all the guys in here; I don't think they've got as much cash in their pocket as me. That's difference number one." Letting go of her wrist, I take out the money. "Difference number two: Even though you've just about bored me to death, I'll still give it to you. Because I can respect hard work. And finally, unlike all the wannabes who come here every day, I'm a real cowboy."

She eyes the cash in my hand, which is much more than a thousand dollars, before snatching it away and tucking it into her cleavage. Then, "You still wanna know my real name?"

"No," I reply.

It's not *her* real name I want to know anyway.

She hops off my lap and I'm out the door, walking to my car, when my phone rings in my pocket. It's Radisson, my cousin and the one person who knows everything about me.

Before I got put away, we used to be partners in crime, working together on the ranch, riding together, starting shit together. Well, I'd start shit and he'd cover for me, but yeah. Growing up, we even had little nicknames for each other: I called him the Quiet Mustang because of his limited speech capabilities, and he called me the Dark Stallion because I was reckless and hence, dangerous. There was a time I couldn't imagine living my life without him in it. Didn't think I'd have to. But then what happened, happened, and here we are, eight years later.

I pick up the call, but before I can say anything, I hear, "Where the fuck are you?"

That doesn't sound like Rad, and it wasn't the voice I was hoping to hear on the other end.

But I guess it makes sense.

I wasn't picking up his calls. Save for the one phone call I made the day I got out to let him know that I was out and safe, I haven't really kept him in the loop. So he got creative; my older brother doesn't like to be ignored. And well, Rad has always been a good boy; he can't say no, especially to Marsden, the head of the family.

"I'm assuming," I begin as I come to a halt beside my car, "you were polite when you asked Rad for his phone so you could call me."

Mars breathes out sharply. "Believe it or not, he wouldn't give it to me. Had to steal it off his saddle when he was makin' rounds in the bunkhouse during dinner."

Along with being our cousin, Rad also happens to be the foreman at the ranch. Meaning, he's in charge of everything from the upkeep and operations to the ranch hands. He's the second-most-important man at Rawhide, the first being Mars since he's the one signing everyone's paychecks. If anyone deserves that role, it's Rad. He's dedicated his entire life to Rawhide. While I've done the same, my goal was never to stay. I wanted to get out of there one day, build my own life, my own ranch.

I shift on my feet. "What do you want?"

"What do I *want*?" Mars bites out, his tone laced with disbelief.

"You called me for a reason, didn't you? What is it?"

I hear a sharp breath coming from the other side. "I called you because you're not home yet. Because you keep avoidin' my calls. Because you were released a week ago but I know fuck all about what you're doin'." Another breath, this one just as sharp as the last. "Well, up until today."

My body goes rigid at that. He could mean a lot of things by that, but somehow I think I know what he's talking about. I'm proven right when he goes on to say, "Cooper called."

Fuck.

Fuck, fuck, *fuck*.

I knew it was a risk enlisting his help. He's got a big mouth and a very weak will. But I needed someone with connections at the city court, and I didn't have a lot of time to go searching for someone who is loyal to us but also isn't a spineless fucking rat. I guess I'm gonna have to make good on my promise to him and cut his throat in his sleep.

"What the fuck were you thinkin', attacking him like that," my brother snaps.

"He crossed a line," I tell him, fisting and unfisting my fingers.

"And what line was that?"

"Disobeyin' me."

"You're not a fuckin' king," he reminds me. "What you are is a felon out on parole."

I clench my jaw at his reprimand. Sounds just like it did back when I was out and riling shit up at twenty.

"You know what that means, don't you?" he keeps going. "You gotta keep your nose clean. Or you're back in, serving your full ten-year sentence. And this time, even I won't be able to help you."

"Didn't want your help last time; don't need it now."

"Christ," Mars bites out. "You just keep diggin' the hole for yourself. You've got no idea the lengths I had to go to, to get you that hearing after how you fucked it up last time."

I did fuck it up last time.

In my defense, though, I stuck to the truth. They asked me if I regretted what I did, and I said no. I said if I got a do-over, I'd do things differently and instead of beating him bloody, I'd focus on choking the life out of him.

They didn't like that.

So yeah, I was surprised when my brother called me about the second hearing. Apparently, the DA has a penchant for paying for sex with schoolgirls, and he's up for reelection. But this time, I was determined to get out. Because this time, I had a purpose.

A plan.

The one my brother wouldn't like, so I couldn't clue him in.

"Especially when the Turners would do anything to keep you in," he adds. "One chance, that's all they need. One slipup and you're back in."

I'm aware.

The Turners would do anything to send me back in. Like they did everything they could eight years ago to get me a harsher sentence. Attempted murder in Montana gets you anywhere from ten years to life. The only reason I got the minimum of ten was because of who I am, a Grayson, and because the Turners wouldn't let it go down to five. Now that I'm free without serving a full sentence, I know they would love to take me out. But unfortunately for them, I've got a plan that's going to end not only what they started eight years ago, but also this fucking feud, once and for all.

"There isn't going to be a slipup," I say.

He scoffs. "Yeah, that's a little hard for me to believe when you're stabbin' cops in broad daylight a week into your parole."

"Cooper's fine. He's gonna keep his mouth shut."

"Yeah, how do you know that?"

"Because I told him to keep it shut."

"That's—"

"And because his son's in the program, isn't he?"

This time when Mars breathes out sharply, it's because he knows I won.

"I'm sure he's not gonna do anything to jeopardize that," I finish.

Which is why I roped him in, in the first place. I knew he'd do anything to keep his loser son out of prison. And if anyone can make that happen, it's my brother and his fucking program.

I don't like to mention it, the little prison program my brother's got going on the ranch. I never did, and after everything that happened eight years ago, I hate it even more. But again, I needed someone who was beholden to us, and Cooper fit the bill.

"Now, if you've got nothing else—"

"Tell me exactly what the fuck you were thinkin' marryin' the Turner girl."

Something shifts in my chest, my gut, at this.

I don't know how to describe it, but it feels like the ground opening up. The ground shaking under the galloping hooves of a thousand horses before the earth gives in and cracks down the middle, breaking apart. Fissures running everywhere.

It happened the night that changed the course of my life.

Something broke apart inside of me, and out came fire and anger. So much of it that it was hard to contain, and I had to do what I ended up doing. Beating a man within an inch of his life because he destroyed mine.

Over the years, whenever it happened and I broke apart on the inside, I'd just find a motherfucker to beat up. It wasn't hard; I was in prison, and there are a lot of motherfuckers in there. I wish I could do the same tonight as well. Beat someone up.

But I'm out on parole, and despite what my brother thinks, I do realize I need to be careful. I can't be caught beating someone up, especially where there are cameras and word could get back to the Turners.

So I don't know how to glue the cracks. How to shove all the things back inside, the fire, the anger. Her voice.

Her *musical* fucking voice.

That snuck into my bloodstream and crept inside the very core of me, despite the fact I only heard it three days ago. And it's the first thing I hear at my brother's "the Turner girl."

I couldn't let you sit here, waiting for me, after everything... we've shared.

I breathe through my nose for a few seconds, trying to calm myself down. Then, "What I was thinkin' is none of your fuckin' business."

A pause and then, in a growly voice, "Come again?"

I clutch the phone tighter. "You heard me."

I'm about to break the heavy silence between us when he does it himself, his voice low and vibrating. "Proved me right."

"What?"

"You," he says. "You like to live wild. You like to live on the edge. 'Watch out for him,' Daddy always said. 'He's worse than those damn broncos he likes to ride. He'll either end up dead or in prison'; and I fuckin' prayed for prison. I guess you should really be careful what you wish for, huh." He sighs. "I just didn't know I'd have a hand in it."

My chest tightens at his regretful tone.

Once upon a time, I worshipped my big brother. He was more like a father to me and our little brother, Axton. Our parents died in a car crash, and the responsibility of the ranch fell on Mars. He was twenty-two and was already working at the ranch, helping our dad with the business and whatever else needed doing. Still, it was a big change for him that he shouldered well. Not to mention, he got a twelve-year-old rebellious teenager and a one-year-old screaming toddler as a bonus. He was strict and somewhat aloof, but I understood that he had to be that way. He had to be author-itative because Rawhide depended on him. I and our little brother depended on him.

He's still my big brother, but we haven't seen eye-to-eye in a long time. Despite all that, though, I still don't like to hear that tone.

"There are days when I regret not namin' you my foreman. If I had, you probably would've been too busy to go off the rails like you did. You—"

"I didn't go off the rails," I growl.

"You beat a man half to death with a hot branding iron," he growls back. "And not just *some* man; you beat up Hank Turner. The family we've been at war with for decades. The family that took our land, the land that rightfully belongs to us, to our forefathers. They'd do anything to destroy us. Anything to take us out. But instead of using your goddamn head, you went in there, guns blazin', and handed them the ammunition to use against us. And for what?"

"Don't," I warn.

He doesn't heed it and keeps going: "I told you eight years ago and I'm tellin' you now, a girl ain't no reason to go stupid and turn your back on your family."

The crack inside me becomes a chasm, wide and gaping, painful and hot.

Furious.

"A girl ain't no reason to lose eight years of your life, to lose your ability to fuckin' think and to be doin' whatever it was you thought you were doin' by marrying the Turner girl. I know you loved her but—"

"Fuck you," I mutter, cutting him off. "*Fuck.* You."

I hang up and switch off my phone.

Pocketing it, I get in the car and pull out of the parking lot. All through the drive back to the motel, my body is tight and my fucking heart is pounding. The chasm inside me gets wider and wider until it feels like I'll never be able to seal it shut again. I'll never be able to bury all the things that crawled out from the underneath.

Bury *her.*

Where she's safe, protected. Like I wanted her to be eight years ago. Like I promised.

By the time I reach my destination—the motel I'm staying at for the night—I'm shaking. Tremors are running up and down my body. The brand on my shoulder burns as hot and as brutal as it did the night I put it there. With a shivering hand, I open the door to my room, but it all stops the moment I see her in there.

The Turner girl.

The girl I've been seeing in my dreams for the past six months. The smart, straight-A college girl who liked to be careful and safe. Until she made the mistake of writing to a felon in prison.

Back in my six-by-eight prison cell, there was no escape from her, her words, her thoughts. I'd dream about the things she wrote, her desk, her room, the library she worked at. Her favorite tree. Her favorite books. It would piss me off, and I'd end up in fights and then get thrown in solitary. Where things would get even worse because there were no distractions except following the cracks on the cement floors and counting bricks on the wall.

Even so, I guarded her letters with my life. I kept them hidden either under the mattress or tucked inside a book. Sometimes I'd carry them in my pocket. There's no privacy in prison, no dignity, very little respect. Didn't matter what my last name was, and most everyone knew who I was, from guards to inmates. The only consolation was that her letters skipped the usual inspection by the guards and were delivered to me with the seal unbroken.

So her secrets were safe.

Or at least safe from the world until they got into my hands. I won't apologize for it, though. I won't say I didn't mean it, because I absolutely did.

My plan *was* to lure her out and seduce her into marrying me. I will admit to an attack of conscience, though, that led me to send her away at the café. But when she found out my real name, I didn't have a choice but to take her.

And here she is now.

In the flesh.

When I left to find a strip club, she was already out for the night. I guess the day took a toll on her. So she's on the bed, sleeping on her back, her head on the pillow with her blond hair scattered around it; one of her small hands is curled by her cheek, and the other rests on her belly. Her cheeks are flushed and her dark blond eyelashes cast shadows on them. Under the dim yellow light, her hair looks like a halo and she looks like an angel.

Like an answer to all my prayers.

I don't pray, but I think she is the answer. It was a pure stroke of luck that she fell into my lap, and now that she has, I'm not letting her go.

I enter and close the door behind me. I'm not exactly quiet, but she doesn't move; she's a heavy sleeper, something I found out last night. Or maybe all that screaming and pounding on the door knocked her out. Either way, I don't think she's going to wake up anytime soon.

I sit down in the chair by the door and take my cap off. Without taking my eyes off her, I unlace my boots. When I'm done, I stand up, snag the T-shirt at my back, and yank it off my body. I walk to the bed as I unbutton my jeans. I drag the zipper down and climb onto the bed.

The lower half of her body is covered by a white sheet, and I take it off, revealing her. She's still got her white dress on, the one I bought her. The one she wore this morning.

Her wedding dress.

Something like satisfaction rushes through my veins. I'm not sure why or what the fuck it even means. But seeing her in a dress I bought, seeing her in a dress I told her to wear like the one at the café, does something to me. It makes me feel…powerful.

Possessive.

Primal.

I take her in now, all sleepy and soft, unaware. I wrap my hands around her ankles and spread her legs. She lets out a long breath but keeps sleeping.

Good.

I don't need her awake for this, for what I plan to do. It wasn't my need that made me find a strip club, but her. I am hard up from prison but not as hard up as I am for *her*.

My wife.

Tiny little thing with curves for days. Hills and valleys, crests and swells and fucking dips. Her body's a landscape. A wonderland. That you want to map with your fingers.

If you were someone else.

If you were me, though, you'd want to more than map. I want to plunder and ravage. Dig my fingers, my teeth. Grab and grope and leave my mark. Brand her in the way her family has branded me.

So that's what I'm doing.

Leaving her my mark.

I've wanted to do it since the very first letter she wrote me, and somehow more than just reading it, I heard her voice in my head. I never could've imagined, though, how fucking sweet it'd turn out to be. Like the strums of a guitar around the campfire after a long, hard day of roping bulls and wrangling horses.

Kneeling between her open thighs, I fist my cock and jerk off, staring at her face. Taking in her pale skin and pink lips. The delicate line of her neck. It was so easy to wrap my fingers around her throat and squeeze. So easy to feel the thrum of her pulse on my palm. If I'd squeezed hard enough, I bet I would've slowed down her breathing, left my fingerprints.

I groan at the thought, pre-cum sliding down my length, lubing up my hand.

With my other hand, I reach down and inch up her dress, careful not to wake her. Her panties come into view, and *Jesus Christ*, they're white too. Something about that color on her gets me going. Like she's an innocent college girl, and I'm the big, bad *criminal* cowboy who wants to dirty her up.

And she *is* innocent, isn't she?

Untouched. A virgin.

Fuck.

Fuuuuck.

Just the thought of breaching that barrier, breaking her in, makes me choke my dick with my fingers like I imagine her virgin pussy choking me, strangling me, molding to the ridges of my cock. And the thought that I'd never feel that, never feel her tight cunt around my desperate and horny dick because she's a fucking Turner, makes me so pissed off that my pumps become faster.

Rougher.

Angrier.

So do the noises I make, my breaths, my need to brand her. And before I know it I'm coming. I'm spurting all over her white panties, her creamy thighs, my hand. My chest shudders and my muscles spasm. I feel like I can finally breathe now that I see my cum striping her skin, soaking her little panties.

But only for a moment.

The next breath I take, I'm full of guilt. I'm full of regret and anger that never seem to go away, no matter what I do. She was right when she told me that revenge won't give me peace. But I'm not doing this for peace, am I? I'm doing it to avenge. I'm doing it to avenge the girl I failed to protect.

Annie.

Disgusted, I move away from the Turner girl and throw open the window before sitting on the floor under it. These days, I need an open window to breathe and hardness that reminds me of my cell, the only thing familiar in this new world, to navigate.

I fish out the marriage certificate from my pocket, unfold it, and take in her signature. Her curly, feminine, *familiar* handwriting. So familiar that I'd recognize it anywhere. And in that handwriting, she's written a name, or a semblance of a name, that I don't recognize.

R Bell.

I don't give a fuck what that stripper's real name was.

But I do wanna know why my wife signed our marriage certificate with a name I've never heard before.

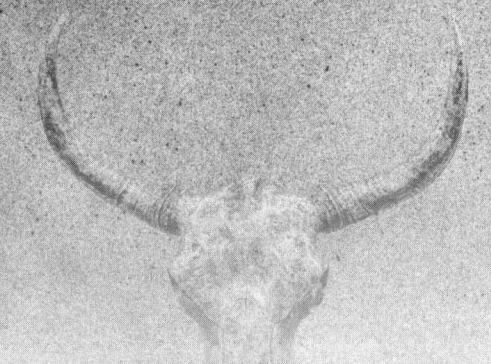

CHAPTER ELEVEN

HE'S THE REASON.

That we left the ranch all those years ago.

Isn't he?

I thought about it after the courtroom. I thought about what he said in the car, about his crime, about him trying to kill Peyton's father. I couldn't put it together before—probably because I was out of my mind with fear—but it all adds up now.

Eight years ago, we left the ranch abruptly, Peyton and her mom, and my mom and me. I remember we were at camp when we got the call that we had to cut it short and leave. And that we weren't going home but somewhere else. They told us there was an attack at the ranch. That someone broke in and beat Peyton's father within an inch of his life. They said he had every intention of killing Mr. Turner, but someone heard noises coming out of the mansion and called the cops.

They also said he wore a mask, a bull mask with horns.

Peyton was understandably upset. She never liked her father, but someone trying to kill him was an extreme she couldn't have imagined herself.

But me; like a traitor, I was happy. Not because Peyton's father and my parents' employer was almost killed but because we finally had the chance to move away from my daddy. I was happy that maybe now my mother would be safe from him and his fists, his cruelty. So while Peyton hated the masked man who came to kill her father, I didn't. I saw him as a savior. I know it's fucked up. I know what an epic betrayal of Peyton this is.

I *know* that.

Not only did that man try to kill my best friend's father, but he was probably from the Rawhide ranch. The family that's full of criminals and bad men. The family that as part of the Grayson clan, I'm supposed to hate.

Even though no one told us that specifically, that the man who broke in was a Grayson, Peyton and I could both figure it out. Peyton's mom tried to keep us away from the news, too, citing that it would have a harmful effect on us. But Peyton, as always, didn't follow the rules. She tried to find everything she could about the trial, the man who was arrested. She never shared any of this with me, though. She thought I was too fragile, and I let her believe that. But I wasn't too fragile.

I was too invested in him.

I already wanted to know everything about him, about the man who got us away from my daddy's evil clutches. Who saved my mother. Who saved *me*. Not that moving away made much of a difference. My father was still very much a part of my mother's life if he wanted to be.

But the point is that he's the one. He's the one who saved me.

The one in the mask, the man I think of as my hero.

I don't know how to feel about that. I don't know how to even *begin* to comprehend what it means. That the same man who saved me years ago is the man who's been lying to me for the past six months. I've dreamed about two men in my life, and turns out, both of them are one and the same.

My asshole *criminal* cowboy. My husband.

No, *not* my husband. He just *thinks* he's my husband and I'm his wife. And if I have my way, he'll never find out the truth. It's more imperative now than ever. *Especially* after I know what he's capable of. Beating a man half to death and stabbing a cop in a courtroom; having his shooter friend at his beck and call, ready to kill people.

"How do I know you kept your promise?" I blurt out, my voice sounding too loud in the space.

We're in the car and I'm watching his hands. They're resting on the wheel, his fingers loosely grasping it as he drives us somewhere. I don't know where we're going; he of course never told me. Like the morning at the cabin, when I found him in the room, fully awake, and this time, staring at the document he made me sign. There was breakfast on the nightstand, and with a heavy look directed at me, he said we were leaving soon and I needed to be ready.

I didn't argue with him.

I didn't ask all the questions I wanted to ask. Like, why do I always find him sitting in a corner, awake, looking like he hasn't slept a wink all night? What was he doing after I went to sleep? Because I think something happened. Something…that I'm afraid to think about. Not to mention, I could've fought him this morning. I could've screamed, gotten someone's attention instead of meekly getting in the car with him.

But I kept seeing the blood spurting out of the sheriff's arm. I kept thinking about how he could get someone killed if I didn't obey him, and my tongue stayed tied. I unglue it from the roof of my mouth once again, and while staring at his throat-grabbing, knife-wielding, and almost-murdering but *savior* hands, I prod, "How do I know he…" I stop and clear my throat before continuing, "How do I know my brother's alive?"

I watch his fingers flex on the wheel. Then, "He's alive."

I lift my eyes to his face, and the first thing I see is the sun's rays hitting him and making his bronzed skin glow. The sunlight falls on his jaw, his throat, the strands of hair teasing his neck in patches, and for a second or two, all I can do is trace the patterns they create. All I can do is think about how the sun chases away the shadows created by his cap.

How he attempted to murder someone, but he's also a savior.

"But how do I know that?" I insist, pushing those thoughts away for the millionth time. "You could be... You could be lying."

His fingers flex again.

As if at the word *lying*. Then, "I was."

"What?"

"Lying."

"I don't—"

"Didn't have anyone waitin' for him," he says, keeping his eyes on the road. "He was fine the whole time."

And my mouth falls open. "He was... You..."

His chest rises and falls with a breath. "Killin' the Turner family's not my endgame. Not anymore. I want them alive. So they can wish they were dead."

I turn toward him fully. "So you *lied* to me?"

His jaw moves back and forth. "That's what I said."

"That's... I don't..." Then, with my hands fisted, I try again: "I can't... I can't *believe* you lied to me."

His face is hard, a pulse beating in his cheek, but his shrug seems casual. "Well, I lied to you for six months. Shouldn't really be a surprise I did it again, don't you think?"

God, I hate him.

I absolutely fucking hate him.

I open my fists and grab the edge of the seat, biting into the leather with my nails. "So, what, if I hadn't gotten in your car yesterday, *your stupid freaking car* that you kidnapped me in, and came with you to the courtroom all quietly and meekly like I did, nothing would've happened?"

"Something would've happened."

"Like what?"

"Like me tyin' you up and throwin' you in the trunk of my car. And drivin' you to the courthouse anyway."

I think a nail breaks at this. "You—"

"I didn't think your wrists could take the abuse," he speaks over me. "Not yet at least, so I made a judgment call."

I stare at him for a few seconds because I don't know what else to do. I don't know what to *say* or think other than the fact that he's insane. He's completely *insane.*

"So scaring me *out my mind*," I begin, glaring at him, "was your judgment call?"

"Your wrists are gettin' better, aren't they?"

I look down at my wrists like an idiot. And again *like an idiot*, I do think they look fine. The redness is still there, but the skin doesn't look as tender or swollen as it did only a day ago. It doesn't itch as much either.

But that's not…

I jerk my head up. "I don't care about my wrists. I *care* that you lied to me."

"Again," he replies, his voice all cool. "Shouldn't be a surprise after everything."

"Oh my God, this is—"

"Plus, it got you to get in the car, didn't it."

"That's not a reason to—"

"The easy way too," he goes on. "So all's well that ends well."

"No," I snap, finally getting my bearings. "All is *not* well. All is *fucked.* All is—"

"Stay in the car."

I draw back at the sudden change of topic, and for the first time since we started this journey, I look away from him. And I realize two things: First, we've come to a stop. And second, we've come to a stop at a ranch. I've been so focused on him that I have no idea how long it took us to get here, but it looks like we're parked on a dirt road and there's a corral right in front of us. There are palominos trotting along the fence and a couple of ranch hands brushing other horses' coats and tending to their hooves. A sprawling house stands against the backdrop of a large field that also holds grazing horses, and then, as always, off in the distance is the ever-present chain of mountains that you find in Montana no matter where you go.

Before I can turn to him and ask what this place is and what we're doing here, he climbs out of the car and prowls away, leaving me stunned. He heads toward the barn that sits right adjacent to the corral, and as he nears it, I see the barn door opening. A guy comes out wearing a Stetson and leather chaps. I watch them have a conversation, and it's so reminiscent of yesterday that ignoring his decree, I jump out of the car and head toward them.

I get there just as the guy walks away and I demand, "Who was he?"

My eyes are on the guy as he heads back to the barn, which is probably why I don't see Arsen move closer to me. So close that I feel him breathing down my neck. I *feel* his big hard chest, which was plastered to my spine yesterday while he held my throat captive, moving. My heart races, and for some reason, instead of turning around to face him, I choose to watch the guy as he disappears inside the barn.

"Is he your buddy?" I blurt out. "Like the sheriff?"

Ignoring me, he rasps, "You didn't stay in the car."

Even though we're not touching, his words vibrate through my body, raising goose bumps. "Are you going to stab him too if I ask him for help?"

I hate that my words sounded more breathy than stern. But he's so fucking close and his breaths are so warm and I want him to get away from me.

"I'll stab him if he touches you."

"That's—"

"Or if you touch him."

"What?"

"So you better save all your pleadin' and beggin' for me," he goes on, his voice deep and sort of hypnotic.

I curl my fingers into a fist, still keeping my back turned and my eyes straight ahead; I have no clue what I'm seeing, though, because something occurs to me. "Did you… Is that why you stabbed Sheriff Cooper in the arm *specifically?* Because I t-touched it."

Because that's what he did, didn't he? He stabbed Cooper's arm, and before that he kept staring at it with a dangerous intent.

A strange kind of intensity wafts from him and his voice. "Don't like when men put their hands on things that belong to me just as much as I don't like those things putting their hands on other men."

My heart jumps to my throat, beating in a mad rhythm. "That's… that's *psychotic.*"

"Maybe."

"And I'm not a thing," I remind him.

He hums. "Semantics."

"And I definitely, *definitely* do not belong to you."

"I've got a paper in my pocket that says different."

At this, along with my rapidly beating heart, the blood starts rushing in my veins like crazy too. "That *paper* does not hold up."

"No?"

"No."

"Why?"

"Because it's a lie. You *forced* me to sign it under false pretenses."

He hums again. "Well, you did sign it, didn't you?"

"That doesn't—"

"It's *your* name on there."

Something about his tone makes my belly churn. It feels *knowing.* Like, somehow, he knows that I'm lying. It's impossible, though. There's no way for him to know. I won't *let* him know.

"Isn't it?" he prods when I stay silent.

Breathing in deep, I straighten my spine. "Yes."

"So then, you're mine."

"I'm—"

"And no one puts their hands on what's mine."

I close my eyes for a second and gather myself. I curl and uncurl my fingers. I fist my dress and suck in my belly. All in an attempt to not fall apart at his rough tone. His *possessive* tone.

Clearing my throat, I change the subject and try again: "Who is he?"

I feel him shift behind me. "His brother works at Rawhide; one of the wranglers."

"What are we doing here?"

"You're about to find out."

"Why can't you just..." I breathe in and out for the hundredth time before I continue, "Tell me about last night."

"What about last night?"

"What happened after I fell asleep?" I ask because for some reason, I can't get it out of my head. "No matter how scary it is, I need to know."

"What do you think happened?" he asks in return.

I clench my teeth. "I don't know; you tell me." Before he can answer, I continue, "And if you lie to me again, I'll lose it, okay? I'll fucking lose my shit."

He waits a beat to answer. "I left."

"Left."

"For a little bit."

"Where?"

Again, he takes a second to reply. "To find someone."

I'm confused. I don't really understand what he means, but then it hits me, and my body goes tight. "You...you went to find a g-girl?"

"Yeah."

My heart clenches so hard, so viciously, that I can't even pretend it's not jealousy. Which is insane on a whole 'nother level that I don't want to analyze right now. Especially when I blurt out, "On our wedding night?"

I can't believe I said that. What is *wrong* with me?

"It was, wasn't it," he says, and I swear he feels closer, and his words sound almost tender.

"I-I shouldn't have said that," I stutter, stopping myself from rubbing my arms and chasing away the goose bumps at his voice.

"Didn't think you'd want my hands on you, though."

"I don't." Then, to emphasize, I add, "I absolutely do not want your filthy *criminal* cowboy hands on me."

"So it's a good thing I found someone, isn't it?"

I clutch my dress, my *wedding* dress, my stomach bottoming out. "You did?"

"Uh-huh. Meaning, you're safe from me, from my hands."

"I'm not safe with you," I say, flinching at his "safe," my chest still tight. "I'm never safe with you; and how do I even know that you didn't?"

"I didn't what?"

"T-touch me."

Again, I can't believe I said that, that I went *there*. I don't know what's happening, why I'm saying all the wrong things. So I go to take it back. I also go to turn around, because this is not helping. Him so close, whispering things; and me, not looking at him, just listening to his words.

It feels like before.

Like when I'd read his letters in my room, lying in my bed, and imagine him saying the words out loud to me. So this is messing with me, with my head.

But before I can do any of that, he whispers, directly in my ear, "Maybe I did."

And I freeze. "What?"

"Touch you."

"You…"

"And maybe I did find someone," he says, unbothered by my loud breaths, heaving chest. "She was willing. No, she wanted it. She knew how to dance too, knew how to writhe and grind and twist on my lap like the top-notch stripper she was. But for some reason, she wasn't doing it for me. So I came back. I raced back to the motel and as soon as I saw you on the bed, unaware and sleeping, I realized why."

"Why what?"

"I realized"—he moves closer, and I swear to God I feel him pouring his words down my ear—"she wasn't the one I wanted. I wanted someone else."

I close my eyes because I know what he's going to say. And I need to brace for it. I need to brace for his lies.

"I wanted a girl with hair like the sun and eyes like the sky. Who smells like the buttercups that grow on my ranch."

My eyes pop open. "B-buttercups."

He hums. "That smell sweet like roses and tart like citrus."

"I…" I swallow thickly, my eyes unfocused. "I smell like t-that?"

"Yeah. It's hard to breathe around you."

"I-It is?"

"It's hard to ride in the car with you."

I shake my head. "I…I didn't—"

"It's hard," he whispers again.

I swallow, unable to say anything.

"Makes me wanna throw you in the trunk just so I don't have to breathe you in."

I flinch. "That's—"

"So maybe when I came back, all hard up and turned on, and found you in the bed, I did touch you." Then, "Like I always told you I would."

I go still.

"You remember that, don't you?" he goes on.

I do. I remember it from one of his letters. I've read that one so many times now that I can recite the words with my eyes closed. I know exactly where on the page that sentence is, the one where he talks about touching me.

I *know*.

But I shake my head again. "Don't. Don't talk about that."

"How I said," he goes on, "that if I ever saw you, I'd have to put my filthy criminal cowboy hands on you. Because I wouldn't be able to stop myself. And I wouldn't just touch you. I'd grab you and grope you and I'd do it *so fucking hard*"—I flinch at the way he says it—"that I'd brand you with my mark."

There's that word again. And God, something is seriously wrong with me because I have to clench my thighs at it. I have to clench my tummy just at the thought of his brand on me.

"I'd brand your skin that I always knew would be like silk. But you wanna know what the kicker is?"

I keep shaking my head. "I don't want to talk about letters."

"I just didn't know *how* silky. I couldn't even *imagine* how fucking soft and rounded and *ripe* your body would be. How much I'd want to bite it with my teeth, squeeze it with my fingers. Eat you like the piece of fruit you are. Like a peach, maybe." I feel him getting even closer, still not touching, though, but so, *so* close. "Or a cherry. A red and juicy cherry that you want to suck on."

"I—"

"And the thing is, you really are a cherry, aren't you."

"What?"

"Untouched and innocent."

"I—"

"Ripe but *so fucking* tight."

I clench my legs again. "Just stop."

"So maybe when I saw you last night, I lost my mind. But there's one flaw in this whole thing."

"What f-flaw?"

"You would've felt it."

"I don't—"

"You would've felt me inside you. Pulsing and throbbing and fucking stretching you out. Even when I tranqed you, you would've felt me breaking you in and making you bleed. Because I'm just that big, darlin', and you're just that small."

Why did he have to say that? Why did he have to call me darlin'
and in a way that reminds me of melted butter and sticky syrup?

"Don't call me that," I protest.

"So no, I didn't touch you," he finishes. "Because if I had, you
wouldn't have slept through it. That place between your thighs
would be so sore and throbbing you wouldn't be able to sit in the car
like you did, driving me crazy with your buttercup scent and your
sassy mouth." Then, "Besides, I don't stick my dick in a Turner. And
you're a Turner, aren't you? So as I said, you're safe."

At last, I spin around and look up at him.

His eyes are dark and lazy, heavy-lidded, and there's a flush up
high on his cheekbones. But I ignore all of it, including the fact that
I probably look the same, and say, "Stop using that word. Stop saying *safe*. I'm not safe with you. How can I be safe with you? You keep
lying. You keep hiding the truth. You keep manipulating me, forcing
me, threatening me. I don't... How am I supposed to *be* with you?
What am I supposed to do? You ruined my life, do you realize that?
Do you realize how hard it is to be with you? And I...I can't...I can't
do this. This is... You have to promise me. You have to *freaking promise*
me that you won't lie. You..." I grab my forehead, looking away. "God,
what am I doing, what am I *doing*? You're never going to promise me
anything. You don't care about me. You never did. You're selfish and
manipulative and cruel and I'm stuck with you. I'm—"

"Okay."

I blink, feeling dizzy. "What?"

His heavy-lidded eyes are back to normal and the flush that made
his cheekbones look all sharp and brutal is gone. He says, "I won't lie."

I take a few seconds to respond: "You won't."

"You *are* stuck with me," he says, his gaze boring into me. "You're
stuck with me for as long as I want because I forced you to sign on the
dotted line. So the least I can do is make a vow to never lie to you."

"A vow?"

He keeps his dark gaze steady. "Consider it my wedding vow."

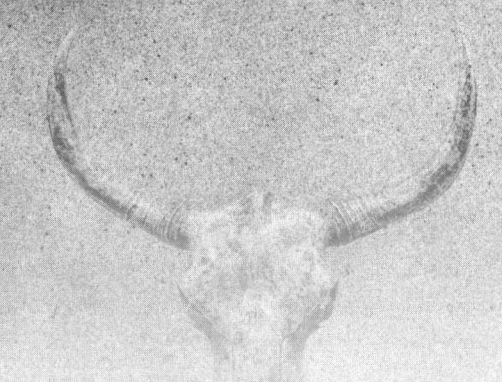

CHAPTER TWELVE

To: Bo Porter
From: Peyton Turner

Dear Bo,

    I just hit submit on my assignment. Like, literally five minutes ago.

    Not that you asked for it but I'm sending you a copy of what I wrote. I do think I've managed to scrape at least a C+ so prepare yourself to be dazzled. Oh and of course, thank you so much for all the help. You did annoy me at times and there were a couple of occasions when I really wanted to strangle you but overall, you were great.

    Now I'm sitting at my usual place—my desk by the window overlooking my favorite tree and I know you didn't ask but they aren't cutting it down anymore; all that neighborhood rallying seems to have worked!—and writing you this letter. I'm also grinning like a crazy person in case you haven't figured that part out yet.

    But I also realized something. There's no reason for us to talk anymore. I came to you for my assignment and it's over now. So we could say goodbye to each other except I don't think I want to.

    I don't want to stop writing to you. I don't want to stop waiting for your letter every Friday. Every week like clockwork, I finish my classes and my shift at the library, and race back to my apartment. I whip open my red mailbox and there you always are. Waiting for me inside a white prison stamped envelope. Usually I tear you open right there, standing on the side of the street because I'm so excited to see you, your words. I'm so excited to find out how they'll affect me.

Sometimes you make me mad because you can be so blunt and rude. Not to mention, so bossy and high-handed. Especially when you tell me to quit my shitty job at the shitty library with shitty hours and the shitty air-conditioning. And I know I freaked out on you when you told me to stay away from my math professor because he asked me to come up to his office after hours. But you were right. He did make a pass at me. So I declined his offer of being his TA. And funnily—and spookily—enough, I heard that he took a job at another university a few days later. You didn't have anything to do with it though, did you? There are times when you make me smile too. You listen to me ramble about my classes, my professors, all the plans I have about grad school, about my future.

And then there are other ways I think about you.

I imagine how you look bent over the piece of paper that I hold in my hands every week. I imagine your fingers—that I think are long and thick, maybe scarred and scrape-y from years of working on the ranch— clutching the pen and scribbling words. For some reason, that picture is so hard to come by. Maybe because after everything I know about you, it's hard for me to imagine you sitting still. Even though I know you do. Even though I know you have to, given where you are right now.

I also imagine your face.

I know we never talked about it, not after my initial confession, but the article I read about you in the Post had a picture of you too. It was grainy and unclear. But I could see you, with your dark head bent, as you were escorted out of the courtroom with a crowd around you. And while I couldn't see your face among the sea of people, I could see that it was raining and some days I feel really sad about that. About the fact that it was probably one of your last days on the outside and the sun was hiding behind gray clouds.

I don't want to stop imagining you. I don't want to stop talking to you. I don't want to stop, period.

Do you?

Until next time (hopefully),

Peyton

———

To: Peyton Turner
From: Bo Porter

Peyton,

This is a bad idea. Straight up.

It was a bad idea when you first wrote to a felon, asking for his help, and it's a bad idea now that you want to keep writing to me when there's no need for it anymore. This is the opposite of the careful life you want to lead. The opposite of what a straight-A student might do. I want you to remember that. For later. Remember that it was your idea because my answer is no. I don't want to stop.

Instead, I want to tell you about my Tuesdays.

My Tuesdays go like your Fridays. Every Tuesday when one of the guards moves through the rows of tables in the dayroom, distributing the mail, he knows to come to me first. He knows I watch him like a hawk until he makes his way over. And he knows not to let anyone disturb me when I get your words in my hands.

But unlike you, I don't skip sentences. I go slow. I take my time. I take in every word, absorb paragraphs. Then I close my eyes and sniff your words in through the nose like cocaine. Call me crazy but they smell like flowers. Sweet and rosy. And when I'm high on you, I see you in my head too.

There you are, sitting at your desk with your head bent. I think you'd have your hair up and away from your face. You're a straight-A student, aren't you, so you don't want anything to break your focus. Maybe you also wrinkle your forehead when you're deep in thought. Or when you have a hard time coming up with the perfect word or the correct phrase.

Or maybe you bite your lip?

When you're sassing me, I imagine you doing it with a lifted chin. Your hand getting heavy on the paper, your breaths picking up speed. Your cheeks red and flushed with anger. I imagine you frowning as I tell you that I don't want you working so hard at the library, your nose buried in a book. I want you to have an adventure. And if I could, I'd give it to you. I imagine that frown getting thicker as I ask you what if it really was me, who scared that professor away? Like I did with those inmates.

Would you be scared of me?

And now I'm imagining the flush of anger spreading through your cheeks because you're not afraid of anything, least of all a felon hundreds of miles away. And I want to touch it, that flush.

I want to touch you.

I untie your hair first and let the silky strands fall down your back. And it is silky, isn't it, your hair. It's soft and rich and so long that it teases your lower back. I imagine you sucking in a breath at this. You probably weren't expecting me to. But maybe you should have. I'm a felon doing time; following the rules isn't how I got behind bars. After eight years of my life in this hard place, I'm thirsty for something soft.

I'm thirsty to run my fingers—that you already guessed are scarred and rough—through the soft and smooth mass of your hair. Then I move those strands to the side and expose the nape of your neck. It's the color of the moon that I sometimes see through the barred window of my cell. But I know just by looking at it that instead of it being cool, I'm going to find your skin all warm and cozy, probably from all the sunlight streaming in through that window of yours. And well, you already know my last day on the outside, the sun was hiding, so now I crave it like I've never craved anything before.

I touch that fragile spot on your neck, all soft and warm.

I'm rubbing my finger up and down, back and forth, in circles, trying to soak up the feel of you. Trying to memorize it just like I memorize your words so I can make it last for a whole week before I get to touch you again. So when I touch my own fingertips, instead of rough skin, I feel your phantom softness.

But maybe you don't want me to. Maybe you don't want a roughened con touching you with his rougher fingers.

But then again, I warned you, didn't I?

Bo

PS: Unlike you, I'm not much for reading but I read your paper and if your professor gives you anything less than a B, he's a moron. But maybe I don't have to tell you any more. You already know how all professors are fucking morons, and you should stay away from them.

CHAPTER THIRTEEN

I NEED TO steal his knife.

That's the only way. I need a weapon so I can get away from him—because no matter his vow, I am *going* to get away from him—and his knife is my best shot. All I need is an opportunity.

It's just that I'm so *freaking* tired right now. I'm the kind of tired that I've never been in my life, and it's all his fault. Because like everything else, he forced me to do it. He *forced* me to ride a horse.

With him on it.

Apparently, the reason we were at the ranch was because my husband needed a horse so we could ride on it and go home.

That's what he said.

Those were his exact words, *We're going home*, when he, despite my loud protests, picked me up and deposited me on the saddle. And then before I could ask any other questions or just take a breath, he pulled on the reins and made a clucking sound with his mouth and took off at a gallop that I swear to God caused him to bark out a laugh. Like he was finally doing something he'd been dying to do.

And I guess he was.

Eight years is a long time to stay away from something you love so much. And I'm not going to lie, I finally understand what the fuss is all about. Why people love riding so much. I think it's the freedom. The wind in your hair; the sun on your back. It's the fact that it feels like flying. Like throwing your hands up and just soaking up the world. The peace. The nature.

The *adventure.*

Gosh, is that what it feels like, being on an adventure? Like the blood is rushing in your veins and the adrenaline is going. Like you're flying, and even if you crash and burn, it'll be worth it. At one point, I wanted to turn around and tell him that. It would be the kind of thing I'd tell Bo, but then I realized—for the thousandth time—he isn't Bo. He never was; he never will be. So all I could do was hold on and let him have his moment.

Now here we are, hours later, still riding. At a more sedate pace, however. But still through the woods. I take in the canopy of branches and leaves above me. There are bits and pieces of sunlight streaming through the gaps, and I try to figure out what time it is. I have no clue if it's early afternoon or late, or how far away we are from Black Rock. I guess I fell asleep and now I'm awake, and every-thing hurts.

My back. My thighs. The place between my thighs.

There's a kink in my neck, too, that I try to get rid of by stretch-ing the length of it. Which is when I realize something. That I'm still in the same position that he put me in. I mean, why would I be in a different position; we're literally stuck together on top of a horse, but still. Now that we aren't galloping or I'm not lulled to sleep, I'm becoming aware of certain things.

My back is all but melted into his front, the side of my face is cradled between his pecs, and my spine is sagging and settled cozily into his pelvis. And then there are his thighs that are hugging mine; his arms that blanket my arms. With one of his hands grab-bing the reins while the other, *God, the other,* is splayed wide on my belly. It's so large that his thumb goes up and grazes the underside of my breast and his pinkie is almost tucked into my belly button.

Not to mention, the heel of his palm.

He's pressing it into my belly, using it to keep me all locked in and tethered to his hard body. Did it get harder over the course of a day? Or maybe it's the fact that I'm not afraid for my life like I was yesterday when he was threatening me, so now I'm finally realizing there's no way he's made of muscles and bones, no.

I think he's made of steel or iron.

Really hot iron with ridges and grooves that I want to rub up against. I don't know where the urge comes from, but I want to. I *need* to. So I arch my back, pressing my head back on his chest, and wriggle my hips, whimpering.

I can't believe how good this feels, moving against him, rubbing up against his torso and twisting my hips in the confines of his thighs. Which is why it comes as a shock when he abruptly stops me. His large hand on my tummy grows rigid and pushes in even more as he effectively traps me against the cage of his body.

Then, dipping his face down, he growls into my ear, "Stop moving."

My eyes are wide as I blurt out, "I wasn't."

It's a total lie, of course. And in the face of the vow he made to me only a few hours before, no less. But I couldn't think of anything to say when I'm trying really hard to ignore the scrape of his stubble against the side of my face. It's just as sharp as it was yesterday, but somehow I don't mind it. And his scent of leather and musk, which I inhale with every breath I take, is still as aggressively masculine as it was before. But all it does is make me feel all soft and feminine rather than weak and terrified.

It grows even thicker when he exhales sharply at my lie and flexes his fingers on my belly. I eye that hand, big and bronzed with veins going up and down the back of it, and find myself saying, "It's just that, uh, you're very hard."

His chest jerks behind me. "Rubbin' up against me isn't gonna make me any less so."

"And very big," I continue.

His fingers on my belly flex again. "Again, writhin' on my lap like a goddamn stripper isn't gonna make me any less big."

I'm not an idiot.

I know what he's saying. I know what I'm saying too. I just don't know why I put it that way. Probably residual sleep and all my aches and pains, and whatever is happening to me at this proximity and how secure he keeps me against his body on my first horse ride. But that stripper comment was uncalled for. Especially after what he did last night.

So I try to sit upright as I say, "And you'd know that, wouldn't you."

He keeps his hand firmly placed on my belly, refusing to give me even an inch. "I would and I'd probably slide a twenty-dollar bill into your thong and send you on your way because you're just wastin' my time."

Gasping, I elbow his gut and he grunts, flinching. "That was extremely offensive."

"No less true," he murmurs. "I did vow I wouldn't lie to you."

"Yeah, well I'd never dance for you anyway," I throw back, ignoring the racing of my heart.

"I think you just did."

I elbow him again. "And if I'm a twenty-dollar stripper, why are you so hard?"

I can't believe I'm talking about this so casually. Or that I actually want to wiggle some more and feel that hardness on my back. Maybe being kidnapped and fake-marrying-by-force a criminal cowboy is breaking my brain.

"Because," he replies, his voice low, "I spent the last eight years behind bars with just my hand for company. Not to mention, didn't find the relief I was lookin' for last night either so anything from a little breeze to a soft, buttercup-smellin' body wriggling in my lap could get me hard."

I bite my lip at the mention of that flower again and blurt out, "Did you...really not do anything with that stripper?"

His chest shifts again with a breath. "No."

At his answer, my heart soars, but then I kick myself in the head for melting at it when it's not as if his fidelity—even if you could call it that—means anything. Instead, I go back to the topic at hand and accuse, "It's your fault that I was moving."

"Pretty sure it's yours," he murmurs, pulling on the reins to guide the horse away from a particularly large rock. "Since you're the one with all the moves."

I ignore how expertly he does that. "That's because I hurt, okay? In case you don't remember. I've never ridden on a horse before."

"I don't."

"What?"

"Remember," he finishes while maneuvering the horse around yet another roadblock. "That it was in your third letter you told me you've never ridden before. But since you've read about it a fuck ton and seen other people do it, seein' as you live in the Wild West, it's probably the same thing." Then, "How's that workin' out for you though?"

What an ass to not only poke fun at me but to also *remember* what I told him and in which letter. Even *I* don't remember that.

I ignore the racing of my heart and dig my nails into his forearm as I mutter, "You probably remember it because you wanted to draw up an elaborate plan to torture me. As evidenced by this…"—I growl, trying to think up a word—"this whole traveling-by-a-horse bullshit and *ow!*"

All of a sudden, the horse jerks underneath me, making *me* jerk and almost lose balance. And I have to grab on to him even more tightly.

"You did that on purpose," I accuse because he did.

"His name's Rocky," he tells me.

"What?"

"The horse. Learn to use it."

I breathe out sharply, scratching his arm. "Oh right, you're a cowboy."

"That I am," he drawls with exaggeration.

"*Of course*, you'd be more concerned about your ho—Rocky than me."

"Ain't no use denyin' it."

I scoff. "I knew it. I *always* knew cowboys made the worst boyfriends."

"Well, what can I say; we don't like to be tied down."

I roll my eyes. "Okay, tell me this: If your barn was burning, what's the first thing you'd save?"

"Pretty sure I'm about to find out."

"Your horses."

"Yeah?"

"Yup." I nod. "You'd get all your horses out first and *then* go in for your girlfriend."

"You got me. I do love my horses."

"Who, by then, would probably be dead."

"Yeah, I don't think you need to worry about it."

"Why is that?"

"Because you aren't just my girlfriend."

"I—"

"You're my wife."

"I'm not. I'm—"

"And cowboys may be the worst boyfriends but we make the best husbands." I open my mouth to protest, but he doesn't let me get a word in as he continues, "So I won't let anyone burn my barn down with you in it. And if someone even thinks about it, I'll burn him down first. That clear enough for you?"

At last, I glance up at him.

He's looking straight ahead, his features blank but sharp. The hat still perches on his head, casting a shadow over his eyes. But just like in the car, every few steps, sun pours down on him like honey, lighting those dark places up. Setting them on fire, making his dark eyes glitter and his bronzed skin sparkle.

He has to be the most beautiful man I've ever seen.

I just didn't know beauty could be dangerous too. Dangerous and lethal and *lifesaving*.

I open my mouth to say something, I'm not really sure what. Hopefully not about how his crime changed my life in so many ways; I'm not about to tell my forced fake-husband that I thought of him as my hero for the longest time when he's nothing more than a criminal. But it doesn't matter now because before I can utter another word, we come to a halt.

I look away from him to find that we've come upon a clearing of some sort. A large gap surrounded by trees where the earth looks covered in heaps and mounds of dried leaves. Up ahead, through the thick trunks of trees, I see a lake. Or more like a large body of water because it's too small to be called that. The water is shimmering under the sunlight and looks so pretty that it takes my breath away.

Behind me I feel a movement, and before I know it, he's climbed off the horse, and I have to grab onto its neck to keep myself from falling. It's more from the sudden turn of events than losing my balance, but still. Then, standing beside me, he lifts his arms, his palms open as if ready to receive me.

And help me down.

It's a testament to who he is, criminal enough to kidnap me, and yet careful enough that he doesn't want me to fall. And it's a testament to what I feel for him, too threatened to feel safe around him, and yet I trust him enough that I accept his help without a word.

However, as soon as he brings me down, my knees tremble and give out, and I have to hold on to him for balance. I fist his T-shirt and crane my neck up to look at him. "W-Why are we stopping?"

His fingers dig into my waist as he replies, "Because we need to make camp."

"Camp?"

"For the night."

I blink and grab his T-shirt harder. "We're…we're staying *here*?"

"Yes."

"But I…" I look around as if I'll find something other than the woods surrounding us. "Can't we just keep going?"

"No."

"Why not?"

His chest moves with a breath as he says, "Because Rocky needs his rest."

"But I—"

"And you do too."

I pull at his T-shirt, trying to get through to him. "But I've never gone camping before."

Another breath while his features stay as cool as ever. "Well, you better get used to it because Black Rock's still a few days away."

"Wait, what?"

"And we'll be '*going camping*' every night until then."

"But…" I go up on my tiptoes. "It can't be that far away. It can't—"

"It's not," he assures me. "But we're taking the scenic route."

"What?" I shriek.

He jerks his chin at something behind me and deadpans, "You can wash up in the lake when you're ready and there's a bush behind you when you wanna go pee."

"*I'm not peeing in the bushes!*" I say, shrieking again. "I'm not… This is a joke, right? It has to be. What century is this? Why did we have to take the scenic route or—"

He shifts on his feet, shifting me with him as he says, his eyes flicking back and forth between mine, "There are no asshole cops here that you can turn to for help. Nothing but bears and wolves for *miles*. Wild animals that'll tear into you and leave you for dead the moment they catch your scent. So we're takin' the scenic route because your only safe bet in these woods is sticking close to me. And if you're as smart as you think you are, this time, you'll stay exactly where I put you. No ropes. No drugs. But most importantly, no lies." Then, straightening up, "Welcome to your first adventure."

———

Fire burns bright and hot between us.

Orange embers flicker in the air, lighting up the night, casting burning shadows on his face. On his entire body, making it glow.

He looks to be in deep thought, his eyes staring into the flames. I can see them dancing in his eyes. If I tried, I could almost convince myself that he himself is made of fire. With lava flowing in his veins and flames flickering just beneath the surface.

We're having dinner right now that *he* cooked while I watched him from the log that I'm perched on. I also watched him take Rocky's saddle off and unload the saddlebags before tying Rocky to the tree behind him. He combed Rocky's mane, then massaged his back while whispering sweet nothings in his ear. All I heard was the low tones of his rough voice, hypnotizing enough that I couldn't take my eyes away. He gave Rocky his feed and put out a bowl of water for him before moving on to our dinner.

But first, he gave me a pill.

He said it was for my pain, and I believed him. Because he's right: There's nowhere for me to run, so he didn't need to drug me. Besides, if he wanted to, he could've found a different way. Plus, he said he wouldn't lie to me. And he wasn't. Hours later, I'm still awake and my pain has retreated into the background.

Even though neither of us has eaten all that much, I can't help but think this is the very first meal we've shared despite being together for three days now. Before this, I'd either miss meals because I was sleeping, or he'd leave a plate for me on the nightstand with him nowhere in sight.

I don't know why it feels so monumental, but it does: our first meal together.

"I've imagined this before," I blurt out. Then quickly add, "Foolishly."

He's on the opposite side of me, sitting on a log of his own with his thighs sprawled and his elbows resting on them, his hands holding the paper plate with his untouched dinner. At my words, he lifts his eyes and focuses on me. "Imagined what?" Then, he adds much like me, although in a drawl, "Foolishly."

I shift on my seat, my own dinner plate in the lap of my dress. "This. Having dinner. With you."

If he finds this surprising, my revelation, he doesn't show it. His features remain unmoved and glowing as he repeats, "With me."

I exhale sharply. "With *Bo*."

Something flashes through his face, tightening up his features for a second.

"I mean, of course, stupidly," I add before he can say anything.

"Yeah, you said that."

"There were times when," I find myself divulging, "I'd sit down with my food and read your letter."

My confession is followed by a light grunt from Rocky and the fire crackling. Which, to be honest, is fine. I don't want him to say anything. Not that there's anything to say other than how stupid I've been, but still.

"I'd order takeout, light candles, and read your letters out loud. I guess I wanted to pretend we were having a conversation over dinner." I shake my head. "And for the third time, I know how crazy it sounds and—"

"It does sound crazy," he cuts me off.

My heart drops.

His jaw clenches before he adds, "Because he'd be too high to hold his head up at the table, let alone make dinner conversation with you."

God, what an asshole.

"Forget it." I stab a potato with the plastic fork. "I don't even know why I told you that."

"Me neither," he says. "Thought we weren't talkin' about letters."

That gets my back up, and I stab the potato-laden fork at him. "Well, *you* don't get to talk about them. I can do whatever I want."

He studies me a beat, then he straightens up and sets his plate aside. "That so?"

"Yes, actually it *is* so." I lift my chin. "In case you forgot, I'm the injured party between the two of us."

"Injured party."

"Yes, I am. I'm the victim here. The forced; the silenced; the *kidnapped*. I'm allowed a few concessions."

"Fine."

I raise my eyebrows in disbelief. "What?"

He throws out a short nod. "You're allowed a few concessions."

Despite myself, I smile a little. "Does that mean I can call you an asshole whenever I want?"

His gaze drops to my mouth for a second before he drawls, "Don't you do that already?"

I wrinkle my nose. "Criminal cowboy."

"Used that one before too."

"I—"

"If that's the extent of your imagination, college girl, we're in a lot of trouble."

In his low and drawling voice, it sounds exactly like I wanted it to, "college girl," and yet nothing like I imagined it would.

I blink myself awake and ask, "Why?"

"Might get old after a while," he tells me, his eyes boring into mine. "Since we're gonna be spending the rest of our lives together."

"We're not."

The determined lines on his face make me shiver, and I glance down at the food. "You know I'm not a vegetarian, right?"

"I'm aware."

I look up to find his eyes pinned on me. "So then why do you always make sure I have no meat in my food?"

For the record, I don't care. I'll eat whatever is put in front of me and be grateful that I wasn't the one who made it. Growing up, I had to do all the cooking myself because my mother was either too busy with making my father happy or too beaten up to do anything else but lie down. So I'm not picky.

"Just coverin' my bases on the off chance you were." Then, "You didn't want me feedin' you somethin' against your will, did you? Like I did with the tranq."

I was in the process of putting a deliciously cooked potato in my mouth when I stopped. I put down the fork and asked, "Is this an apology then? For drugging me? You know, how you sometimes apologize in a weird way. Like when you read my favorite book."

"It's a fact," he tells me. Then, as if muttering to himself, "Still don't know why that's your favorite book though."

I keep my eyes on him for a few seconds more, as if by doing that I'll learn all his secrets and solve the mystery he is. Not that I want to know him, but I think I *need* to. Keep your friends close but your enemies closer. Isn't that what they say?

I'm trying to get away from him. Shouldn't I know about any potential weaknesses or vulnerabilities that I can use against him? Like the fact that I now know where he keeps his knife.

Tucked in his boot.

I've been watching him retrieve it to chisel the twigs and fallen branches in order to make the firepit; to cut the rope to get the saddlebags down; even to skewer the meat while cooking. Every time he's done using it, he puts it back in. I can see it even now. The black handle peeking out the top.

I've never used a knife before, and I don't know how I'll react if I do need to use it. Either on him or those wild animals he was talking about. All I know is that I have to try. I have to get away from him, and I need a weapon for my protection.

And all the information I can gather.

"So," I begin, breathing in, "where'd you learn to cook like this?"

He keeps looking at me for a few seconds, his eyes roving over my features. As if he's mulling something over. Just when I think I won't be able to take his scrutiny any longer and he's probably never going to answer me anyway, he speaks, surprising the hell out of me.

"My folks died when I was twelve. And my younger brother only wanted to eat applesauce like our ma used to make it. Since my older brother took over the ranch and our cook couldn't get it right no matter how hard she tried, I was the only one left." His lips tip up but there's no humor in his tiny smile as he continues, "Apparently, Ma used to put a pinch of cloves in it and for some goddamn reason, no one could figure it out except me. Everyone kept puttin' cinnamon in it and Ax kept throwin' away the bowl. So I guess I learned cooking a long time ago."

I try to swallow, but something feels stuck in my throat.

I didn't know about that. I mean, I knew about the Grayson family. I knew there are three Grayson brothers and that the oldest is the head of the family. Which means their parents must have passed. I think they died in a car accident, now that I recall. But I never thought of it in these terms. In the terms of three boys losing their parents when they were really nothing more than boys. Three boys learning to live their lives again.

Twelve years old is *too* young to be doing something like that; I know. I was doing something similar: cooking and cleaning up, bandaging my mother's wounds, trying to disappear the rest of the time.

"I didn't know," I say lamely.

His eyes had moved over to the fire, but now they come back to me. "Now you do."

I lick my lips. "I always…"

He watches me do it before taking a deep breath and asking, "You always what?"

I blush and squirm in my seat. "All I've heard are horror stories. About the Graysons. About how all Graysons are criminals. How they'll do anything to take our land. Steal, cheat." I swallow. "Kill."

He keeps his gaze locked on me. Unblinking and intense. I wish he'd look away, though. Just so I'll have some reprieve. But I don't think he's going to give me that mercy.

"All true," he murmurs at last.

"But the Turners would do that too," I jump to say.

They would.

It's not one-sided; I know they're not the good guys. I knew it when I was living with them, and I know it now that I haven't been to Black Rock in years. I want nothing to do with that place anymore. A place made of land wars and family feuds and abusive fathers.

"What's your point?" he asks, breaking into my thoughts.

I have absolutely no idea what my point is. Except that I don't think the Graysons are as monstrous as I've made them out to be.

Which is a ridiculous and dangerous line of thought. I cannot think this way. I cannot warm up to them. I don't even know them other than what I've been told all my life. I don't *want* to know them. Or humanize them. Besides, shouldn't it be the other way around? I'm the captive.

"What's your younger brother's name?" I ask, cursing at myself because didn't I just decide to not do this anymore?

Before I can take back my question, he replies, "Axton."

"How old is he?"

"Just turned eighteen."

"And your older brother is Marsden, right?"

"Right."

"How old is he?"

"Forty."

"How old are *you?*"

"This twenty questions?"

"No, this is me getting to know the family I was forcibly married into," I say with my eyebrows raised. Although, inside, I'm still going *What the fuck.*

He keeps watching me as he throws back, "Old enough to say this is past your bedtime so you should go to sleep. We've got an early day tomorrow."

"But I thought you wanted me to have an adventure," I retort, pasting a sweet smile on my face.

Which he takes in before something passes over his features and he takes a deep breath. "I did, didn't I."

"Yup," I reply, popping the *p* at the end. "So then—"

"So then," he cuts me off and repeats my words. "How about you tell me a little about your family?"

I pause. Then, "What?"

"We're married, aren't we?" he says, his lips turning up a bit, but again, I don't think there's any humor in it. "So I should get to know them too."

I narrow my eyes at him. "You already know everything about them."

He nods his head slowly, accepting my words. "So then how about I get to know your best friend?"

This time my voice is higher and squeakier. "What?"

"Does she suck at sociology too?"

"I don't... What?"

"What about adventure?"

"What about it?"

"Does she like adventure or is she boring like you?"

"I'm not boring."

"Boring. Careful. Same thing."

"It's—"

"Bet she's never read a book in her life."

"Are you implying my best friend is illiterate?"

"No. I'm implyin' your best friend knows how to have fun."

I don't know where he's going with this. Or why it would even enter his *brain* to talk about my best friend. But I know that I need to venture carefully. Very, *very* carefully. I can't show fear. I can't raise suspicion.

"You know," I begin sweetly, even though I'm sort of quaking on the inside, "if you keep talking about my best friend, I'm going to take offense. We're married, remember?"

His dark eyes glitter. "And if you take offense, I'm gonna assume you're jealous. Like you were about the stripper."

I scoff. "I was not jealous about the stripper."

"No?"

"No," I say sternly. "You can do whatever you want with *whomever* you want."

His lips pull up in a slight smirk. "That your wedding vow?"

My heart races. "No, it's me saying: I don't care about what you do because I'm running away the first chance I get."

"You've got nowhere to run, remember?" he taunts, his words dripping danger.

I do. There are woods everywhere, and again, I don't know if I'll ever be able to make my way out of this place. But just like stealing the knife, I need to try.

"Well, I'd rather take my chances with the wild animals than stick by the side of a man who's hell-bent on using me for his revenge plans." I pause and then add, "Plans that, by the way, I don't even know about. Like, what the hell do you want *me* for specifically?"

This makes him draw a breath, his chest swelling up and down. "Why don't you let me worry about that part?"

Clutching the fork, I frown at him. "Are you listening to yourself? I'm involved in this too. You *got* me involved. Without my say-so. You ruined my future for this. I think I have a right to know."

He clenches his jaw for a second or two before clipping, "Future."

"Yes," I insist. "Did you think about that for even a second, how this affects me? You know what I want to do with my life, don't you? I told you. I *told* you when I've never, not once, told anyone. You know I want to work with domestic violence victims because of my history. I was going to volunteer at the shelters this summer. That's why I wasn't doing a shift at the library. You *know* all this and you still—"

"You can still do that," he cuts me off.

"What?"

"Not gonna keep you tied to my bed, if you cooperate," he says, his nostrils flaring. "You wanna volunteer at the shelter, be my guest."

"This is your solution? Keep me married to you until you get your revenge and in the meantime, I go fulfill my dreams?"

"Isn't that what you wanted?"

He throws that at me so casually and in such a calm voice that mine goes up. "What I wanted was to not *be* here, okay? What I wanted was to not be lied to and kidnapped and forced to marry a criminal, to not be used for your revenge. What about love?"

Something about him goes unnaturally still at this.

I can see his chest moving with his breaths. I can also see his jaw pulsing. Those flames are still dancing in his dark eyes, but something about him, within him, *around* him, has gone still. Maybe the night air. Maybe the earth has stopped moving. Again, all I know is that I feel this change in him and I'm forced to go still too.

Then, with a harsh clench of his jaw that I feel in my own teeth, he goes, "What about love?"

"I"—I swallow—"want it."

I loved you.

I don't know where that thought comes from. Although, it shouldn't be a surprise because it is the truth.

His eyes narrow. "Thought you said you didn't wanna be like your mother."

I wince. "I don't."

He watches me for a beat. "So this is perfect, ain't it?"

"What's perfect?"

"There's no chance in hell you're ever gonna fall in love with a criminal."

I already did. Once.

But I keep my mouth shut and my spine straight under the massive ache in my chest and belly that's begging me to curl into myself.

"Because love's worse than any wild animal in these woods," he continues. "A wolf would kill you but love's the kind of animal that'll eat you up but won't let you die. It'll keep you alive and in pain for the rest of your life."

CHAPTER FOURTEEN

IS HE SLEEPING?

I can't say for sure because he's sitting up against a tree and not lying down on a sleeping bag like me. His back is leaning into the trunk with one leg drawn up and his face dipped low. So much so that his chin touches his chest. A softly breathing chest, I should add. I watch it go up and down for a few moments in the dying embers of the fire. Then I watch his arms. They're folded across his chest, and they're locked so tight that I can see the hills of his biceps. He appears more like someone keeping watch than someone in a deep slumber.

Plus, I don't think he ever sleeps, as impossible as that sounds. But then, I watch as one of his arms goes slack and falls to his thigh. Followed by a low release of breath. And my heart starts pounding because he's asleep after all.

This is my chance.

My own slumber that I'd given in to while waiting for *him* to go to sleep is washed away, and I'm ready to go. Slowly, I unzip the sleeping bag and sit up. My eyes are on his face, looking for any movement, *any* indication that he heard me. But he keeps sleeping. Letting out a small thankful breath, I climb out of the bag. He's only a few paces away from me and I can see the knife handle sticking out of the boot on his bent leg.

Tiptoeing, I make my way toward his sleeping form and crouch by his boot. I reach out with my hand, and slowly, very slowly, I slide the knife out. Once I have it, I take a step back, and then, out of nowhere, the hand that was sitting limp on his thigh strikes.

Like a rattlesnake, lying in wait, his fingers coil around my wrist and squeeze so hard that a gasp and a squeal escape me. At my sound of pain, he snaps his eyes up. His dark gaze is alert and his features are sharp, and I realize that he *was* lying in wait. He probably wasn't asleep at all; he knew I was coming for him the whole time, and like a wild, dangerous animal, he lured me in.

Like always.

"Not so fast," he murmurs, his voice hardly sleep-ruffled and just as alert as the rest of him.

God.

What a fucking monster. I was wrong to think the Graysons are anything but evil and criminal. And I feel so foolish for thinking it that I go manic.

I absolutely lose my fucking shit.

I launch myself at him and crash-butt my shoulder into his chest. He's momentarily shocked at my sudden burst of energy, and I'm able to knock him back, his spine hitting the tree. He curses at the impact as his fingers loosen around my wrist, and I'm up on my feet in a flash *with* the knife. I'm already spinning on my heels when he wraps those wretched fingers of his around my ankles and takes me down. I scream as I fall to the ground, my elbows and forearms taking the brunt of it all, along with my knees. I think I even have cut skin in places, but I can't be sure and I don't even care right now.

Because *right now*, as my skin smarts and possibly bleeds, I feel him on top of me. His wildly breathing chest pressed to my shuddering back. Starting to feel suffocated, I struggle harder under him. Despite giving it my all, though, he manages to flip me over.

And our eyes lock in the darkness.

His, fiery and angry; and mine, probably just the same except there may be a hint of panic too. For a second, *less than* a second even, it feels like our chests move in tandem. His swells up when mine swells down, and mine goes up when his goes down. It feels like our breaths, like our eyes, are tangled together. But then I feel his fingers wrapping around my wrist, the one holding the knife, and the moment breaks.

I start thrashing under him, and he bears down on me.

"Let me go," I bite out with heaving breaths, and then I keep chanting it like a prayer.

Let me go let me go let me go letmego.

"Calm the fuck down," he tells me, all the while tightening his hold on me like a vise, suffocating me with his muscles and bones. "You're gonna hurt yourself."

I headbutt him at this.

Hard.

Just to show I don't care what happens to me as long as he gets hurt. I cry out at the impact and see stars, and he curses again, this time loudly, as his hold on me loosens and I twist my hand with the knife free. And then I swing it down, and holy God, *holy fucking God*, I hit something.

Something like muscles and bones.

And everything stops. My head stops spinning. My vision comes back, and the first thing I see is blood.

Dripping on me.

Granted, it's only a few drops, but they plop on the center of my heaving chest, warm and thick. Before scattering every which way. Sliding along my collarbone, seeping into the bodice of my dress; sluicing up to the triangle of my throat. I watch for a few seconds, hypnotized, but then gather enough wherewithal to look for where it's coming from.

Him.

It's coming from his chest, higher up on it, just under the globe of his left shoulder. Where his knife is lodged, and dear Lord, my fingers are still wrapped around the handle.

Did I do that?

I did that, didn't I? I stabbed him. *I stabbed my husband.*

I gasp, finally letting go of the knife, my sweaty fingers grabbing his bicep. "I… You… Are you… Oh God, did I kill you?"

I clap my other hand—the non-knife-wielding hand—onto my mouth at my own horrific words as I look up at him. Only to find him staring at my trembling chest. At his blood, the trails of it all over my skin.

"Not yet," he grunts in reply.

Then he goes for the knife. A flash of tightness passes through his face as he heaves himself up a little and dislodges it from his body. His frame jerks and he grunts at the action. Throwing the knife away, he comes back down, pressing the length of his body against mine.

My eyes skitter to his wound and my hand on his bicep flies over to cover it for some reason. "I've never…" I press on the spot, feeling the blood ooze, making my fingers sticky, and he grunts. "I've never s-stabbed anyone before."

"Clearly," he bites out.

I press on it harder, making him wince over me. "S-shouldn't we do something?"

"Like what?"

"To stop the bleeding."

"That why you're tryin' to jam your fingers into my wound?"

I ease up on the pressure and jerk my gaze back to him. "I-I wasn't. I was just… I was trying to keep the pressure. I'm s-so sorry."

He breathes through his nose, his chest shuddering over mine. "Yeah, are you?"

"I didn't mean to."

"No?"

"No."

"What were you gonna do with my knife then"—he grunts again—"swat butterflies in the meadow?"

"I'd never swat a..." I begin hysterically but think better of it. "I just... I wanted to protect myself."

Another wave of pain flashes through his face, tightening his features and shuddering his chest. "Against me."

I swallow. "And w-wild animals. You said there were bears and w-wolves and—"

"And you thought a pocketknife would help you fight bears and wolves." He growls low; this time the tightening on his features is anger rather than pain.

"You were going to do it."

"There's a difference between you and me."

That gets my back up, and I instantly regret any remorse about stabbing him. He deserved that. And more, I decide, as I say in disbelief, "Oh my God, so you're a sexist too?"

"I am whatever the fuck I am when it comes to knowin' that a mere girl like you doesn't stand a chance against a wild animal with—" He pauses here, his words slowing down, probably to scare me. "A. *Fuckin'. Knife.*"

I grit my teeth. "The knife was the only option I had."

"The other *option*, as always before you fuck everything up to where someone ends up getting stabbed, is to just *stay. The fuck. Put.*"

I dig my fingers into his wounded flesh again, making him jerk and wince, probably spilling more of his blood. Before I lean up and state, "Or the *other* other option is you don't use me for revenge like I'm some object and let me the fuck go."

He emits a wordless growl in response, which I think is the

result of me pressing on his wound again. Despite everything, guilt stings me, but I don't ease up on the pressure. No matter how much blood I seem to be getting on my fingers. He needs to learn his lesson. He needs to *hurt*. Shame on me for wavering.

Frustrated, I ask, "You weren't really sleeping, were you?"

His nostrils flare again with a large, painful breath. "Just nodded off for a second."

"You never sleep."

He grunts his agreement.

I frown. "When was the last time you slept?"

"In my cell."

I gasp. "So you… You haven't slept in a *week*?"

His jaw clenches for a second. "Quit lookin' at me like I'm a freak."

My eyes go wide. "No, I wasn't. I—"

An expression passes through his features that bunches his brow and makes his cheekbones seem even darker and flushed in the dying embers. "I can't seem to fall asleep, all right? Not on the outside. Where everything's so fuckin' open. There's so much fuckin' air and sky and goddamn people that I'm choking with it all. The only time…"

I flick my eyes back and forth between his. "The only time what?"

His brow bunches deeper and that flush on his cheekbones grows. And for a few seconds, all he does is look down at me with irritation bordering on anger. Then, "The only time I seem to drift off is when I"—he takes in a sharp, angry breath—"when I'm able to smell you."

"What?"

His jaw moves as if he's trying to grind his words into dust. "Your scent."

"W-what about it?"

"It's thicker," he grunts, the words ripped out of his chest almost. "When you sleep. You also seem to toss and turn. A lot.

Spillin' your hair everywhere. Sometimes I can smell you from across the room and I"—he pushes out another breath—"I can sleep for a bit, thinkin' about those fuckin' buttercups."

This is not real, is it? People can't smell you from across the room, can they? If they can, your scent can't lull them to sleep. Not *my* scent, the little college girl. And not *him* being put to sleep because of it, the asshole criminal cowboy.

Even so, words leave my mouth before I can pull them back. "Is that why…you drifted off just now? Because of m-my scent."

A pulse beats in his cheek. "Yeah."

This is insane. This is… I don't even want to think about what this is. So I pivot and bring up something else important. "Do you think…"

His stomach hollows out with his next breath, alerting me that maybe we should be doing something about his injury and soon. "Do I think *what?*"

"That"—I swallow, my throat tight—"maybe you have, uh, PTSD?"

His body stiffens over me and his eyes flash. "What?"

"I-I mean, you spent eight years in prison so—"

"Why don't you save your psychobabble for all those women you're gonna help," he says, cutting me off. "And focus more on what I'm gonna do to you."

My breath snags in my chest. "I'm…I'm sorry?"

Instead of answering me, he lets his eyes wander.

He lets them go from the top of my head to the bottom of my chin, taking detours on the way to stop at the crests of my cheeks, the tip of my nose, the curve of my lips. Everywhere he pauses, I feel that spot tingling. I feel it getting heated.

He moves on to my throat, then my chest, slowly setting me on fire as he goes along. His blood on my chest has dried now, making my skin itchy and restless. But no more restless than when I realize how we're arranged. I knew that he was on top of me, of course, but I was too scared to notice details before.

Not anymore, though.

I notice how my chest grazes against his every time we take a breath and how I feel the ridges of his abs on my own belly. How I can *feel* the ladder of his sculpted muscles pressing into my soft, pliant flesh. If I stopped to focus, I'm sure I'd be able to count how many rungs that tight ladder in his abs has.

Probably eight.

But right now, my focus is taken up by how he's settled into the juncture between my thighs. My body is wrapped around him, my calves all tangled up with his and my thighs hugging the outside of his meaty thighs.

This is too intimate.

More intimate than riding on the horse together. And instead of being utterly terrified, I feel what I felt back then. This quickening in my belly. This restless current in my veins. This urge to move. I try to push him away then, my fingers still all sticky, streaked with his blood. "Get off me."

He doesn't.

In fact, he goes ahead and stares at my heaving chest a little bit more before his eyes make their way up, all lazily, almost defiantly. Then, when they reach my eyes, he replies, "No."

My heart beats like I'm a scared little bird, scared but excited. "You know I had to do that. You *know* I had to make a run for it. I can't…"

"You can't what?"

"I can't let you use me."

His eyes look molten as he says, "I know." Then, "You probably wouldn't be you without all the sass."

Something squeezes in my chest at his tone, and I have trouble breathing for a second. He sounds exactly like Bo in this moment. Like *my* Bo. Like those two people could be the same.

"I was right though," he keeps going.

"R-right about what?"

His lips pull up slightly. ~~It's too little to call a smile but still too~~ blatantly there to ignore it. Then, "Your cheeks flush when you talk back. You go all red."

"Don't," I blurt out, swallowing. "Don't talk about the letters."

Especially not now. Not when this moment feels so precarious. When it feels like I know him after all.

"Yeah? Well, I'm the injured one now," he says hoarsely. "Think that gets me a few concessions."

I swallow again. "Just let me go, *please*."

"Can't."

I push at him again. "You *can*. You—"

"Maybe I'll keep you."

My heart thuds. "W-what?"

"Forever."

"No. That's... You said you'd let me go after your revenge. You—"

"Maybe I changed my mind. Maybe you're growin' on me. You did sign on the dotted line, didn't you?" Before I can say anything else, he murmurs, "Till death do us part."

"Absolutely not. You—"

"You know what I did before I got put away?" He asks the question on a rasp, his eyes going back on their journey down my body.

I'm so thrown by his off-topic question and his perusal that all I can do is whisper, "W-what?"

"I broke horses," he replies, his eyes on the base of my throat, studying my fluttering pulse.

"Horses?"

He licks his lips, staring at the spot. "Stallions, colts mostly. A filly or two sometimes."

I jerk at a peek of his tongue. "Okay. But—"

"Been workin' on the ranch since I was fifteen," he says, cutting me off, his eyes moving from my throat and going back up to my trembling lips. "I would've started sooner but we had Ax. Someone had to take care of him. So I started late but I saved up everything

I could. Just so one day I could buy my own land, probably away from Rawhide. So I could start my own business, breakin' horses for money."

I swallow thickly and before I can think about it, my hands move, my arms wind around his neck, and my fingers, bloody and all, fist his hair. I don't know why I do that. It's the *opposite* of what I should be doing, but I can't help it. I can't help but wrap my arms around him because he just told me his dream.

It was his dream, wasn't it, his future that got interrupted.

God, I wish I knew why.

I *wish* I knew why he did what he did. Why he thinks love is an animal that kills you. I haven't forgotten about it, the words he said to me at dinner. I wonder if love has anything to do with his thirst for revenge.

He finally looks up, breaking whatever moment we were sharing, and brings us back to the present. With him on top of me, keeping me trapped, refusing to let me go. And I resume my struggles, twisting under him, trying to get away.

"But that's not here or there. The point is, even though I haven't been a cowboy in a very long time," he says, his body just as dense and heavy over me, "any cowboy worth a damn knows that there ain't no tamin' a wild little filly with a lasso. You wanna get her in hand, you gotta let her ride and get it out of her system."

My breaths scatter. "What does...what does that mean?"

His eyes glitter. "You don't want me to drug you, do you?"

My arms around his neck flex. "What? No. No, please. You—"

"And like I said, ropin' you like a wild little filly hasn't worked either."

I go to take my arms away from his neck and put some distance between us, but he sinks into me more. Making me realize he was still keeping a part of himself away from me. But not anymore.

I can feel it.

That part, the one I wanted to feel earlier in the day, back when we were riding. And holy shit, I was right. It's hard. Harder than those ridges of his abs. And it's big. Although I don't think I imagined it to be *this* big. Or thick. Or that it'd be throbbing. There's a distinct pulse that I feel on my tummy, and something inside of me, some primitive feminine part, makes me arch up into it.

"So if I wanna keep you, I'm gonna let you ride," he drawls.

"Ride?"

"Uh-huh."

"What?"

"My mouth."

"I... *What?*"

He licks his lips then, as if highlighting them, making them all shiny so I can't look anywhere else but at his mouth. And he's successful, because for the life of me, that's all I see.

"You want that, don't you?" he goes.

Still staring at his mouth, I shake my head. "No."

His shiny, dusky-pink mouth tips up. "Well, you're right. My bad."

My gaze skitters up. "I'm right?"

"Yeah," he says, staring into my eyes. "You are. You don't want to ride my mouth. You want somethin' else."

"What?" I ask, staring back, barely aware of what I'm saying.

"Judging by how you're attempting to give me another desperate and horny lap dance, I'm gonna say you wanna ride the heat I'm packin' in my pants."

And I stop. Because this is when I realize I've been moving against him. All this time, I've been rocking against that hard thing stabbing my tummy. My feet are hooked around his thighs and I'm almost off the ground, hanging onto him like a desperate, horny girl, but I'm *not*. I'm absolutely, one hundred percent *not* horny or desperate.

This is not me at all. This has never been me.

I shake my head again. "No, I—"

He cuts me off with, "And you're doin' a good job too." His voice is thick and heavy, just like this thing on my belly that I can't even think of the proper name for. "Way better than what you did this mornin'. Guess it pays to be desperate, huh? You keep that up and you're lookin' at a huge tip."

"Tip?"

"Yeah," he keeps rasping, and I think he's doing it on purpose because his voice is slowly driving me crazy. "And by that I meant cash. Not the other kind."

"What's the other kind?"

His lips twitch and something wicked passes through his features. "The tip of my big, hard cock." I flinch, but before I can do anything, he goes on, "Because the thing is you can't have it."

His words give me a pause. "Why not?"

"Because you're a Turner, remember?" he says, his eyes dark and flashing. "And I don't stick my dick in a Turner."

Right, of course. He told me that this morning. And for some reason, I have to bite my lip really, *really* hard so I don't spill out the truth. Especially when after declaring that rule, he rocks his *dick*— oh God, just the thought of it makes me blush—into me. And he does it in a way that, despite everything, I can't help but rock back. Since this time I'm doing it more consciously, I feel something else. I feel another throb and not just the one on my belly due to his thick length.

I feel a pulse between my legs.

I'm wet.

"I also"—he keeps rocking into me and I keep rocking back— "don't stick my dick in a liar."

"W-what?" I ask, even though what I want to do is throw my head back and moan.

"You lied to me, didn't you?"

I know I should be more alarmed right now, and I am. But for the life of me, I can't stop doing what I'm doing. I can't stop rocking back and forth, side to side as I leak and leak and freaking leak like a faucet.

"You…" I swallow, pulling at his hair, dragging my heels up and down the backs of his thighs. "You m-mean about the vegetarian thing?"

His eyes flash. "Is there anything else you're lyin' to me about?"

I shake my head. "No."

"You sure?"

I close my eyes to shut out his probing gaze and pull his hair harder. "I was just…I was just trying to protect myself."

I don't know if what I said made sense or not, but he hums, his chest buzzing. "Yeah, and trust me, no one regrets it more than me."

"Regrets what?"

"That you had to lie to protect yourself and now you're a Turner."

"Okay," I say uselessly, without thinking about it.

"Meaning you're off-limits," he growls, his tone suddenly laced with anger. "*Meaning* all I could do last night when I came back from that deadass strip club, all angry and jacked up, was jerk off to your sleepin' body like I was still back in prison, reading and rereading your letters, trying, *goddamn fucking tryin'*, to hear your voice in my head."

If anything could pierce through the fog my mind seems to be under and make me realize what's happening, it would be this. This crazy, *crazy* thing he's said. Even so, I can't seem to let go of him, and I'm tightening my limbs around his body. I breathe out, "You what?"

He clenches his jaw, his eyes glittering with a furious light. "All I could do was kneel between your soft *silky* thighs and fuck my fist like I've been doing for the past six months."

"Six…"

"The only difference was last night I had somewhere to dump all my cum, instead of letting it run through my fingers."

"Where?"

"On you."

"Me?"

"Your juicy thighs."

My juicy thighs flex around him. "You came on my…"

"And your white little panties."

I feel them now, all drenched and sticky, and it reminds me of something. I pull at his hair and ask, "Is that why…my p-panties were all sticky this morning?"

"Yeah."

"Oh."

There was a hint of regret in my tone. Because I think…I think I would've liked to be awake for that. To watch him come.

"Was it a lot?" I ask before I can stop myself.

"Drenched your panties and painted your thighs," he whispers. "What do you think?"

"You—"

"And if instead of *on* you, I'd come *in* you, you'd be drippin' for days."

I fist his hair, twisting my hips under him. "I think we s-should stop."

"You'd be swollen and full and hurting for days. And I'd be walkin' around hard as fuck knowin' you felt me sliding down those juicy thighs of yours that I wanna bite every time I get a flash of them through your dress. So yeah, it was a *fuck* of a lot."

I arch and moan and whisper, "I really think—"

"So as much as I liked paintin' you with my cum and makin' your body my canvas, I'm not a delicate fuckin' artist. I'm a hardened cowboy with a record and I wanna dump my load in a juicy warm cunt." I flinch and whimper, but he keeps going. "Apparently, though, that's not possible. Because you're a Turner. So instead of givin' you what you're askin' for, I'm gonna suck your little college girl snatch through those drenched panties of yours and we'll see if that doesn't keep you in your place and finally get you to behave. A word of warning though"—he pauses to let that take effect—"I know I said I'd take my time with you. Go slow and savor. But that was just somethin' I said to not scare you. In all honesty though, I like it hard and fast and that goes for everything including eating pussy."

Before I can even attempt to respond, he gets up.

He pushes his large body off me and comes up to his knees. My fingers mourn his loss and in his absence grab the dead leaves on the ground. I wonder if this is what he looked like last night, kneeling between my thighs. All big and hard, his chest vibrating, his stomach hollowing out. Without taking his eyes off me, he goes for his T-shirt. He fists it with the hand on his uninjured side and again, before I can attempt to put things together, takes it off.

My eyes go wide and I'm all ready to take him in. But he doesn't let me. All I am able to do is catch a glimpse of all the blood on his shoulder before in a flash, he's over me again. But this time, his one hand is by my head and his other at my throat.

Holding that knife to my pulse.

My heart dives. I was so busy staring at him like a lunatic that I never realized he had retrieved the knife and now is holding it to my throat.

His eyes shine as he says, "I know you wanna deny it. I know you wanna say you don't want this. But how about we cut the bullshit?" He presses the tip of the knife on my pulse for a second and my breaths are suspended. Then, in a surprising move, he flips it and offers the knife to me, handle first. "How *about* I give you a chance to kill me. You wanna stop me, you stab me with that knife. And I'll be down there, eatin' your pussy and makin' you come until you pass the fuck out and can't lie to me anymore."

As if in a daze, I take the knife from him and blurt out, "But—"

"Shut the fuck up."

"No, it's, uh"—I gulp when his eyes narrow—"you're bleeding."

"Yeah?"

"So, uh, d-don't you think we should do something about that?"

He watches me a beat. Then, "If you think a little blood's gonna keep me off your pussy, then you need to learn a lot of things and learn them fast." I open my mouth again to say something, but he commands, "Now, shut the fuck up, hold on to that knife, and keep those legs open."

I purse my lips and wrap both hands around the handle of his knife, hugging it to my chest, and open my legs wider. Like I'm some kind of a good girl and this is not the most bizarre and the most erotic thing that's ever happened to me. Then I watch him move down my body and flip up the skirt of my dress. Before I can draw another breath, he bends down and puts his mouth on me.

The first lick of his tongue, even through my panties, makes me jump and almost stab myself. The second lick is when I try to close my legs, but he holds me down and laps at me.

Which is when I come.

It's embarrassing, but I can't help it. I can't help but rock and undulate on the ground as my channel pulses and pulses in his mouth, flooding my panties even more. At which point, he takes the wet fabric in his mouth and sucks on that alone as if trying to soak in the juices. Before taking the fabric between his teeth and giving it a pull.

And holy God, I come again.

Probably because of the scrape of his teeth against my panty-covered pussy, or the bite of the waistband. Or maybe his growl—because he growled something fierce when he did that—or just my body surrendering to him, to his mouth, to my own desires, because it's not as if he was lying.

I did—do—want this.

Despite my better judgment and everything he's done, my six months of feelings haven't been erased. It's not my desire alone, though. It's his, too, that's turning me on so much.

Because look at the way he's eating me.

He's using his tongue. He's using his teeth. He's using his voice, too, slurping and gulping and growling. Plus, his fingers are digging into my thighs, keeping me open and available to him. He's using his *entire self* to suck on me, and even though there's a barrier between his mouth and me, I can still feel his hunger reaching. I can still feel all his pent-up desire from the last six months.

So what choice do I have but to give him what he wants. To come and come and just flow into his mouth. What choice do I have but to writhe my hips, dig my head into the ground, scrape my skin against the dirt. I clench my thighs around his head, feeling his stubble on my innermost tender skin, feeling his blood making everything more slippery and stickier.

And I come again.

And again and again and fucking again until I *almost* pass out. Just as I'm slipping into dark slumber I realize the knife is still in my hands, clutched tightly and held securely between my breasts. And it never occurred to me to use it.

CHAPTER FIFTEEN

The Dark Stallion

IF YOU KILL once, you can maybe explain it as an accident.

A moment of insanity. A moment of weakness. But if you kill twice, then you've got a pattern. A precedent. A history. You can't explain it away as a mistake.

It's deliberate. Premeditated.

Although nothing about what happened just now was premeditated. I've thought about it a lot, yes, but I didn't pin her to the ground with the explicit intention of doing what I did. And what I did was betray Annie.

I'm the reason she isn't here anymore, aren't I?

Because I failed to protect her. I *failed* to keep her safe. So I don't get to do what I did. I don't get to feel peace. I don't get to feel a moment's relief like I did when I tasted my wife's snatch. Not until I avenge Annie. But I can't even do that right. Because for some fucked-up reason, I can't keep away from Peyton.

I dab the knife wound with an alcohol pad as I watch her lying on top of the sleeping bag. She looks exactly the same as she did last night, the answer to all my prayers. An angel with a halo around her head. Except, turns out, this little angel is also a hellcat.

With blood and dirt streaking her dress and her body; her fair skin tanned from being in the sun all day, and that long blond halo-like hair all tangled up, she looks like a bloodthirsty princess, sleeping peacefully after a long day of causing chaos and mayhem.

And, well, from being eaten the fuck out.

Apparently, my little hellcat of a wife squirts.

Not sure if she noticed that, but she's gonna wake up with drenched panties again tomorrow. And *fucking apparently*, I'm hard as fuck again.

I clench my teeth and focus on dressing my wound. Not that it helps all that much, because every little sting and the resulting grit of my teeth remind me that she did this to me. That she stabbed me and I ate her out. By the time I finish, I'm angry and agitated all over again, and itching to do what I've been wanting to do since I saw her signature on the document.

I get my cell out of my pocket and turn it on. I've never really been a fan of cell phones, not even before I got put away. Always thought they made this crowded world a little more crowded. And now that I'm out, I fucking detest the thought of being surrounded by more people than I already have to be. Even if figuratively. Which is why I like the woods. Bad reception and no one to bother for miles on end.

Nowhere for the Turner girl to run.

Engaging the phone, I put it to my ear.

Rad picks up on the third ring. "Hey."

His voice, as always, sounds unused. Full of thick gravel and sand.

"What does Peyton look like?" I ask without preamble.

There's a moment of silence on the other end. Not unusual; sometimes Rad needs time to get his words together. We're all used to being patient with him. This silence, though, feels different. Thicker, fraught with things.

Even though I'm impatient as hell for his answer, I don't blame him for taking his time. I probably threw this at him out of nowhere. Just like when, months ago, I called him and asked him to look into the Turner girl. He was surprised back then too. But like a loyal brother, even though he's just my cousin, he didn't ask questions. Just went about gathering all the information he could for me. And what a revelation that information turned out to be.

"You don't know what your *wife* looks like?" Rad says finally, breaking into my thoughts.

"Look, I know you're pissed," I tell him.

"You know that, do ya."

"I didn't tell you that this was what I was plannin' on."

"No, you didn't."

"But just answer the question."

"Thought we covered this," he retorts.

We did. That was the very first question I asked him when I told him to look into her. Not that it would've mattered, what she looked like. But for reasons unknown, I wanted to know the moment I got my hands on her letter.

Blond hair, blue eyes, fair skin.

That's what he told me, and again, for reasons unknown, every time I sat down to read her words, that's what I pictured. Every time I sat down to write a letter back, I pictured a generic shade of blond and an average pair of blue-colored eyes.

I was wrong.

Her eyes aren't average blue; they're the blue the sky gets just after the rain, crisp and crystal. Her hair isn't the generic blond; it's the kind of blond that's a mix of sunflower and gold. And her skin is like the cream you put in your coffee when you wake up the first thing in the morning. It's also soft and pink like the roses. She's a goddamn Montana morning with clear skies and the golden sun and roses swaying in the breeze.

Oh, and along with the goddamn buttercups.

"Just answer the fuckin' question," I growl.

"Blond hair, blue eyes," he finally indulges me.

I'm not sure what makes me go there, but I ask, "And her best friend?"

"What about"—he pauses for a fraction of a second; the length of time is negligible, and to someone unpracticed, it wouldn't seem like a pause at all—"her best friend?"

"What does she look like?"

"Why?"

"Look, Rad, I'm sorry, yeah?" I sigh. "I'm really fuckin' sorry I didn't tell you what I was planning, but what the fuck did you expect when you read the Turner will?"

He scoffs. "Yeah, shoulda seen that comin'. You marryin' into the family that killed your girl."

I clench my teeth as a piercing pain flashes through my body. As I feel my insides splitting apart.

I know Annie's dead. I know she died eight years ago, the same night I went to kill her murderer but didn't succeed. I know all that. I just don't like hearing it. I don't like hearing she's gone.

Forever.

I also know it probably wouldn't make sense to anyone else, what I've done when it comes to the Turner girl. But it makes perfect sense to me. There's a will, old and ironclad, that was made by one of the original Turners who first settled in Montana. It states that the heir to the Turner ranching business shall always be the oldest-born Turner son; in this case, Brecken. Moreover, the land on which the business sits is to be divided equally among all Turner children when they turn eighteen. When the daughter marries, however, the power of attorney of the land will go to her husband. Meaning, the land might be hers, but the husband is the one who controls it.

And that's what I want.

I want the *control* of the Turner land. Because the one who has

BRANDED

the land, has all the power. *Because* eight years ago, the Turners started a chain of events that led to Annie's death and changed the course of my life, so now I'm going to change everything for them.

"But even knowin' you," he goes on, "and…how fuckin' reckless you are, I couldn't…have imagined you d-doin' something this…*fucked.*"

This shows how agitated he is by what I've done, because usually he's able to mask his struggles with his speech unless he's upset. Something like regret leeches into my veins, but I push it back. I have to. I have no choice.

"So no, I'm not gonna…give you any more *information*," he finishes on a biting tone.

My nostrils flare with a breath, and even though I don't want to, I do it. "Listen to me, this is important, okay? I need to know. Trust me when I say—"

"Not gonna trust you with her."

That feels like a kick to the gut. Rad's always been my only confidant, so when her letter fell into my lap, he was the first person I called. Back then I didn't know what I wanted to do, but then he found the will and my plan became clear.

First, I had to keep her safe. And away from any other men who might become a problem later on. That included motherfuckers both on the inside—fuck yeah, I told every asshole to stay away from her letters and promised retribution if they even thought about writing back to her—and on the outside. Which means I did have a hand in making her math professor disappear. Had a couple of cops put the fear of God in him and tell him it'd be in his best interest if he took a job somewhere else. And then I had to make sure I did everything I could to keep her writing to me every week so I could do what I did.

So I understand where he's coming from, but it still doesn't feel right. Until I realize he's not talking about *her.* The Turner girl, or at least who I thought was the Turner girl, my wife.

He's talking about her best friend.

And with that, another realization dawns and I straighten up. "Tell me you don't have feelings for the friend."

There's silence on the other end. As unusual as the one before because I think he knows I've figured it out. "Are you fuckin' kidding me? Tell me you *don't*."

"Gonna hang up now," he growls.

"The fuck you are," I bite out. "You want her. You want the best friend."

How the fuck did that happen, though?

All I told him was to look into the Turner girl. Where she lived; who she hung out with; what she did; if she had someone, a boy, because if she did, I'd have to get that taken care of. He told me she had a best friend. That they were more than best friends; they were like sisters. Even though they were different from each other, they still managed to do things together. They lived together. They went to classes together. From what I remember, very early on, Rad also told me about seeing guys going in and out of their apartment, which made me lose my shit, even though I knew they probably were connected to her best friend and not her. Because I knew she was inexperienced with guys; I had her letters to prove it. But I never involved Rad more than asking him to get me information.

So again, how *the fuck* did this happen?

"I'm done," he growls again.

"So, what, I tell you to look into the Turner girl and you end up fallin' for the best friend?"

"Least I didn't kidnap a girl...and stab a cop to marry her."

"Jesus Christ." I scrub a hand down my face. "This is fucked."

"You're tellin' me."

"I thought she had a boyfriend."

"Took care of him."

"Took care of him how?"

"You don't need to know that."

"He breathin'?"

"So far."

"Fuck." Sighing, I tunnel my fingers through my hair. "Okay, look, just… I need to tell you something, yeah? But I can't. Not yet. Not until I know for sure. So just…don't do anything else that's fucked. Not until I get back to the ranch."

Because I don't think the girl he's fallen for is the best friend at all. I think Peyton Turner's best friend is sleeping right in front of me.

CHAPTER SIXTEEN

To: Bo Porter
From: Peyton Turner

Dear Bo,
    You're right. This is a bad idea. This isn't how I usually live my life. If my best friend were doing this, I'd tell her to stop. I'd tell her to open her eyes and come back to reality. Because all of this seems like a dream.
    A daydream.
    This only happens in my books and books usually have a happy ending. Unlike life. You could very well have nefarious intentions. You probably had them all along. Maybe this was all a ploy to lure me in. So you could either ask me to send you money in the next letter or to run drugs for you to your buddies. But I don't think that's your plan.
    First, I don't have any money; I'm a college student and you already know that. And if me running drugs for you was your ultimate goal then reading pages and pages about my mundane life for months is just too high a price to pay. Plus in order for me to run drugs to your friends, I kinda need to know who your friends are.
    And I don't.
    You never tell me.

Now that I think about it, I hardly know anything about you. Anything personal, that is. Except your crime and your name. Oh and that you're a cowboy with a deep love for the horses. Which could be in itself a point against you but I think I'm going to take my chances with you.

Besides, if I didn't, you'd never know that some of what you imagine is right. I do smell like flowers. But it's my perfume. I borrowed it from my best friend years ago and loved it so much that I've been using it ever since. My hair's long and thick and yes, I usually have it up in a bun or a ponytail. Mostly because I find my hair annoying and it's always in the way. And as for the nape of my neck, I have to admit that I never thought about it a lot. What it felt like or looked like. I never thought anyone would be interested. But I touched it for you. I ran my fingers over my pulse and I think you may be right. The nape of my neck is soft and warm. Most of all though, it's ready.

For a roughened con to touch me with his rough fingers.

For you.

You said that you want soft things but I've lived my entire life being all soft and docile. So my hunger runs for hard things. Things with sharp edges. Things that bruise and bite.

I think your fingers could do that, grip me, grab me, wrap my long hair like rope around your wrist. I think your fingers could leave their mark on me and so to answer the question you didn't ask: I want your hands on me, rough and strong. Rough and strong, when it comes to you, doesn't scare me as much. Which is a surprise because of how my daddy was but yeah.

What I'm afraid of is that I don't want you to stop there.

I don't want you to just put your hands on me. I want something else too.

I want your mouth.

I think your mouth will be soft. It will be just as soft as the rest of your body is hard. In fact, your mouth will be so soft that I'll wonder how a man so hard can have a mouth so plush and hot and oh so wet.

But then you'll show me. You'll show that it's not about the texture of your mouth; it's about how you use it.

You already know that I've never been kissed. Not once in my life. Which means I've imagined my first kiss about a million times by now even though I pretend that I haven't. And every time I've imagined it, I've imagined it to be demanding and passionate. Possessive and owning. And I think that's how you'll use your mouth on me. Even when you're going slow, it'll feel like you're going fast. And when you're going fast, it'll still feel like you're being thorough.

What I'm really afraid of is that you won't want to.

Kiss me, I mean. Because I've never been kissed before and there's a reason for that. A very good reason and some days I think why should you be any different? Why should you look at me differently than the rest of them?

But then again, this is a daydream, right? None of this is real. None of this will ever happen. I'll probably never see you and you'll probably never see me. So maybe you could be my first kiss, after all.

Until next time,

Peyton

PS: You know what they call a daydream? A reverie. And reverie, along with daydream, is my favorite word.

To: Peyton Turner
From: Bo Porter

Peyton,

What if I do have nefarious intentions? What if I'm playing a really long game? A game where, as you said, I lure you in and then ruin you. Although if I really was, I wouldn't tell you.

Like I never tell you about anything else. Other than my crime and that I'm a cowboy. Or was. I was a lot of other things too but they don't matter anymore. In here, I'm just a number in an orange jumpsuit. So maybe you already know everything there is to know about me.

Another thing to know about me: I'm not like your daddy. I'm not going to hurt you. Not physically at least. My rough hands may leave marks on your body but they won't be the ones you'll cry over when you look at them in the mirror. My sharp teeth may bruise your skin but only because you asked for it.

I'm also not like all the other motherfuckers out there. Those little college-going pissants who don't know their asses from their elbows. I'm torn between beating the shit out of them until they stop existing for making you feel the way you do and letting them live because their loss is my gain.

Even though I haven't been on the outside for eight years now and things may have changed, I know some things remain the same. A man getting to put his rough hands on a woman whose soft skin has never known any other fingers is one of them. I thought I knew hunger. I knew craving. I knew what it's like to starve in a place like this. But I didn't know the first thing about it until your last letter.

Hunger is when there's a deep ache in your stomach. When every breath you let out hollows out your gut and leaves it clenching. Craving is when your fingers shake while standing in the chow line, and your fucking knees tremble in the exercise yard. Starving is what happens when the slightest thought of you makes my body sweat. And hard.

I've been so fucking hard all week.

You want hard things, don't you? Well, here I am: all hard up and in pain. And I may sound like a big man right now, boasting about taking it slow; taking my time with you, absorbing you, dissolving you on my tongue; strumming you and stirring you with my fingers, but I already know it's going to be a struggle.

It's going to be a struggle to control myself.

So maybe it's a good thing that I may never get to see you because if I do, I don't think I'd stop with just a kiss on the lips. I'd want things from you that you probably aren't ready to give.

Bo

PS: A reverie, huh. So maybe that's what you are: my reverie. My dream girl.

CHAPTER SEVENTEEN

AS ALWAYS, I wake up fully aware.

I slowly sit up on the sleeping bag with the early morning sun at my back. There's dirt under my fingernails and twigs in my hair. There's streaks of blood on my body and my dress, dried up and so stark against the white backdrop. Rocky's still tied to the same tree, his head bent, mouth grazing in the bucket on the ground. There's breakfast waiting for me, warm and fresh by my sleeping bag, along with my own bucket of water and a small towel. I notice the smoke rising from the firepit he built yesterday, alerting me that he probably cooked those breakfast sausages while I was sleeping. At least he isn't going along with my fake vegetarianism anymore.

The only thing that's missing from this scene is the man who put all of this together.

Then I hear a splash in the close distance, and beyond the trees and the foliage, I spy flashes of arms cycling in and out. I guess I found him then. He's taking an early morning swim. But how is he doing that after what I…

Regret drowns me for a few seconds. I honestly did not mean to stab him. Yes, he deserved it. He probably deserves *more*, but daydreaming about plunging a knife into someone and actually doing it and watching the blood spurt out is something else.

I never want to do that again. And yes, I will admit that I never want to do that *to him* again. I also don't want to think about what came after.

What he made me, basically *forced*—as always—me to do.

Three times. Or was it four? Whatever it was, I'm not thinking about that. Instead, I spring up on my feet. Bending down, I reach out for the bucket of water and a little washcloth he's left for me. It's not as hard as I thought it was going to be with my hands tied.

Oh yeah, my hands are tied.

That was the very *very* first thing I noticed when I woke up. Even before the sun and the dirt and all the other things. But I decided to not dwell on that because I guess I can't blame him after what I did last night. I mean, he's my kidnapper, isn't he? He's using me for revenge. I'm nothing but an object to him. Just because he made me come…No.

Absolutely not. Stop. *Right now.*

The point is, nothing has changed. Even though it feels like it has a little bit.

Even though, I can't help but feel my heart clench at the fact that he tied the rope in a way that has enough of a give so I can easily wash up and eat. Or that every morning, no matter where we are, he always remembers to feed me breakfast.

Just as I'm done eating, I hear another splash and my eyes jump over to the lake-type-thing. Only to have them go wide and for my mouth to drop open because holy God.

Holy fucking *God.*

There he is, emerging from the water. Last night, the fire was too low and he was too fast for me to see anything, but not anymore. Now I can see *everything.* Every powerful, masculine, *wet* inch of him.

So, *so* wet.

The water is sluicing down his thick, dark hair and sharp face. It tunnels through the arched planes of his pecs that seem like the expanse of a land that can probably withstand a thousand galloping hooves. Before splashing along the grooves of his abs that I thought were ladderlike but that I realize now look more like the harsh terrain of a mountain. And don't get me started on the dark dusting of his chest hair. Lighter at the top but growing thicker along the abdomen with the thickest trail disappearing into the waistband of his...

A literal gasp escapes me when I realize the only thing he's wearing is black-colored shorts. I mean, of course, he was swimming. But now they're wet like the rest of him and they fit him like a second skin.

Which means several things.

First, I can see every flex of his thighs—and this is what Peyton means when she says tree-trunk thighs—as he walks out of the water. The way his thickly muscled thighs tense with every step he takes makes me wonder how the ground isn't shaking beneath his feet.

Because *I* am. I am shaking. My heart is shaking, and I haven't even looked *there* yet.

By there, I mean the thing that is the hardest on his body, or at least gets the hardest when the occasion calls for it; and before I can talk myself out of it or more *into* it, I skitter my eyes to the spot and freeze. Why was I wasting my time checking out his abs of steel or his iron-welded thighs when I could've been looking at that...*bulge* in his shorts?

I lean forward a little, squinting at it. It's big, that rounded bump. It's almost stretching the fabric of his shorts to the max, sticking out almost. Sort of like a tent. Was it this big last night? And how does it fit into a girl? All I know is that I have to squeeze my thighs hard. Like, really, *really* hard. And even though I washed up, my thighs still feel sticky. Or maybe it's because I'm wet again. I'm leaking all over, just at the sight of his nearly naked body.

So it's a good thing when he bends down to pick up the pile of his clothes from the ground and I lose sight of it. It's even better when he puts his jeans on, covering his magnificent muscles, the fabric getting soaked in places from the water. Then, as he straightens up, I watch him rake his fingers through his wet hair, slicking it back before heading toward the camp. Actually, he first spears me with his dark eyes, and he does it in a way that makes me think he knew I was sitting here all along, watching him like a perv.

Even though I'm embarrassed at being caught, the closer he gets, my embarrassment is overcome by concern. I see the cut on his body, just by his collarbone. An angry-looking, reddened gash.

I'm staring at his wound so hard, all wet and dripping with water, that by the time he makes it back to the camp and takes his place on the opposite log, my own shoulder is throbbing with a phantom ache. He picks up the saddlebag by his log—something I hadn't noticed before—and retrieves a first aid kit.

Before I can stop myself, I call out, "I can do it."

He was in the process of fishing out alcohol pads and a bottle of disinfectant, but he stops and looks up. I blush under his dark gaze and swallow. "I know how to…"

There was no need for me to trail off there, but it's hard to talk when he's looking at me like that. With *so much* intensity that it doesn't feel like looking at all but touching. It becomes harder when I realize exactly *what* he's looking at.

My hair.

My loose, finger-combed hair.

Every day since I've met him or rather since he kidnapped me, I've taken the time to braid my hair. Just because every morning, that's what I do. I even went to the café with my braid hanging over my shoulder. This morning, though, I left my hair loose, the long strands falling down my back and over my shoulders. It feels strange, heavy, like there's a weight on my shoulders, but also freeing because I can feel the wind in my hair.

I don't know what made me do it. But now that's he's staring at me like that, I'm starting to wonder if maybe I should've done what

I usually do. Squirming in my seat, I clear my throat. "So as I was saying, I know how—"

This time, I stop talking because something zips through the air, and without thinking or hand-eye coordination, my tied hands reach out and catch it. It's the pack of alcohol swabs. Good. Now I have something to do instead of blushing and feeling awkward.

With the swabs in my hand, I come to my feet. Slowly, I make my way around the smoking firepit, my feet crunching the leaves, stepping on the dirt and twigs. I should probably be watching where I'm going, but I'm not.

Because I'm watching him watch me.

I'm watching him take me in as I walk toward him. My loose hair, my bloodstained dress. My tied hands in front of me and my bare calves. I'm also watching the stubble on his hard jaw. It's grown thicker over the course of the last few days, now bordering on a light beard. But more than seeing those whiskers that cover his beautiful face, though, I'm feeling them.

Between my thighs.

I didn't dare look when I was washing up, but I think he left marks down there. From his stubble. And they're all pulsating right now, burning up, the closer I get to him. It should hurt, all of this. My bare feet walking on the dirt, those little rash marks of his stubble, and it does. But it hurts so good that I can't help but curl my toes every time my inner thighs brush together. I can't help getting wetter.

When I finally reach him, there's a moment when I'm taller than him, and he has to crane his neck up to look at me. It should make me feel powerful for once. That I'm finally looking down at him. But then he goes ahead and widens those powerful thighs of his that I just saw on full display, making a place for me between them, and I lose whatever illusion of power I had.

My knees feel weak and I go down to the ground.

I kneel in front of him, but it's okay. It's so I can be at eye level with his massively broad shoulders. And thereby his injury.

It has nothing to do with whatever craziness is going on in my head and between my slippery legs. That his eyes flare at my new position, and his bare chest swells with a large breath, is something I'm choosing to ignore. Then, before I can draw another breath, he touches me.

Or rather, my hair.

He reaches out and runs his fingers through the loose strands and goose bumps rise all over my body. I clutch my dress with my tied hands and whisper, "What are you...doing?"

"Touchin' your hair," he whispers huskily, staring at his fingers strumming through the mass like the strings of a guitar.

"But—"

"Only ever seen you in a braid," he goes on. "Didn't know your hair was this long. Or this thick."

"My hair's always been this long and uh, thick," I say lamely.

He fists the ends, tugging at it, making me gasp. Before wrapping it around his wrist, once, then twice, making me whimper and clutch my dress harder. Licking his lips, he rasps, "Long enough to use it as a leash and thick enough to pull that leash hard."

He accompanies that with a hard tug of my hair that almost makes me lose my balance, but his thighs around me keep me safe. Still, I whisper, "Please."

Which makes him look up and find the result of his ministrations. My neck is stretched back, and my spine is bowed. I'm clenching my thighs, and even though he can't see that, I still think he knows. He also knows how wet I am and how close to exploding. Something like satisfaction passes through his features before he lets go.

I'm just about to draw in a relieved breath when he produces his knife from somewhere, probably his pocket, and my heart thuds. Flicking it open in his hand, he orders, "Hands up."

I look at the knife for a second. "What?"

"Can't do this with tied hands, can you?"

I blink. "Y-you… You're going to untie me?"

His eyes narrow a bit. "You gonna run out on me?"

I shake my head. "No."

"So then," he repeats with a dip of his chin, "hands up."

I open my mouth to tell him that it's okay. The rope has enough give to allow me to work on him with my hands tied, but then I realize how crazy it sounds. Nothing has changed, remember? I'm still his captive. If he wants to untie me, I should jump at the chance, not politely decline. So I curl my fingers into a fist and put them up in front of him. And without taking his eyes off me, he cuts the rope in the middle, all deftly and quickly.

But before I can go free, his fingers wrap around my wrist, just under where the rope left its mark. "It worked."

His touch makes me flinch and raises chill bumps up and down my arm. "What worked?"

His dark eyes rove over my features. "Lettin' you ride my mouth last night."

I gasp. "That… You… What?"

His fingers squeeze my wrist slightly. "The wild little filly ain't so wild anymore."

My cheeks burn. "I don't…"

"Shoulda done it sooner."

"You shouldn't have done it at all," I retort finally.

"If you say so."

"It was a mistake."

"Not from where I was lookin'."

"And where were you looking from?"

"From between your juicy thighs."

"You're such a—"

"While gulping down your orgasm number four," he finishes.

"You…" My cheeks burn harder as I correct, "Three. It was only t-three times."

He leans forward, and I try to ignore how his abs contract with the motion. "I'd believe you, if drinking from your cunt didn't feel like shooting tequila. And trust me when I say, I know how many shots I had. By the time you were done squirting into my mouth, my jaw was drippin' and my chest was drenched. I was so drunk on your ripe little pussy that you could've stabbed me with the knife I gave you and I wouldn't feel it."

"I-I forgot I had it," I confess like an idiot.

His eyes flash with heat. "I forgot the whole fuckin' world and everyone in it while eatin' your pussy, darlin', so I guess we're even."

"Please don't," I hiccup, "call me darling."

"You tell me what to call you and I'll call you that."

"My n-name."

"Yeah, what's your name?"

I almost tell him then. I even open my mouth, sound out the syllables in my head, before I realize what I was going to do. Then, whispering, I say, "You know what my name is."

His eyes grow intense and so does his hold on my wrist. "Tell me again anyway."

With a pounding heart, I lie, "Peyton."

"Peyton," he repeats.

I don't know why, but again, for a second I think he *knows*. Somehow he's figured it out, my lie, and he wants me to admit it. But I remind myself that's impossible. Still, it scares me so much that I blurt out, "Can I please just…dress your wounds?"

He runs his eyes over my features for one last time before letting my hand go, and I breathe out in relief. I finally break eye contact and focus on the task. I pick up the kit and fish out the rest of the things I need to clean and bandage his cut. Then, I try to switch off everything. The fact that he smells like the woods, the water, and clean and crisp leaves; his skin is all damp and bronzed, and there are still droplets clinging to his tight muscles. Or how small I look on my knees before him. How his body seems mountainous and towering, giving me shade under the sun.

My hands tremble when I reach up and dab his cut with the swab. I go about it lightly because I know it must sting. I also mutter a quiet *sorry*, but if it does hurt him, he doesn't show it. He sits there, still as a rock or as the mountain I just compared him to. Still and staring. And honestly, why not, because he's had a lot worse with that brand on his back. The first letter of revenge, Rawhide, and Reverie. I wonder if the Turners did that to him and if that's why he's so hell-bent on revenge.

"The land you talked about buying," I say, surprising myself.

In the light of day, the moment when he shared that with me seems to have been very raw and vulnerable. And maybe I should just let it lie. I shouldn't get myself involved. It's none of my business. And by his reaction, it definitely seems so. He goes all alert, his tanned muscles going taut. Still, I keep going: "Is that… Do you still want that?"

It's hard to maintain matching his gaze, so I look down to where I'm almost done rubbing in the antiseptic when I hear "No."

I so want to look at him, but I can't or I'll lose my courage. "Is it because some time has passed?"

"Eight years," he clips, and even though I'm looking at his cut rather than at his face, I still know he said that with a clenched jaw.

"Of course, I-I know that." I swallow, keeping my eyes on the task. "But it sounded like a…a good plan. A goal. A dream. And I…I was just wondering if you could maybe still do that."

"I can't."

"Why not?"

A few seconds go by, and I'm finishing up with putting the last tape on a fresh bandage while losing hope. But then he says, with a voice so tight and low that I have to strain to hear it, "Because I don't get to."

"What?"

"Because I don't get to buy land and be done with the Grayson-Turner bullshit. Not when the reason I wanted to do it is gone."

I snap my eyes up then. And good thing I'm done with dressing his wound, because there was no way I could've continued with a steady hand after getting a look at his face. It's harsh and tight, dangerous, but that's not the reason why I'm afraid or why there's a deep clench in my belly. It's the fact that his eyes look…desolate.

They look vacant.

They're dark as always, but there's an emptiness to them that I've never seen before. It's like all the fire inside of him has leached out and he's gone cold. I have this bizarre feeling that if I looked now, the brand would have disappeared from his body. That nothing hot and scalding ever touched him to begin with.

Which is ridiculous. All of this is ridiculous. But I can't help it. I can't help the thoughts running through my mind and how my entire body shakes with the urge to get closer to him. I stay put, though, and ask, "A girl?"

That seems to jerk him awake from whatever place he'd gone off to. And thank God—thank *fucking* God—his eyes don't seem empty anymore. They glitter, and even if I can see it's anger at my question, I don't mind it. "That's enough of your questions."

"I was just"—I go to take my hands away from him, but he stops me by wrapping his fingers around my wrist again—"wondering."

"How about," he goes, squeezing my wrist, "you answer some of my questions for a change?"

Unease washes through me, and I struggle to get away. "What questions?"

He only tightens his hold on me. "Your father."

My heart jumps in my throat. Why are we talking about him? I don't think we've ever talked about him. As in, *specifically*. Where he's staring at me like I'm under a spotlight, a lens that he's peeking through. And I'm good at lying—of course I am—but I don't think I'd be good at it under this kind of scrutiny. So I try to break out of his hold. Even though I know I won't be able to. His grip isn't bruising but it's firm, and I'm not getting out of it until he allows me to.

Still, I keep trying as I ask, "W-what about him?"

"You know this, about dressin' wounds and shit, because of him," he declares. "Because of what he did to your mother."

I swallow, my unease still not going away. In fact, for some reason, it's growing by the passing second. Not only because of my deception, but also because there are certain things I don't like to talk about. Or to be asked about.

"I don't know why we're talking about this," I say, looking anywhere but in his eyes. "You already know that. And you already know everything there is to know about my father, because you almost k-killed him eight years ago and you're hell-bent on destroying him, so I don't—"

"And you," he cuts me off.

"Me what?"

"He did this to you."

I was in the process of twisting my hand in his grip when he spoke, and I go still. Did he just... How did he know?

"Didn't he?" he prods when I don't give him the answer.

I wince and resume my struggle to get away from him. "I don't know what you're talking about."

His features darken. "He did."

"Why would you even think—"

"Because a man fucked up enough to beat his wife is not gonna take mercy on his daughter."

"Can you please let me go?"

"How often?"

"I just want you to let me go."

"How often," he repeats, his voice so low that I can see his chest vibrate with it, "did your father beat you?"

My heart is racing and racing and *freaking racing*. No one knows anything about this. I never ever talk about it. I try to never ever *think* about it, let alone talk about it with anyone. Not even Peyton, who knows every single thing about me and my life. Well, not every single thing, not *this*, but everything else. Over the years, we've bonded over evil fathers and negligent mothers and how crazy it is that we not only share similar looks but similar stories as well. Except she doesn't know the whole story.

No one knows the whole story.

"I don't want to talk about this," I keep insisting.

I absolutely don't, because for some *insane* freaking reason, I do want to tell him.

If there's anyone in this whole wide world that I'd want to tell, it'd be him. Because somehow my heart thinks I owe him that. I owe him the truth about my life because he saved me from it. Without knowing, he gave me and my mother a second chance. His crime saved us, or at least me, and revealing all my hidden truths to him seems like a very small price to pay. But if I tell him that, then I'm going to have to tell him the whole truth. And I *can't* tell him the whole truth because I'm supposed to be lying and pretending and playing a stupid role that's getting harder and harder to do.

"How. Fucking. *Often?*" he roars, jerking me closer to him.

My hand goes flying and lands on his wildly breathing chest to find my balance. And before I can stop myself, I practically shriek, "It doesn't matter, okay? It doesn't fucking matter how often. My father is a monster and that's what he does. That's what he's always done. It's not even the point. I don't care about that. I don't care how many times my father beat me. That's not the right question."

"What's the right question?"

If I was more in possession of my faculties, I'd consider my words carefully. If I wasn't holding on to him like I'm falling apart and he's the one holding all my pieces together, I'd pare my words, try to tread carefully, so I don't expose too much or accidentally ruin everything.

As it is, I don't.

My heart pounds with its own rhythm and my lips let the words flow. "The right question is about why, instead of protecting me from my father, my mother used me as a shield to protect herself. Why did she provoke him against me when he was in a bad mood; why did she put him in a bad mood in the first place so he'd focus his wrath on me and not on her? So he'd take his f-frustrations out on me and not on her. The *right question* is"—I keep going, even though I'm running out of breath—"why didn't she love me enough to protect me? Am I even worth protecting?"

Because if my own mother didn't protect me, then maybe I'm not. Maybe I'm expendable. I'm forgettable and dispensable. I don't matter to anyone.

He leans forward, jerking me out of my thoughts. When I get a look at his eyes, my fingers dig into his shoulders like claws. It's probably painful to him, but again, he doesn't show it, and neither can I loosen my grip on him. Because there's fire in his dark eyes, but it's not like the kind I've seen before.

It's the kind that'll burn these woods down.

"I want you to listen to me," he says, his skin burning hot just like his words and his stare. "When we go back, I'm going to hunt him down, and I'm going to kill him. And I'm gonna do it with my bare hands. Because shootin' him down like an animal or stabbin' him with a knife isn't enough. It isn't enough to make him regret putting his hands on you. So I'm going to wrap *my* hands around his throat, and I'm going to squeeze every tendon and crush every bone in his neck. And I'll do it slowly, so he has enough time to watch his entire life flash before his eyes and all the choices he made that led him to his death. Do you understand what I'm sayin' to you? When we reach Black Rock, I'm gonna kill your father for hurtin' you."

I was wrong. The fire in his eyes won't be contained to just these woods. The fire in his eyes will burn the world down. And all the people in it.

Including my father.

"But you…" I whisper, hypnotized by the darkness in his gaze. "You said you wouldn't kill him."

I don't know which *him* I'm referring to. My father or Peyton's father, the man on whom he's intent on exacting revenge. I don't even know if I'm playing a part; and if I am, then how do I keep doing it when he's promising to kill people.

For me.

"That was before I knew," he says.

"K-knew what?"

"That you're worth protectin'."

His words sound sweet. They sound like the light at the end of a tunnel, the first drop of rain on cracked, scorched earth. They sound like they're meant for me.

For the *real* me.

The one I'm trying to hide away from him—and I can't have that. I absolutely can't. So I need to find a way to run before we reach Black Rock, and I need to find it quickly.

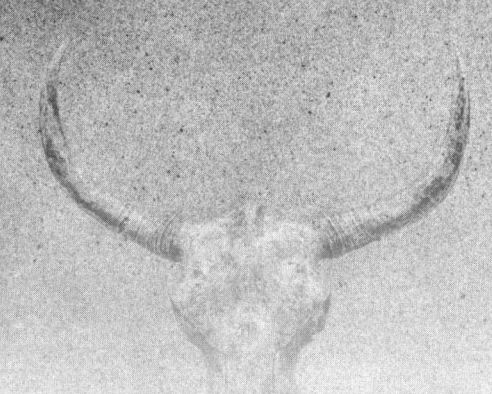

CHAPTER EIGHTEEN

IT COMES TWO days later.

The opportunity for me to run.

We're in another camp, much like the first one, and once again, it's the middle of the night with the fire burning low. This time I definitely know he's sleeping, even though like always he's propped up against a tree because his PTSD doesn't let him sleep.

Except when he can smell you…

My heart clenches at the thought and what it means that he's finally drifted off. But I ignore it and focus on his hand lying on his outstretched thigh. It's limp, and I know that for sure because it's tied to both of mine.

It's his way of making sure I don't run.

It's also his way of killing me slowly, because every night before he ties me to him and every morning when he unties me, he makes sure to put an ointment on my wrists. To make sure my skin doesn't chafe. It's torture, the way he cares for me one second and the next reminds me I'm nothing more to him than a pawn. And if I was smarter—which I'm not, not where he's concerned—I'd focus on only the pawn part. As it is, I can't, but I do tell myself to stop thinking about it right now.

He doesn't know that for the past two days while he was tying me to himself, I was looking for a chance to break free, and I made a breakthrough today. It was pure luck, but while washing up this morning, I found a piece of glass lying under the foliage. And it's a sharp piece, too, that I think will cut through this rope with only a little effort.

We reach Rawhide tomorrow. I always thought I'd be long gone before that, but here I am. In any case, I need to make it this time, because as soon as we reach his ranch and he puts whatever twisted scheme he has for revenge into motion, he's going to find out I'm not Peyton. And I don't even want to think about what he'll do when that happens.

So I get to work. I very meticulously, with small motions so as not to alert him in any way, go about cutting the rope. Once free, I slowly get up and, as quietly as I can, walk out of the camp. And then, when it's safe, I run.

With only the moon to guide me, I take off into the woods with that piece of glass in my hand. I try to remember where we came from. I try to remember landmarks or signs, a fallen tree or a crooked branch, anything to tell me that I'm going in the right direction. The direction where freedom lies. At this point, I don't even know what it looks like, this far-fetched idea of freedom that I have, and I don't even care. All I care about is trying. So I keep zig-zagging through the woods, ducking under branches, leaping over logs. Sometimes landing on my feet; other times falling. I skin my knees; I scrape my palms. I think I lose my makeshift weapon some-where, too, but nothing is going to deter me.

Or so I think until my hurtling body comes to a jarring halt.

It's a miracle I don't fall face-first from my own high veloc-ity, and now I'm standing in front of the one thing I hadn't really given much thought to tonight. Or any night, to be honest. Mostly because he was always with me and I knew he'd protect me from something like that.

A bear.

A big black *scary* bear with glittering eyes.

I don't know where it came from. Or maybe in my mad panic, I didn't pay enough attention to watch where I was going and ended up in his path. However it happened, I'm utterly petrified now. I don't know what to do. I don't know what to think. I don't know how long I stand frozen, simply staring into the eyes of death. Until I hear a low growl and I flinch, my heart jumping up in my throat.

The bear moves. Its paws thudding on the ground, crunching leaves, and I spin around and take off running once again. Only this time I'm running toward him. Because he's the only one who can save me now.

What was I *thinking*? Why did I run away from him? Why didn't I listen? I know he's dangerous, but he's the only one who's ever made me feel safe. God, I'm such an idiot, and I'm going to die now.

I *know* it.

So I call out his name. "Arsen!"

And I don't stop.

Arsen. Arsen. *Arsen.*

I use it as a chant, a prayer almost, that I send up to the night sky. But I'm not sure if he or anyone up there can hear me over the stampeding feet of the beast chasing after me. I'm just about ready to give up and let it take me when I crash into a tree. Or something really, *really* hard. My body ricochets back, but before I can go down, the thing I crashed into—my kidnapper, my husband, the man I was calling out for, *Arsen*—catches me around the waist. He pins me to his hard body and saves me.

Just as it's sinking in that he's here, he's *really* here, and I'm sagging with relief, I hear a loud crack. Followed by another and then one more.

Gunshots.

My body freezes, but my eyes are frantic. They go to his chest first; he's breathing wildly, as if he's been running too. Before I take in his shoulder, all alert and taut, and then his outstretched arm, which I follow all the way down to his hand that's holding the gun.

It's smoking. The gun, I mean.

It's the first time I've seen something like that in real life, wisps of smoke coming out of the barrel. I think this is also the first time I've seen a dead bear. It's lying on its side, and I can see three holes in its body. One in its temple and two in the side, blood dripping from all of them. Its eyes are open, though, just like its mouth, revealing sharp teeth shining in the night, and I have to look away.

Panting, I glance back at him. "You... Y-you came."

His chest moves at my words, almost like a shudder, and he finally looks down at me. His features are tight and sharp, but other than that, they're blank as a slate. I don't care, though. I don't care that I can't read him. That I can *never* read him. Or that he wants to use me for revenge, and I'm back to where I started for the *third fucking time.*

Maybe I'm not meant to leave him. Maybe I'm *meant* to be at his side. Till death do us part. I know it all sounds crazy, but I don't care about that either. All I care about is that he's here and he saved my life and I...

I throw my arms around him.

I wind them around his neck and without ever—*ever*—having done this move before, I hoist myself up on his body. I jump up and my thighs go around his very narrow, very cut and muscular hips. And he helps me. I feel his hands go under my butt so he can give me a boost and now I'm completely, irrevocably, wrapped around him.

Good. Perfect. This is exactly where I want to be.

With him.

I shove my face against his neck and breathe him in. I breathe in his clean scent, ripe with sweat and musk, as I whisper, over and over, "You came. You came for me. You came... You..." I nuzzle my nose in his pulse. "I was so scared. I was so... I thought I was going to die. I thought this was the end and... God, I can't believe you have a gun. I can't believe you shot him. I can't... You never said anything. You never..."

Both his arms are wrapped around my body, and at my words,

both of them squeeze my waist. Almost suffocating me. It feels so good, getting my breaths cut off after breathing like crazy, that I melt into him even further. My body finally relaxes and my curves drape over his hard muscles.

That's when he starts walking, but I have my nose buried in his neck and my fingers fisted in his hair so I don't really pay attention to it all. In fact, I think I close my eyes at some point, being lulled to sleep by immense relief and his rhythmic steps. By his rising and falling chest; his arms that are still squeezing me, cutting off my air.

It's glorious.

But it's over too soon when he comes to a halt and forces us apart. He does it with a hard jerk, unlocking my limbs from around his body and putting me down on my feet. And while I'm blinking awake, trying to catch up to his abrupt actions, he spins me around.

I teeter on my feet, my shoulders crying out in pain at his rough ministrations. "What are you…"

I get my answer when I feel him sliding the rope around my wrists. The coarse material chafes around my skin, but I don't make a peep. In fact, for a second, I feel comfort. I feel safe being his captive. But then that illusion is quickly broken, too, when he ties the knot so tightly that a gasp escapes me. My skin burns and I try to look behind me, but once again, he dominates my body with his and lifts up my now tied hands.

Again, he does it so hard that my shoulders scream in agony and tears of pain well up in my eyes. But I guess I should've saved them for what he does next.

He takes the long end of the rope he used to tie my hands and throws it up in the air. I watch it go over the branch of the tree up above before he catches the tail when it comes down. And *then*, I watch—no, I *feel*—him pull it down and down, that rope, as my arms go up and up and holy God, *up*.

Until my feet have almost left the ground and I'm up on my tiptoes.

Essentially, hanging me from the tree.

When he's satisfied with how my body has been stretched and arranged, he takes the rest of the rope, throws it up and over the branch again, and makes a noose that he then finishes off with a knot. Crazily, I think he's so tall that he didn't even have to stretch himself all the way up while doing that.

I also think I'm dreaming. That this is not real. I'm not really trussed up from a tree, my arms outstretched above me, my toes grazing the ground. It's not my body that's stretched to its limit, and it's not my eyes burning with tears, not my heart that's quaking.

Not *my* savior who's done this to me.

Finally, he locks his dark eyes with mine, and I realize this is real. So very real. It's in the way he takes me in. From the top of my tied hands to the bottom of my flexed feet. It's in the way he goes for his T-shirt. His arm reaches back and fists the neck of it before he takes it off. I lose my breath at the sight of his bare chest, all large and strong, dusted with dark hair and stacked with dense muscles. If I thought that bandage on his shoulder would make a difference in the sheer power and dominance he exudes, then I was wrong. In fact, it makes him look even more dangerous.

Just like that brand.

Letting his T-shirt drop and still taking me in like I'm his trussed-up piece of art, he prowls toward me. Shivering, I twist my hands in the bonds. "Please."

Please take me down. Please don't do this. Please just let me hold on to you like before so I can feel safe.

I don't say any of it, but I know he hears me nonetheless. Because his perusal ends and his eyes come back to mine. And they come back with a look so bright and blatant that I'm hit with it in the center of my chest. It's like a rope around my wrists, my heart, binding me, choking me.

It's a look of pure ownership.

Pure possession. It's a look that says I'll take what he gives me because I have no choice. Because he holds my free will in the palm of his hand.

My arms shake in the bonds. "Don't... Please don't do this. Whatever it is that you're thinking. I'm sorry. I'm sorry I ran. I'm sorry I didn't listen to you. I promise I won't do it again. I won't run. I promise. Please, just—"

I feel a jerk then.

In my body, in my *dress*, and that makes me stumble, even though I'm all tied up and my toes barely touch the ground. I glance down to see his large hands fisting the strap of my dress, right where it meets the bodice. And then I watch his knuckles jut out and his hands shake as in one clean go, he rips it right off. He tears that flimsy ribbon of a strap that holds my dress up right in front of my eyes before going for the second one and doing the same thing.

Just as I feel my dress rustling down my skin and collapsing around my body, I snap my eyes up to look at him. "That was my... Y-you just tore my wedding dress."

His thickly stubbled jaw clenches in response, but other than that, he doesn't say anything. Instead, I feel another jerk around my body. This time I don't have to look to know what he's doing.

He's tearing off my panties; I know that. I know his rough hands are fisting the waistband at my hips, and just like the dress, he tears it off my body like tissue paper; and all I can do is blink as I feel the night air brushing through my bare curves. As humiliation burns a path through the center of my chest and belly, all the way down to that pulsing place between my thighs.

The only consolation so far is that he hasn't looked at me yet. My thick, curvy, source-of-all-shame body. He's busy taking in my face with impassive features.

No, not impassive.

There's a pulse in his jaw that looks painful. Or maybe it's my humiliation that's an ache in my chest. Whatever it is, I want it to be over. I want us to not hurt anymore. And straining on my toes, I arch my body up. I raise my chin toward him and whisper, "I'm sorry. I'm so sorry. I've learned my l-lesson. Just p-please put me down. *Please*, Arsen."

Once again, his name on my tongue feels like an aphrodisiac. A sweet elixir that I was denying myself for so long. I was, wasn't I? I didn't want to say it because I was so angry at him for lying to me. I still am, but now that I've said his name, I never want to stop.

Especially when hearing me say it, he leans down. He brings his face—God, his *mouth*, soft and pillowy—so close to mine that we're breathing the same air. And I realize I want to kiss him. I realize I've *wanted* to kiss him since that night. Since the night he put his mouth on me.

My pussy.

Because how is it that he kissed me down there but never on my lips? How is it that I've spent the last six months imagining his lips on my lips, and I've yet to taste them?

When he grabs my jaw, I realize I've wanted him to touch me since that night too. Because he hasn't. Which is a feat in itself since we've ridden on the same horse for hours; I've sat with my spine almost fused to his chest; he's lifted me onto and off the saddle with his hands around my waist; I've redressed and bandaged his cuts, but still it feels like we haven't touched at all.

He stretches my neck farther up, tilting my head back and bowing my spine, and I think it's going to happen. I think he's two seconds away from kissing me. But then he cocks his head to the side as a cruel light flashes through his face. He tightens his fingers on my jaw, and using his grip as leverage, he gives me a push and my body goes swaying.

Back and forth like a pendulum. Like a piece of meat.

A swinging doll, naked and humiliated, at his mercy and his whims.

My shoulders scream in protest. My wrists are flayed, but the most painful thing is the shame in the center of my belly. The most *painful thing* is the thump of my naked spine against his bare chest when, after letting me swing for a few seconds, he rounds my hung body and brings me to a stop with his splayed hand on my trembling belly.

He plasters himself to my back as he rasps the very first words he's spoken to me since he rescued me from the bear. "Do you know how long I've waited to hear you say my name?" Through my broken and heaving breaths, I try to look back, but he presses his hand on my belly, making me arch up as he commands, "Eyes up front."

"A-Arsen, you—"

My words stop when I feel something pressing at my pulse.

When he *uses* that something to inch my head up. I don't have to look to know what it is. I know *exactly* what it is, even though I've never—not *ever* in my entire nineteen years on this earth—had it pointed at me.

A gun.

He's holding my chin up with the gun pressed just under my jaw, and I don't know how, but it still feels hot from when he used it to save my life. My muscles are locked tight in fear and I know my eyes are open, but I don't think I'm seeing anything other than dark spots. And in that darkness, I hear him say, "Back when we were writin' to each other, there were so many times I wanted to tell you my real name. Wanted to see it written in your handwriting. I'd sit there, in my bunk, and hunt down the letters of my name in the words you wrote. And then put them together in my head, tryin' to imagine what my name would look like in your small fancy handwriting. But then"—he breathes out behind me, grazing his stubble along the side of my cheek—"I get out and I meet you, but you refuse to say it. You *refuse* to say my name."

I swallow. "I-I was angry. I was angry that y-you lied to me. That you—"

He presses the gun harder and I flinch. "I know you were. I am too."

"I—"

"I kept thinking about it. I kept imagining it. The moment you'd say it. The moment I'd *make* you say it. But then you did and I—" He takes another deep breath, his hot chest sliding along my spine. But this time, when he exhales, I hear a slight hitch in it, a little shudder that I probably wouldn't have noticed if we hadn't been plastered to each other. "You screamed my name. In fear. In panic. And I thought I'd lose my mind. Thought I'd come out of my skin if I didn't find you. If I didn't get to bring you back where you fuckin' belong."

My heart clenches then, clenches and clenches, and I try to look back at him again. But he presses the gun harder, and I have to stay put. I hate it. I absolutely *hate* it, but I do. Instead, I dig the back of my head into his sweaty chest. "I-I'm sorry. I'm so, so sorry."

"I thought I'd tear this world apart. Turn it upside down until I found you. And the only time that's happened was eight years ago," he continues, his words hot, his breaths hotter. "I didn't like it back then and I like it even less now. So do you understand what I'm sayin' to you?" He inches the gun up, pressing it against my lower lip, as he continues, "I'm sayin' don't fuckin' say my name, yeah? Not my name, not another word. Until I tell you to. Is that clear?"

My heart's racing, and amid the chaos in my body, I jerk out a nod.

His growl is satisfied. "Now, do you know what this is? Just yes or no."

My chest shudders when he skims the mouth of his gun over my lower lip. "Y-yes."

"It's a gun," he says in a rough tone. "But it's more than a gun, isn't it?"

I bite the inside of my cheek to keep quiet, but it's hard.

"It's the thing that saved your life."

"Arsen, please, I'm—"

He shakes his head slowly. "*Tsk, tsk.* If you keep breakin' the rules, darlin', I'm gonna have to cut this short. And the fun's just gettin' started." My breath comes out as a broken sob, and he pushes the muzzle into my lip even more. "So how about you put your pink little mouth to better use and thank the gun that saved your life?"

My heart drops, and my eyes scamper up to meet his. This time around, he doesn't stop me. He doesn't tell me to keep my eyes up front, and I know why. It's because he wants me to see the cruelty in them. The meanness, the danger.

The fire.

I don't know what he sees in my eyes—I don't know myself what's reflected right now except for sheer humiliation and pain—but it hardens his already harsh jaw and sharpens his already unforgiving features. It makes him push the mouth of the gun at the seam of my lips as he says, "You called for me, didn't you? With this mouth. You screamed my name to come save you and I did. So it's time you pay the price. It's *time* you open it when I tell you to open it and do exactly what I tell you to do with it, you got that?"

I somehow manage to nod.

But it only enrages him further because he clenches his teeth as he continues, "So open those goddamn lips of yours and wrap them around the muzzle of this gun. And wrap them good, yeah? Because I want you to suck. I want you to suck it like I know you wanna suck me."

"I d-don't—"

He presses the gun so hard to shut me up that my lips get smushed against my teeth. Then, with flaring nostrils, he says, "You like lyin', don't you, baby? We're gonna talk about that too. I'm gonna teach you what happens when you open your mouth and the first thing that comes out of it is a lie. In fact, we'll start now. Just for that pathetic fuckin' lie, I'm gonna leave the safety off."

My eyes go wide and I start to shiver. Or maybe I was shivering this whole time, I don't know. All I know is that I can't look away from him and his brutal but hypnotizing eyes. "Because you know it's a lie, don't you?"

I nod again.

His eyes go back and forth between mine. "Yeah, you do. That's why for the last two days, I can't fuckin' escape you. Everywhere I turn, there you are, your big blue eyes, your golden hair, your buttercup fuckin' scent. *There you are*, lookin' for ways to touch me. Bandaging my wounds with your soft hands; pressin' your ripe little body up against me on the horse, rubbin' up on me like a cat in heat. Asking for it, begging for it, drivin' me fucking insane. That's what you wanted just now. You wanted my mouth."

I did. I *do*. He's right. I didn't realize it myself, not until a few moments ago, not until he spelled it out for me, but yes, I've been doing all those things for the past two days.

"Yes," I whisper.

"Yeah," he rasps. "It's because I ate your pussy so good that you're addicted to it now."

It should be embarrassing, but it's not. Somehow none of what he's saying is embarrassing to me. Maybe because I'm past all that now. He's stripped me of dignity, tied me up naked so that I don't have any shame left.

"So how about you show me how much and maybe I'll give it to you. Suck the mouth of my gun like you wanna suck me." His voice drops lower. "And I'm not just talkin' about my lips. Suck it like I know you wanna suck somethin' else, somethin' much harder. As hard as this loaded gun that just saved your life. That fuckin' saved my sanity."

If words alone had the power to do it, I'd branded. I'd be tattooed with them. Every single depraved and humiliating word would be written on my skin. As it is, I know I'll never forget them. Not until the day I die. Or the fact that as depraved as they are, I still find myself obeying him, and I do it because I could hear the hitch in his voice at the end there.

His *sanity* sounded like *s-sanity*.

And I know somehow, as scary as he seems right now with the gun in his hand, he's also *scared*. *Still* scared of what could've happened. So I open my mouth and wrap my lips around the muzzle of his loaded gun.

And *suck*.

His nostrils flare the first time I do it. The second time, his jaw clenches, and on my third suck, I feel his chest vibrate with a low growl. When I notice a flush painting his sharpened cheekbones next, something happens to me. Something strange and new but also old and familiar. Something that tastes like this metallic object he's making me suck but also like a quickening in my lower belly.

It's heavy and sticky, swollen and wet.

It's my pussy. It's pulsing down below, throbbing from this lewd thing I'm doing. From the way I'm swirling my tongue around the barrel, vacuuming it in my mouth, trying to drink from it like I would if we were really kissing.

I have to clench my thighs at that. And since my thighs are bare just like that throbbing place in between, I make a mess. I'm all wet and leaking and my thighs slip against each other. They also make a wet, slick sound that causes me to suck the gun harder. It causes me to open my mouth wider and go up and down the barrel, gagging myself on it. Or maybe it's him who's making me gag on his gun, shoving the thing in and out of my mouth, pumping and pumping.

I don't know. All I know is that I can't just pretend that I'm thinking of kissing his mouth. This is a full-blown sucking, and yes, I'm pretending to suck his dick. And at this, my body goes in search for it outside of my imagination and I begin to rock against him. Or rather, against that bulge in his pants that I swear is growing harder by the second.

Just like his breaths.

They are wild and violent, gusting against my spine. I moan and writhe and suck the gun harder. I realize my chest is wet with my saliva, all greased up and slippery, and I wish my arms were free so I could wrap them around the gun and go at it even harder. I wish I could hug it between my breasts and use my spit to go up and down.

I wish I could suck on his real dick the way I'm sucking on his loaded gun.

It's a harsh wake-up call when he pulls the thing out of my mouth and leaves me bereft. I hate it so much that my eyes open and I whimper. I roll my head back and forth in protest, but he shushes in my ear. "Shh... It's okay. It's okay."

"But I—"

"I know," he whispers, his arm around my waist tightening and squeezing, pressing me against his frame even harder. "I know, darlin'. I know you want it."

"I do. I do. Please, please," I whine, grabbing the rope and trying to arch and rub up against him.

But instead of bringing it closer, he moves the gun even farther away from where I want it. It goes lower and lower on my body, leaving a wet trail of my own saliva as he whispers against the side of my face, "I know you wanna suck it, but it isn't the real thing, yeah?"

"But—"

"Shh," he goes again, his tone gentle and soft, a little bit amused too. "I know. But listen to me, this isn't my dick no matter how much you want it to be, baby. And trust me when I say you don't want it goin' off in your mouth like my dick either, okay? So how about you calm down some and let me give you what you want."

I know what he's doing.

I know he's trying to *handle* me. Because this is what he does when Rocky gets agitated about something or doesn't want him to check his hooves. He talks to Rocky, using the same gentle, indulgent tone that he's using on me.

I probably should say something, something like I'm not his horse or filly or whatever it is that he keeps calling me, but I don't care. I don't care how crazy I look right now or how amused he is at my desperation; I want it.

I want *him*.

So still writhing against him, I ask, "Your d-dick?"

His breath escapes in a low chuckle. "My baby's got a one-track mind, doesn't she."

"You—"

"Not a big fan of guns; I like my knife better. But my baby made me a convert. All I had to do was point a gun at her and she went from being a sassy, pain-in-the-ass *wife* to my personal little porn star."

I jerk at his words and from the fact that he's brought his gun down to my tummy, and at *porn star*, he presses the muzzle into my belly button. "You—"

"Nah," he corrects himself. "She became my personal little porn star the moment I licked her pussy." I moan and twist my hips as he keeps going, making imaginary circles on my belly with his gun. "If I had known that, darlin', instead of stabbing that motherfucker for touchin' you, I would've just flipped your dress up and ate you out in front of him. You moaning out my name while squirting down my throat would've probably sent a better message that you're mine. And you are, aren't you?"

"Yes."

"Yeah, you are." He nuzzles the mouth of his gun in my tummy as he chuckles again. "And I can tell you one thing, that sheriff would've creamed his pants watching you come for me but he wouldn't have dared come near you. Because everyone knows, no law, no country, not even God is allowed to come between a man and his wife's slutty pussy. And you're that, aren't you?"

"Yes," I whine again, rocking and rocking and *rocking* my hips, every curve in my body jiggling.

"You're my wife."

"I am."

"And yet you keep runnin' from me."

"I won't. I won't. I promise," I say, rolling my head back and forth on his chest. "I won't run. Till death do us p-part."

"That a vow?"

"Yes, it is."

He hums. "What else?"

"I'll listen to you," I say, my eyes almost in a trance, blinking open and shut.

"Good. What else?"

"I'll do what you tell me to do."

His chest goes up and down with a satisfied breath. But then, he goes, "That's all good, baby, but that's not what I want and you know that. I *know* you know that."

"But I…"

I feel him going down with his gun, lower than my belly button, skimming my pelvis before actually touching me there. Right where I'm wet and pulsing. And I'm so wet and pulsing that the barrel almost slips through my core. It almost slides through it, and just as he begins to run it up and down, he says, "Give me what I want."

"But Arsen, I—"

"Give it to me."

I hear his words. I do. But I don't know what they mean. I don't know anything anymore except how good this feels. How I want him to keep doing this. Keep running the length of his gun up and down my core.

At my continued silence, he repeats, "Now, baby."

My eyes are scrunched shut. My mind is a whirlwind. My hips are rocking against that gun, and I'm powerless against his demands. "I won't lie to you. I-I promise. I won't."

I feel his chest vibrate with his breaths before he whispers, right in my ear, "Then tell me your name."

At this, awareness slams into me and my eyes snap open. "What?"

"Because we both know it isn't Peyton," he whispers.

I try to stop twisting, but he's still pumping the gun along my core, and all I can do is stutter back, "B-but I…"

"Because the name you signed on that piece of paper starts

with an *R*, and if you don't tell me what it is, I'm gonna lose my fuckin' shit. I'm gonna lose it, darlin', yeah? I need to know your name." He keeps pumping as he confesses, "I *need* to know the name of the girl I'm jerkin' off to every night and blowing my load like a teenager. And then, satisfied, I sleep in her scent. I know the taste of her cunt, but I don't know her name. I know I'm gonna kill her daddy for her, but I don't know what to call her. And for the past eight years, every time I close my eyes, I see fire. I see blood and concrete walls and barred windows. But six months ago, somethin' happened. My nightmares went away and I'd see skies as blue as her eyes, sun as golden as her hair. I'd see rosy skin and soft curves instead of cinder-block walls. So I need to know the name of the girl who made me dream when I thought all I was destined for was nightmares."

Later, I'll think about the repercussions of this. I'll think about how foolish I've been. How *dangerously* stupid. For now, it slips out of me.

"R-Reverie," I whisper at long last. "My name… It's Reverie."

And then I come.

Because he flicks my clit with the muzzle of his loaded gun and because he says with a long breath that he's been holding for ages, "Like a dream."

And I feel such a relief. Such lightness at finally telling the truth, that I don't have to pretend anymore; not to mention, from having an orgasm that, when I finally come down from it, has left my eyes closed and my lips loose.

"Peyton's best friend. My mother was her nanny and my daddy worked on the ranch. She asked me to do her sociology paper because she was failing. And I said yes b-because I'd do anything for her. But then I wrote to you and I…I kept writing. I kept writing even when I didn't need to because I couldn't not. Because I liked it. I loved it. And then we met and I wanted to tell you. The t-truth. At the café, but you… But then I found out who you were and…I ran. I had to. I couldn't tell you the truth because I had to protect Peyton. Because of who you are." Still blinking up at him, I continue, "I lied to you because you're just like him. You're just like my father."

I feel him stiffen behind me, but I don't let it stop me now because I need to get this out. All of it. Every little piece of my sordid history.

"Which is so crazy because I always thought that the man who saved me and my mother could never be like my daddy. You're that man. You saved me. Eight years ago, we left the ranch because someone broke in, in the dead of the night. Someone in a mask. He tried to kill Mr. Turner and so they said it wasn't safe for us to live there anymore. They took us away and I was so happy because I thought we'd finally be safe. That finally my daddy wouldn't get to us. But I was wrong."

I think I feel both his arms going around me at this, but again, I don't let it deter me because I need to get this out. "He did get to us, to her. He pushed her down the stairs. I saw it. They were arguing about something like they always would and I *saw* him push her. I tell people I wasn't home the night my mom died. I tell them it was probably an accident that she fell down the stairs. But it wasn't. I was there. I was hiding behind the couch because I thought he was going to come for me. But he didn't. He left. He saw her go down. He stood before her bleeding body and then he left. And I...I never thought you'd be like him. I never thought that the man who saved me eight years ago would kill me one day. You're going to kill me now, aren't you? Because I'm not who you thought I was. I'm not a Turner. So can I ask you something?"

"Anything."

I hear him say it in a ragged whisper, and I ask the question I've been dying to ask. "What's her name?"

I don't have to tell him who I'm talking about, and I don't know how much time passes before I hear, "Annie."

I smile slightly, my head too heavy for my neck now. "That's pretty. She's lucky. That you love her so much to do this for her."

"I made a promise."

I nod, my head lolling now, grazing my outstretched arms. "Can you make me a promise too?"

He grasps the back of my neck to give it support and repeats, "Anything."

"Promise that when you kill me, you'll make it quick. I don't want to lie in a hospital bed, in a coma for days before they pull the plug. Like my mother did. So promise me you'll kill me right away so it doesn't hurt. So it doesn't…"

I forget what I was going to say. Probably because my body gives in and I sag against him. The last thing I remember before I float away is him cutting the rope up above and bringing my limp arms down. Before picking me up off the ground and winding his arms around me so tightly that for the first time in my life, I feel safe.

Even from him.

CHAPTER NINETEEN

To: Peyton Turner
From: Bo Porter

Peyton,

I've never beaten around the bush before and I'm not going to start now. In fact, I've been blunt with you to the point of being an asshole. So before I say anything to you, I want you to know that I've been granted parole.

I'm getting out Friday.

My hearing was last week and I admit I should've told you. I didn't because I'm an asshole. Because I know this is just a dream for you. A fantasy on paper. A safe way to have an adventure. The felon you've been writing to suddenly on the other side of the bars is the opposite of that.

I get it. I also get that what I'm about to say is probably the last thing I should say to you. If someone else had said this to you, I'd tell you to run. Or call the cops. I'd tell you to tear his letter into pieces and never write back.

But I have to.

I will be at the university cafe, next Tuesday at 11AM (around the same time I usually get your letters on the inside). I'll order a cup of coffee, and I'll find a seat in the direct view of the entrance. I'll sit there for an hour, until the clock strikes twelve, looking at the door, hoping to see a girl come in wearing a white dress.

I'm telling you this because I want that girl to be you. The girl who filled my lonely days with her words.

Bo

PART II

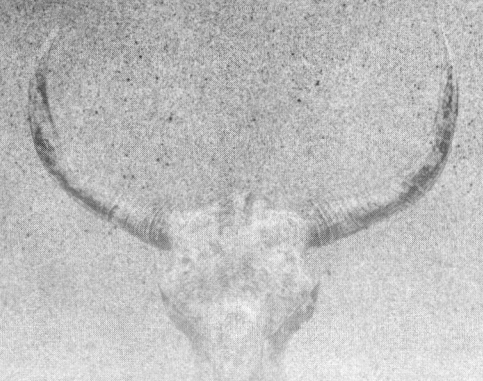

CHAPTER TWENTY

I SEE IT before we get there.

Rawhide. The Grayson ranch.

Written in white on a hanging sign made of dark wood. The words are flanked by a fancy *R* on both sides, just like the one on the cap he wears. It looks old, the sign, with cracks running through the wood, creeping into the painted letters. Like it's been here for years, decades. Maybe that's why it looks so grand despite those little dents and chips. For its tenacity to keep standing year after year.

Or maybe it's the fact that it stands against the backdrop of a vast blue sky and rolling green fields. Not to mention, the mountains that jut out in the distance. I lived in Black Rock for the first eleven years of my life, but I don't think I've ever seen a sky so blue or the ground so green. Or the tips of the faraway mountains so sharp and snowy-white.

I don't know what I was expecting at Rawhide, but… Actually, scratch that. I *know* what I was expecting. Something dilapidated. Something neglected and, yes, fraught with danger. Rusted signs, broken fences, scorched earth. But it's something out of a picture book.

As we ride up to the entrance, more things come into view. Tall trees in full bloom; a winding dirt road just beyond the sign that leads to a log mansion so sprawling and majestic that it puts the bungalow on Wildfire to shame. I mean, just look at the wraparound porch on this thing and those thick polished pillars. There's a wide set of stairs that lead up to the porch and cushioned rocking chairs that look like the most comfortable chairs I've ever seen after riding on a horse for close to a week. But the most striking feature of this mansion/house has to be the massive front facade. It's made of stacked horizontal logs the same color as the sign—although the wood here is more polished and looks restored—giving it both a rustic and a modern look.

The mansion isn't the only building on the property, however. As we follow the path, I notice a bunkhouse up ahead and a barn. There's also a corral, just off the barn, with horses circling along the wooden fence. It would all be very normal-looking if not for the fact that a bunch of ranch hands in their leather chaps and cowboy hats are leaning against the fence, watching as a horse tries to throw off its rider. The man on the saddle is trying to hold on, his hands gripping the reins, but it's obviously not easy. The horse keeps kicking his hind legs back, his body bucking like a wave.

Over the loud neighing and thudding hooves, I hear the men cursing and hollering. They clap when the horse bucks so hard that the man bounces off the saddle and boo when, despite that, he still manages to stay on. Then, a second after that near miss, the horse jerks so hard that his front legs leave the ground in a cloud of dust; and no matter how hard the man was gripping the reins, his hold slips and he flies off the saddle in an arc, hitting the ground with a thud. Followed by a round of applause and whistling.

I'm so invested in all of this that I sit up straight and gasp. And then I hear a muttered, "Fuckin' show-off."

Which reminds me of my own dire situation.

Behind me, I feel him move and then dismount as gracefully as ever. Like we haven't been riding for hours on end and every muscle in his body isn't screaming with a deep-seated ache like mine are. And as always, he stands there, with his arms up and his features impassive, to help me down as if things are normal. Like the last week didn't happen. Or last night. Like he doesn't know my real name and I'm still his wife—not really.

He does and I'm not.

I have zero energy; I have no inclination to pretend otherwise. I didn't even think I'd be alive to see today, and I'm just over all the lies. So I accept his help without a word and get down. As soon as my bare feet hit the gravel, I hear someone exclaiming from behind me, "Holy fuck."

I spin around to find the group of men facing us, now watching us as a spectacle. Some with confusion, and others with shock and familiarity. One of them, though, is on the move. He's already pushing through the group and striding toward us. I think he's the one who said those words. As he takes off on a run, I realize he's the rider who got thrown off if his dusty clothes and scraped-up cheek are any indication. Also, he's not a man. Or rather he's too young to be called one. At least way younger than the man standing beside me. Before I can make any other judgment about the newcomer, though, he reaches us and throws his arms around Arsen, holding tight, his Stetson falling off his head with his actions.

And when I say tight, I mean it.

Although his hold on Arsen has nothing on when Arsen winds his arms around him and squeezes. He does it so hard that the younger guy's feet almost leave the ground and he emits a loud bark of a laughter. The younger guy I mean, not Arsen.

I think he's too busy feeling a surge of emotions to laugh or even crack a smile in this moment. I wouldn't believe it if I wasn't watching it with my own eyes, but Arsen's usually impassive and hard features are scrunched up slightly and are lined with what I can only call longing. There's a wet sheen to his dark eyes that's so bright, just like the midday sun, that I have the urge to blink my own eyes against the glare.

But I dare not because I don't want to miss this reunion.

That's what this is, isn't it? A reunion after eight years. I also think I know who this younger guy might be: Axton. He's the first to break away, and as soon as he does, he rears back and lays a punch on Arsen. The sound alone of flesh meeting flesh makes me flinch, but Arsen, other than his head jerking to the side, hardly moves. He doesn't even reach up to touch the spot or acknowledge it in any way.

"That's for being an asshole every time I came around to see you and you wouldn't see me," the younger guy growls.

Arsen simply looks at him and dips his chin. "Noted."

I watch as maybe-Axton's shoulders go up and down with his heavy, noisy breaths. "You look...*old.*"

At this, Arsen finally barks out a laugh. "Eight years's a long time, huh."

His shoulders heave again. "Yeah. A fuckin' long time."

Arsen's jaw clenches for a second before he dryly delivers, "You look the same, though."

The guy chuckles. "Fuck off." Then, his head shaking, "I can't fuckin' believe you're back."

Another flash of longing moves through Arsen's features before they go impassive like always with a hint of condescension. "Yeah, well, eight years and nothing's changed. You're still gonna get your neck broken and end up dead before you can legally drink."

"What, that?" He motions with his thumb over his shoulder. "That was just a little bet to see who gets to break that bronco first."

"You don't really seem to be winning."

"Are you kiddin'?" Axton waves his objections away. "I'm the only one who's been on that sucker for close to thirty seconds. It's been a week since Rad rescued it from some real hillbilly type. Ain't no one been able to touch it let alone ride that bad boy."

Arsen shoots him a look that I can only call superior. "Well, that's about to change, ain't it? Because as you said, I'm back."

I don't really see it because Axton's back is turned, but I feel him rolling his eyes. "Think you should probably worry less about me and more about you. Because where the fuck is your shirt?"

Before Arsen can say anything, we hear a shout—a woman's—bursting from the direction of the mansion. Thankfully. I wasn't prepared to hear his answer.

"Axton Jonah Grayson, get your lazy ass back in the house and pick your tighty-whities up off the floor right now or I'm gonna lose it. I'm not your fucking…"

The voice trails off, because the woman it belongs to bounds down those wide stairs and stumbles upon the scene in front of her. By that I mean, she catches sight of Arsen and comes to a sudden halt. Her eyebrows scrunch up and her mouth falls open, a reaction similar to the younger guy's.

Is this Annie?

As soon as the thought flashes through my mind, I'm ashamed of it. For a variety of reasons. Including that this potential moment is much bigger than my useless fascination with a girl that I know for a fact is important to the man I was forced to marry. *So* important that he's ready to burn down the world in his quest for revenge for her. So important that I think he loves her.

He does, doesn't he? Because you don't go to such lengths for someone you don't love.

And this woman here, she's beautiful. She might be the most beautiful girl I've ever seen. She has the blackest, shiniest hair, which goes past her hips, and her skin is a beautiful shade of bronze, making me think she may be of Native American descent. Her eyes are catlike, with arched ends and a dark fringe of lashes. And her lips are plump and dark pink with an enticing curve. With a plaid shirt, skinny jeans, and cowboy boots, she looks at home here. Like she belongs on this ranch. I wonder what that's like.

I watch her mouth Arsen's name before she takes off just like Axton. She runs up the path, her long hair flying behind her, and right in front of my eyes, she jumps into Arsen's arms. Her feet lift off the ground and her arms wind around his neck like she'll never let him go.

Despite myself, I press a trembling hand to my belly. There's an acute pain down there that only increases when I see Arsen rocking her in his arms. I hear a soft sob escaping her as she hides her pretty face in the side of his neck.

Like I did.

Like I *have* for the last week. I've burrowed my face there while we rode for hours through the treacherous woods. I've slept with my nose buried in it. I found comfort in it last night when he saved my life. But now it's hers, that spot, and God, I…

I want to punch something. I want to punch him. He's responsible for this. He's responsible for *all* my misery and these crazy conflicting feelings.

She finally breaks away from him, and he puts her down. And then, just like Axton, maybe-Annie rears back and punches him in the face. This time the sound isn't as loud as before, but I still wince. She grimaces before shaking out her wrist. Then, pointing that same hand in his direction, she declares, "You deserved that."

This time, he does touch the spot on his jaw as he drawls, "Apparently, that's the consensus."

She's not amused, however, and swats his chest. "Do you have any idea how scared we all were?" She doesn't wait for Arsen to reply as she keeps going, *"Any idea* at all? All Mr. Grayson said was you weren't going to be home for another few days. That you got held up."

This time, Arsen does try to intervene. "It's—"

"After eight years," she cuts him off. "You were in prison, Arsen, for eight years. And then you get out and you can't come home? What are we supposed to make of that?"

"I'm fine," Arsen says in a low voice.

"No, you're not," she insists. "You can't be. You're out of your mind is what you are. I overheard Mr. Grayson the other night, okay? I did. Your brother never shares anything, but I overheard. You married the Turner girl. Are you crazy? Are you *absolutely* insane? Are you out of your mind? Because *those people*—"

At this point, all proceedings come to a halt, because finally, they all notice me. It's not their fault, though, for not doing so before. I've been kind of shrinking away since Axton broke into the scene. It just didn't feel right to be standing so close to them. To all the Graysons. Not because of who they are but because they're clearly a family. The kind I've never experienced before. No matter how or under what circumstances I'm here, it still feels like intruding. In any case, there's no hiding now. I'm the center of their attention.

Axton leans toward the girl and mutters, loud enough for me to hear, though, "Think it's time to shut up."

She turns toward him and punches his arm, which makes Axton go, "*Ow!*" Then, turning back to me, she apologizes. "I'm so sorry. I didn't…" But then she trails off as she really looks at me. Her pretty dark eyes go from my unruly, messed-up hair to my dirty bare feet, and everywhere in between. My scraped-up knees, my dirt-caked arms. But mostly my attire.

The T-shirt I'm wearing that's too big on me and clearly belongs to someone else. Like the man standing behind her. My forced-husband and her…whatever.

Annie turns back to Arsen then and pushes at his chest. "What did you do to her?"

He takes a deep breath and his nostrils flare. But before he can respond, his eyes fall on something behind my shoulders and his face hardens. Actually, his entire demeanor goes on alert. Not only his, but Axton's too. Even maybe-Annie's. They all sort of fall in line, with Arsen widening his stance and Axton clearing his throat. But the biggest change comes over her. She goes from being this spitfire of a girl to a demure-looking one. She tucks her gorgeous hair behind her ears and lowers her eyes, wiping her hands on her thighs.

Somehow it makes her look younger than before, and I had put her in her early twenties. I follow their gaze to discover the reason for this sudden change, and there it is.

A man.

Tall and broad, even more so than Arsen, and very grave-looking. He has dark hair—from what I can see, because he has on a black-colored Stetson—much like Arsen and Axton, but it's threaded with silver. It also curls like Arsen's, not like Axton's, though, whose hair, now that his hat's off, I see is straight and spiky. His eyes are dark as well but with a little bit of brown. Which is more similar to Axton's eyes, as Arsen's more often than not appear pitch-black. But unlike both his brothers—because I think I'm looking at Marsden Grayson right now—he has a mustache. A classic horseshoe shape that makes his square jaw look even more angular and broad.

Silently, he takes in the scene, his eyes going from one end of the line, starting with Axton and then to Annie and then to Arsenal, where his gaze stays for a long moment. Then, with a gravelly voice that also matches Arsen's, he goes, "You made it."

Arsen stares back at him for a few more seconds before jerking his head in a nod. "Looks like it."

Marsden exhales a breath, shifting on his feet. "Welcome home."

I notice Arsen's chest shudder with his next breath. It's a very subtle movement, but I've been so close to that chest for such a long time that I can make it out. I'm not sure if anyone else did, though. Or if they catch a little extra roughness in his voice when he replies, "Good to be back."

Then, without further response, Arsen's older brother turns toward me, and I draw back a little at his sudden attention. I hate that I cower, but there's something about his quiet authority that makes me fall in line too. While Arsenal Grayson reminds me of an ever-burning fire that can roar and engulf me at the slightest provocation, Marsden

Grayson makes me think of hard, cold marble that will freeze me with one look.

Not to mention, my state of undress makes me even more timid than usual.

Before I can get my bearings back and straighten my spine, I'm suddenly looking at the mountainous, branded back of my husband. I don't know how that came about because he was standing all the way over there, but now, he's here in front of me, and between me and his brother. I'm not going to lie, it does ease a little bit of my trepidation and I can breathe easier. Even though I don't think his safety net is going to last much longer. How can it when he knows the truth now?

From over Arsen's shoulder I hear Marsden ask, "This the girl?"

I notice his shoulder blades twitching with a breath before he replies, "Reverie."

"What?" his brother says.

"That's her name," Arsen replies back in a low tone.

I should probably be paying more attention to the conversation; this could be where they decide my fate. But I'm still reeling from the fact that this is the first time he's said it.

My name.

Last night when I told him the truth, he repeated my words from the letter and called me a daydream. But he never actually said it. I can't decide if it's a good thing or bad. Because if he *had* said my name last night, I probably would've died right then and there after how he wrung me out, both emotionally and physically. And if I had, I probably wouldn't have to face his entire family standing here in his T-shirt.

As it is, I'm about to pass out from how fast my heart is racing right now. How different my name sounds in his voice, how new. Like this is the first time I'm hearing it. Like no one has ever said *Reverie* before him.

"What? But I thought her name was Peyton."

This comes from a confused Axton, and my heart skips a beat. I knew it was bound to happen. In fact, I thought that moment was upon me. But now that it's happening *in real time*, I'm not really prepared for it.

Their obvious bond with each other aside, I know they're all dangerous and capable of bad things. And while I still strangely don't care what happens to me anymore, I do very much care about protecting my best friend. How I'm going to do that, though, I have no idea. I spent the entire morning today thinking about it, but I still have no clue. The only reason I'm not completely freaking out right now is because Peyton is still far, *far* away from this mess; and God, I hope I can somehow find a way to keep her safe before it's too late.

Or before they all kill me. Whichever comes first.

"Isn't that what the Turner girl is called?" Axton continues, a frown bisecting his brow.

Arsen whips his attention over to his younger brother, and with a hardened jaw and a growl, he replies, "She isn't the Turner girl."

A chill runs down my spine at the way he says it. It's anger, pure and clear, fiery. I can feel the heat of it focused on me, even though he hasn't even looked at me once during this whole exchange. Which makes me realize he hasn't said a word to me all morning, not one word.

I was so engrossed in my own thoughts that I didn't notice it until now, and I know why. He's absolutely enraged at the fact that I ruined his plans. I mean, I knew he would be, but I didn't know to what degree. I also didn't know I'd feel…*guilty* for ruining things for him. But I can't help it. He's doing it for love, isn't he? And I can't blame him for it.

People do crazy things for love.

"What the fuck? Then who is—"

"Okay, can I please say something here?" the girl interrupts, the girl he's most probably kidnapped me for.

Like Arsen, she breaks the line to make it to where I'm standing, fisting the hem of my T-shirt, trying to disappear. Arsen, watching her approach, shifts and maneuvers himself between me and her, and God, I have to say that I'm thankful for this as well. I'm not really proud of it, but I'll take it. Because I know I'm not going to have his protection for much longer.

The girl throws me a small smile before shooting Arsen a look. Then, surprisingly, she moves her focus to Marsden. "I know we all have questions, but they both look really tired. I think we should at least get them inside and give them time to freshen up and get something to eat before we all descend upon them."

Before Marsden can reply, Arsen jerks his chin at her. Apparently a nonverbal way of communicating that she well understands. Because she throws him a small smile before turning back to me. Her beautiful brown eyes are soft, much like her smile, as she introduces herself in a tone that I can only describe as gentle: "Hi, Reverie. It's nice to meet you. Welcome to Rawhide. My name is Haven, okay? Why don't you come inside with me, and I can show you where to freshen up."

I blink. "H-Haven?"

Oh God, she's not Annie. The relief I feel makes my knees weak and my lips tremble.

To her credit, her smile doesn't falter at my strange reaction. "Yes. Should we go? I bet you want to get out of here."

I do. So much.

And before I can really think about the repercussions or whether I can trust her or not, I nod. Her smile widens, and she motions for me to follow her. For a second before I leave, I get this crazy urge to look at him.

The man who brought me here.

For some reason, this feels like a big moment. The moment where our surreal, out-of-some-drug-induced-nightmare journey that started back in the alley where he grabbed me—no, that started with the first letter I wrote him—is coming to an end. Like this is some sort of goodbye now that he knows the truth and we're at Rawhide.

I wave it off, though. This is not goodbye. I'm still stuck here, aren't I? My best friend is potentially still in danger. No matter how my chest is clenching as I walk away, I don't look back. Not even to check if he's looking my way, because I can feel the Grayson brothers watching me go.

Once we're inside the mansion, Haven takes me through an open-concept living room and dining area that leads to a series of hallways that I have no hope of ever remembering. But even so, I can tell that the interior of this place is as grand as the exterior. Ceilings as high as the sky with wooden beams running parallel to one another; the walls and the floors made of the same dark wood as the front facade. The room she takes me to reminds me of the hunting cabin I woke up in my first day. Except the bed is even more grand, with a large wooden headboard and silky dark sheets, and the wooden walls are thankfully devoid of any bear heads.

I watch Haven make a beeline for a door that she opens to reveal a huge bathroom with two large sinks and a tiled floor. Before I can see anything else, she comes back out with a couple of fluffy white towels.

Throwing me a smile, she says, "Good thing I had everything prepped for his return." She offers me the towels, and without knowing what else to do, I take them. "So as you can see, the bathroom is through there. You can take a shower, or there's a huge bathtub in there that you can make use of too. I've also put out a new toothbrush, and all the toiletries and things are stocked." She scrunches her nose. "Fair warning, though; they're all very basic. Like a bar soap and a bottle of shampoo, not even a conditioner. But that's what he uses, so that's what I got for him. I just…" She sighs, looking far away. "I wanted him to feel at home, you know? Wanted to make him think no time has passed at all and that things are the same. So I got all his favorite things, put out his favorite sheets, even though all his sheets are practically the same color; got him new clothes, the kind he likes; ironed some of his favorite old ones. Although, honestly, I don't even think they're going to fit him anymore, and I just…"

She goes silent for a few moments, her brown eyes shining in obvious pain. Then, she seems to shake it off and continues, "In any case, if you want I can lend you my own stuff until we can get you yours, okay?"

I know an answer is expected of me, but I can't seem to focus enough to give it to her. Instead, I ask a question of my own: "W-who are you?" Then, embarrassed, I clench my eyes shut. "I-I mean, I know you're Haven. But I…I don't—"

She seems to get the trouble I'm having, so once again, she helps me out. "I'm Mr. Grayson's wife."

I frown in confusion. "M-Marsden's?"

She raises her eyebrows. "Yup, he's the only Mr. Grayson on this ranch." Then, to explain, "The other two are just two guys I grew up with, Arsen and Ax. If they ever told me to call them Mr. Grayson, they know I'd punch them in the face."

This is…strange. All of it.

It raises more questions for me rather than answer them. Why would she call her own husband Mr.? Also, how old is she? I know the oldest Grayson brother is forty and Haven can't be more than twenty-two or twenty-three. But more than that, if she's Mrs. Grayson, essentially the mistress of this ranch, why is she helping me?

I can't trust her, can I? No matter how strangely kind and friendly she seems.

"I see that raises more concerns for you," she observes correctly.

I clutch the towels to my chest. "I can't… You're *married* to one of them. You're…you're probably in on the whole thing and…"

Her features soften even more. "I know you have no reason to trust me, but I'm not. I don't even know what this *whole thing* is. I don't know why he…" She seems to be searching for words as she takes me in. "I don't know why he brought you here. If it's any consolation, none of us do. We all thought... Well, you *saw* what we thought, and I apologize again for getting carried away back there. All I know is that you don't want to be here. And that you're scared. I can see that. And you're hurt"—she looks pointedly at my wrists and my bare legs—"and it doesn't matter if you're a Turner or not, I can at least offer you a shower, some food and rest. That's all. It's not a big deal. You won't owe me anything and after this, you don't even have to talk to me if you don't want to. But I figure we're girls, right? Girls need to stick together and this is the least I can do."

She's sincere; I can see that. And if she's not, then she has to be an excellent actress. Either way, I nod, towels still clutched to my chest. "Is this"—I lick my cracked lips—"his room?"

Her eyes go wide at this and she gasps. "Shit, I didn't think of that. You probably don't want to be here after everything. Let me find you another—"

"No." I stop her, my heart somehow both racing and squeezing at the same time. "It's, uh... It's okay. I-I don't mind."

As crazy as this sounds, I *want* to be in his room. It makes me breathe easier. But I don't know how to explain it to her. Turns out, I don't have to because she somehow gets it completely. "Okay then. I'll leave you to it. But I'll make sure he stays away." She searches my face. "Okay?"

A relieved breath escapes me and I nod jerkily. "Yes. Please."

Her smile is both sad and understanding. "You got it."

And then she leaves and I'm here, all alone in this room that was his before he got put away. Feeling both nervous and safe.

CHAPTER TWENTY-ONE

The Dark Stallion

THE DOOR TO my brother's office opens with a groan.

I step in, and the gap between the third and fourth floorboards creaks as I walk over it. I get in farther to see that while the left wall is completely flooded with photos from our childhood, the right wall has end-to-end bookshelves, bulging with heavy texts and paperbacks. On the third shelf from the right, there's a book called *Wild Montana*, a text about Montana's wildlife. It's probably the fifth book or maybe the sixth, depending on what mood Mars is in while reading it. If I found the book in the fifth place, I'd generally assume he was pissed off. Because it usually goes in the sixth, but when he's angry, he'll mess up the order. Which is a big deal for my organized-to-a-fault brother.

There's a large desk with thick legs in the center of the room. The front left one has a slight chip in it from where an eight-year-old Ax kicked it when Mars wouldn't let him go to the rodeo with his friends. The wall above the desk is the home of a portrait of our parents. If you take it down and flip it over, you'll see the names of all three of us, Marsden, Arsenal, and Axton, written in red Sharpie on the cardboard backing. Ax's doing.

Not gonna lie, I'm happy this is the first room of the house that I'm stepping into after eight years. Because creeks and groans may be louder than before, but other than that very little about it has changed. Unlike the living room and the dining area that I just walked through. But I'm trying not to dwell on all that. Or any of the changes that might have occurred in the last eight years.

To that effect, I glance at Ax, who's sprawled on one of the armchairs by the desk, playing on his phone. Then, looking at my older brother, seated behind the desk, I ask, "What's he doin' here?"

Ax doesn't give Mars a chance to reply. "Ah, you got your shirt back on. Good." Then, "This is a family meeting, ain't it? I'm family."

I inhale a sharp breath, glad to notice that the air still smells like leather and whiskey with a hint of the woods. Perfect embodiment of my brother who rules all from behind this desk, but from what I can remember, before our parents died and our lives changed, wanted to be just a cowboy instead of a landowner. He didn't get that freedom, though. Not like me and definitely not like Ax.

I wave those thoughts away and say, "This is not a family meeting."

Finally, Mars gets a chance to reply: "It involves family. And Ax is eighteen now. He gets to sit in."

I know how old Ax is. If Mars or anyone else thought I forgot that my younger brother turned eighteen five and a half weeks ago, then they were wrong. I remember. I also remember that when I got put away, he'd reach my chest—even at ten years old—but now he's as tall as me. His voice was still childlike then, only starting to turn deep. He was all elbows and knees, but now I can see the definition of his muscles through that blue T-shirt he's wearing. He's more tanned now, and the lines of his face have matured under the sun, telling me that eight years ago, he was a cowboy-in-the-making whose hat would sit too big on his head, but now I bet he's as good a cowboy as any one of those ranch hands out there.

Mars would've made sure of that. Like he did with me and Rad. And speaking of which, I know my older brother has aged as well. There's silver in his hair, and the lines on his forehead and around his eyes are deeper. When I left, there was no indication that he'd end up marrying the girl me, Rad, and Ax grew up with. But a little over three years ago, Mars called and shared the good news. I know they celebrated their three-year anniversary two months ago. Well, celebrated may be a stretch, given that she calls Mars Mr. Grayson, like she still works for him and he still signs her paychecks.

I did have a chance to meet them during visitations, but after the first few times, I refused to see them. In the beginning, they'd still come, especially Axton, but like an asshole, I wouldn't budge. It was just too painful, to look them in the eyes and see sadness and regret for me. For what I lost. For how my life changed. I didn't need that from them.

I didn't need their pity, their grief. I was there because I deserved to be there, and once all of this was over, I would still be stuck. In the past. In that night eight years ago. So no, I didn't need their sympathy. I also didn't need them to waste their time on me. I wanted them to move on with their lives. It was just that I didn't know how hard it would be to witness that, all these changes in my brothers.

Ax looks up from his phone, tips his hat at me in salute. "Lookit, bitches; I got a seat at the table now."

Mars has a million rules about things. Probably the only way he knew how to deal with our parents' sudden death and all the responsibilities that he inherited. In our family, when you turn eighteen, you get inducted. As in, you get to find out business secrets, land secrets, secrets about the bloody history of the Graysons and the Turners. I'm not sure how much Mars has shared with our younger brother—probably not much, since he just turned eighteen and I can still see some youthful innocence in his eyes—but it's coming.

Mars sighs, possibly praying for patience when it comes to Axton. And I decide to fuck it. The sooner I accept that things changed in my absence like I wanted them to, the better. So I take a seat, indicating my silent agreement. I regret it a second later, though, when Ax asks, "So first question, what happened to your shirt anyway?"

I shoot him a warning look.

"Ax, son, enough," Mars warns.

He raises his arms in surrender. "Fine. Whatever."

Finally, Mars sits back and rests his elbows on the arms. "Now, care to explain who she is?"

I fist my hands, digging my blunt nails into my skin because I know what's coming. It's like an electric shock every time it happens, every time thoughts of her run through my head. Or like sticking your hand into scalding-hot water.

Reverie.

Like a daydream. I couldn't have picked a better name for her myself. The girl who brought my dreams back is called Reverie. Suits her much better than the name Peyton ever did. But that's neither here nor there. The point is that I've tried to escape her these last few days. Her buttercup scent that I fall asleep to; the shape of her curvy little soft body that seems to be imprinted on mine after riding with her for close to a week; the goddamn memory of her *taste* that rises up at the least opportune moments. I've tried pushing all those things away, but it doesn't work. So now I simply let it all pass through me, let it electrocute me, burn me before moving on.

Although I don't think there's any moving on from what happened last night. What I did. I keep my tone neutral and my mind at task. "She's the best friend. Her mother used to work for the Turners."

Mars doesn't bother to hide his confusion. Tipping his hat up, he asks, "If she's not the Turner girl, what is she doin' here?"

It's hard to hold on to a calm composure, but I do it. "She's here because I made a mistake."

At this, Mars's eyes turn sharp, and I notice Ax putting his phone aside. Several seconds pass while they scrutinize me, and soon I'm losing my patience. I need to get this done so I can get out of here. Because as it turns out, my fucked-up brain thinks family's a crowd, too, and I'm starting to suffocate within these walls. I'm not sure, though, where I'll find relief or where I belong because it's not as if I can take an easy breath when I'm outside either. Out there, there's too much fucking sky and air.

Actually, I do know where I find relief. By her side.

When she's with me, all my focus is on her. On looking at her, smelling her, keeping her safe. I don't feel useless. Like a sore thumb sticking out whose only place is behind bars. But the thing is that I don't deserve relief. And neither do I know how to keep anyone safe, let alone her.

Mars is the first to break the silence. "Are you sayin' to me that you brought home the wrong girl?"

I clench my jaw and let another one of those electric shocks jolt through my system. This one stems from anger at myself. At my absolute fucking incompetence.

"Holy shit." Ax sits up in his chair, his mouth open in a way that makes him look like the ten-year-old kid he was when I left. "You fucked up."

Before I can respond to Ax's conclusion, Mars speaks: "Did you?"

Exhaling a short breath, I admit grudgingly, "Apparently."

I see his mustache twitch in growing anger. "So instead of putting her back in the right place, you brought her here."

"She's not a bridle that I misplaced," I snap. "She's a girl. Couldn't leave her by the side of the road when I found out she was useless, now, could I?"

"So you shouldn't have picked her up like the goddamn bridle in the first place."

"Well, hindsight is twenty-twenty, ain't it."

He grinds his jaw. "How does that… How the fuck could you not know?"

I've been asking myself the same question. How the fuck did it happen?

Last night, after I found out the truth and she passed out, I gave Rad another call and told him everything. He was just as shocked as I was. Apparently, both girls look alike, and since they're always together, it never occurred to him, or to me, that there was a chance of mistaken identity. Not to mention, when I called Rad about the Turner girl, I gave him some pointers, and all of them were based on the letters. How she loves books more than people. How she spends most of her time at the library. How her best friend has a habit of falling for the wrong guys. So, like me, he assumed Reverie was the Turner girl.

But that's not the worst part. The worst *fucking* part is that when I did suspect something, I didn't immediately follow through. What the fuck was I thinking?

I wasn't thinking, though, was I. I got distracted. I got fucking stupid the moment I saw her at the café and heard her voice. That was the moment I started thinking with my dick. There are no two ways about it. Something about her, something that I can't put my finger on, does it for me. Maybe it's that face, all beautiful and innocent; those blue eyes full of wonder and fire; maybe those lips that tremble with shyness even as they sass me; or maybe it's her abundant curves that I want to lose myself in. Or it could be the very fact that despite being at my mercy, she managed to get one up on me.

She managed to fool me good.

I may have made a mistake in kidnapping her, but she's the one who stood strong. Who stood firm and determined without cracking despite every ordeal I put her through. Without once wavering and confessing the truth. While most men I know would've crumbled, she took it all and she did it with dignity.

And fuck, I respect that.

I'm attracted to that. I'm attracted to my wife.

Well, not my wife after all, like she claims.

The thought somehow pisses me off more than the fact that she ruined my plans. And that is *exactly* why I need to focus. Because I want her too much. I want her with an intensity that I have never felt before. Not even with Annie. The girl I thought I loved. The girl who loved *me* but lost her life because of me.

Coming back to the moment, I reply, "What can I say, she fooled me. She was tryin' to protect her friend and I was too stupid to notice."

"Yeah, you were," Mars snaps before turning toward Ax. "You. You're gonna stay on her. If she puts a toe outta line, it's your hide I'm tannin'."

Before Ax can reply back, I say, "No, he's not."

Mars snaps his eyes over to me. "You brought a Turner into our home. Doesn't matter if she ain't really a Turner as long as she's loyal to them. What do you, in your *infinite fuckin' wisdom*, suggest we do with her?"

I ignore his sarcasm and take a long breath. "Haven can watch her."

"My wife," he bites out, "doesn't work for you anymore. She's not gonna do your bidding."

"And *my wife* won't be chased around by a fuckin' horndog who'll be more inclined to look up her skirt than watch her."

"Hey, I'm sittin' right here," Ax interjects.

"She's not your wife now, is she?" Mars reminds me.

I let a few moments pass so his dig won't sting me too much, before I can respond calmly. "I brought her here. She's my responsibility. And yes, I fucked up and I fucked up big. But she's already been through a fuck of a lot because of me. She doesn't need a fuckin' watchdog following her twenty-four seven. She doesn't need to feel more unsafe than she already probably does, given she's from the Turner clan and we're the Graysons. Haven's a better option."

Mars's jaw pulses as he stares at me for a few seconds. "Fine, Haven can be with her. But I want him"—he tips his head toward Ax—"close by. We ain't taking any chances."

I don't like it. But I know my brother won't budge until I give in. So I shoot him a short nod before turning to Ax. "Close but not too close, yeah?"

Ax watches me with a smirk. "You're awful jealous about a girl who ain't your wife."

I give him a dark look. "You're awful amused for someone who's this close to gettin' his ass kicked."

Not that it fazes him. He's still a little shithead like he was eight years ago as he goes, "I'll treat her like my hot adopted sister; ya happy?" Then, "On the other hand, doin' your adopted sister does have a very strange taboo appeal, so—"

"Son, stop," Mars commands.

He quiets down, but that fucking smirk still lingers on his face.

"I'm assuming you have a plan to fix your mistake," Mars prods, and I shift my focus away from the thoughts of punching my younger brother on the first night I'm back from prison after eight years.

"Rad's already on it. He should be here tomorrow," I tell Mars.

He wasn't happy about it. About what I told him to do. Not only about my mistake—which he thinks is his, too, and in his typical good-boy way, which he feels guilty for—but also about the fact that the girl he fell for is the real Turner girl. And hence belongs to the family that took almost everything from him including his speech. But I didn't give him a choice. I should feel guilty about it as well—and I do—but I'm an asshole. I'm selfish and I'm fucking determined to see it through.

"First," Mars begins, "I don't like the way you keep draggin' my foreman into your shit; and second, then what? What the fuck is your mysterious plan?"

"They did it for the land," I tell him. "So I'm gonna take it away."

"You are," he goes, his expression barely changing.

"Thought you'd be happy about it. You've been vyin' for that land for years."

He has been. Even though we all grew up on the same stories about the feud, I always had a hard time understanding Mars's drive to follow the same path as our father. Especially because I never wanted that for myself. Yes, I was loyal to the ranch and to the cause, but I was always going to move away. I was always going to buy my own land one day, land that was far away from all this Grayson-Turner bullshit, and chart my own path. But then it occurred to me. My older brother doesn't want to follow in our daddy's footsteps, yet he *is* like our daddy, which makes sense because Mars was closest to him. He also was very close to our granddaddy. Both of whom I knew very little about because they passed when I was too young. So I know this is a dream come true for Mars.

"And I'm givin' it to you on a silver platter," I finish.

"Are you?"

I look him in the eyes and lie, "I am."

I may be taking away their land, but no, I'm not giving it to Mars. But these things are for later. "Now, if I've answered all your questions, I'm gonna go."

With that, I stand up from my seat, ready to walk out. I'm at the door when I hear him call out to my back: "This won't bring her back. Nothing ever will. You know that, don't you?"

My chest is so tight that it feels like it's about to split open. "I'm not tryin' to bring her back. I'm tryin' to avenge her."

"You've done enough."

"No, I haven't."

"You send them money every month." At this, I turn back to face him, and he goes on, "I know you do. I know you told Rad not to say anything, but eight years is a long time. I figured it out when money started disappearin' from your account. Same amount, same time."

"You think money makes up for everythin'?"

Before she died, Annie was the one her family depended on. Her family being her sick mother and her younger brother. And yes, I told Rad to make sure they're covered. She gave up college to work full-time so she could look after them, so me depositing some money into their account monthly was the least I could do when I was the one responsible for her being gone.

"No," Mars says. "But you never wondered, did you?"

I stiffen then. "Wondered about what?"

He watches me a beat. "She was new in town. No one knew where she came from. You met her once at the town fair and took up with her."

"And?"

Again, Mars takes his time with it before saying, "So did it never occur to you that maybe, just maybe, she was takin' advantage of you? Of who you are."

It's true that when I met her Annie was new in town. She'd just graduated high school and moved two towns over with her sick mother and her younger brother to start a new job as the wrangler at one of the ranches. So when I met her at the local fair, she had no idea who I was or where I came from. Other girls wanted to tie me down and take advantage of me being a Grayson. So even though she was the one to pursue me, I found her ignorance refreshing. Whatever the case, though, my brother has no business talking about things he'll never understand.

I clench my jaw for a few seconds before somehow gathering myself and my anger and clipping, "Don't talk about what you know nothin' about."

He shoots me a grave look. "I may know more than you think."

I study him for a few moments. "Eight years is a long time, ain't it? Maybe that's why you don't remember. That you're responsible for her death too. Turners have always wanted our land but they never stood a chance. Not until you. Not until you took over and started that little program. I told you to shut it down. We all told you to shut it down before it was too late, before they came for it and used it to take your precious fuckin' land. But you wouldn't listen. And Annie paid the price for it. So let me remind you: You don't know anything about her. You don't know anything about my relationship with her. But like me and the fuckin' Turners, you killed her too. Which means it doesn't matter if she was takin' advantage of me or not, her death is on all our heads. And I'm gonna do everything I can to avenge her. The only reason I'm lettin' your little program survive is because we're blood and you weren't the one who rigged the barn that night. So I want you to remember that or the next thing I'm comin' for is you."

I don't wait to find out what his reaction is because I don't give a fuck. Besides, I've been inside this house long enough and I need to get out. But once again I'm waylaid.

"Hey," Haven greets me as she comes up the hallway.

I jerk my chin up at her.

"I got her settled," she tells me.

Again, I let the current pass through me. "Thanks."

"In your room."

"What?"

She raises her hands in surrender. "She insisted. I offered her another room but she wouldn't go."

For a few seconds, I tamp down the urge to go in search of her myself. To bust down the door of my old room and demand to know what the fuck she was thinking. Why *the fuck* would she stay in a place that belongs to me? To the man who kidnapped her. Who forced her to marry him. Who then *dragged* her through the woods, put her through the kind of trauma that she'll have nightmares about for the better part of her life. She should be running away from me, from all reminders of me. She should be trying to find a way to call the cops, or the Turners.

I wouldn't blame her.

But then it occurs to me that maybe she's trying to cling to the familiar. This is the ranch she grew up hating and dreading. She doesn't know anyone here except me. And I may be the devil, but it's better to stick with the devil you know than the devil you don't. Besides, even if she wanted to contact the outside world, I wouldn't let her.

Turner or not, she's still the enemy.

"Fine," I say. "If that's—"

"Although," she continues, "she wants you to stay away from her. So you're going to have to find somewhere else to sleep."

Fantastic.

At least she's thinking straight. That makes one of us, because despite just getting all worked up over the fact that she still must want to be close to me, I now feel a piercing pain in my chest knowing that she doesn't want me around. That tonight, I won't get to smell her buttercup scent or watch moonlight hit her velvet skin and make it sparkle.

Fuck.

I'm losing my fucking mind, and once again, that's the last thing I want. "Wasn't plannin' on goin' anywhere near her anyway."

"What did you do to her?" she asks.

"What do you think I did to her?"

She leans closer and lowers her voice. "You came here with no shirt on because she was wearing it. Did you—"

"Jesus, fuck, why's everyone so concerned about that?" I burst out. "What I do with my wife is none of your fucking business."

"From what I hear, she's not your wife."

I scrub a hand down my face. "Yeah, people keep remindin' me of that." Then, sighing, "Just do me a favor; keep your nose out of my business and look out for her, yeah?"

She frowns and folds her arms across her chest. "Why can't you do that?"

"Because like you said, she ain't my wife," I retort. "And she doesn't want me around her."

"Does that bother you?"

"Does what bother me?"

"That she doesn't want you around."

I clench my jaw. "This ain't keepin' your nose out of my business."

She isn't deterred, though. "I think you should be nice to her."

I give her a look. Then, sighing, I turn my back to her and get on my way.

"Hey, I was talking to you!" she calls out.

"I wasn't," I call out.

"You know I'm right. *You know* you need to be nice to her," she calls out again, but I choose to ignore her and keep walking.

I don't need to be anything to her. In fact, for all intents and purposes, our association is over. She should forget about me, and I sure as fuck will try to forget about her. But first I'll kill her daddy, her real daddy. It won't erase the years of abuse and her mother's death, but the world will be a safer place for her. And *then*, I'll do whatever I can to forget about her.

CHAPTER TWENTY-TWO

I'M WAITING FOR the other shoe to drop.

So far it hasn't happened, but I know it's coming. After Haven left me in his room, I took a long, hot shower. I stood under the water and let it wash away all the caked dirt and blood. The only reason I got out was because my skin was beginning to prune and I was hungry. Which Haven had already predicted because when I got out, there was food waiting for me on the nightstand, along with some clothes on the bed. I was slightly nervous about the clothes, but Haven somehow found me ones that fit me perfectly: a pair of jeans that I'd usually wear if I were going to classes and a simple T-shirt with a hoodie.

Somehow, though, instead of making me feel relief after wearing a dress for almost a week, the change of clothes made me feel sad. It made me feel like things have really come to an end. That I'm Reverie once again. Plain and lonely with a careful, safe, *boring* life.

Just as I was finishing the food, Haven came in and told me she was supposed to watch me. And that occasionally, Ax might pop in when Haven needed to be somewhere else, but someone would be with me at all times. She said she didn't like any of it, and I could see she was telling the truth. It made her feel that I was a prisoner—which I am essentially—but she needed to do it because she had promised Arsen.

After breaking the news, Haven asked me if I wanted to help her with dinner and I said yes. I didn't want to sit in my room, or rather his room, all day worrying about my fate. Only I didn't know the dinner she needed my help with was going to be all about him. His favorite dishes, his favorite dessert. His favorite everything.

After that reunion I'd seen earlier, I probably should've guessed that Haven would make a homecoming dinner for the man who lost eight years of his life behind bars. As I helped her, I wondered if she knew who Annie was. And if I asked her, if she would tell me. But I refrained, of course. It was none of my business, and no matter how friendly she looked, she was still in the Grayson camp. Although, I did feel bad for her because she took such pains in cooking dinner for him and he never showed up.

Nope, he was nowhere to be seen at dinner.

Marsden wasn't there either, but I was glad about that. Marsden Grayson is scary, and the more I get to know Haven, the more I wonder how in the hell they ended up together. Ax did show up, though, and even though he kept his distance from me, saying only a couple of words, I could feel him watching me with a glint in his eyes.

In any case, I excused myself as soon as I could. Ax escorted me back to my room because Haven had to clean up—where are the maids, though? Turners wouldn't survive without them even a day—and when he closed the door behind me, I knew it was locked. Again, I understood. It'd be stupid of them to not do that. I could do any number of things if left unsupervised, like make a phone call to the Turners, to warn Brecken of what's coming and make sure Peyton remains safe in the Bahamas.

Although I'm losing patience now. It's the next morning and they still haven't said anything about what their plan is. What do they intend to do with me? I'm not of any use and they know that, so what happens now?

Also, where is he? Why didn't he show up for dinner last night? What was he doing? Where did he sleep? *Did* he sleep?

"Don't come near me, you filthy Grayson asshole!"

The scream echoes through the space and my heart drops. I wish I could pretend it was all in my head, that screeching voice, but I'm in the kitchen with Haven, who's at the stove sautéing veggies for a Mexican casserole, but at the shout, she stops right alongside me. Meaning that she heard it too.

Meaning, it's *real*.

I start running before I know what I'm doing. I dash through the kitchen, turn the corner, and zip through the hallway leading to the living room where the voice came from, and the sight that greets me knocks the breath out of me. Somehow it's worse than looking a deadly bear in the eye. Probably because back then, as scared as I was, I knew I could go to him. I knew he'd come save me. But I don't have that luxury now. In fact, *he's* the one responsible for this.

For bringing my best friend here.

An enraged Peyton stands in the middle of the living room, looking around frantically. I know she's searching for me, because as soon as she sees me standing at the mouth of the hallway, her eyes, which are a color similar to mine, widen. And she breaks into action, heading toward me.

I go to her as well. We both meet in the middle somewhere, our arms instantly going around each other and holding tight. I'm aware of the noises coming out of us, too, the screams and squeals, the exclaims all filled with a variety of emotions—shock, surprise, utter fucking relief. But most of all, our embrace is filled with joy that we finally have each other. It's always been us against the world, and I really, *truly* thought I'd never see her again.

She's the first to break the hug but keeps her arms around me. "Oh my God. Oh my God. *Oh my God*, you're okay. You're"—she roves her teary eyes over my face—"alive. You're... God, I was so *worried*, Riri. I was..."

She trails off to give me another tight hug. Which I return, but this time I'm the one to break it. "What are you doing here? What… Why aren't you in the Bahamas?"

She pulls a face. "Because I didn't go."

"Why not?"

"Because that doofus broke up with me."

"What… Ben?"

"Yuh-huh." She's enraged. "With me. Can you believe it? With *me*."

I'm so confused right now. "But I thought *you* were going to break up with him and—"

"Yes." She cuts me off in turn as if we're in a race to get all our questions answered, and frankly, we are. "But he got there first. He left me stranded at the airport, Riri. Like, the motherfucker didn't even call. *I* had to call him and he didn't pick up. And then he had the fucking audacity to send me a text and say that it was over and that's it. God, I was so mad. I went back to the apartment to find you so I could vent but you weren't there and…" She shakes her head, swallowing. "At first, I thought you went to the library but then you didn't come home and God, Riri, I was so scared. I was so freaking scared. I kept calling and calling but your phone kept going to voice mail and… I looked everywhere for you. *Everywhere.* I knew it had something to do with Bo so I went to that café where you said you were going to meet him. I went to the *cops*. I told them about this guy you were going to meet. I told them he just got out on parole but they wouldn't listen to me. They said you must've run away. No one would take me seriously. *No one.* I was this close to calling my brother. This close and I—"

At this, I hug her again. Because finally the fear of the unknown is washing over me and I need to hold on to her, and it looks like she needs to hold on to me too. "It's my fault, isn't it?"

I shake my head, my eyes stinging. "No, absolutely n-not."

She hiccups. "It is."

"No."

"First, like an idiot, I don't stop you from writing to a fucking c-convict. Then I tell you it's okay to g-go see him and then you go see him and he breaks your heart and makes you feel bad about yourself. And I know you, Ri. I know you don't show pain and you never cry and you're always strong. But that a-asshole got to you. And I—"

I scrunch my eyes closed, keeping my tears at bay. "No, it was me. I went looking for him that night after you fell asleep on the couch. It's my fault."

She leans away from me then, her face blotched. "*You* went looking for him?"

I nod, my cheeks burning in shame.

"But what… What happened? How did you…"

Her questions make me realize that we have an audience. There's a man standing a few feet away from me that I've never seen before. He's as tall and broad as the rest of the Graysons, but he's got them beat in the muscle mass. His neck alone looks thicker and more corded than those of the three men I've met here.

I realize that when people say burly, he is what they're talking about. Also mean. It's probably due to that wicked scar running down the side of his face. From the top of his forehead all the way to the bottom of his left jaw, going through his thick dark eyebrow and both his lips.

But mean can be pretty, too, can't it?

And he has to be the prettiest man I've ever seen. His eyes are a glimmering green, and those scarred lips are thick and plush. He has a killer jawline and the most stunning cheekbones I've ever seen on a man. Or rather, a cowboy. Given he has a Stetson on his head and is wearing a plaid shirt with cowboy boots.

I have no idea who he is or why he's staring at my best friend with a focus that sends chills down my spine. I'm about to break the hug and push Peyton behind me so I can figure out what's happening, but then my gaze falls on someone behind the stranger and I freeze.

Because there he is, the man who brought me here.

Looking the way he did eight years ago.

I don't know how I know this for sure, but I do. Maybe he wasn't as built and thickly muscled as he is now, but I bet this is exactly what he looked like before he got put away. When he was just a cowboy, all cocky and confident, and not hardened by prison.

He has on a washed-out denim shirt that clings to his broad shoulders like water clung to his bare chest whenever he got to go swimming. The sleeves are folded up to his elbows, displaying his corded forearms that always made sure I stayed safe while we rode. His thighs are encased in a darker-colored denim that fits him so well I can practically see the thighs that hugged mine for the past week. I can practically feel them rustling against mine right now.

But that's not what makes my heart skip a beat, several beats, actually.

It's that brown-colored Stetson on his head, sitting with the brim tipped low. Pair that with his rugged boots so big that I'm sure I could fit both my feet in one of them, and he has to be the hand-somest cowboy I've ever seen. He's not classically pretty like the other guy, but he has this roughness about him that I want to rub up against. Scrape along and come out with black-and-blue bruises.

Well, I did, didn't I? And now he's brought my best friend here.

"You," I begin, gathering myself and moving away from Peyton, "brought her here."

At my words, his eyes snap back up to mine. And I realize that while I'm seeing him for the first time like he was before I met him, he's probably meeting me for the first time too. As Reverie. The girl who always wears loose hoodies that hide all her curves and let her live a safe life. Although the hoodie I'm wearing is not that loose or large, but I'm guessing he gets the picture. Because his jaw clenches and something like anger passes through his features.

Well, I'm not his problem anymore. Whatever happened between us back in the woods was probably his way of making do after eight years in prison. I mean, if he really found me attractive or thought I was pretty, instead of just jerking off over my body, he would've at least kissed me, right? Yes, he said he wouldn't kiss a Turner, but that didn't stop him from…doing *other* things.

And oh my God, what is wrong with me? My best friend's life is in danger. *My* life is in danger, and I'm thinking about how my kidnapper didn't kiss me. I glance at the stranger before going back to him and prodding when he chooses to remain silent. "Is he your guy? Does he… Does he work for you?"

Before he can respond, Peyton barges into the conversation. "I know who you are. I saw you on TV. You're Arsenal Grayson. You're the one who tried to kill my father that night." She doesn't let him respond. "You kidnapped my best friend? What, is Bo your buddy then?" Again before anyone can respond, she keeps going: "What is this, huh? Some kidnapping scheme? First, you tell your friend Bo to trap my *innocent* best friend with letters, then you kidnap her? And then your other lackey comes in and kidnaps me?"

Finally, Arsen deigns to respond: "Somethin' like that."

"Look," Peyton goes, arms folded across her chest. "If you guys think my brother is going to give you money in exchange for us, then you're fucked in the head, all right? Which we all knew anyway because you're the Graysons but I want you to think this through."

"Yeah?"

"Yes." She raises her chin. "My brother, I hate him, but he calls me like clockwork every Sunday. So if I don't pick up my phone tomorrow, do you know what he's going to do?"

"I'm sure you'll enlighten us."

"He's going to think something is wrong. And then he's going to think Graysons are behind it."

"That doesn't sound good."

"No, it doesn't. So you better let us go before my brother—"

"Think it's enough," the stranger interrupts for the first time.

And his voice makes the house shake. Or it should because of how deep and unused it is. I thought Arsen's voice sounded unused the first time I heard it, but this stranger's voice is really a bunch of put-together guttural syllables.

"Oh, *now* you talk," Peyton snaps. "I kept asking you and *asking you*, for the past hour since I woke up in your filthy cowboy truck, what the fuck's going on and who the hell are you and what do you want with me and *what the hell* am I doing at the Grayson ranch and you didn't have the decency to say a word. *Not* a word. I don't even know what the fuck's your name and you think this is enough." She scoffs. "Oh, you sweet summer child, you haven't seen the kind of havoc I can wreak. By the time I'm done with you, you'll be cursing the day you ever laid your eyes on me."

Silence follows her threat. Broken by a snort coming from the left. It's Axton. Which creates a domino effect in the sense that the stranger lets out a long breath, as if he's praying for patience. Haven, who's also here, clears her throat and ducks her head to hide her twitching lips. Arsen is the only one who doesn't show any outward reaction except tipping up his chin. "Haven."

This gets Haven moving and she heads toward us. "Hi, I'm Haven. I can't believe I'm having to do this a second time, but would you like to freshen up before you start threatening people?"

Peyton frowns. "I'm not going anywhere with you. I don't even know who you are."

"Peyton, lets's go," I tell her.

"But—"

"Just"—I squeeze her arm—"trust me."

It takes her a few seconds, but she nods and just as we're leaving, I hear him say to Haven, "They've got thirty minutes."

With that, he turns around and walks out. Just like that. And as I walk away with Peyton, I realize that in this whole exchange, he never said a word to me.

Not one word.

"So you're married," Peyton goes.

I don't know how long we have until our thirty minutes are up, but I tell Peyton everything. From the night he grabbed me by the motel to yesterday, which I spent waiting for them to tell me my fate. I'm not proud of it, but I may have broken down here and there, trying to catch my breath and swallow down my tears. It's just that for the entire last week, I thought no one was coming for me. No one even knew I was missing.

But I was wrong.

Peyton did look for me, and she's here now. She's with me, and I know it's not what I'd planned for, but God, I really wanted someone by my side. I wanted my best friend to be with me, and I'm just so happy and *relieved* that she's here. And that she's been holding me tightly through my entire story.

"No, you are. You're the real Peyton," I reply back.

My belly clenches in pain, and I don't have it in me to even pretend that those words didn't hurt, but I can't focus on it right now. I'll deal with my insanity later.

"But there's no way a document like that would hold up in court," Peyton says, protesting the same thing I did once upon a time.

I break out of her embrace. "Do you think he cares about what's going to hold up in court? He stabbed a cop, Peyton. *At* the courthouse. He has judges and police in his pockets. Whatever it is he wants out of this marriage, he's going to get it."

Even as I say it, it seems so far away. That courthouse thing. It feels like it happened in a faraway universe. Along with so many other things. They might as well have happened to someone else, and I have a hard time figuring out why that's such a bad thing.

"So you know what we need to do, don't you?" Peyton asks, breaking my thoughts.

"Yes, we need to run."

She gives me a look. "No."

"What?"

"We need revenge."

I draw back and repeat in a high octave, "*What?*"

"You've tried running, remember? And if what you say is true, that everyone is in his pocket, who are you going to run to?"

"Your family," I reply, my heart racing now. "Your brother will kick their ass. Didn't you just say that yourself? All we need to do is somehow get the message to him that we're being held here without our consent. Or"—my eyes go wide as I continue—"he's going to call you tomorrow, right? And if you don't pick up, he is going to get freaked out and sooner or later, he's going to figure out Graysons are behind it all. So if we really think about it, we probably don't even have to run. We don't need to do anything but sit here and wait for your brother to come rescue us."

"But don't you see," Peyton says urgently. "My family is the same. Do you think my brother is any better than these Graysons? Do you think my father is any better than all these monsters in this house? They're all criminals, every single one of them. And why do you think you're here in the first place? Because of them. Because of their decades-old feud."

"Look," I sigh. "I know. I know they're all the same—"

"Yes, they are and I'm not taking a thing from my family. Not a single thing, Riri, including their help that probably will come with strings attached anyway."

She's right. I *know* she's right. It's not as if it hadn't occurred to me. That Turners are as bad as Graysons. Or that her brother won't help us without trying to further his own agenda with Peyton. I know he's been trying to get her back to Wildfire for ages now. He wanted her to go to college in Black Rock instead of staying in Bozeman. He's also increasingly trying to butt into her dating life, which is why she hates picking up his weekly calls.

But this is bigger than that. The stakes are much higher in this case.

"But Peyton," I say, trying to convey the seriousness of this situation, "these people are dangerous. *He* is dangerous. We need to figure out a way to get out of here, okay? We have to. Before it's too late. Before something bad happens. We need to be smart here. We—"

"And we will be," Peyton assures me, cutting me off. "We'll be smart and we'll wait. Until the time is right and then we strike."

"What, strike with *what?*"

There's a glint in Peyton's eyes that I don't like. It's diabolical; I've seen it before, and it always ends up causing more trouble than anything else. I open my mouth to tell her exactly that. That I don't like the look in her eyes and that she really needs to reconsider, but she speaks first: "I don't know yet but I'm going to figure it out."

"Peyton—"

She squeezes my shoulders. "For now, just follow my lead. I'm going to find a way."

"But—"

"Do you trust me?"

I look into eyes as blue as mine, and even though I have a very bad feeling about this, I know nothing I say will deter her. If history is any indication, I *know* that already. I have countless stories about her reckless behavior, and while as I said, the stakes are much, *much* higher here, there's no way that past events will be an incentive for her to stop. I don't know what *will* make her stop, but I know arguing right now is not the solution.

So I say, taking a deep breath, "Yes."

Peyton looks at me for a second. "I've taught you well because I almost believed you."

"I—"

"It's fine. I'll prove it. You'll see."

Before I can say anything else, she springs up from the bed and skips to the door. She pounds on it with her fist as she calls out, "*Hello?* Anyone out there, especially, you evil, criminal Graysons who are keeping us here against our will? We're done braiding our hair and plotting your murder. Get in here so we can talk."

She spins around, raises her eyebrows, and winks at me before skipping back to the bed, looking extremely proud. Despite myself, I can't help but chuckle, and I'm just about done shaking my head at her when the door to the room opens and in comes a voice.

"If you're serious about killin' us, can I ask to go last? I wanna see how you take this big guy down. My money's on you talkin' him off a cliff."

It's Axton, and by "big guy," he means the pretty cowboy whose name we still don't know. They both walk in at the same time. Or rather, the nameless cowboy walks in first, looking slightly aggravated while Axton is right behind him, clapping his hand on his shoulder and chuckling.

While Axton makes himself comfortable in one of the armchairs in front of the bed, the big guy shoots Axton a look before making a beeline for the farthest corner where he settles against the wall, folding his arms across his chest. For some reason I think that's what he always does, looks for corners and nooks and crannies that he can use to disappear. But I don't think he's the kind of man who can go unnoticed. Especially by Peyton, who's glaring at him from beside me.

The thud of the door shutting brings me out of my useless thoughts, alerting me that he's here. The air in the room changes, thickens and becomes heavy. Probably with his scent of musk and leather.

I watch his long strides, taking him across the room where he finds a wall to stand against too. But not like the big guy. He doesn't hide or want to disappear. He wants to command the room, be the center of attention without *being* in the center. He wants eyes to follow him wherever he goes as he *shifts* it, the gravity.

At least he shifted mine, because now I don't know how to keep sitting here with him in front of me without collapsing on myself. I don't know how to look away from him even when he hasn't spared me a single glance. His eyes are on his target, the object he's going to use for his revenge. My best friend.

"I hear I'm your wife," Peyton goes, leaning back and propping herself on her arms.

I tighten my muscles in anticipation of his answer. I even look away and wring my hands in my lap, waiting for him to say the words that I know are going to feel like a blow, no matter how crazy or unwarranted it is.

But it never comes because he replies, "No, you're not."

And I jerk my eyes up to him. Even though he's still not looking at me, I can't help but wonder if he read my thoughts. If he somehow knew how insanely I was hanging on to his answer.

"If this is your way of proposing," Peyton drawls. "Then I don't even want to see the ring."

"Good," he clips, shifting on his feet and folding his arms across his chest. "Because there ain't one."

Sitting up straight, Peyton narrows her eyes at him. "You're kind of an asshole, you know that?"

His features remain blank as he murmurs, "That's the general consensus, yes."

She looks at him for a few seconds before taking a deep breath and asking, "So? Why do you want to marry me? What the hell is going on?"

"Because I want your land."

Peyton watches him with narrowed eyes. "My land?"

"Yeah."

"How does marrying *me* get you the land?"

"Because half of it belongs to you now," he says, his eyes dark and alert. "According to the Turner will, it automatically became yours when you turned eighteen. But the power of attorney is still your brother. Meaning, you can't make any major decisions about the land without his signature."

"What? That's bullshit."

He shifts on his feet. "Well, until you get married. Then, the power of attorney gets transferred to your husband."

Beside me, Peyton's spine snaps straight. "What kind of sexist crap is that? Do they think I can't take care of their stupid land? Why, because I'm a girl?"

"Yeah, well, you're gonna have to take that up with your father." His chest moves up and down with a large breath. "The point is, the man you're married to controls half your family's land. In this case, me."

"So, what, you just want me to roll over and *hand* you my share of the land?"

"Well, it already belongs to me so you're a little late with your protests. And I don't just want your share of the land; I want all of your land."

Peyton scoffs. "Right? Because my family is just going to give it to you."

"If they know what's good for them, they will."

"What is that supposed to mean?"

"It means"—he shifts on his feet again—"your family business is goin' under. Your daddy ran it to the ground and your brother's been tryin' to revive it. But even he knows, he can't. You're drownin' in debt and if something doesn't happen soon, you're all going down."

"Oh, I see," Peyton says, raising her eyebrows. "You're going to swoop in and save it. Buy the other half and give us the money. Is that your plan?" Before he can respond, Peyton leans forward to say, "My family will die before selling our land. They will die *twice* before selling it to a Grayson. So good luck with that."

Arsen watches Peyton for a second before murmuring, "You're not as dumb as I thought you'd be." Peyton gasps beside me as he keeps going: "But you're forgetting somethin'. I don't wanna buy your land. I just wanna control it. Especially now."

"Why now?"

"Because there's oil in it."

"Oil?"

"Yeah. The thing that's gonna solve all our problems. Your brother's meetin' up with an oil-drilling company in three weeks. If the deal goes through, they'll break ground, dig oil wells all over your land and you'll be swimmin' in money for generations." He pauses before stating, "Unfortunately for him, I control half of that land he wants to drill on."

"You're going to stop the deal," Peyton breathes out in realization.

He nods his head. "If they don't agree to my demand."

"And your demand is gaining control of the entire land."

With his eyes flashing, he declares, "You're right. Turners will never sell their land to Graysons. But the thing is, your land already belongs to us. Always has, always will. But we're not heartless. We'll let you keep your business. We'll even let you keep the percentage of the profits from the oil that you so kindly found for us. The point is that we could all be swimming in money. All your brother has to do is agree."

"So ultimately," Peyton bites out, "this is about money."

He tips his hat up with his finger. "You know it."

"What a cliché."

"Cliché for a reason."

Peyton is outraged; I can feel it. I want to calm her down, but I'm dealing with my own rage. I can feel my pulse pounding in my temple. I can feel it in my face, in every part of my body. Because I know he's not telling the whole truth. I somehow know he's hiding something.

Isn't he?

I know he doesn't care about the money. There's no way this is about money. He has an agenda. Which means he's still lying. Even after he *promised* he wouldn't. He made a vow, our wedding vow.

Here's the proof then.

That everything that happened in the woods was a lie. Just like those letters were, and I…I don't know how to deal with that. I don't know how to deal with the fact that he doesn't have the *decency* to acknowledge my presence. To look me in the eyes as he *lies* about his grand plan of vengeance.

"And you're doing this for revenge," Peyton concludes from beside me, and I have to really focus to be able to hear her.

"Yes. Eight years ago, your family started somethin' and I'm going to end it."

"Am I allowed to ask exactly what happened that led you to almost kill my father eight years ago?"

At this, I have to look up. Somewhere during this whole conversation, I averted my eyes and started staring down at my lap. I stared at my fisted fingers, my jutting-out knuckles. I stared at my jean-covered knees, my borrowed boots, anywhere but at him, because if I did, he'd probably know the effect he's having on me. He'd probably see that I'm still affected by what he does when he's so totally unaffected by me.

But I can't *not* look at him right now. I can't pretend that this isn't what I wanted, this isn't what I've been waiting for. To find out why. What happened to his Annie.

His features are set in stone, and even though the brim of his hat's up, his eyes still seem hidden in the shadows, mysterious and dark as he replies in a low tone, "No. Because you don't get that story."

I wince. Not outwardly but on the inside.

My insides clench, my belly and my chest. Even my fisted fingers flex and my nails almost break the skin with how tight I'm curling them into my palms. But I'm proud to say that he doesn't notice. He wouldn't anyway because he's still staring at Peyton, and even though I'm sitting right next to her, I'm almost convinced he doesn't even know I'm here. Which, in this case, is fine, really, because his *no* somehow felt personal.

After this, I straighten my spine and try to focus on things that matter. Such as the fact that Peyton agrees to their scheme. She agrees to go along with it and act married because she doesn't really care about the land or the feud either. If Arsen wants to end it all, she's not going to stand in his way. Or at least that's what she tells them.

I know she's lying.

Ax and the pretty cowboy interject at certain points as well, but the gist of it all remains the same: Peyton and I will cooperate.

He pushes off the wall and unfolds his arms. He brings the brim of the hat low as if he's about to step into the Montana sun, hiding his eyes from view as he concludes, "You go along with my plan and help me get the land and in three weeks, you and your *friend* can go free."

CHAPTER TWENTY-THREE

I KNOW EXACTLY where he is.

Even though I'm not looking at him. Instead, I'm staring at the bonfire that's set up in the center of the large rolling field behind the Grayson mansion. It's for a party. If someone had said to me a few days ago, or even yesterday when I arrived at the ranch, that tonight I'd be attending a party at Rawhide, I probably would've called them crazy. But it doesn't seem too crazy now. Because it's a homecoming party.

His homecoming party.

Even though I'm staring at the flames, I know he's all the way across from where I am standing, and he has a group of guys—all ranch hands I think—around him. His back is to the field beyond and I know he's tensed.

He's uncomfortable.

His stance is wide, and his shoulders are unusually rigid. And his Stetson sits low on his head, hiding his eyes. I think that's the sign, his brim being too low, of his discomfort. When he doesn't want anyone to see his eyes or gauge his thoughts.

I know he hates this. He hates all these people around him. He hated when one of them wanted to hug him. He backed off and offered his hand. Probably because he can't stand being touched after being imprisoned for eight years. Just like he can't find sleep easily. He hates that they're all flocking around him, and he hasn't had a moment's peace since this thing started. He hates the music, too, cowboys playing guitars around the fire. He hates that it doesn't look like this is going to end any time soon so he can be alone.

I don't want to feel sympathy for him, but I do. I also want to go over there and *punch* him in the face. Then I want to fist that denim shirt of his and demand that he call me by my name. He did that on purpose, didn't he? He called me *friend* on purpose. Probably to take revenge on the fact that I didn't call him by *his* name for so long. Because he's that twisted. Because that's all he thinks about: revenge and getting even and everything that's evil.

"What's his name?"

Peyton's voice gets me out of my musings, and I come back to the moment. She's asked this question of Haven, who's following her orders and keeping an eye on us. Axton is around, too, somewhere, keeping us all in his line of vision, even though from what I saw before he has some friends from his school attending the party. Apparently, he'll be a senior in high school when they open after summer and is quite popular from what Haven's been telling us; Peyton asked.

Right now, though, Peyton's focused on the group over to our left that consists of Marsden, a bunch of suit-wearing, important-looking men, and that pretty cowboy. To be specific, though, she's solely focused on the pretty cowboy, her eyes narrowed and her lips pursed.

Haven follows her gaze and smiles. "Radisson. Radisson King. But everyone calls him Rad."

Peyton takes a sip of her beer. "Does he work for you all?"

"Well, he is the foreman but he's family," Haven explains. "He's their aunt's son. They all grew up together."

"Why doesn't he talk to me?" Peyton asks next.

Haven chuckles. "Because he doesn't talk to anyone. Well…"

She trails off because at that very moment, he does begin speaking, and I think he talks for about half a minute if not more, with all of us watching him. Which, thank God, he doesn't notice because it would make anyone uncomfortable.

When he's done, Haven continues, "He was in a car accident when he was young. Hit his head really bad and suffered from TBI. Traumatic brain injury. It affected his speech. Took him a really long time to be able to talk again, a couple of years at least and… They were hard, those years. He struggled a lot. The *bullying* in town, at school…" She shakes her head. "You know how kids are. They can be so cruel. Plus his scar didn't help either. He was the town's monster, a beast. He still is to some and he just… I guess, he got used to not talking."

Peyton swallows thickly, her features stricken and eyes misty. I probably look the same. Because when he told me about the Quiet Mustang, he didn't put it this way. I know he brought him up to scare me—and I did get scared—but I couldn't have imagined, not even in my wildest nightmares, that Radisson's story would be so tragic. It's their parents' death all over again. It was just a simple fact to me until I got a glimpse behind the curtain.

No, actually it's everything about Rawhide. All my life I heard so many horror stories about the family that I never considered them to be anything other than the monsters we were told they were. But just look at them. They're truly a family, all these brothers and Haven. They care about one another. Or at the very least, they don't hit children or abuse women like Peyton's and my father did.

"And you know, he's really gentle. I know he looks all big and fierce and of course, he kidnapped you and all that," Haven says to Peyton, drinking her own beer and wrinkling her nose. "But he really is the sweetest. He detests violence; he really does. He's the only one among them who won't go hunting. He *refuses*, says killing animals for food is enough, doesn't want to kill them for sport too. He hates guns. He—"

"What?"

That's me. So far, I've been really quiet. I've been given a lemon-ade, my drink of choice, but I've yet to take a sip. All I've done ever since we arrived at the party is stand in this very spot, staring at the fire and *not* at him, and occasionally murmuring a noncommittal sound as Peyton and Haven talk about things.

So I get that both of them are a little shocked at my sudden interruption. Plus, I was a little loud, too, but I can't help it. Not at what I just found out. "He doesn't like guns?"

"Uh, yeah, no," Haven says, overcoming her shock quickly and smiling. "I don't think he's ever shot one. Or maybe once or twice but—"

"Can you hold my drink?" I turn to Peyton, cutting Haven off.

I know it's rude, but again, no helping that. I thrust the drink at Peyton, and she has no choice but to take it as she asks, "Riri, you okay? What—"

"I'll just be a second," I say to them both and take off.

Toward him.

Toward that *asshole* who lied to me. Again. And again and *fuck-ing again.*

Halfway through my journey, I realize he isn't there anymore and I come to a halt. Frantically, I look around and see a flash of his Stetson disappearing around the barn. The one just by the corral where Axton was trying to break the bronco. I make a beeline for it, and soon I'm rounding the corner of the barn. I don't care if Axton or Haven or their entire Grayson clan follows me and then locks me up in his stupid room after I'm done with him; I'm not going to let him get away with this, with lying. He doesn't—

I scream the moment an arm wraps around my waist. Or I try to, but the sound gets muffled because simultaneously, a hand wraps around my mouth, too, and I'm picked up off the ground. And then I'm being taken somewhere. All of this happens so suddenly and in under two seconds that I should be reeling. I should be confused and panicked out of my mind.

But I guess he trained me well.

He taught me how to react to a sudden grab in a dark alley–esque situation. So I'm freaking out, yes, but not because I'm afraid but because I know it's him; and how *dare* he grab me again like a freaking criminal? Like this is the first time we've met and he hasn't done all the things he's done.

As he takes me wherever he wants to take me, I twist and struggle in his grip. I scratch his arms. I elbow his ribs. I even try to kick back and hit his thighs and calves. Not that it has any effect on him. He still keeps walking, keeping me plastered to his hot and hard chest, without once breaking his stride.

When he finally arrives at the destination, all the way to the back and away from the party, he puts me down, spins me around, and pins me to the wooden wall of the barn. And I finally lock eyes with him in the dark, both our breaths hard and fast and noisy. His Stetson is gone and his hair's all mussed up, strands falling over his forehead, so I guess I did *some* damage.

But why does he look so beautiful, still?

And why does his voice sound so much rougher than it did only a few hours ago when he says, "Thought I told you not to tail an ex-con."

My breaths are still loud, but at his words, irritated like I'm some kind of a bother, they grow even faster and instead of replying back, I do what I've wanted to do all this time. I punch his face. It's not as hard as Axton's was yesterday or even Haven's, and I think it hurt me more than it did him, because all it did was make him blink and breathe through his nostrils, but I'm glad I did it.

I'm also glad that I go ahead and smack his face.

And then it's like I got the taste for it, and I can't stop so I keep going. I keep hitting him. Slapping his face, hitting his chest. I even knee him in his thighs; I was going for his stupid junk, but I miss it.

I would've tried again, but I think he's had enough so he takes both my arms and pins them to the wall by my head. He also leans into me with his hard body, trapping my legs with his, his belt buckle digging into my upper belly.

Then, with his fingers squeezing around my wrist, he rasps, "You get that out of your system?"

I twist between him and the wall, trying to dislodge his grip. "Let me go."

"Not until you calm down," he says with authority.

"Don't tell me to calm down."

"I will if it looks like you're on the verge of hurtin' yourself."

"I'm trying to hurt *you*, asshole."

"Yeah, don't think that's happenin'."

"You're such a…" I breathe in deep before proceeding with, "You're a liar."

A light frown emerges between his eyebrows as if he's confused. "Thought we covered that too."

"Your *shooter* friend," I bite out, getting up in his face, "the one you told me was waiting to shoot my best friend's brother but was really not? Now as it turns out, he isn't a shooter at all." At my words, his frown clears off and he breathes out. "Apparently, he doesn't like guns all that much." I keep going: "He won't even shoot animals."

He breathes out again, this time muttering as if to himself, "Yeah, forgot about that."

At his acknowledgment, I jerk in his hold again, trying to get free and smack him across the face some more, because I'm not done yet. But he overpowers me, and all I can do is glare and snarl, "Of course you forgot about that. You've told so many lies, it's a wonder you can keep them all straight."

His jaw—which I can't help noticing is even more stubbled now and has crossed the line over to a light beard—clenches as he pushes out a breath. "So is that why you were followin' me? Because you found out Rad won't touch guns?"

"Yes," I snap. Then a second later, "No."

He watches me for a few beats, his frown back and thicker than before. "Why don't you figure it the fuck out first and then launch yourself at me?"

He loosens his hold on me then. Big mistake. *Huge.* Because the moment his fingers leave my wrist, I launch myself at him again. I smack and slap and punch and kick and even bite. I'm not sure what part of his body I managed to get my teeth into, but it felt like the side of his neck; now I'm subdued again.

This time with brute force. That he still doesn't physically hurt me, even with the way he has his fingers so tightly wrapped around my wrist, is something I don't want to put a lot of thought into. Not right now when I'm so angry at him.

His chest rumbles with his words: "What the fuck's your problem?"

"You," I snap, fisting my fingers in his grip. "*You* are my problem. Everything wrong in my life is because of you."

His nostrils flare and his chest almost shudders with his large breath. "So maybe for once, you should act smart and stay away from me instead of fucking tailin' me the moment I leave your fuckin' sight."

God. I hate him. *So much.*

My own breaths are all large and choppy, too, as I repeat, "Let. *Me.* Go."

"Calm down first."

His answer only manages to enrage me. "If you start talking to me like you do to your horses, I swear to God, I'm going to lose it."

His jaw pulses. "More than you already have?"

"You—"

"And you already know what I like to do to calm you down, so unless you want me to get on my knees and spread your thighs so my mouth gets to work between them while the whole town is just across from the barn, you'll do as I say and calm the fuck down, yeah?"

Maybe I can't stop my thighs from clenching at his threat and my belly from feeling achy. But I sure as hell am going to ignore it. Instead, I glare at him through the darkness. And even though I'm so mad at him, I study his features.

It's been almost two days since we've been this close, and now that I have him here, I try to find signs of his earlier discomfort. Or some clue about what he did yesterday and all day today. Because after he told us about his plan, he disappeared. Rad gave Peyton some papers to sign, something to do with the power of attorney and the land. And Peyton promised to pick up her brother's weekly call tomorrow so as to not arouse suspicion about what the Graysons are planning until they're ready to reveal it.

"You promised you wouldn't lie," I blurt out after a while.

His eyes shoot up and I realize he was studying my features too. Specifically, my mouth, the jut of my chin. The pounding pulse at the base of my neck. Because all these places tingle and burn.

"What?"

"I know you want revenge on the Turners and taking their land is the perfect plan. But I know you don't care about it," I say. "You don't care about the oil, the money. That's not your end goal."

Something flashes across his face, something like a mix of surprise and...*satisfaction*—for what reason, I don't know—before he says, "You know me so well, huh?"

I look in his eyes, my heart racing. "Yes. I *know* you. You can fool Peyton but you can't fool me. So tell me what you're going to do with it."

At this, his features close down. "You don't need to worry about it."

I twist my hands in his grip. "You're planning something, aren't you?"

"Again, not your fucking concern."

"You said you'd let them keep their business," I say urgently.

"And I will."

"But—"

He tightens his grip on my wrists, his fingers finally digging into my bones, mashing my pulse. "Let it the fuck go, all right? It's not your business. In three weeks, all of this will be behind you. All this bullshit. This war, this revenge, every single thing that I did to you. I ruined your life, didn't I? Well, in three weeks' time, you'll have it back. All of this will be a memory to you. You'll do what you always wanted to do. Help people. Change lives." His jaw clenches here for a second before he says, "Fall in fuckin' love. So why don't you worry about your future more than what my endgame is?"

Right. In three weeks, when he's done taking the Turners' land away and doing whatever the fuck he wants with it, I can have my life back. It will be like none of this ever happened. And I should want that. I *do* want that. That's all I've wanted since he took me.

"What about till death do us part?" I say ridiculously, knowing he never meant it.

At my words, his fingers tighten around my wrists even more. "What about it?"

"You said that," I remind him like he's forgotten. "You said you won't let me go. You made me *promise* that I won't run from you."

He was already smashing my pulse with his thumb, but now he's absolutely crushing it, slowing it down as he says, "Yeah, that was before I figured out you're the wrong girl."

It's like he smacked me, kicked me in the gut.

The wrong girl. The girl who's expendable. I am that. I know it. I've always known it. I don't know why it's hitting me so hard, him saying that. Why it *hurts* so much that I want to double over.

"Jesus, *look*"—he lets me go completely and scrubs a hand down his face—"clue the fuck in, all right? I said that to scare you. To make it look like there was no escape. To make you feel powerless. And honest to fuckin' God, I liked it. I liked scarin' you. I liked knowing I have power over you. And for a second, I liked the idea of never letting you go. Of keepin' you once all of this was over. For myself, for my amusement. Even though, God knows, I don't deserve it. I don't fuckin' deserve any peace in my shitty life after what I did eight years ago. But I'm a selfish piece of shit who wanted it anyway. All that disappeared though when I found out I fucked up. And I'll be the big man here and admit that I fucked up big. I never should've dragged you into this. You're not a Turner. You understand how fucking lucky you are? You've got no business being here. You're not fuckin' tangled up in decades of bloody history. You're clean. You're *free*. So that's what I'm doin'. I'm setting you free."

"But I'm not *free*!" I practically scream.

That's the problem, isn't it? That's the *entire* problem. That I'm not free or clean. It doesn't matter that I'm not a Turner. Because I still have a history.

I have a history with *him*.

A history of blood and lies. Of a cabin in the woods and meals around a fire. Of him scaring me and thrilling me and making me feel fucking alive for the first time in my life. We have a history filled with thirty-seven letters and sleepless nights. So no, I'm not free or clean.

I'm branded.

He *branded* me, and I can't go back to my old life now.

I don't want to go back to it. And *Jesus Christ*, this has to be the most insane thing that anyone has ever done. This has to be the worst case of Stockholm syndrome, and it's all his fault, and I just...

I slap him again. And again and again, and I do it because I want to punish him, brand him like he's branded me. But this time, I have things to say too. Disjointed, broken, rambling things that begin and end in strange places and probably don't make any sense at all.

"*You* clue the fuck in, asshole. I'm not free. I'm not clean and it's your fault. You *did* things to me. You stripped me naked. And you t-tied me to a tree. You pointed y-your gun at me and made me suck it and I..." I hiccup and smack his chest. "I've never f-felt safe in my entire life like I did with you. So much so that I told you my biggest secret. I told you about my f-father and how he… I t-told you about my mother's death and I'm supposed to just move on in three weeks? Like none of it was real, like it never happened." I scratch his jaw at that, drag my nails along his neck. "And you won't even look at me. You pretend I don't exist and I can't stop thinking about if you got any s-sleep last night. And that you missed your dinner yesterday and lunch today and how uncomfortable you were at the party. But you don't care that you left me in your room, told others to look after me when it's y-your job. *You* brought me here. You should be the one taking care of me. *You*, not your sister-in-law or your b-brother who can't stop staring at me. I'm yours. You *made* me yours and I…"

I stop because I run out of steam. I do want to say more things, though. I have a lot more to say, but while I'm hiccuping and trying to catch my breath, he moves. He inches closer to me, and I feel his breath on my cheek, all hot and wild.

And while I'm trying to contend with that, with his sweet breath, I feel his mouth on my cheek. My left cheek, just under my eye, and I feel him licking my tears away. Something I wasn't aware of. That I was crying.

Actually, he's not licking, he's *drinking*.

I can feel him sucking them down and I hear him swallowing them thickly. But there's so many of them, my tears, that he has to catch the stream on his rough thumbs, his long fingers, scraping and rubbing my face. His hands remind me of where my hands are. They've somehow landed on his shoulders and I fist his shirt, sighing under his soft ministrations, thinking this is the first time he's put his mouth on me like this, and oh Lord, it's so soft.

Softer than I'd imagined. Hotter and wetter.

That all I can do is whimper and moan as I cling to his body. "W-what are you doing?"

"Taking care of what's mine," he rasps against my skin, his stubble stinging me.

I twist his shirt and say the exact opposite of what I just said: "I'm not yours."

His mouth laps at my jaw. "Unfortunately for you, you are."

"I—"

"I'm gonna kick his ass."

"What?"

"Ax," he says, his thumbs making circles on the apples of my cheeks. "Told him to stay away from you."

"I don't care about—"

"A cow's delivery was breech," he says next.

"What... What does that—"

"Today, at lunch."

That's when I understand what he's doing. He *is* taking care of me. He's answering all the questions I didn't ask, or rather didn't want to but blurted out anyway, and I just... God, my heart clenches in my chest.

"We were out a hand and the vet was late," he goes on, licking and explaining. "So I had to pitch in."

"Is she..." I clench my eyes shut and arch my back, despite myself. "Okay?"

"Yeah," he whispers at my jaw, his fingers in my hair. "It was hard. But she pulled through."

"And the calf?"

"Tiny little thing but yeah, she's okay too."

"Okay"—I swallow—"good."

"Went to see my parole officer after that," he goes on.

"Your parole officer."

"Now that I'm back in town."

"Oh."

"And Haven told me."

"Told you what?"

"That you didn't want me around. So I made myself scarce last night at dinner."

I move my hands to his hair then and pull the strands. "Did you eat something, though?"

"No."

I pull at his hair. "You shouldn't skip meals."

He rolls his forehead on my neck. "And you shouldn't worry about me."

"You should also see someone."

"About what?"

"Your PTSD." Before he can say anything, I continue, "I know you hate to hear this but I could see. You didn't like being at the party. You didn't—"

"This helps."

"What?"

His chest moves with a breath. "Breathin' you in."

I bite my lip so hard it hurts. "I'm not—"

"And I couldn't."

I think I know which question he's answering, but I still ask, "You c-couldn't what?"

"Sleep last night."

I go up on my tiptoes then, the pain in my chest is so huge. I wind my arms around his neck and whisper, "Because I wasn't there?"

He tucks his face in the crook of my neck and keeps breathing me in. "Yeah. Couldn't see you. Couldn't smell you."

"Oh, Arsen, I—"

"So I came to your door."

My heart skips a beat. "You came to my…"

"Stood there a long time." He sniffs my neck as he says, "Kept taking a whiff of the wood, tryin' to smell you through the barrier."

I swallow. "I didn't… I didn't know."

"Kept tellin' myself to leave," he goes on, rubbing his nose in my pulse. "Kept tellin' myself I couldn't bust down your door, couldn't go in there. Not after everything. Not after how I've fucked up with you. Told myself you needed peace, you needed to be free. From me. That you aren't my wife, not really. It doesn't matter how much you feel like it. I've got no right to you, to go in your room." Then, pushing his forehead against my neck, he goes, "I wouldn't have climbed on though, I swear. I wouldn't have gotten in the bed with you. I wouldn't have touched you. Tell me you know that. Tell me you know I'm not lyin' about that."

He says it so urgently, so *sincerely*, I have no choice but to nod. "I do."

A breath of relief pushes out of him. "Because I wouldn't have. It would've been hard. It would've taken every shred of decency I've got left in me to not touch you, *everything* that my mama taught me before she died, everything my brother taught me about how to treat a girl, but I would've done it. I would've watched you. Smelled your hair. Your skin. Watched the moonlight play with it. Like I've been doin' for the past week. And then fallen asleep for a little bit, just under the window."

"God, Arsen, you—"

He shudders. "So when it became too much, I left. Went for a ride."

I swallow again, flexing my arms around his neck. "On Rebel?"

"Yeah." He nods, his open mouth dragging up and down the column of my neck. "It's been eight years since I saw him but he remembered me. He remembered that I was the first to break him."

Warmth spreads across my chest because I can hear the pride in his voice, the joy, and it sounds glorious. It makes his voice a little deeper and rougher, more of a growl that scrapes over my skin so good that I can hear it for days. I tilt my face and rub my chin in his soft hair. "Like your dream."

Finally, he moves away from my neck and looks up, his eyes heavy-lidded. "Yeah, my dream."

I see the scratches I made on his face. His jaw specifically. A cut on the side of his mouth, his high cheekbone. I bring my fingers to stroke the cuts I gave him lovingly, tenderly, as I whisper, "So it was real? What happened between us?"

A tightness flashes over his face that resembles torture as he replies back gutturally, "Yeah, darlin', it was real."

A relieved breath escapes me. "But you didn't… You didn't say my name."

His jaw pulses beneath my fingers and his fingers in my hair fist. I don't know what it says about him or about me, about *us*, that he knows exactly what I'm talking about. Actually, I do know. It says that maybe we're both branded. He branded me, but maybe I did the same to him.

"I shouldn't get to breathe the same air as you, let alone look at you when you're in the same room as me." My gaze scurries up and I look into his glittery, molten eyes as he keeps going: "What makes you think I should get to say the *absolute fuckin' dream* that is your name after everythin' I've done and everythin' I'm going to do?"

"You—"

"This isn't the first time, is it?" he cuts me off, his voice all rough edges. In fact, ever since we arrived at the ranch, his voice has become even more of a drawl and even deeper. Like he's exactly where he belongs even though he's struggling to fit in.

"What?"

"That you've cried." His eyes rove over my features, his thumbs still circling on my cheeks. "Your friend, she said it. Yesterday. That you never cry. Except when it comes to me."

I shake my head. "That's—"

"Made you feel bad about yourself at that goddamn café when the truth is that I stopped thinkin' the moment I saw you walkin' through that door. I got fucked in the head the moment I heard your voice. And then I put you through hell. Lied to you. Tied you up, drugged you. Stripped you naked, *humiliated* you. I did everythin' to break you, but you didn't break. Not until now. Not until I once again made you feel less than." He moves his jaw back and forth. "Instead of tellin' you the truth, I made you feel like you're the one lacking. You're not. You're a survivor. You didn't let anything that happened to you in the past break you. Your daddy beat you; your mama let him. She used you to protect herself instead of protectin' you and yet you wanna help people like her. Do you realize how beautiful that is? How brave you are. How fuckin' stunning and breathtaking. I told you it's hard to breathe around you, didn't I? It is. It's hard to not look at you, to not ask Haven and my useless brother about you. It's so fuckin' hard to let you go. But I'm tryin', darlin', yeah?" He swallows thickly, his Adam's apple jerking. "Because if anyone's lacking between the two of us, it's me. I'm a piece of shit. You call me your criminal asshole cowboy and that's exactly what I am. I'm a *selfish* fuckin' piece of shit, baby, because I'll take what you give me and I'll steal what you don't. So the reason I don't look at you is because I'm not the kind of man you want starin' at you. I'm not the kind of man you want sayin' your name."

Maybe I should focus on other things. Try to listen to what he's saying to me. But I'm a girl. A girl who's never been called beautiful by a boy before, much less a man who sets her heart on fire. He sets my entire soul on fire, and for the life of me, I cannot focus on anything else but the fact that he called me stunning.

"You really…" I lick my lips. "You really thought that, when you saw me at the café? You really think I'm beautiful?"

His eyes flash bright. "No, because you aren't just beautiful. You're so beautiful that you might not be real. That maybe I made you up in my fucked-up head while starin' at the little piece of sky through the barred window above my bunk. You're so beautiful, you're like a dream. A reverie." He circles his eyes all over my face. "My Reverie."

"But you sent me away," I remind him. "At the café. You…you told me to leave and I thought…"

"I told you to leave because I was tryin' to protect you," he replies. "I was tryin' to do the right thing. Not that I've got any experience in it but…" He swallows thickly again, his gaze pene-trating. "It's on me, yeah? I didn't think. I made you feel like all those fuckin' college boys did. But that's what they are, do you understand? *Boys.* Immature little shitheads. They don't know what beauty is because most of 'em haven't seen the ugliness in the world. They don't know the value of softness when they've never felt hard, concrete walls. They don't know what it's like to close your eyes at night and see fire and blood. Instead of daydreams of you."

I clench my eyes shut for a second before I ask, "What hap-pened to her?"

He freezes. His grip on me goes still instead of rhythmic jerks and pulses. But I can't turn back now. I need to know why he's the way he is. Why he's so determined to get revenge. Why he spent the last eight years behind bars, looking at the sky through a barred window, when I *know* that he belongs out here, sleeping under the stars, riding like the wind, working the land. Being with his family.

So if he's all statue-like right now and unbreathing, I breathe for him. I press my heaving chest to his unforgiving frame. I stretch myself to the bone to get up in his face, bring our mouths together, and breathe out, "What did they do to her? They did something to her, didn't they? Something happened eight years ago that made you this way. You're not this man. You may be hard and rough but you're not a criminal. You're not ruthless and without mercy. You're a protector. You protected me. You've been protecting me so tell me what they did. Tell me what happened to her. What—"

"She died."

His eyes seem faraway now even though they're on me, and it's hard to breathe at his declaration, but I do it for him. I keep hold-ing on to him, pressing my chest against his, giving him my breaths as he says, "She was waitin' for me. At one of the barns. The one where we used to meet. I was runnin' late when I got the phone call." He pauses here for a second and I let him, waiting and *dreading* his next set of words. "There was an explosion. On the north side of the property. At first, Rad said it was way off the pastures, out in the woods. It spooked the cows, the horses, but they weren't harmed. Coulda been a lot worse, he said. So I was relieved. For a second, I let *relief* run through me. But then it occurred to me. The barn. It was on the north side too. Away from everything, out in the woods, her favorite. She loved that place, said it gave her peace after a long day of ridin' and groomin'. She worked for one of the ranches in town, a wrangler." He pauses again as if seeing her in his mind, before continuing, "By the time I got there, it was all gone. All traces of the barn, her. Just ashes, nothing more. She died in her favorite spot, waitin' for me. Probably scared out of her mind. Burned alive, in agony, *waitin'* for me to come save her."

I know I need to be strong right now.

I know I need to hold him, give him strength, but I don't know how to do that when I'm falling apart myself. When my own knees are shaking and buckling. I didn't know what I was expecting, but it wasn't what he told me. I didn't expect to see the sheer pain on his face. Or hear the acute misery in his voice. I didn't expect my own heart to break like this. For him. For the woman he loved.

For *them*.

"I couldn't though," he goes on. "I couldn't save her."

Somehow through my own tears and ache, I grab his face and whisper, "Arsen."

My voice is small and broken, but he hears it still and finally focuses on me. More than that, he finally *breathes*. His chest shudders against mine, and the force in his grip returns. In fact, it returns tenfold. He grabs my face in his rough palms much like I'm grabbing his and says, gutturally, "They killed her. They rigged the barn. And I broke into Wildfire and tried to kill the man responsible for it. Eight years later, I'm still hell-bent on destroying him, destroying the whole Turner family and I'm not gonna stop. Nothin' will make me stop. Do you understand what I'm sayin' to you? These people, the Turners, the *Graysons*, we're all the same. We're all dangerous.

Criminals. We're cut from the same cloth and that's why"—he squeezes his fingers around my face, making me look into his eyes— "you need to leave. You need to get out of here in three weeks. You need to be free. You need to forget what happened here and you need to run, you understand? Far, *far* away. Where no one can find you. Not Turners, not Graysons. *No one.*"

"Not even you?"

"I'm a Grayson, ain't I? But more than that," he continues, his eyes bright and fiery, "I *am* like your father. You were right. I'm cruel, selfish. A killer. I couldn't save the girl I was supposed to love. She died because of me. I can't save anyone. I'm not a protector. So you need to run, you understand? You need to save yourself. From me. Tell me you understand."

I was wrong.

He's *nothing* like my father. While my father killed the woman he loved, eight years later, Arsenal Grayson is still mourning the woman he couldn't protect. While every time my father came around I'd try to hide behind whatever was larger than me, when Arsen puts his arms around me, I feel safe. They both have done their own brand of bad things to me, but only one of them wants me to go free.

No, they're not the same. In fact, they couldn't be more opposite.

So for the first time in my life, I decide to throw caution to the wind and I don't berate myself for it. I don't second-guess myself like I would when I wrote those letters. I wholeheartedly and in possession of all my faculties do what I do next.

I kiss him.

CHAPTER TWENTY-FOUR

HE'S SHOCKED.

Because he doesn't move for several seconds. It should make things awkward. I'm the only one who's moving her lips over his. Closed ones at that. But I'm too busy tasting him. I'm too busy finally, *finally*, breathing a sigh of relief because I've been waiting to kiss him for a long time now.

Years, it feels like.

And even though I know nothing about kissing, I'm still forging ahead. I'm still licking the seam of his mouth. Curling my tongue over the ends. I'm still sucking his lower lip into my mouth because it's so soft, almost bouncy. And every time I take a little bite of it, I think I taste lemonade. I want to ask him if he was drinking it like me at the party and do we have the same favorite drink. I also want to ask him a million things about himself, now that I'm not holding myself back and I have no shame left in me when it comes to him. And also, when I know he'll tell me; I'll *make* him tell me.

But then I discover how fucking amazing his stubble feels on my tongue, all scrape-y and stingy in contrast to his plush lips, and I put everything else on the back burner. There's time for that later. Three weeks' worth of time. Just as I'm about to lick his stubble more, though, my head's yanked back and his face, all angry-looking, fills my vision.

"What the fuck are you doin'?" he growls.

I grab the collar of his shirt and reply, "Kissing you."

"Kissing me."

"Yes." I swallow, my cheeks blushing. "Was that not…c-clear?"

His eyes narrow. "It was."

"So—"

"I'm just"—he flexes his fist in my hair—"not sure about the why."

"Because I want to."

His nostrils flare with his breaths. Three breaths. I count them, and I know he's taking them to calm himself down because he was starting to breathe a little heavier back there. Then, "Did you listen to anythin' I just said?"

I go to nod, but his grip is too tight so I switch to a verbal response. "Yes."

"Tell me."

"What?"

"Fucking"—he shakes my head a little, his fingers mean and brutal—"repeat it to me. What I said to you."

I cup his jaw, caressing his stubble, those cuts as I whisper, "I need to be free. I need to run."

His nostrils flare again. "Run where?"

"Away from here."

"Far away," he corrects.

"F-far away."

"And from who?"

"You."

"Me."

"I—"

He shakes my head again to shut me up. "Why?"

"Because you're…you're bad for me."

"And why am I bad for you?"

"You're"—I hiccup—"cruel and selfish."

"You forgot one," he reminds me and pulls my head back even more.

I have to wait a second so I can clench my thighs at his rough grip, the harsh stretching of my neck. "A-and dangerous."

"Try again."

"I don't—"

He leans closer to me, hovering. "The one where I put my bare hands around the throat of the motherfuckers who've hurt you and squeeze really fuckin' hard."

God.

I suck my belly in, butterflies buzzing down there. "A killer."

His chest moves with satisfaction. "Yeah. A killer."

"But—"

Again, he shuts me up by inching closer, bringing his mouth over mine, not touching, though, only tempting. "So tell me again, why *the fuck* are you kissin' me?"

I take him in. His harsh face, every line standing taut and sharp. His eyes dark and glittering, brutal. And I think to myself that I wasted so much time. *So much time*, lamenting the fact that his eyes weren't blue like I imagined them to be. Or that his voice was too deep the first time I heard it, and his shoulders were broader than I thought. I wasted so much time thinking he was nothing like I'd dreamed about for the past six months, nothing like my Bo. When I should have been thinking that he was—*is*—everything I needed him to be.

Cruel, selfish, and dangerous, yes.

But also, fierce and protective and God, capable of so much love. This is what people call love. This is what people call loyalty. That he's still willing to go through hell for the woman he loved. So isn't it obvious why I'm kissing him?

I'm kissing him because I love him.

I fell in love with him when I only knew him as Bo and could barely imagine the fire inside of him, and I'm even more in love with him now when his flames have touched me. I keep rubbing my thumb in his stubble as I say, "Because I realized something."

"What?"

"That I'm still mad at you."

That gives him a pause. "You're mad at me."

"Yes," I whisper, skimming my thumb along the curve of his lower lip. "If you think that I've forgiven you for all the things you've done because you wiped my tears, tears that *you* gave me, then you're highly mistaken."

His jaw pulses and I know he's remembering my tears in this moment. Remembering and *regretting*. It's plain as day on his face. It only makes me more determined to do this. "I keep the letters you wrote me in my desk drawer. Just beneath the window because Bo"—his frame tightens at the name and I clutch his face harder— "told me that he likes to watch the sky through his barred window. So I figured he'd like that. But now I know it wasn't Bo; it was you. *You* liked to watch the sky through the window. I know I'll never have the heart to move them, no matter how much I might want to. So they'll just sit there, as a reminder. Your reminder. As the reminder of all the lies you told. I could fill a book with all the lies you told, all the crimes you committed, and still not be finished. I'll have nightmares about you for the rest of my life. So yes, I'm mad at you and no, I haven't forgiven you yet. But I want to."

I can see his cheek pulsing as he stares down at me. "You shouldn't."

"That's not up to you," I say, arching up to him. "The only thing that's up to you is apologizing."

His hands move and go down to my waist where he grips me so tightly, I teeter on my toes. "How?"

I move my hands, too, and bury them in his hair before fisting the strands tightly. "You want me to be clean, don't you? You want me to be free, to forget all about what happened. So then, you're going to have to make me."

His brow furrows. "*Make* you."

I pull at his hair. "Yes, because you brought me here, remember? Against my wishes."

Understanding finally dawns on him and his brow clears. His fingers on my waist grope and pull, *pinch*. "So you're the victim."

My heart flutters at him throwing his words back at me. But we're way past that now, so I squeeze my arms around his neck and whisper against his lemonade-tasting lips that I can't wait to get back to, "No, because I may not be a Turner but when you forced me to sign on that dotted line, it doesn't matter what I wrote—I became a Grayson. And I don't care if you did it for revenge or that I'm the wrong girl. All I care about is I'm your wife. You *made* me your wife. So now it's *your* job to turn my nightmares into dreams."

He has to make up for all the things he did because I don't want my love for him to be tainted by my anger, by his lies and crimes. I don't want to remember him as my kidnapper. I want to remember him as my husband and the man I love.

Something passes through his features, through his entire body, which becomes larger somehow. His broad shoulders stretch out and his chest swells up to massive proportions. His eyes glitter in the dark, and I swear his fingers on my body go all heated and so, *so* tight that I'm this close to moaning under them. Even his voice grows gruffer and more growly as he says, "You've got no clue what you just did, do you?"

My heart, already pounding, starts knocking in my chest so hard, I lose my breath for a second. "Yes, I do."

He circles his glittery eyes over my features before refuting, "No, you don't."

"I—"

"You just opened the door."

"The d-door?"

"The one I was trying"—he kneads my flesh again, all impatiently—"*really fuckin' hard* not to bust down."

"Last night?"

"Last night."

"I think—"

"And guess what," he rasps, his mouth so close to mine that it feels like I'm already drinking the lemonade. "I'm not just watchin' anymore."

"You're not?"

"No, I'm climbin' in the bed with you."

A current runs down my spine and I pull at his hair again. "I-I want you to."

"I'm throwin' away the sheet you've got on."

"I don't care."

"And I'm tearin' off the clothes you're wearing."

"O-okay."

"You're not gonna need them anymore."

"Why not?"

"Because if you want somethin' to cover your gorgeous little body with, it's gonna be my body. And you know why that is, don't you?"

I shiver. "W-why?"

His fingers on my waist dig and *dig* into my flesh as he growls, "Because you're my wife and if you wanna be warm, it's *my* job to make it so."

I swallow again and hold on to his shoulders, my nerves finally getting the better of me. "Okay, but…but let's talk first."

"Yeah?"

"Yes because I thought—"

"I know what you thought."

I lick my lips. "What?"

"You thought I'm a man but I'm not just a man."

"No?"

He shakes his head slowly. "No, I'm not just a man. I think in all your girly fuckin' excitement you forgot that I'm a man who spent the last eight years behind bars. Six months of which I spent dreamin' about you."

"I didn't. I—"

"And when a man's locked up and dreamin' for that long, he starts to change," he goes on, his words all rough and rippling with danger. "He becomes harder, rougher. Aggressive. So that when they finally let him out, he doesn't come out a man; he comes out a bull. And you know what a bull does, don't you?"

"What?"

He waits a beat to answer, and I know he does it to keep me on my toes.

In fact I do just that. As I wait for him to tell me, I go up on my toes and I plaster my body against his. And in response, he pulls me up even higher. He slides his corded arms around my waist and squeezes them to bring me up so my feet leave the ground and my toes barely graze it. So all I can do is completely and absolutely depend on him to keep me upright.

When he's done overpowering me this way, he finally goes, "He fucks."

I flinch, or I would have if he'd let me. But he has such a hold on me that all I can do is curl my toes as he continues, "And he fucks like it's his job. Like that's all he knows how to do, fuck and rut and fuck again until he can't do it anymore. Especially when there's a ripe little pussy around. And you know you've got a ripe little pussy, don't you, that pops off like a firecracker just by me lookin' at it."

"That's not—"

"So I know what you thought. You *thought* you'll kiss me and I'll kiss you back and it'll be like the movies. It'll be like the books you read. But, darlin', you already know I never read a book I liked and this is as real as it gets. I jerked off to your body just because your tits shake when you breathe in your sleep. I licked your pussy and gulped down your juices under the bullshit guise of calmin' you down. Which you loved so much that you humped my mouth to kingdom come and squirted down my throat like a fuckin' hurricane. So you wanna kiss me, baby, I'll kiss you back. I'll kiss you back all you like but then we'll do the things that *I* like. And that's not gonna end well for you."

He's doing it on purpose.

He's trying to scare me, even though he's right. I *was* thinking I want to kiss him because I love him, and I want him to kiss me back after everything he's done to me. Because I have zero experience with guys, and he knows that. So I just wanted to take things slow for tonight.

I swallow before saying my thought out loud: "You're just t-trying to scare me."

"You think so?"

"Yes." I try to sound confident. "I'm not an idiot. I *know* the things you like and I'm not scared of them. But I—"

"Yeah, what do I like?"

"Eating my pussy," I blurt out before I lose courage.

He takes my features in—I bet they're all flushed and red—for a second before saying, "You think I'm just gonna eat your pussy tonight?"

I try to swallow again, but that becomes a hiccup and I tug on his hair. "As I said, I'm not an idiot. I know you'll want to do other things but I thought we'll start slow and—"

"Yeah, no," he says, his chest vibrating with his words. "There's no slowin' this down if I get anywhere near that college girl snatch that turns slutty the moment I lick it."

I tug on his hair again as my thighs clench. "Don't call it that. And you have to because I'm a virgin."

Something like satisfaction crosses his features, and the side of his mouth pulls up in a lopsided smirk that makes my belly clench in both desire and fear. "You are, aren't you."

"Yes, so we need to slow down and—"

He squeezes his arms around me. "Yeah, that's the thing, see. You know the color that riles a bull up, don't you?"

My heart skips a beat then, and whatever courage I'd gathered vanishes as I breathe out, "R-red."

He squeezes his arms around me again, his eyes flashing. "Yeah, red. The color of roses. The color of your cherry when I pop it. And it'll be the color smeared on your thighs and runnin' down my dick, when I'm done with you. So if you think that's gonna slow me down, then maybe I really should have mercy on you and tell you to go back to your books."

Fear pierces my chest instantly and I tighten my hold on him. "No, no. no. I didn't mean that. I—"

"But I won't," he cuts me off, whispering over my trembling mouth, and I breathe out a sigh of relief. "Because mercy is for men who haven't laid eyes on you yet and good for them, because if they do, that'll be the last thing they see. But my dick got hard the moment I saw you and only got harder the moment I sucked your pussy juice off your panties. So virgin or not, be prepared to stay on your back because I'll be workin' off my hard-on between those silky thighs for a long fuckin' time."

I think I came.

It's a shock because I've been so busy being scared and angry that I somehow forgot I was wet. I was so freaking turned on that I was creaming my panties, but I think I just flooded them. I feel my pussy fluttering in the aftermath; or maybe this is just the beginning of what's to come. But I guess that's what he does. He makes me so insane, so conflicted, and yet so alive that I don't know what to do with myself except fall for him even more.

He's my adventure.

The one I've been waiting for my whole life.

So I guess slowing down was never in the cards for us. I mean, he kissed me down there long before he ever kissed me on the mouth, so I should probably just accept my fate and rejoice in it.

"But you'll be gentle, won't you?" I whisper.

A puff of a breath escapes him. "I'll let you pretend I'm being gentle."

"Arsen, you're scaring me again."

"Shoulda thought of that before you decided to become my wife, dream girl."

My eyes pop wide. "You called me dream girl."

That lopsided smirk comes back. "Your name's Reverie, ain't it?"

"Yes."

"Like the dream."

I smile, but then it occurs to me: "Also, you forced me to marry you."

"Nah," he rumbles, his lips twitching. "I just forced you to sign those papers. You became my wife the moment you decided to open the door."

"You're such a—"

He shuts me up then and kisses me.

And I forget everything else but his mouth and lemonade. His soft and hot lips and that tongue that demands entry into my mouth from the get-go. If I was the old Reverie, Reverie from maybe even two minutes ago, I would've hesitated. I would've fought him before giving in anyway because he always makes me feel so good. But I'm the new Reverie now, his dream girl, so I open my mouth the moment he wants me to and let him take over. I let him touch the corners of me that no one has ever touched before. I let him lap and lick on the inside. I let him suck on my tongue and bite my lower lip until I moan and arch up against him.

I let him teach me things.

I mean, this is my first kiss and he's the one with all the knowledge. So I let him hoist me up, and I climb his body, my thighs going around his slim hips and my ankles crossing at his back. I let him knead my ass with his large hands and long fingers that stretch and pull apart my cheeks so roughly that I moan into his mouth.

That moan is a lesson, too, actually.

Because when I make noises into the kiss, it makes him kiss me even harder. It makes him take my lips into his mouth and suck on them like *I'm* the lemonade. Like I'm the drink he hasn't had in eight years, and that's true, isn't it? He hasn't kissed anyone in so long, hasn't felt the softness, the fullness of a woman, that my heart clenches in my chest. I start to feel selfish for asking him to slow down. What was I thinking? It's okay, though. I'll make up for it now.

And I do that by moaning harder, louder. By pressing my mouth into his even more, kissing him back even harder than before. I do it by arching my back and squeezing my thighs around him. By twisting and moving against him, dragging that place between my thighs they say is the softest part of a woman against the hard ridges of his abs, so he can feel more of me.

All of me.

And it works because he groans. His chest shudders, and for a few seconds, his breaths are so large that my lungs feel all swollen with them. Like there's too much air in me, too many beats in my heart, too much life in my veins. Too much fluttering and quickening in my belly.

Amid all this, he begins to walk without breaking the kiss. Which is good because I don't want to come up for air, and I don't really care about where he's taking me. I've ridden on a horse with him, been through hell with him. He's the most dangerous destination of all, and I'm wrapped around him like he's my safe space. Nothing scares me anymore.

So we kiss and kiss until he does break it.

But at least he doesn't set me down. He keeps me around his body, and so in lieu of his lips, I kiss his jaw. I lick his stubble like I wanted to do and suck on the sharp jut of his chin. I move to the side and suck on that soft place just beneath his ear, and this one makes him shiver.

Shiver.

My big, bad criminal cowboy husband *shivers* at something.

I'm so amazed by it, by this little weakness I've found, that I do it again and again until he growls and yanks my head back. I blink up at him and look at his face. It's all kinds of turned on. His cheeks are high and slashed with red. His eyes are hooded and heavy, and God, his lips look swollen.

Stung.

By me, the vicious little bee that I am. Except I probably look the same as him, my victim, all puffy and bitten.

"You tryin' to make me blow my load too soon?" he growls.

I flex my thighs around his hips. "It'll make you do that?"

"You lookin' at me all doe-eyed will make me do that."

"I know you call me college girl and—"

"You are a college girl," he cuts me off and tightens his arm around me.

"And you think I'm too y-young but—"

"I wasn't the one who wanted to slow things down back there."

I go to bite his lip then, for always interrupting me. "But I'm a straight-A student, you know. And I was just trying to learn a new trick to make *my husband* shiver."

Heat flashes in his eyes, and his jaw pulses with it. "You wanna learn new tricks, darlin', I'll teach you all the tricks to bring me to my knees. But tonight, it's my turn to make you jump and all my wife needs to do is ask how high."

"You—"

"Up you go, now," he commands.

I frown in confusion, but before I can ask what he means, he puts me up himself and deposits me on what I realize is a saddle. "Where…where are we going?"

He climbs up behind me, wraps his arm around my belly, and jerks me up to his hot, wildly breathing frame. "Somewhere I can make you scream and I'm the only one to hear it. Because I don't share."

Then he snaps the reins and we take off into the night.

CHAPTER TWENTY-FIVE

AGAIN, I HAVE no idea where we're going, but I don't care. Because he says the sweetest things in the scariest of ways, and because I'll go anywhere with him.

So I turn on my side, do what I wanted to do for the longest time while we were riding all last week. Kiss his pulse. His jaw, the triangle of his throat as I nuzzle my nose in it and fill my lungs with his scent. And he does what *he* probably wanted to do all last week: fist my hair to pull my head back and put his mouth on me.

I want to warn him then. Tell him that it's probably not very safe to ride on a horse while kissing, but again, I don't much care. Even if we crash and burn, it'll be the best death anyone could ever meet. Besides, the man I'm kissing is made of fire so even if we did burn, he'd save me. So I kiss him back as we ride, my eyes closed, my heart pounding, and I keep going until he stops the horse.

Only so he can get down and bring me down with him.

Then I'm wrapping myself around him again and fusing our lips together. I feel him walking and coming to a halt. I hear him unlocking a door that opens with a groan. I smell the fresh hay and leather as he floods the space with yellow light, still kissing, still connected. I realize it's a barn but different than the one we were just at, farther away from the main house. I see flashes of bales of hay, chopped wood, metallic tools as we keep going. Then I hear him climbing. I guess there are steps here and he's taking them, all the while carrying me in his arms, his boots thudding on the wooden treads.

This is when I want to take my mouth off him and get away. I want him to put me down because I'm me. I'm heavy. And I know he's carried me to places; he carried me back to the camp after the bear attack; he puts me on and takes me off the saddle all the time; and he's been carrying me all this while that we've been kissing.

But steps are different. Steps are harder.

My heart will perish with embarrassment if I hear him heaving and breaking a sweat. Which I realize is a lot of pressure on him when I'm the one with the problem so I try to push away from him, but he growls and grabs the back of my head, keeping my mouth pinned to his.

We reach the landing that way, fighting with our lips, and soon I find myself being lowered to what I realize is a little bed. Only then does he let me go. When I'm on my back and he's on top of me.

"I'm…" I say with sore lips as I open my eyes, my cheeks blushing. "I'm h-heavy."

His mouth looks sore, too, as he takes me in with dark eyes. "The only thing you are is perfect."

My heart squeezes as I shake my head. "I'm not—"

"Let me make somethin' clear to you because maybe it wasn't before," he cuts me off with another growl. "This is my home. This is my ranch. The bed you're lying on is the one I made last night but didn't sleep in because you weren't with me. Everything you see here belongs to me. Including you. Which means I'm the one who gets to make all the rules, yeah? And you're the one who gets to follow them. So if I say you're perfect, you better believe it. You better believe you're the most perfect thing I've ever seen, and instead of arguin' with me, you say *thank you*, all polite and sweet-like. Is that clear?"

I want to kiss him. And then I want to smack his face for being a dick about something that he could've said nicely. So all I do is nod my head as I whisper, "Thank you."

His chest pushes into mine with a satisfied breath. "Good girl."

His praise twists me into knots and I breathe out, "But I'm not c-calling you 'sir' or anything like that. So get that out of your head."

He roves his eyes over my features before rasping, "I can live with that. Sir ain't somethin' I prefer anyway."

"There *is* something you prefer?" I ask, feeling all kinds of young and naive again, wondering if sex is really that complicated.

His bee-stung, or rather Reverie-stung, mouth pulls up in a smirk and he leans down, his lips skimming over mine as he replies, "Daddy."

A shocked gasp falls from my lips, and he catches it with his mouth. I know he said that to scare me again, but I don't care. Because for the next several seconds, he makes me dizzy with another one of his kisses. Soon he breaks it, though, and untangling himself from the web of my limbs, he pushes off me.

Panting, I come up on my elbows and watch him walk back a few steps. I want to look around, try to take in the space we're in. All I can tell from the corner of my eye is that there are bales of hay stacked up to the wall here as well, but this space could also be someone's bedroom with an armchair in a corner. Not to mention the bed on the floor that I'm sitting in. But I'll explore it later because for now, I don't want to miss a single thing. So I keep watching him.

My husband.

And he keeps watching me as he unbuttons his shirt. One by one, those silver buttons on his denim shirt open and I see the sliver of his massive chest peeking through. I see his dark hair that I can't wait to feel on my fingers. Halfway through, though, he stops. I'm about to protest because my favorite part was coming up, his ridged abdomen and the trail of dark hair that thickens around his belly button. But before I can say anything, he reaches back and snags his shirt, taking it off in one go and giving me the glimpse of everything that I was dying for.

His boulder-like shoulders. The expanse of his chest, that eight-pack ladder, his tight, dark brown nipples. And that hair. All dark and springy. I don't even know where to look first so I look at all of it, in no particular order. Which is why I think I miss what he does next.

Unbuttons his jeans.

I'm only alerted to the fact that he's doing it when he lowers the zipper and that sound rends the silence in the barn. Or rather silence fraught with heavy breathing. *My* heavy breathing.

I see another peek then. Of darker, springier, much thicker hair beneath the open zipper of his jeans. I know what that is even though I've never seen it, not in real life. So I sit up. I clutch the sheet, press the heel of my palm into the mattress, waiting, and I swear I gasp when it finally happens.

Because when he reveals it, his cock, it slaps against his stomach with a thwack. And it feels like the loudest sound there ever was. Probably because his dick has to be the *hardest* dick there ever was.

Mind you, I have zero experience to make that judgment, but still I know his cock is *so* hard it has to hurt. It's thick and long, that's not even in question; I've felt it so I was expecting that. I was expecting his cock to be something that would need its own ruler, like my forearm—I mean that thing reaches up to his belly button—so I'm not really surprised to find out I was right. The thing that really gets me, that makes me clench my thighs and squirm where I'm sitting, is the fact that it's dripping.

Constantly.

It's all wet and glistening, the head, the length, the root even. And God, it's so darkened, a mix of red and purple and throbbing. Even as I watch it, I see a pearl of pre-cum oozing out and sliding down his rod, dripping down to his balls. Two heavy sacs that look all tight and just as ruddy as his dick.

"You're…" I breathe out, swallowing. "It looks like you're in… pain."

He brings his hand, his large, scarred, *beautiful* hand, down and squeezes his balls. "Yeah, this is what six months of dreamin' about you looks like."

I look up then, at his heaving chest, now all flushed just like his cock. His abdomen that hollows out with every breath he takes. His face, all sharp lines and needy angles. His entire frame, all large and dark and slashed with lust against the backdrop of the yellow light.

"Looks like torture though," I say.

His chest heaves and I watch him tugging at his balls again before he grips the length of his cock and starts slowly, oh very slowly, going up and down. "The most exquisite torture I've ever felt."

I follow his hand on his cock as he jerks himself off and starts walking toward me as I whisper, "Are you trying to sweet-talk me?"

"I'm a lot of things, darlin', but sweet ain't one of them," he bites out, pinching the head of his cock.

I tear my gaze off his length and look into his heavy-lidded eyes. "You can be sweet though."

"Yeah?"

"Sometimes."

His nostrils flare. "Good that you think so because this is all the sweet you're gonna get."

With that, he kneels at the end of the bed, all naked and glorious, his muscles flexing and bulging with his actions. And I blurt out, "This is our wedding night."

At my words, his eyes flash and flicker with possessiveness, making my skin break out in goose bumps. He grabs both my ankles and slides me closer as he growls, "Yeah and tonight, I pay for my crimes."

"Crimes," I whisper.

He leans over and places a soft kiss on my mouth. "Yeah, for every little crime I committed against you, your body." Another kiss as he goes to unzip my hoodie. "For druggin' you and kidnapping you. For blowin' myself over your sleepin' body like the horny, desperate ex-con I am."

He pushes the hoodie off and goes to remove my T-shirt, and I raise my arms without him telling me to. He takes it off and places another kiss on my mouth, and my hands clutch his shoulders. "I pay for every night I tied you up with rope instead of using my arms to bind you to me like I should have."

I'm shivering now, at his words, at his soft kisses. At him unhooking my bra and taking it off in the next breath. Before whispering against my mouth, "I tore off your wedding dress, didn't I?"

I clutch my eyes shut and nod, still hurting from that.

He cups my breasts and squeezes, making me moan. "And made you ride my gun instead of my cock like you wanted. Like you *deserved* for being my sweet"—a small kiss on my mouth—"slutty"—another kiss—"glorious wife."

"Arsen," I whimper against his lips.

And he swallows it with another kiss as he whispers, his hands going down for my jeans, "Your body's my crime scene, isn't it, baby, so on our wedding night, I pay for violating it instead of worshipping it like I should've done from the start."

I arch my back and he makes quick work of pulling off my jeans and panties. And then I'm naked.

I honestly wouldn't have known about it at all—which is a marvel in itself—if I hadn't heard the rustle of my clothes falling onto the floor. Because as soon as I'm all bare curves and rolls—another thing that I'm very chill about—he leans over and lowers me down onto the cool sheets, draping me with his body. I guess he was right when he said he's all I'll need to stay warm and covered.

Besides, he's doing the thing he said he would.

Worshipping me.

With his lips on my lips. I know everyone calls it kissing, but *this* is worshipping. He's worshipping my lips, sucking and sipping on the taste of my mouth like that is his religion, before moving down to the side of my neck. He spends some time there, around my pulse, doing the same thing, taking little bites of my skin, savoring my taste as my limbs wrap themselves around him. My arms go around his neck and my thighs hold on to his hips. And it's the most amazing thing I've ever felt.

My bare body tangled up with his.

My heels digging into the backs of his thighs, scraping against the dusting of his hair. My nails scratching his shoulders; his hard, leaking cock throbbing against my tummy. I'm so busy reveling under all these new sensations that I don't realize he's gotten down farther.

To my tits. Until he takes a nipple in his mouth and I arch up.

Holy fuck.

I didn't know how fucking sensitive my nipples are. Or how fucking sensitive my breasts would be when he lets go of my nipple and sucks on the flesh itself. It's like there's a direct line from my tits to my belly and down to my pussy. And that line is tugging with every suck of his mouth and every pump of his fingers as he squeezes my flesh.

So much so that I've completely come off the makeshift bed and now I'm hanging on to him. I keep scratching him with my nails as he sucks on my tits, plays with them, and I drag my wet—soaked—pussy along his stomach, the ridges of his abs, the thick thatch of his hair. I'm moaning and twisting and *leaking*, quite possibly as much as he is, my toes curling in ecstasy.

God, yeah, this is what worshipping is.

This is what a goddess must feel like. Cherished and devoured in the same breath.

But he's only halfway done because after he sucks on my tits, he moves down to my belly and does the same thing. I'm not going to lie; I'm the most conscious about my tummy. About its endless rolls and doughy flesh and impossibly pasty skin. But the second his mouth touches my belly button, I forget all about it and moan so loud that the roof seems to shake.

God, how is it that my belly button is so sensitive?

I'm about to snap my thighs closed and practically jump off the bed, but he holds me down. He grabs my hips like handlebars, his blunt nails making dimples in my flesh as he laps and laves at my rolls, eats them up like he's been starving for ages, for eight years, six months of which he spent dreaming about me, and I'm his first feast. My body and its abundant curves are his sustenance.

I swear to God, just that thought—the body that I always hated being his meal—makes me come. Or maybe it's the fact that while he's been feeding on my belly, I've been humping his chest. I've been writhing and grinding against him, and I've finally fallen over the edge. God, it's still so embarrassing, how easily he makes me come. So it's almost a relief that he's finally down to the place that's actually supposed to be this sensitive.

My still-pulsing pussy.

Although my relief is short-lived because gosh, I never stop coming. The whole time he's down there, eating me out, I keep climaxing. My orgasm stretches out like a coil of rope that seems endless. My thighs keep shaking. My belly contracts, and I'm undulating like a wave in the ocean.

And it doesn't help that he's making all these sounds. Back when he was sucking on my tits and my belly, he did groan and grunt, and it all felt needy and horny, *arousing*. But this is different. This is so much more intense and Jesus, *lewd*. He's slurping too. All unabashedly and with abandon, which gets me going even more. Like he's actually drinking from my pussy. Not to mention, his head goes up and down and side to side and his stubble scratches my inner thighs.

I think I pass out.

Or at least lose all concept of time and space. Because the next thing I know, he's rising from between my thighs and crawling up over my body. He's covering me once again, the length of his sweaty body pressing against the length of mine, settling himself with his hips between my trembling thighs and his hands framing my heated face.

"Eyes on me," he commands in a gruff voice.

I blink them open and try to focus.

"This is it," he says, his eyes looking all drugged and wild.

For the first few seconds, all I can do is take him in. His ruby red, *glistening* lips. I'm a little shocked at how wet his mouth looks, but then I glance at his jaw, at the actual droplets clinging to it, to his throat even, and oh my God, is that me?

Did I do that to him?

I bring my hands from where they were clutching the sheets in a death grip and cup his jaw on both sides. "Did I... Did I do that?"

Possessiveness is so thick on his features that it might as well be another presence in the air. "Yeah, my baby like to squirt."

"Oh no," I breathe out.

"Oh *fuckin'* yes."

I caress his jaw with shaking fingers. "But I'm sorry. I—"

His stomach hollows out with his breath as he rasps, "I'd drown a thousand times if it meant I'd get to taste your sweet little snatch on my way over to the other side. So your *sorry* is what I call my heaven and I never wanna come up for air, yeah?"

"Arsen," I moan, twisting under him, which is when understanding dawns. I know what he meant by this is it because his cock is *right there. Right* at my entrance. At my restless movements, his head brushes against my pussy and we both shudder.

He presses his thumbs on my cheeks. "You hold on to me now, yeah? This is gonna hurt and I don't wanna hurt you more than I need to. So you're gonna do exactly as I say and—*fuuuck.*"

That was me. I did that, making him break off mid-speech because I took matters into my own hands. I arched my back and put my hands on his ass, pushing him inside on my own. I'm pretty sure that wasn't what he was going to say, but whatever. I didn't want him to waste time talking and educating me when I needed him *in* there. When I needed the hard part to be over.

Namely, the taking of my virginity.

And it was hard, I'm not going to lie.

I jerk at his entry and gasp, my eyes going wide at the stretch. He curses before dropping his forehead to the crook of my neck. His breaths are gusty, creating a mist over the column of my throat. I blink up at the wooden ceiling as I wait for the pain to pass. It's like a sting, like a needle piercing through. Sharp in the beginning but now dulling out. When I think it's gone, I tilt my face to the side and whisper, "It's done."

He stiffens over me. Not that he already wasn't all rigid, but at my words, his frame snaps tighter and he looks up. "What?"

My hands are still on his ass so I dig my nails into the hard globes and reply, "You're in."

His eyes narrow farther.

"The h-hard part's over, right? Now it's all…it's all smooth sailing."

I swear I feel him throb inside of me and the pain comes back. Okay, so maybe it won't be all smooth sailing, but at least I'm not a virgin anymore, and everyone is always talking about how that's the most wonderful thing. Plus, I don't think I bled at all. So I'm sure it'll be okay.

Only he doesn't think that because slowly, he rises up from my body. He pushes himself up on his arms, his shoulders straining, looking like he's going to do a push-up. He looks down at me with what I can only call an angry expression.

Angry and aggravated, pained even.

Then, with flaring nostrils, he says, "If you think"—he comes down, his biceps bulging with the action, his torso pressing into mine, sort of pinning me down with his weight—"I'm *in*"—he pulls out of me a little, and my limbs tighten around him, refusing to let go—"then, baby, you're in for a very rude awakenin'."

Before I can say anything, he pushes back in and *holy fuck*, what was that?

I jerk as if electrocuted, my spine bowing with the kind of

stretch I've never felt before. I scream and thrash, or at least try to, but his weight is pinning me down and I moan, "Arsen, I—"

At the plea I don't really get to make, the pain lessens. And I realize he's pulled himself back and given me a second to breathe as he says, "Because that was just the tip."

I'm panting. "The t-tip?"

"Yeah. Remember the kind I told you about? The one that you give to a stripper for givin' you a lap dance."

"Uh-huh."

"That's not the one I'm talkin' about here."

"Arsen, please, I—"

"This is the other kind of tip and you've got"—he pushes back in again, making me moan and arch because the pain flares up—"about eight more inches to take."

My eyes go wide and I scratch his sides, my knees coming up on the bed. "But I don't think I can...take it."

His chest swells with his breath. "Oh, you'll take it."

"You won't fit. You—"

His dick throbs inside my pussy, and I moan again as he growls, "I'll fit. Even if it takes the whole goddamn night, I'm gonna make it fit."

I roll my head side to side. "It's t-too much. You're too much."

He leans down, his muscles vibrating, droplets of his sweat plopping down on my body, his bronzed skin glowing in the yellow light. "Yeah, I am. So this time, instead of being a fuckin' brat, you'll listen to me and do as I say, yeah?" He pulls back again, relieving the pressure. "Because as I said, you'll take it. You'll take every goddamn inch of my cock in your college girl snatch because I don't wanna imagine a world where I don't get to be inside of you. Where I don't get to be as fuckin' close to you as I possibly can."

Tears well up in my eyes and I nod. "O-okay."

His stomach hollows out over me once again and he clenches his jaw for a second. "Now, hold on to me and let me fuckin' do it right."

Nodding desperately, I hold on to his shoulders and get ready.

He breathes out a sigh of relief and pushes back in. This time, deeper, *so much deeper* that I can't help but moan again. But I'm not alone when I do it. He's right there with me, coming down over my body, framing my face with his large hands again and putting his mouth over mine so he can swallow down my painful noises.

So he can kiss them into moans of pleasure.

Which doesn't take too long, or maybe it does, I don't know. All I know is that he keeps kissing me and pulling out and pushing in, deeper and deeper with each pump. My thighs spasm and my belly cramps as he gains inch over inch, and I think I even bleed a little when he busts through my cherry. But after a while, it doesn't hurt too bad. After a while, he slides in and out like he was always meant to be there. Like his dick was always meant to slide into my channel and carve it and mold it to make space for him.

After a while, we're both so sweaty and our mouths are so swollen that we stick together. Our bodies fuse with each other, and I don't know where he starts and where I begin. I don't know if I'm the one moaning or if it's his noises. Or if I pull at his hair or if he's pulling on mine. Whose breaths are filling whose lungs or whose limbs are tighter. All I know is that we move as one. Our hips twist and slam into each other. My tits shake and his chest scrapes against mine. My heels dig into his back and his knees dig into the mattress for more leverage.

So he can go faster. So his cock can reach the parts of me that I didn't think existed. Or if they did, I didn't think anyone would be able to get there. Maybe this is what he was talking about back there. Being *this* close to someone.

Being this close to his wife. To *me*.

That's when I come. At this very thought. That he's *making* me his wife. He was right when he said he only forced me to sign those papers; I became his wife the moment I accepted my fate. And with his cock inside of me, my initiation is complete. I'm truly his now. Always. Forever.

Till death do us part.

So I fly over the edge and come all around him. My channel pulsing, making me moan out so loud that I drown out my own heartbeats. Not his noises, though. Because I hear him grunt and growl before he jerks over me, his hips losing their smooth rhythm and his cock throbbing inside of me.

I know there will be a lot of moments from tonight that I will remember for days to come, but I think the most memorable one will be him, coming inside of me. And then wrapping his arms around me and tucking his face in the crook of my neck, sighing.

Long and hard.

As if after eight years, he's finally home.

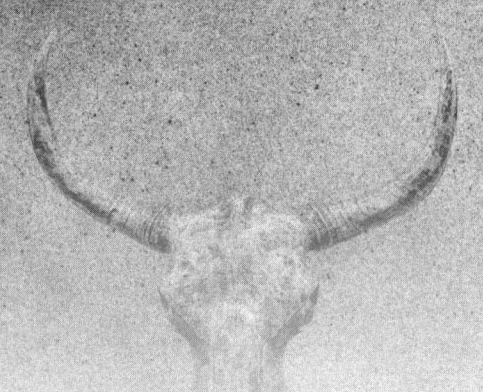

CHAPTER TWENTY-SIX

HIS BREATHS ARE the first thing I hear.

They are what wakes me up. All heavy and harsh, growling. I open my eyes and there he is, all lit up by the first light of dawn, kneeling over me. With his hand on his cock and his eyes on my naked curves.

My tits to be exact.

God, he's so beautiful like this. All sweaty and tanned, his eyes feverish, his chest heaving. His biceps bulging and twitching with his movements. Is that what he looks like when he jerks off over my sleeping body? As if he's in a trance, unaware of everything around him except me: The most beautiful thing in the world. The most tempting, the most *perfect*.

I know he said that to me last night, but I didn't believe it. Not until right this moment. Not until I caught him in the act. I don't think he knows that I'm awake. It feels like intruding almost. Especially when his other hand, the one tugging at his balls, creeps up and he rubs himself on the chest, restlessly, almost shaking with the sensation. Or when he rubs his throat like he's getting too hot and sweaty. So much so that his breaths are misting everything up and he has to wipe his mouth with the back of his hand.

Before he spits on the palm of it.

On the very hand he was rubbing his body with and *oh lord*, now he's using the same hand to blow himself. While his other goes down to his balls as he leans back some, thrusting up his pelvis. Humping the air, going up and down like he's actually fucking.

Like he fucked me last night.

In the back of my mind, I'm thinking how easy it is to think these words now, without blushing, without blinking an eye. I guess I'm *really* not a virgin anymore. I'm really his.

His wife.

And that thought makes me so horny, so restless that I writhe on the bed, twisting in need. Which is what alerts him that I'm awake and his eyes snap up to mine. I should look away now, shouldn't I? I should be respectful of his space, give him privacy, but the thing is I don't want to. I don't want to have any secrets from him, and I don't want him to have any secrets from me. And I know it's crazy, but that's how I feel and I want him inside of me right now.

Right this second, or I'll pass out from this lust.

I'll get crushed under its weight and the weight of his stare. So maybe that's why he says, all gruffly and low, "Touch yourself."

My eyes go wide in shock, but I don't think I'm as embarrassed at his request as I should be. Because first, he hasn't stopped touching himself. No, in fact, I think his hand has sped up and his jaw has clenched harder at being caught as if it's the hottest thing ever. Being caught by me while he's doing things to himself.

And second, I am horny. Even though I've never done this in front of anyone, it makes total sense to do it now in front of my husband. So keeping my eyes on him, I unclench my hand from my side, bring it down to my tummy. I widen my legs some more and twisting my hips again, touch my pussy. The moment I do, I feel an electric current passing through me because gosh, I'm so wet. So so *so* wet. I'm all slippery down there. And so fragile-soft. Softer than velvet. Softer than roses and more swollen than I've ever been.

I wonder what I look like to him right now. Probably all slutty and whorish, my legs spread and my pussy dripping. But it's okay. Not only because I don't mind being slutty when it comes to him, but also because what he's seeing, he's liking.

He's loving it because he's shaking.

There are great big shakes that run through the length of his body, making his hips jump and movements all haphazard. And his breaths have become all choppy and broken. I think more than my own fingers, he's the one who's turning me on, and he's the one who's going to send me over the edge.

I'm proven right when on a groan, he begins to come. His entire frame shudders and I notice his ruddy cock jump in his fist as it spills cum all over my body, my trembling belly and my shivering thighs. Even my hand that's playing with my pussy, and then I'm coming too. I'm moaning and writhing and arching right before his eyes as I feel his orgasm sliding down my fingers, mixing with my own juices, all hot and musky. Making everything even more slippery and drenched.

But it's not over because in the next moment, he falls on me. He knocks my hand aside and replaces it with his mouth. He latches on to my clit and sucks and sucks and makes me come again.

Harder than the first time.

Because he's not only eating me out, but he's also tasting himself on me. He's tasting his own cum and I think that's the hottest thing anyone has ever done to *anyone*.

No, I spoke too quickly, because when he's done lapping his cream off my pussy, he goes up and swirls his tongue over my belly, right where more of his cum has landed. He laps at it, and before I can contend with that, that he's eating his own cum off my body, he climbs up even more and in the next breath, grabs my jaw. Putting pressure on it, he forces me to open my mouth, and before I can gauge his intention, he spits his cum onto my tongue, making *this* the hottest thing I've ever experienced.

So much so that I moan, and winding my arms around his neck, I latch onto him and kiss him. He shoves his tongue inside my mouth, and then we're both tasting each other. We're both swallowing each other down. And our flavor mixed together becomes my instant favorite. We're sweet and tart. Like sugar and lemonade.

He stays kissing me for a long time, and I'm sleepy and satiated once again. When we finally stop, he tucks his face in the crook of my neck and breathes me in, his heavy arm draped across my chest, fingers playing with my hair all lazily and possessively. I swear he feels like a sleepy, satisfied beast right now as he mutters on a grunt, "Fuck, you always smell so fuckin' *good.*"

He drags his "good" out as if he never wants it to end. He never wants to stop smelling me. Biting my lip, I tilt my head to the side and rub my chin in his hair. "Were you able to sleep last night?"

He breathes out, his chest moving over mine, and grunts. I'm taking that as an assent, and I smile. "Will you take me to see those buttercups that you talked about?"

His grunt is accompanied by a nod this time and a whiff of my neck, as if he's smelling those flowers right now. And I smile even harder than before. "Is that what you did? Before? When I'd be sleeping."

He hums.

I keep rubbing my chin in his hair as I whisper, "You know, you could've just…"

He turns his head and looks up at me, his eyes all stoned. "I could've just what?"

I trace his jaw, his cheekbone, with my thumb and reply, "Fucked me."

I'm not going to lie that it does feel freeing, saying these things, talking to him in this way. But at the same time, I can't help but blush when his eyes go slightly alert and he roves his gaze over my face. "Fucked you."

"Uh-huh," I say, nodding, caressing his beautiful face. "I was right there, my pussy all open."

He flicks his eyes over my face for a second before his mouth lifts up in a lopsided smirk. "So what, I fucked you once and you're all grown up now. That how it works?"

I blush harder, but I'm determined not to back out. "Uh-huh. You've made me a woman."

"That so?"

"Yup." Then, I think of something better and say, "Actually no, you've made me a *wife*. So get ready for all the wifely things."

At this, he goes totally alert and maneuvers himself away from my body so he can prop his head up on his palm. "And what are these wifely things?"

I turn on my side, too, as I crane my neck to look up at him. "Um, let's see. Okay, starting now, I'm always right."

"You're always right."

"Yes. So if we fight about something, you're the one who has to say sorry first."

"Why is that?"

"Because you're the husband."

"So?"

I pat his jaw as if he's an idiot. "So it's always the husband's fault."

He grabs my wrist and squeezes it. "Startin' to see why that is."

I roll my eyes at him. "You always have to say yes to everything I want to do."

"Like what?"

"I don't know. Like, if I want to buddy read a romance novel with you, you have to do it."

At this, he frowns. "What the fuck is a buddy read?"

"It's when two buddies"—I motion to him and me—"read the same book together and freak out about plot points and such."

His frown thickens. "Yeah, no."

"Arsen. You have to. It's the rule."

"Fuck rules," he grunts. "I ain't readin' jackshit."

"Fine, whatever." I roll my eyes again. "But you're writing me letters."

He grabs hold of my wrist and keeps it pinned to his chest. "What?"

"You're still paying for your crimes, aren't you?" I remind him. "All those letters you wrote, they didn't even have your right name on them."

His eyes flick back and forth between mine. "Didn't have your name either."

I bite my lip. "So then, you'll write me a letter every day and you'll start with *Dear Reverie*."

"Dear Reverie."

"Yes, and then end it with *Your Arsen*."

His fingers flex around my wrist. "What else?"

"And then you'll tell me one true thing about yourself."

He watches me a beat before saying, "Yes, ma'am."

My pussy spasms at his words, and I lean up and put my mouth on him. He still tastes like me and himself, and it's so intoxicating, my favorite flavor, that I can't help but moan. And I guess we're his favorite flavor, too, because at my moan, he presses into my mouth harder and takes over. He rolls me to my back and settles between my thighs as we make out for the next several minutes. I'm so horny and desperate that when he breaks the kiss, I writhe under him, trying to rub my pussy against his hard dick.

But before I can beg him to fuck me, he pushes away from my body and gets off the makeshift bed. Coming to his feet, he starts to walk away when I come up on my elbows and call out, "Where are you going?"

My words sound breathless probably because I am that way. But also because I'm watching him move in his space, all naked. His back, broad and branded, is muscular as ever, rippling with so much power that I'm as stunned as I was the first time I saw it. It tapers down to his narrow hips with the cutest two dimples that I want to lick and poke my tongue in, that then give way to his ass, and I think I'm dying. I move restlessly on the bed, clenching my thighs as I stare at the work of art that is his ass.

So muscular and rounded. Like he spent all eight years behind bars doing squats. Or rather he spent his entire life doing squats, and maybe he did. My cowboy husband. Not to mention, his ass is tanned as well. As much as the rest of his body, and for some reason, that makes me even more desperate to bite into it, his honey skin. He goes to a small dresser at the far end of this bedroom-like space and grabs a bottle of water along with something else that I don't get to see. And then he's turning around and heading back to the bed, and I'm watching his dick.

That looks just as hard as it was last night.

All ruddy and leaking and the place between my thighs gets even wetter, if possible. I'm sure that I'm leaving a stain on his sheets, but after last night, I don't care. All I care about is his dick, hard and pointing up, throbbing and slapping against his hard abdomen, leaving a trail of cum on his dark hair and bronzed skin.

He gets to the bed and kneels down at the end. "Eyes up here."

Caught at being a perv, I snap my gaze up. "I wasn't staring."

"Somethin' down there says you're a liar."

I blush. "Well, you were staring too."

He drops his gaze down. "I was."

I follow it and gasp.

He's looking at my breasts. My naked breasts because I am… *naked*. I knew that of course. But I haven't thought about my clothes since yesterday, and while it was okay in the heat of the moment, now I just feel awkward. So coming up to my knees, I go to snatch the sheet, but he grabs my wrist. "No."

My cheeks are flushed. "But I—"

"Not a chance."

"I need to cover myself. I—"

His fingers flex. "Not from me."

There's so much possession in his gaze, so much ownership, that I wonder if every husband stares at his wife like that. If he does, then how does a woman not spontaneously combust, both from embarrassment and from lust.

"You have your rules and I have mine," he says. "And it's that you won't hide your perfect, absolute dream of a body from me."

I squirm and bite my lip. "But I'm not—"

"Don't," he commands, his jaw clenched. "Don't finish that sentence."

I swallow. "But I'm really not."

His chest moves with a large breath as he vows, "You *are* and before these three weeks are out, I'm gonna make you believe it. I'm gonna make you believe you're worth protectin' too. Because your parents did a shit job of that."

I ignore his "three weeks" decree and say, "I didn't protect my mother either. I hid behind the couch. I never even t-told anyone what happened—"

"You were a kid," he reminds me. "The burden of protection was on her, not on you. You did what you had to, to survive. You're a survivor, remember? Brave and magnificent. You did what you had to do to stay alive because of the monster who was your daddy."

"I—"

"And I'm gonna kill him for that. But I'm not broken up about your mother being dead either."

I shake my head. "I don't want you to kill him. I don't want you to kill *anyone*."

"Well, you've got no choice in the matter."

He's insane and I love him. I love him so much that my entire chest spasms with it. Breathing deep, I say, "Fine, I don't want to fight with you right now. But I need my clothes, Arsen."

"Yes," he says, squeezing my wrist again. "But not the ones you wore. I'll buy you new ones."

"What was wrong with what I wore?"

"You used them to hide yourself and you're done hiding."

I open my mouth to say something, but I don't know what I could say to that because he's right. I did use my clothes, even the ones Haven got me, to hide myself. I even hid myself in the dress I wore for him that day at the café. I guess the only time I haven't been able to hide myself was when I wore my wedding dress, the one he bought me.

"Is that why you bought me that dress?" I ask then.

"I bought you that dress because I was goin' to ruin your life," he says after a beat, his eyes dark. "And maybe through some miracle, there was enough goodness left in me that told me that I should at least buy you a new dress for the day that most girls consider one of the most important days of their lives. Even though it was all a sham."

This is when I realize something. I don't think he knows it. That the goodness left in him isn't there by some miracle. It's there because it's a part of him. It's a part of him that survived the night his life changed eight years ago. It's the part that survived the fire.

"You did it to yourself, didn't you?" I blurt out.

"What?"

I don't know if I should say it or not. But I'm going to. I don't care if I'm stepping on a land mine and it's going to blow me to pieces. "The brand on your back. You did it to yourself, didn't you? *You* put it on your back."

He did it as penance. I couldn't figure it out before, but now I know. I may not know everything about him, but I know this is who he is. I mean, he's ready to pay for his crimes against *me*. "You burned yourself for her."

His eyes flash fiercely. "I'll do anythin' for her."

The pain in my chest is so huge that it's a wonder I'm not crying out. It's a wonder my words are clear enough for him to understand. "It means revenge, doesn't it, that 'R.'"

He stares at me for a beat. "You don't need to know what it means."

Because this is all a sham.

I knew that. I *know* that. All these games that we're playing, they are just that, games. I'm not really his wife and he's not really my husband. I'll be gone at the end of three weeks. He said so himself just now. But at some point last night, I pushed it to the back of my mind. I lost myself in his kisses and his body. In his worshipping hands and penitent fingers.

But he didn't. He never did.

"What is that?" I ask, motioning to the bottle of water in his hand along with a white pill.

He follows my gaze and replies, "For your pain from last night."

Even though we're so far past it all, I still ask because I'm trying to make a point: "You're not trying to drug me again, are you?"

He looks up, and whatever he sees on my face clues him in on what I'm doing because he says, "Don't need to."

"Because you know I won't run?"

"No." He shakes his head. "Because you'll be gone at the end of three weeks anyway."

See? He never forgot. Not even for a single second. And I have further proof. There's something that I spy from the corner of my eye, lying discarded by the end of the bed. I motion at it with my chin. "And what is that?"

He doesn't need to look to figure out what I'm pointing at. "The wrapper that the condom came in."

"You wore a condom last night," I say in a flat tone, but I know this is an accusation.

I had no idea until I caught sight of the wrapper that he'd used a condom. I was so lost in him, so gone that I wouldn't have cared. I *didn't* care. It didn't even enter my brain; old Reverie would scoff at my carelessness. My new self, however, is enraged that he *betrayed* me in this way. That he thought I needed protection from him, and I'm going to explain just what kind of protection in a second.

"Yes."

"Because you thought I might be crawling with diseases?"

"No."

"Because you thought *you* were crawling with diseases?"

"No."

Of course not. He hasn't touched anyone in eight years. So I keep going, "Because you didn't want to accidentally get me pregnant?"

I'm super close to the reason, and his next clipped words hit the nail on the head. "Yeah and because I don't want anything connectin' you to me beyond these three weeks. *Because* I want you to be free."

"Where were you?" Peyton asks me sometime later, and I freeze.

It's still early in the morning, and I'm coming out of my room, or rather *his* room, that I'm staying in. After our less-than-pleasant conversation, Arsen said he'd drop me off at the mansion because he needed to do some things today, and I agreed without arguing because really, what choice did I have. I'm not sure if what happened there at the end meant that it was over. This thing between us. I can't even call it a thing, though.

It was just one night.

And some imaginary games that didn't *mean* anything. Besides, I've already forgiven him for everything he did. How can I be mad at him when he did it all for love? I know I always wanted a careful kind of love, a love different from my mother's, but I don't think what my parents had was even remotely similar to love.

Love is branding yourself in penance because you couldn't save the woman you loved. It's doing anything to exact revenge for her death. Love is what he feels for Annie even eight years later.

Love is what I feel for him. So he's off the hook. Anyway, I come back to the moment and reply, "In my room." Then, looking around, I add, "Are you sure we should be talking to each other without supervision?"

So apart from all the new information about the will and the Turner business, yesterday it was also decreed to both of us that we'll be staying in separate rooms, away from each other. That we are allowed to be in each other's company only if someone, either Haven or Axton, is with us. It's probably to keep us from colluding and coming up with our own plan of escape, even though we both agreed to cooperate with them. I guess taking chances with the Turners is not something the Graysons are willing to do.

I don't blame them, because Peyton *is* trying to plan something, but I also think it's bullshit. In any case, I wasn't aware that we were breaking rules first thing in the morning.

Peyton rolls her eyes. "What are we, five? I don't care about what they want. And I checked about half an hour ago; you weren't in there."

Yes, because Arsen dropped me off about twenty minutes ago, and since then, I've been taking a shower and getting ready for the day. In the clothes that Haven got me. So a pair of jeans, a T-shirt, and a hoodie. The clothes that I use to hide myself, the ones he didn't want me to wear. It doesn't matter now, though. I have other things to think about so I wave my thoughts away. "Probably because I was in the bathroom."

I hope she buys my lie, but when she does, almost immediately, it doesn't give me the relief I'd hoped for. Instead, it makes me feel shitty because I've never really hidden anything from her. Well, except how my mother died, but that's different.

"Why, is your stomach upset?" she asks sympathetically. "Because I think there was something fishy in those sausage rolls we had at the party."

I wrinkle my nose. "Peyton, focus."

She shakes her head. "Right. Sorry."

"Why are we meeting in the middle of the hallway, in broad daylight, when anyone can stumble upon us? We need to be smart, remember?"

She looks up and down the hallway before sharing, "I'm here because we need to go."

My heart starts racing because this is it, isn't it? This is where things turn even more dangerous because my best friend has a plan.

"Go where?" I ask carefully.

Once again, she looks this way and that and leans closer to me. "We're going to check out Marsden's study."

"What?" I exclaim loudly.

Which makes Peyton squeeze my arm. "Are you crazy? Lower your voice."

I slap a hand over my mouth before taking control of myself and whispering, "No, *you* are crazy. We're absolutely not doing that."

That's like walking into a lion's den. Because if we get caught, I'm pretty sure Marsden Grayson, with his mustache and his cold eyes, will eat us up and spit us out.

"Yes, we are," Peyton protests. "I have a feeling we're going to find all kinds of things in there."

"Exactly," I protest back. "Which means if we get caught, it's game over for us."

"We won't get caught."

"How do you know that?"

"Because you'll be my lookout while I poke around."

I breathe out sharply. I should've known. Because I'm *always* the lookout. And that's because I refuse to break into her mom's liquor cabinet or into a teacher's office. Or make out with the security guard at a club so we can get past him to see the band backstage.

"Absolutely not," I refuse.

Peyton gives me a look. "Do you want to find something on the Graysons or not?"

"I absolutely *do not* want to find something on the Graysons."

"So, what, we're supposed to just stay here and not do anything? We're supposed to just trust them that they'll let us go in three weeks."

Yes, because they will. They absolutely *will* let us go.

There's a stabbing pain in my chest at the thought that I somehow breathe through. But before I can say anything, she goes, "Because what if they don't? They're not exactly trustworthy, are they? They kidnapped us. They kidnapped *you*. He wrote you letters from the freaking prison so he could seduce you. Can you imagine the level of"—she searches for a word—"*evilness* that takes?"

I want to tell her then.

Tell her his reason, about his Annie, but I can't. Because it's not my story to tell, and I don't think he'll appreciate me blurting it out like that. And if I tell her about Annie, I probably will need to tell her about…*us*.

Or rather what happened between us last night, and I know for a fact that Peyton will lose her shit. Not because she's a Turner and she has any familial hatred toward the Graysons. But because she's my best friend, and I know she'll see this as me going crazy and acting completely out of character. In fact, it'll probably push her to get us out of here and me away from my evil kidnapper even faster.

As if to prove my point, she adds, "God, I could strangle him for what he did to you. Like, *actually, literally*. That alone is reason enough to find something on these assholes and send them all to hell."

So no, I can't tell her anything. Not until I come up with my own plan about what to do next. Because I think I may have to. The one that sets us *all* free, even him. From his past, from this revenge, from all this hatred and pain he has in his heart. Even if it's all over between us, there is no way I'm going to let the man I love suffer any longer.

First, though, I need to calm down my best friend. "Look, Peyton. I think we really need to be careful here, okay? I don't think we can be—"

"No, you listen," Peyton interrupts and looks me in the eye. "We can't trust these people, Riri, okay? We can't trust my family either. Who knows what they're going to do when they find out about this stupid marriage. I can tell you for a fact that my father will leave us to die here if it comes to that. So we need to look out for ourselves. We need to get our own leverage somehow. We *need* to save our own selves because no one is coming to save us."

I know she's right about her family, her father. Her father is like my father, and they'll both kill us themselves to save their own asses. But I also know that no matter what, *he* won't let anything happens to us. But since I can't tell her that, I sigh in defeat and ask, "How do you suggest we do this? How are you even here? You're supposed to be in the kitchen with Haven and she's expecting me to be there in like, ten minutes."

As soon as I made it to my room this morning, Haven knocked at my door. Thank God for timing. She'd come to wake me up for breakfast and said Peyton was there with her as well. I told her I'd be there after my shower. So if I don't show up, she's going to come looking for me. Plus, now Peyton is gone too.

"She thinks I'm with Axton," Peyton replies.

"What, why?"

"Because he wouldn't shut up about this bronco he's trying to break at breakfast, so I told him I wanted to see it. He took me out back to the barn, and I snuck away when he got too busy measuring his dick with other guys about who can stay on longer." Peyton shakes her head in disgust. "Why are guys so stupid? It's just a horse, for God's sake. No, actually, it's just the cowboys who are this stupid."

I open my mouth to ask her about the rest of the Graysons, but she gets there first. "And Marsden is dealing with something in town. I heard Haven say that to Axton. And I don't know where your husband is except he's not in the house." Then she adds, "Well, technically *my* husband but whatever."

It's hard, but I manage to not show any outward reaction at her words. Inside, though, my heart clenches. "And what about Rad?"

"Why would I know where he is? I'm not his keeper. I don't know what he does or where he goes. He doesn't even talk to me, remember?" Peyton says, a little too quickly and too defensively.

I look at her with confusion. "What? I just meant if—"

"Look, the sooner you come help me look, the sooner we can go back to where we're supposed to be, okay? So are you going to stand here and ask all these questions or are you going to come with me? Because I'm going in that study either way."

Her eyebrows are raised, and she has that dreaded determined expression on her face that means she's not going to budge. So I sigh again and nod, and we take off. I'm not sure how it happens, but we make it to Marsden's study without getting noticed.

As soon as we get in, Peyton bursts into a flurry of activity, buzzing around the room. I try to focus on my job of standing at the door and keeping an eye on things through the sliver of an opening I've left for the purpose. But it's hard because there's a wall to my immediate left that's full of Grayson family pictures that I can't help wanting to take a look at. I want to see him, how he was. Before. Eight years ago, even earlier. I want to see his life, his past. I want to see if he smiles when he's in pictures. Things that are important to him. Things that make him happy. I want to see him with his family.

I realize how mundane all of this sounds in the face of everything that's happening right now. But it's not really mundane to me. In fact, it's extraordinary because it has to do with him. I remind myself that it's over now, though, and I need to focus because this has to be the most dangerous thing I've ever done in my life.

Even more dangerous than falling in love with an ex-con hell-bent on revenge.

"Oh my God," Peyton exclaims, breaking into my thoughts.

Jumping, I spin around. "What happened? What's wrong?"

Peyton is looking down at a sprawling piece of paper on the desk. "I think I found something."

I know it's not really advisable to leave my spot, but I close the door and dash to the desk. "Found what?"

The piece of paper that she's looking at is a map, and from what I can deduce, it's the map of the ranch, the complete Rawhide ranch. Moving her finger over a zigzagging line that is apparently a creek, Peyton says, "I don't know but I think it could be something."

"Something like what?"

She flips the paper to reveal another map, this one slightly newer-looking, and somehow, she follows the same zigzagging line that she was following on the other map. She gets busy going back and forth between maps and pointing at things and tapping stuff here and there, mostly gibberish to me. Apparently when it comes to mischief and mayhem, Peyton is super detail oriented and I have zero imagination.

So I prod, "Something like *what*, Peyton?"

"Okay, look"—she points to something, a little box kind of thingy—"this little barn wasn't here before. They built it recently."

"O-kay," I say, nodding, trying to follow her fingers and all this back and forth she's doing. "So what?"

"So"—she does some more pointing—"there are a ton of such structures that weren't on their land twenty years ago, which is how old this map is." She points to the top to show me the date on the older map. "But on this one"—she points to the newer map—"they suddenly crop up and they're everywhere."

I slap my hands down on the maps and make her stop. "Okay, English, please. I don't know what it means. So they didn't have as many barns twenty years ago as they do now. So what?"

Peyton looks at me with shining eyes. "Do you remember, years ago, probably before we moved to Bozeman"—she pauses to let that take effect—"I came to you because I overheard my brother talking to my dad. About something related to Rawhide."

I try to cast my mind back, but only bits and pieces of memory arise. "Something about some stuff happening on Rawhide. And that your dad was looking into it."

But then, her family had always looked into the Graysons because, according to them, something illegal was *always* happening at Rawhide. So I don't know why this is important.

"Yes," Peyton, all excited, says with a nod. "It was something my brother found out. People were disappearing, Riri. All these men. And their trail led to the Graysons. To Rawhide."

"What people?"

She is even more excited at my question if possible. "This is the best part. They were inmates. Prison inmates."

A chill goes down my spine. "What?"

"I think the Graysons did something to them," she says, straightening away from the maps. "To these inmates."

"That's... I don't think that's—"

"Look, you said he stabbed a cop. In a courthouse, right? And he was like this big guy in prison, wasn't he? Everyone knew who he was. What if it *means* something? What if there are people in the police force that work for the Graysons and together, they're all involved in whatever is happening here on this ranch."

I open my mouth to say something but close it. Then I try again: "So what do these barns have to do with all of this?"

"It could be where they're hiding these men," Peyton speculates.

"Why would they... What do you think they want with these men?"

"I don't know." She gasps then, as if something just occurred to her. "Human trafficking."

"*What?*"

"That's what makes the most sense," she says in conclusion.

"How does it... I don't even... How did you even get to that point?"

Peyton looks at me with grave eyes. "Because they want money."

"Money."

"Yes." She nods, all calm-like, and I don't like it at all. "They want money, remember? *He* wants money. He said it himself. That's his bottom line. He's willing to do anything for it. Including kidnapping a couple of girls and using them to get more land. Land with oil in it. If they can do that, why can't they also run a human trafficking ring out of their ranch."

"Because this is…" I shake my head. I even put a hand on my forehead, trying to calm myself down. "Because this is really extreme, Peyton, okay? And because he…"

He doesn't want money. I don't know what he wants from that land, but it's not money.

Peyton narrows her eyes at me. "Because he what?"

My heart hammers in my chest. "He could be…killing these people? Or punishing them for their crimes or whatever."

It's thin, my lie. Also, how is killing someone better than trafficking them? Oh God, I don't know, but I didn't know what else to say.

Peyton gives me a look. "So you think the Graysons are vigilantes? That they're cleaning up the streets of Montana because their hearts are so big and noble and just?"

"I don't know, they could be. It makes more sense than *your* theory."

She breathes out sharply. "Fine, let's see who's right then."

"Okay, wait; now what is that supposed to mean?"

Her lips stretch out in a slow smile. "We're going to check out one of these barns."

My heart slows down. It almost stops at her crazy, *crazy* plan. "No."

"Yes."

"Peyton. *No.*"

"Reverie, *yes*. Because we have to."

"Why do we have to? Why…" I pinch the bridge of my nose. "You do realize all of this is *wild* speculation, don't you? These could just be barns. Because in case you forgot, this is a ranch. A ranch usually *has* barns. And—"

"Okay then, these are just barns. But if these are something more, then we hit the jackpot. And I'm not willing to let that chance go. Are you?"

Before I can respond, we hear footsteps and our eyes snap to the door. Peyton mouths *Shit*, looking freaked out, but somehow I go calm and grab her hand, pulling her away from the desk. She gathers her maps and we head toward another door that I scoped out as soon as we got here. And thank God for that because it's a bathroom, and just as the knob on the office door turns, we make it inside.

For some reason, I keep the door slightly ajar so I can peek out. It's Axton. And he's making a beeline to the desk. He rounds it, though, and keeps going until he reaches the big portrait on the wall behind the desk. It looks like a portrait of their parents. Axton removes it, and underneath is a wall safe with a keypad. It's clear he knows the code to it because the door opens with a click, and then he reaches in. I can't really see what he's doing in there, but I get a strange feeling.

A strange calling, if you will.

Probably like what Peyton felt when she wanted to check out the office. A hunch that says I need to be in there. I need to look into that safe. I have a feeling that all the Grayson secrets are locked up tight in that safe, and I should probably be sifting through it if I want to do something about this whole mess.

My thoughts break when Axton pulls out a bundle of cash. It's not huge or anything, a very thin stack, and the way he looks back at the door before pocketing it makes me think he's stealing. He slowly shuts the door, enters the code to lock it, and puts the portrait back up. Then he's walking out the door just as fast as he came in.

Twenty minutes later we stand in the kitchen with Haven, and my heart is still racing from what we just did. I'm putting my dishes away in the sink when I notice something through the window. It looks over the backyard where the bonfire was held last night, and I see a uniformed officer standing there along with Rad and Arsen. They're all talking peacefully, or rather the cop is talking to Arsen, but something about how the cop is looking at him has me all on alert.

I feel Haven stop beside me and say, "That's his parole officer."

I look at her to find she's witnessing the same scene as me. "But didn't he go see him yesterday?"

"He did."

"So then, what's he doing here now?"

She shrugs. "They can visit anytime. It's within their legal rights." Then, sighing, "But I have a feeling he's going to be checking in on him more often than he usually does with his other parolees."

My heart clenches when I realize why. "Turners."

She looks at me and smiles sadly. "Yes. They won't let him be in peace now that he's out." She adds, muttering, "God, I so want this to be over for him."

Me, too, because Haven is right. Just like him, the Turners won't let this go either. So I really need to do something and do it soon.

CHAPTER TWENTY-SEVEN

The Dark Stallion

THE TURNERS ARE the family of golden children. Blond hair and blue eyes. And Brecken Turner is no exception.

He sits behind his desk in the glass-walled conference room, his body stiff. Those blue eyes of his, much like his sister's, are narrowed into slits and on me. He was in the middle of a meeting when we walked in, me and Rad, and he understandably wasn't really happy about it.

Me neither.

I don't want to be stuck in a town packed with concrete buildings, much less *in* one such building crawling with people, *much much* less in a room where the same people have sucked out the very air. Even though they cleared out pretty quick, their smell and body heat still remain, and I can't wait to get out of here.

"How did you get past security?" he asks, his tone sharp, the syllables crisp.

While most of the assholes in Montana want to be a cowboy, there are a few exceptions. Like Brecken. He's the rare breed who wears suits and hires people to do his dirty work for him. Kinda like my own brother, but at least Marsden was a cowboy first before he became a landowner. He knows the land he owns, unlike Brecken.

I take a deep breath. "If I tell you, I may have to kill you."

A keening sound fills the room at my words, and I look to my right: Hank Turner.

Last time I saw him, he was lying on the ground in his front yard where I dragged him out of his bedroom. His face was smashed in and his body was covered in blood. He was half dead and barely recognizable.

Sitting here in a wheelchair, he still looks the same today. He's lost much of his weight, and his shoulders are hunched. There are tubes sticking out of his nose and his throat, and he looks like he's going to drop dead any second. The only reason he doesn't is because there's still venom lurking in his eyes that's directed toward me.

I broke twenty-seven bones in his body that night. They had to keep him in the hospital for over six months. I was already in prison by the time he got out, my trial and sentencing completed at an expedited pace. Not that I care about that. All I care about is that they had to reconstruct his jaw, but there was no saving his larynx. I crushed it too bad and damaged it permanently. Along with paralyzing the fucker for the rest of his life.

So now he has to pee in a bag and shit in a pan. And do this thing called esophageal speech. Where, apparently, you produce sounds using the muscles of your esophagus. I didn't know what it meant until I looked it up. I'm not gonna lie, it gives me great satisfaction in knowing I took away his voice when he was the one responsible for fucking with Rad all those years ago. Sometimes the universe can really be poetic.

Looking away from the pathetic waste of space, I focus on his son. "And I'm not here for that."

Brecken looks at me for a beat before glancing over to Rad, who as always has picked a corner spot to stand in with his arms folded and his eyes hidden beneath the brim of his hat. Coming back to me, Brecken says, "You're not supposed to be here. I'm sure your parole officer told you that."

He did. It's one of the conditions of my parole. Stay away from the defendant I beat up with a branding iron.

"I'm aware." I tip my hat back and settle in the chair. "Good move by the way, sendin' my parole officer to the ranch."

His jaw clenches. "I could call him right now and have you sent back to where you belong."

"You could," I agree. "But then how will you ever get what you need?"

"And what do you think it is that I need?"

"Money."

His jaw clenches again. "What do you know about it?"

"I know you don't got it."

He watches me for a few seconds before breathing out. "If this is another bid to get a piece of our land, I'm afraid you're going to be disappointed. We don't need your money."

"I know. You already have someone lined up who's going to drill on your land and bring you all the money that you need."

"So then I don't understand the purpose of your visit."

"The purpose of my visit," I say, continuing to look him in the eyes, "is to tell you that the land you're gonna drill on belongs to me. Or at least half of it."

"What?"

I throw the file I brought with me on the table. It skids across and makes it all the way to him where he slaps a palm on it to keep it from falling to the floor. He glances down at it for a second before looking up. "What is this?"

"Readin' material."

His jaw moves back and forth before he once again glances down and opens the file. What he reads in there makes his body go even more rigid, his fingers fisting the edge of the page. Then he slowly breathes out, lets go of the file, and reaches for the phone. Looking up at me, he presses a button on it and says, "Yeah, Beth. Can you send my father's nurse in? He needs to go home."

Another keening-like sound from Hank Turner that makes Brecken clench his teeth. He doesn't look away, though, and neither do I. Not even when the door to the conference room opens and those sounds become louder as the nurse wheels him out as she murmurs soothing words.

Then, Brecken asks, "Is this some kind of a joke?"

"Depends." I shift in my seat. "Are you laughin'?"

His chest moves with a large breath. "You're married to my sister."

"You could ask her yourself."

His breaths are getting faster, harsher as he once again reaches for the phone and dials a number. This time, though, he puts it on speaker and the room is filled with a loud ring. That a second later gets cut off by a shrill voice: "Breck?"

"Peyton?"

"Oh my God, Breck," Peyton goes. "Thank God, you called. Thank God; I was so scared. I was so—"

"Where are you? What—"

"God, Breck," Peyton cuts him off. "These Graysons are crazy. They've k-kidnapped me. They're holding me against my will and he"—a sob echoes in the room—"*f-forced* me to marry him. Gosh, I'm married to a *Grayson*, Breck. He said if I didn't sign the papers, he'd kill me. He said he'd make it hurt. Like really hurt, Breck. He said if I didn't listen to him, he'd cut my body into pieces and hide it all over his ranch so they'd never find me. And to prove his point, he killed a bear in front of me. He took off its head and chopped it into pieces. *Pieces*, Breck."

I have to clench my fists in order to suppress a sigh. I glance over at Rad, and I notice his jaw is ticking. I don't blame him. If he's really into her, he's in for a very rough ride. That girl is something else, a fucking hurricane. There's acting and then there's overacting.

"I'm so scared," she keeps going in her fake sobbing voice. "I'm so fucking scared. You—"

"Tell me where you are, Peyton. Where—"

"You have to save me. You have to get me out of here. Just please do whatever they tell you to do. Just—"

Someone on the line—Axton—cuts her off and commands, "Enough."

And the line goes dead. The silence that follows is filled with Brecken's heavy breaths and his anger. I can feel it. I can even relate to it. That's what I feel every time I think of a Turner. He slowly puts the phone down as he asks, in a voice that's gone really quiet, "What do you want?"

My jaw clenches. "You know what I want. I want your land."

"Apparently, you already have half of it," he says, his body almost vibrating.

"Yeah, but I want all of it. I want your share of the land too."

"Is that right?"

"You sign your half over to me, your sister goes free and that oil company you're meetin' up with in a few weeks gets to drill."

"And if I don't?"

"I take it all away. I fuck it all up. Your meeting, your business." I force myself to add, "Your sister."

My proclamation is followed by a silence so thick that when Breck speaks next, his voice sounds too loud and jarring. "She doesn't deserve this. She doesn't deserve to be a pawn in your game."

I already fucking *know* that.

I know she doesn't deserve what I'm dishing out. And no, I'm not talking about his sister; I'm talking about *her*. Not because I think his sister, the real Peyton, deserves to be toyed with, either, but because I dragged the girl, the one I *thought* was Peyton, through the fires of hell just for trusting the wrong man. Just for coming out of her shell for once in her shitty life. I'm the one who committed the crime all those years ago, but she's the one who got punished for it.

Even so, I keep my voice light: "That's up to you now, isn't it?"

"I didn't know."

"You didn't know what?"

"What my father was doing," he says, his eyes frothing with something. "All my life he groomed me to take over the business, this land, everything he and my ancestors ever built. When all this time, he was burning it to the ground. Just like he did with my family. My mother and my sister."

I don't know a lot about Brecken Turner. Except that we're about the same age and he thinks his degrees from Harvard and wherever the fuck else will help him run his ranch. But right now, in this moment, I almost feel sympathy for him; looks like he got screwed over by his father too. *Almost.* Because sympathy is for better men than me. I'm just a man burning with hatred and driven by revenge.

"Any particular reason you're sharing your sob story?"

He grits his teeth and draws his shoulders straight. "As I said, I didn't know. I had no idea he'd rigged the barn that night. Or that he was going to kill that girl. So—"

I spring up from my seat then, cutting him off. I don't need to hear this. I don't need to hear how he *didn't know* his father was going to blow up an innocent girl so maybe I should take mercy on him. On his family, on his *sister.*

"You've got until the meeting with that oil company to decide which way you wanna go. And trust me," I state before leaving, "if you pick wrong, I'm gonna destroy everythin' you Turners have ever built and I'll do it in a way that's gonna make your pathetic father look like a saint."

I'm going to destroy everything the Turners have ever built anyway. But he doesn't need to know that. Not until I *take* everything from them and make them *watch* as I blow it up and set it on fire.

Literally.

We're just out of the conference room when Rad grabs my shoulder and pins me to a wall by the elevators. Fisting my shirt, he growls, "He's right."

I know what he's going to say, and I'm really not in the mood to hear it. Especially not when I'm still getting over the jitters from being in an enclosed space again.

"Get off me," I say as calmly as I can.

"She doesn't deserve this," he says, ignoring me.

"Get *the fuck* off me," I warn, my hands fisting by my sides.

I don't want to punch him, but I will if I have to. He pulls me forward and slams me into the wall again. "You know which *her* I'm talkin' about, don't you?"

I try to breathe deep. Try to seal the cracks I feel opening up inside of me. "Rad, I'm not fuckin' around right now. You need to get off me or I'm not gonna be responsible for what I do."

"You think I'm scared of you?"

"I think you need to be."

He scoffs and shakes his head. "You fucked her."

I stiffen then. Or rather feel the fissures vibrating inside of me.

"Didn't you?" he prods.

Fuck it. I jerk out of his hold and grab *his* collar. I spin him around, and then it's me who's pinning him to the wall. "What'd you just say to me?"

His nostrils flare with an angry breath. "You fucked—"

I slam his spine into the wall, cutting him off. "Don't talk about her like that."

"And why the fuck not?"

"Because I fuckin' said so, that's why."

"Because she's your wife."

I slam him into the wall again. "Yeah. So you better show respect or I'll fuckin' kick your teeth in."

He leans toward me and growls, "No matter how many times you say it, it ain't gonna come true."

"You—"

"And you better tell her that too."

I push him into the wall once again. "What the fuck's that supposed to mean?"

"What do you think it means?" he taunts. "What do you think *she's* gonna think when you walk in there with all those pretty dresses you bought for her?"

Heat creeps up the back of my neck, but I don't let go of him. "She knows what the deal is."

"Does she now?"

"Yeah, she does. She knows this is bullshit. She knows none of this means anything."

And it doesn't. I bought these dresses for her because she needs something to wear, and I'll be damned if she'll use clothes to hide herself. She doesn't need to hide. She has *no fucking need* to hide. She's too gorgeous for that. Too beautiful. Too much like the sunrise you can't look away from, all bright and glowing.

Promising.

Fuck, exactly. That's *exactly* what she is.

She is *promising*, like the morning sun. That makes you think anything is possible. That makes you look forward to the rest of the day. That makes you *excited* for the future. She's like the morning sun dressed up as a dream. So I bought the dresses for her because she needs to shine bright like the sun you see in your dreams, not hide away in dark corners like she doesn't belong.

Nothing more; nothing less.

And yeah, maybe it did look like she was starting to get the wrong impression this morning, but it was probably because of what happened between us. Last night and again this morning. The mind-blowing fucking; only *I* get to call it that; no one else gets to use that word in regard to her. Actually, it wasn't just mind-blowing; it was life-changing. It was goddamn religious in its intensity.

Her pussy could be my religion, and I could be on my knees for it, licking it, sucking it, fucking it, *worshipping* it till the end of time. But that's neither here nor there. The point is that it was her first time. Even *I* didn't know how intense it would be so I get that she was confused, which is why I set her straight.

Not to mention, I told her things.

I told her all I could, all the ugly secrets of my soul. Or at least the ones that I could tell. But they were enough. Enough to make her understand that there is no future here for her. And my wife—*fuck yeah*, she's my wife, and I dare anyone to contradict me—is smart; she gets it. She might have slipped up once, but she's not like her mother. She won't be stupid and read into things again. She knows she needs to leave and build a life for herself, away from all this, away from me.

That every time I think about it, about her leaving in less than three weeks, it makes me want to break things and then tie her to myself is not something I'm focusing on. It's not something I'm *ever* going to do. I've already ruined her life too much.

"You don't think it means anythin' that you spent upwards of three hours in a clothing store lookin' for pretty dresses for a girl who isn't your wife, not really, but you keep callin' her that," Rad says, interrupting my thoughts. "When you've never, *not once*, set foot into a mall, *willingly*, let alone bought thousands of dollars' worth of clothes."

Who the fuck cares how many clothes I bought or how much I spent? I've got money, don't I? I could've bought her the entire store if I could carry it in my truck. Or if they had a good selection. Which is why it took so long to get everything.

Which is why I'm so fucking antsy to get out of here, out of crowded buildings and suffocating concrete because I've sweated and shaken too much for one day. Not that I'm going to share all this with him, because he's pissing me the fuck off.

"You need to—"

"And what do you think it means that you've been askin' about her daddy?" he keeps baiting.

"It means," I bite out, "I'm keepin' my promise of huntin' down the man who abused her."

"What?"

My jaw clenches for a second, just thinking about it. "Her daddy used to beat her. He used to beat her ma too. Not that she was a saint or anythin'. Instead of protecting her, her ma used her to protect herself. Egged on her daddy to beat on Reverie, rather than on her."

Rad's brow furrows. "Fuck."

"Yeah, so *my wife* grew up getting abused by her monster of a father and I'm lookin' into him because I'm gonna end his life."

And I would have by now. But the pissant is in Texas for some ranch business. And given that I can't leave the state, not when the Turners are keeping such a close eye on me, I'm going to have to wait until he comes back into town.

"You know," I begin, letting go of his collar and stepping away, "ever since you got up all in your feelings for that girl, you've turned into a real fuckin' pussy. And you know which girl I'm talkin' about, don't you."

I'm not surprised when it comes.

His fist. That he plants on my jaw.

I was counting on that. It was either him laying it on me or me laying one on him, and I didn't want to. Not after how I used him before. So riling him up was the only solution. Although I wasn't prepared for what he says next:

"And for a man who's doin' all this for love, you've got no fuckin' idea what love really is, do you?"

He's right. I don't. I quite possibly never did. Which is why none of this, these three weeks, these dresses, can ever mean anything.

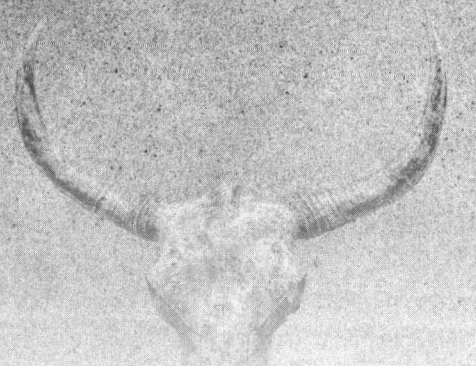

CHAPTER TWENTY-EIGHT

HE DIDN'T COME.

Not that I was expecting him to, but still. He didn't show up for lunch. Which was okay because he did say he had some things to do, and if what he said was true and not just an excuse to get me out of there after what happened this morning, then his absence was almost expected. I'm just not sure how to explain his absence from dinner once again when Haven lets it slip that she specifically told him she wanted him there after she slaved over the pot roast all day. Even Marsden showed up for it.

So basically, I haven't seen him or heard from him all day, not after that parole officer incident, and it's the middle of the night now. I think it's safe to say it's over and I should stop overthinking and overanalyzing things. It's only going to hurt me more. Besides, I have a lifetime to drown in my sorrows, so I should probably focus on what's happening right now.

Seeing as how my best friend is dragging me through the woods in the middle of the night with a map and a flashlight.

We've been walking for what seems like hours, but I'm sure it's only been about thirty minutes. I'm hot and sweaty and extremely anxious, cursing that I ended up here when I promised myself I'd never set foot in the woods again. Actually, no, I promised myself I'd never set foot in the woods without *him* to keep me safe. Something I'm only realizing now as I jump over yet another fallen branch. Woods are scary, but he's scarier. I need that and…

Don't think about him.

I crash into Peyton when she stops, her nose buried in the map with her flashlight shining down on it. I mutter my apology, but she doesn't care because a second later, she looks up and goes, "This is it."

I look at what she's looking at. "This doesn't look like a barn."

No, it looks like a cabin. The kind that he brought me to in the beginning. Although this one's more unkempt and dilapidated than his hunting cabin, with a broken railing and rickety stairs. There's also a couple of slats missing from the very small front porch. Not to mention, this one seems to be deeper in the woods than the other one was. Or maybe it just looks that way, with thick trees surrounding it in the middle of a half-moon night.

Peyton lowers the map, folds it, and puts it in a small pack she's carrying on her back. I still can't believe she came *this* prepared. When she shared her plan while we were cleaning up after dinner, I once again reminded her that she's reaching. That maybe we should find another angle because I don't think there's anything here.

But she wouldn't listen.

And honestly, after that crazy hunch about the safe that I got myself, I couldn't blame her. Which was probably why I didn't really sound as convincing as I could have. But I never thought she'd sneak out to my room when it was time to get me. She even brought a bottle of water—*two* bottles—with her in a backpack, as if we were really just going camping or hiking in the dead of night.

"I know," she says, almost skipping on her feet in excitement. "The only reason I picked it to check out first was because it was so deep in the woods. I thought if they were trying to hide something, they'd probably go for a spot like this."

"If they were trying to hide something, why would they put it on a map?" I retort, glancing at her out the corner of my eye, trying to sound all bold when my heart is racing in my chest.

"Maybe because they thought hiding in plain sight is better than actually hiding something," she retorts back, glancing at me the same way.

I let out an anxious breath. "So what do we do now?"

"We do what we came here to do," she says, walking forward as calm as you please like we're not doing anything remotely dangerous and troubling. "We check it out."

By that she means going around the front porch, spying a dirt-streaked window on the side, and going on our tiptoes to look inside. Well, she's at least being *a little* cautious about things. Even though I don't think there's anything here worth finding, I still don't want us to walk into something dangerous. Besides, spying or not, neither of us is supposed to be here at all.

Except as soon as we look through the window, I discover I was wrong and there *is* something to find. And for the first few seconds, all I can do is stare at it.

At a head.

I almost get a sense of déjà vu from Arsen's cabin, but it's not an animal head. It's the head of a *human*. A *human man*. That seems to be tilted to the side. Then I stare at the body it's attached to. Or whatever I can see of it, since it's sitting in a chair.

No, the body is *tied* to the chair, and it looks...dead.

"Holy shit," Peyton breathes out from beside me.

"I don't..."

I let my words hang in the air because I have absolutely no idea what I was going to say or what all of this means. I can't even believe that what I'm seeing is real. Before I can gather my thoughts, Peyton moves. She goes around me, heading to the front door, and my heart drops down to my stomach. I already know what she's going to do. She's going to try to get in. And I don't think that's a very good idea.

"Peyton," I call out, going after her, keeping my voice low but urgent.

"We have to go in," she says in the same tone and without looking back.

"No, we don't."

She's already climbing the stairs, her steps careful. "We have to."

"No, we do not." I catch up to her at the landing and snatch her arm, halting her in her tracks. "You need to stop and think about this for a second. We don't even know who this man is and—"

"Do you really care who this man is when it looks like"—she drops her voice to a whisper—"*he's dead*."

"But—"

"And what if he's not and we still have time to save him?"

"Peyton, I don't—"

She straightens her shoulders. "Can you really live with yourself knowing that you could've helped him but you didn't?"

No, of course not. But I was thinking more along the lines of getting help.

Which basically means getting *him* help instead of barging into a situation we know absolutely nothing about.

But of course I can't say that to Peyton when she already thinks the Graysons are trying to hide something. Plus, I mean…there *is* a man tied up in here. Even if there might be a good explanation for that, I can't think of a possible one right now. I can't think of anything except that I want Arsen, and I want him to tell me what the hell is going on. Since none of these things can happen and everything is over between us anyway, we have to take matters into our own hands.

I stare at her for a few seconds. "Fine, okay, *damn it*. But I think"—I look around—"we need a weapon. Or something. Something to protect us."

I'm not sure how helpful it will be, but we do need something, some semblance of protection, and after a few seconds of looking, we each find a broken wooden slat. She then uses hers to break the door open, the sound of which seems to echo in the quiet night, but we didn't have a choice because the door was locked.

And then we're in.

The only light is streaming through the dirty window so we can't really see all that much, but now that we're inside, we notice all the blood that's streaked and pooled on the wooden floor. Not to mention that the man's clothes, a torn shirt and a pair of pants, are stained with it too.

God, this is not good at all. Why would he be in here like this, all beaten up and bloody? Who *is* he?

We both rush over to him, and while Peyton tries to ascertain whether he's alive or not—he is, she says—I tackle his tied hands. It's a tight and intricate knot, one that Arsen would use to bind me, and my heart jumps in my throat. That doesn't mean anything, right? Lots of people can tie a rope the same way. I mean, there are only so many knots in the world that you can do.

Oh *God*.

Okay, I need to focus. While I'm tugging and pulling at the knot, Peyton is shaking him and tapping his cheek to wake him up. Just as I'm successful in untying the rope, he grunts. His shoulders move and his tilted head straightens up.

"Oh my God," Peyton exclaims, still bent over him. "Are you okay?"

He groans again, and just as I'm rounding to the front, his eyes blink open and I ask, "Can you hear us?"

Now that I'm not distracted by other things, I notice that his face is all banged up. One of his eyes is swollen shut, and there are bruises and cuts all over his face. What happened to him? His one good eye slowly finds focus and he stares at us, one by one, as Peyton says, "You're fine, all right. You're gonna be okay. We're going to help you."

He frowns, and his gaze moves over to me. Something about it gives me a bad feeling. I can't say why because his eye is all blood-shot and still foggy, but alarm bells are going off in my head as he takes us both in, all silently. Still, I swallow and assure him, "Yeah, it's going to be okay. Do you... Do you know where you are?"

"Yeah, do you know what happened?" Peyton adds.

He swallows, rolling his shoulders. At which point he realizes that he's free, and his good eye goes alert and my internal alarm starts blaring for some reason. Slowly, he brings his arms forward and looks at them. The ropes are still tied around his wrists in a loop, but he can use his hands just fine.

As he looks up at us, I pull Peyton away from him because she hasn't caught on to the vibe yet. He notices my apprehension, something scary flashing through his features that even Peyton can't miss, and slowly comes to his feet. We both take a step back, and he moves, keeping his eye pinned on us. I look for our forgotten weapons as we keep moving back, clutching each other's arm. The slats are now lying neglected on the floor and out of reach.

This is not good. Not good at all.

I think we made a grave mistake. Whoever he is, we never should've come in here. We never...

My frantic thoughts break when he lunges and grabs hold of Peyton's arm. She screams as he pulls her toward him and they begin to struggle. I run for our makeshift weapon, and grabbing it off the floor, dash to where he's trying to subdue Peyton and her kicking feet. It's hard to find an opening between two grappling bodies, but the instant his back is clear, I slam the wooden slat into his head.

But it's not hard enough.

It hardly slows him down. In fact, he pushes Peyton back so hard that she slams into the wall, and he then spins on his heel to come at me. I raise my arm to hit him again, but he easily takes the slat away from me and grabs my arms. I'm twisting and kicking to get out of his hold, but with me, he does things differently. He doesn't try to subdue me with just his grip; he puts his whole body into it and tackles me to the ground.

And fucking shit, it knocks the breath out of me.

My spine hits the wooden floor, and a howl of pain escapes me. But it's cut short because his weight is suffocating, and oh my God, he won't let me breathe. He's crushing my lungs and my arms. He then pulls my hands overhead and pins them to the ground with only one of his hands. While the other, *God, the other*, goes lower. It searches blindly for something that freezes my heart for a second. But just as his hand grazes it—the button of my jeans—Peyton lunges at him with a scream.

She attaches herself to his back and starts pulling at his hair viciously. While he's distracted with Peyton, I try to buck him off, but he manages to break Peyton's hold and push her away. Then he's back on me, and I think this is it. This is where all my nightmares will come true, things every girl tries not to dwell on but that are always there in the back of her mind. The R word that I don't even want to think about. He's going to force himself on me, and the only thing that comes to my petrified mind is him.

Not God. Not my mom. Definitely not my daddy.

"Arsen!"

I scream out his name like I did in the woods. Like that night, I keep chanting it as I struggle and scratch my attacker, even though I have very little hope of my forced-fake husband swooping in to save me. He doesn't even know I'm here. He probably doesn't even *care* anymore, and—

Suddenly, I feel a burst of air rushing through my lungs because the man who was crushing me with his body weight is gone. He's thrown across the room, and like someone breaking the surface after being underwater for a long time, I gasp and cough as I sit up.

He is here.

Like I conjured him up with my words. I chanted his name enough times in the middle of the night, deep in the woods, and now the devil is here. But I'm not afraid of this devil. I know he's here to save me.

I watch as Arsen prowls toward the man who's crouching by the wall, struggling to get up, his eyes full of fear. My husband bends down, grabs his collar, and jerks him to his feet. The man tries to push Arsen away. He even tries to say something, but it's all garbled because Arsen slams him into the wall before swinging his other arm back and hitting the man's jaw. He grunts painfully, but it's drowned out by Arsen's second punch.

After that, the man doesn't get to make sounds, because Arsen doesn't give him a break. He starts raining his fists down on him, and I'm so mesmerized by how fast he does it, how he keeps the man stuck to the wall with one hand while the other works nonstop to just anni-hilate my attacker, that I belatedly notice my husband didn't come alone. Rad is here, too, and Peyton is wrapped around him in a hug in a corner. At which point I come out of my fog and slowly stand up.

What just happened? How are they both here? And God, if he doesn't stop right now, Arsen is going to kill that man.

I think he probably already did because when Arsen started hitting him, I could hear the man making noises, even though they were mostly drowned out by his head hitting the wall and bone hitting bone, but now he's completely silent. He's also completely slumped over, his head is sagging like it was in the beginning, and his arms lie limply by his sides.

"Arsen," Rad grunts from where he's standing. "Stop."

He doesn't, though. It's as if he didn't hear Rad at all.

So Rad tries again, still holding on to Peyton, who's gone all fro-zen, witnessing the brutal scene before us. "Arsen, fuck. *Stop.*"

Nothing.

Arsen doesn't even slow down, so Rad thunders, "Listen to me, you're gonna kill him and—"

"Arsen," I call out then, my heart pounding in my chest. "Please. Just stop. *Stop.* Stop it, *right now.*"

I'm screaming by the end of it, my fists clenched at my sides, my body almost bent in half, but I don't care. He needs to stop, or he's going to jail. And he already did that once. He already went to prison for eight years for the woman he loved, and I'm not letting it happen again. Not for me. Not for *anything.*

I'm about to dash over to him, consequences be damned, when my voice finally gets through to him and he stops. His shoulders move up and down, his back swelling like waves with his heavy and thick breaths. After a long, tense moment, Arsen lets him go, and he falls to the floor with a thud. The sound echoes in my bones, and I can finally draw a full breath.

It immediately dissolves the moment Arsen turns around, his eyes homing in on me.

I was probably expecting to see anger. Danger and threats. And all of those things are there, of course. All of those emotions, along with a hundred others of the same variety, are lurking in his eyes, but what gets me is the fear. No, wait, it's despair.

Yes, it's fear mixed in with despair.

It's subtle, and I don't think anyone else has noticed it, but it punches me in the gut. I've seen it on him once before. Last night, in fact. When he talked about Annie. And I also know why it's there now. It's because he's stuck in the past. His brain went back eight years to when the worst thing that could happen to a man happened to him. He lost the woman he loved because he couldn't get to her in time.

He's probably thinking the same thing right now. His dark, gorgeous eyes have grief in them because of me. Because I was so stupid. I didn't think. I didn't...

"What the fuck happened?" Rad asks, his voice angry, but I'm not looking at him right now.

I only have eyes for my husband. Who stands there, his breaths still wild, his frame so tight it looks brittle. Like anything could shatter it instantly.

"I… We…" Peyton struggles, but again, I can't help her.

I can't look away from Arsen. I can't stop telling him with my eyes that I'm okay. He saved me. God, he *saved* me. Again.

"You tryna run?" Rad asks, his voice even gruffer than before. "That's what this was?"

My eyes go wide, and I shake my head, my answer for Arsen. I promised him I wouldn't run, and I didn't. This wasn't about that.

And Peyton confirms, "No! No, absolutely not. It's… We w-weren't running. We…"

"Then what the fuck were you doin'?"

Rad's voice is the loudest here, and it makes Peyton squeak. Not me, though. I'm steadfast. I'm unafraid. My spine is made of steel so I can lend strength to the man who looks like he once again lost everything.

"I… It's… *fuck*," Peyton begins again, but to no avail.

"Listen to me, yeah?" Rad growls. "We just saved your fool asses. So you tell us what you were doin' here or I'm really gonna fuckin' hog-tie you and leave you in my room."

"Fine, okay," Peyton snaps. "First, it's not Reverie's fault. She didn't want to do this. She didn't want to come here. *I* dragged her. It was me."

"Why?"

"Because." Another deep breath. "*Because* we don't trust you, okay? We don't fucking trust you. Can you blame us after every-thing?" I see her hand waving and snapping from the corner of my eye. "After how you forced me to fool my brother on the phone today. And while I don't care about my family, because frankly they're just like you guys, I do care about myself and my best friend. So we came here because we know your secret."

"Secret."

"Yes. You guys are hiding something," she accuses. "There's something fishy going on at your ranch and we came here to get proof of that."

I hear a sigh and the shifting of feet. Then, "Proof of fuckin' what?"

"Who is this man? Why was he beaten up and tied to a chair in a cabin in the middle of the woods?" Peyton asks instead of answering.

Rad responds with silence. But I see something flicker across Arsen's face. I can't say what it is, and honestly, in this moment, I don't care about any secrets. Maybe it's selfish, but I can't hold my silence and let him suffer.

"We came here because..." I say, keeping my eyes on him. "We know about the men. About them going missing, prison inmates. And we know somehow Rawhide is involved in their disappearances. So we came here because we wanted to find out what exactly was going on."

I hear Rad sigh again, but at the end of it is a growled curse.

"She's saying *we*," Peyton decides to chime in then. "But she really means *me*. As I said before, she didn't want to do this, and I mean it. She mostly came to protect me because I have a habit of making questionable choices. But I didn't think we had a *choice* but to look out for ourselves and get leverage against you. So if you want to hog-tie me, then go ahead. But don't blame Reverie. She's already suffered enough because of me. Because of this asshole here. She's not even a Turner. She's not *in* this."

Arsen's jaw clenches then. All this time, he hasn't looked away and neither have I. And it almost feels like we exist on a different plane. On a different dimension than the other two people in this room. Like we have a tether between us, secret and invisible. A connection no one sees, no one knows about.

And why not? It's because we're branded.

So my question—that Peyton already asked—is just for him. "Who is this man?"

And I know his answer is just for me. "An inmate."

My heart thuds. "An i-inmate."

"Missing."

Sweat is pooling in the small of my back, even though I feel cold. "Why was he…tied up and beaten?"

"Because he robbed a liquor store."

"And then fucked up his girlfriend," Rad adds, his voice laced with anger.

Peyton gasps.

"W-what?" I breathe out choppily.

"Only got convicted for the robbery, though," Arsen adds. "Didn't find out about the other thing until tonight."

"T-tonight?"

"When I beat him up and tied him to this chair."

I put a hand on my belly. "Y-you did it?"

"Yeah."

"Why?"

He stares at me for a beat before shifting on his feet. "Had a bad feeling about him the moment I saw him at the bonfire yesterday. Didn't think he'd be a good fit for Rawhide. Mars didn't agree, so I took matters into my own hands. Brought him out here, beat him like the little shit he is until he talked. And told us the truth about what he really did the night he got arrested."

My heart is beating so hard that it's a wonder I can stand all still like this without clutching my chest. "But I…I still don't understand what he was doing at the ranch. W-why would he be here in the first place when he should be in p-prison?"

Arsen's jaw starts ticking. And in the periphery, I see Rad looking up at the ceiling, sighing. Peyton is the one to break their silence. "What the hell is happening here? What's this big secret?"

Still staring at Arsen, I whisper, "Please."

His features tighten up at my plea. "Because Mars has a habit of pickin' up strays. Or rather caged dogs like this motherfucker here. The ones who commit crimes and get sentenced. Only instead of doin' time in prison, they pay their penance here. At Rawhide."

"Penance," I murmur, the word jumping out at me the most,

for obvious reasons. He's paying his own penance, isn't he, in his own way.

His features tighten further, probably because he knows what I'm thinking. "There's a system. A program. A series of hurdles they have to pass. To prove they've changed. To prove their loyalty to the ranch."

"Wait, what?" Peyton exclaims in disbelief. "This is… It sounds insane. Like a *training* program?"

Arsen still doesn't look at her, like no one exists except me, as he corrects her: "A redemption program. Rawhide Redemption. Mars picks men he thinks need a second chance at life, a clean slate so they can start over. Only they start over here. They make it out of the program, they get a new identity and a job at the ranch."

"But that's… That's crazy," Peyton repeats.

"It is what it is."

"But you guys are *lifting* people off the prison system, right? That's illegal. That requires some *serious* involvement from, God, I don't even know from what. Like, every level of the law. Judges, cops, lawyers."

Arsen's jaw pulses. "Politicians. Probably the reason why your brother and your daddy are so concerned about it."

But somehow *I'm* not concerned about all this. I should be, but I'm not. Not really. I have something else on my mind. "What happens to the ones who don't make it through the program?"

Arsen studies me for a few seconds, his features tightening once again. "They disappear. For good."

I somehow knew it. I'm having a hard time grasping what the program, this Rawhide Redemption, could even mean or what it entails, but I knew this. I *knew* if you didn't make it, you'd disappear off the face of the earth. But even *that* isn't something I'm concerned about. Death doesn't concern me anymore. I'm not afraid of it like I was before because of what happened to my mother. It wasn't love that killed my mother; it was my father. I know now that I'm in love myself. And while love is certainly capable of killing, there's something else that's more important to me: him.

"Do *you*..." I go to swallow, but my throat is too dry. "Do you make them... Were you going to..."

Kill him?

I can't say it, but he gets it. And locking his gaze tight with mine, he shakes his head. "Mars. He likes to do his own dirty work."

At last, ever since we arrived at this cabin and saw that man tied up through the window, I breathe in a sigh of relief. It's so huge that my entire body seems to have taken part in it. Even the tips of my fingers and my toes.

I don't care what's happening at Rawhide. I don't care how many laws these cowboys are breaking, I just don't want *him* involved in it. Not because him being a killer would diminish my love for him, but because I don't think he'd be able to live with himself if he took a life.

I know he wanted to eight years ago, but I don't think he'd ever be able to come back from that. The reason that goodness in him survived the fire was because he failed to get the job done, and God, I'm thankful for it. I *am* even if it makes me the most selfish person in the world, but I don't want my Arsen changing, not even a little bit. Which means it's even more imperative that I find a way to stop him. *He's* the one who needs to be set free from this anger, this fire inside of him, this pain that's making him do this.

"So now you know," he says finally. "There's your fuckin' leverage. Keep it. Use it. Do whatever the fuck you want with it." Then, for the first time since he arrived at the scene, he looks away from me and commands to Rad, "Take 'em back."

With that, he heads to the door. Or starts to, but I say, "It's my fault too."

He stops in his tracks, his gaze coming back to me, emotionless now. Hard and dark. But still I continue, "I thought...I thought it was over."

There's nothing on his face or his body that says he heard me, let alone understood me. But I have to keep going: "When you dropped me off at the main house. This morning."

Again, he gives me no reaction, and I'm hoping that'll change soon because I'm blushing like crazy. I can feel the other two people, Peyton specifically, staring at me with wide eyes. Wide, *questioning* eyes. But I can't think about that right now. I have to forge ahead. "And then you didn't show up for lunch or for dinner and... You never came back to the main house and I thought"—a deep breath—"I thought after what happened this morning that it was over."

Finally, he breaks his silence and utters one word: "Over."

Oh, thank God. At least he's *saying* something. It doesn't matter that he still looks detached from the situation, aloof and cool. I'm just glad he's *listening* to me.

I wipe my hands on my jeans. "Yes, I thought you didn't want me anymore. And Peyton's right. I didn't want her to do this but maybe somewhere in my head, I was m-mad at you. I was mad that...you didn't care. You didn't... You didn't think about me all day like I thought about you and so maybe I came here because I knew it'd piss you off. If you cared about me, that is, and... It was a mistake. I didn't think it through. I didn't think things would end up like they did. So it's my fault too and I..."

It is, and I'm only finding it out now. I'm finding out that when it comes to him, I'm all emotion and no thought. I'm all heart and no head. All love and no care.

"You what?" he prods, and I notice his stubbled—bearded now, actually—jaw clenching at the end of his question.

It makes me breathe easier, his outward reaction. "I'll do anything."

His eyes narrow a fraction. "Anything."

And again, my words come easier, more confident the more he lets his emotion slip free, even if it's anger. "To get you to forgive me."

I know what I've done. I know I've handed him all the reins.

And I know he'll make me work for it. I *want* him to make me work for it after how I scared him.

He lets a few moments pass in silence, and I can hear the imaginary ticking of a phantom clock. Then he moves his eyes. His dark gaze travels up and down my body quickly and almost dismissively. Then, "Thought I said I didn't want you to wear those clothes."

My heart drops a beat, and I have to breathe for a second before I can answer. Because I think, I *think*, I know where this is going.

"You did," I whisper.

His chest moves with a breath, swelling up, becoming larger, formidable. Like the rest of him as he decrees, "You've got five seconds to rectify your mistake and drop 'em on the floor."

CHAPTER TWENTY-NINE

THE OPENING OF the zipper of my hoodie is loud in this dark, abandoned place.

It might even be the loudest, louder than my own heavy breaths, if not for Peyton's gasp followed by her tirade. "You asshole! Just when I thought you had redeeming qualities!" I hear her struggle in the background, as if she's trying to break free of Rad and fly over to me. "Are you actually asking her to get naked? What the fuck is wrong with you?"

Arsen doesn't pay her any mind. Like he hasn't all this time. His eyes are mean and they're only for me. They watch me unzip my hoodie all the way before I roll my shoulders and take it off, letting it fall to the floor.

Peyton's voice echoes in the room again. This time, addressing me: "Don't do it, Riri. Don't you fucking do it." Then to Rad, "Let me go, you asshole. Just let me go to my friend. She needs—"

"Arsen," Rad growls over Peyton. "Stop this shit right now."

"Yes, *Arsen*," Peyton snaps in a mocking voice. "Stop this shit right now and let my friend go. She has *nothing* to do with this."

I want to correct her and say that I do. I may not be a Turner, but I'm a Grayson.

I'm his.

Even if for the time being; and somehow, I got in my head and forgot about that. I fucked up so big that taking my clothes off for him in front of the world doesn't seem like a big deal. Or rather only two people, but with my body issues, they might as well be the whole universe. I can't say anything, though. Whatever energy and willpower I have is going into fisting the hem of my T-shirt so I can pull it off.

"Don't you fuckin' do somethin'...you're gonna...regret later," Rad says with heavy pauses.

I don't think they'd be noticeable to anyone else. Except the people who know about his speech issues. And I think it's happening because he's angry on my behalf. Again, I want to say something, but I can't.

The only thing I see is Arsen. He looks so tall, so broad and large, standing in front of that dirt-streaked window. The barely there moonlight filters in and highlights the shape of his body, making him look like a phantom almost. A fever dream with a silvery silhouette.

The only thing I *feel* is his stare as it follows my fists pulling the T-shirt up and up and over my body. The moment it comes off, leaving me in just my bra and my jeans, my heart explodes in my chest and my skin is riddled with goose bumps. The night suddenly turns cold.

"If you stand here a second longer," he growls without taking his eyes off me. "Lookin' at my wife and what's only meant for me, I'll carve your eyes out." Then, glancing at them, "Goes for both of you."

Peyton screeches. Rad growls.

But I don't pay attention to any of them. I don't even care when Rad drags a screaming, cursing Peyton out of the cabin a moment later. I'm more focused on the fact that I don't feel cold anymore. In fact, the moment they slam the door shut, it feels like I've been licked by fire. And maybe I have been.

If his eyes are flames and his stare is more like a touch.

It travels from my face, through the fluttering pulse at my neck, along my heaving chest and shaking breasts, all the way down to my jeans. I know what he wants me to do, and so I get to it. I unbutton my jeans and without much thought, push them down. I take a step toward him, but he shakes his head.

Then, with the tip of his chin, he commands, "Lose 'em too."

"M-my bra?"

"And panties."

"I—"

"Anything, yeah?" he asks with flashing eyes.

My breath hitches. "Yes."

He shifts on his feet with a deep breath. "Let's get to it then."

Didn't I say he wouldn't make it easy for me? Even so, the actual act of stripping down to nothing makes me a little nervous. Especially when there's no reaction from him, not a single emotion or a sign that this is affecting him in some way. It's like walking barefoot on glass. But then I think about how he must've felt, what *he* must've gone through tonight because of my recklessness, and my arms reach back.

If he can walk through fire for me, I can walk on broken glass for him.

My fingers are surprisingly steady as they unhook my bra and lower the straps on both arms. Then, with another roll of my shoulders, I get rid of the garment and let it drop to the floor to join my other clothes. The instant his stare brushes my bare tits, my nipples go hard. So hard that it hurts. So much so that it takes effort on my part to not reach up and touch them. To not pull at them and twist them and just...*do* something to them. And it only gets worse when I go for the panties and pull them down my legs. Because I realize— as always, belatedly, because he makes me feel so many things and all of them at once—that my panties are wet. They're leaving streaks of cream down my thighs, making them glisten in the moonlight.

Now that I'm naked, he traces the shape of my body with his eyes, and for the first time I notice a little shudder in his chest. That small reaction from him puts me a bit at ease, and I take a step toward him again. But he shakes his head once more. This time, it's physically painful to stop, but I do it because it's his show, not mine.

"Get down on your knees," he commands.

I dig my nails into my thighs. "What?"

"And crawl to me."

"Crawl to y-you?"

"*Anything*, remember?" he growls, his face hard, his voice harder. "This is anything, darlin', so you either drop your knees to the ground and crawl to me like the sweet little wife you're tryin' so hard to be or stop wastin' my time." My thighs clench at his raspy voice and he keeps going, "Because you are, aren't you. Tryin' to be a sweet little wife for me."

I jerk out a nod, feeling a drop of my cum pulsing out of my core and running down my thigh. I *am* trying to show him I can be a good wife who listens to him.

"So again, let's get to it or get the fuck out."

As soon as he finishes, he moves. He heads to the right, his mud-streaked boots thudding on the floor as he drags a chair and proceeds to sit on it. With his shoulders straight and thighs sprawled, his hands resting so casually on them, waiting for me to choose an option: commit or leave.

But there's really no choice, is there? I'm not going to leave. I don't want to. And neither will I let him go, so I drop down to the floor and do as he said.

I crawl.

And every move I make toward him makes my pussy even wetter. It makes my thighs more slippery and slick. My tits are heavy and dangling, and my nipples still want to be pulled and played with. It doesn't even matter that the wood is hard and the floor is all dirty. Or that the dirt grinds into my kneecaps and my palms as

I move. It also doesn't matter that halfway to him, I realize there's a possibly dead body on the floor, lying in a pool of his own blood that I may have to pass through to get to him, but it's okay. It's the proof that Arsen came for me.

He *saved* me.

He keeps saving me over and over and *over again*, and he needs to know that. So when I get to him, I don't just stop at his feet. I go all the way. I get between his sprawled, jean-covered thighs, and as soon as I do, they snap into action and hug my sides, making a café of his body.

And God, he's hard. His muscles feel rock hard, harder and tenser than they've ever been. So I rub my hands up and down, trying to massage them as I look up. "You came."

His features flinch at my whisper and he leans over. He reaches for me, for my braid, and captures it in his fist as he rasps, "You called for me, didn't you?"

"Yes."

He tightens his fist. "Does that make you feel good?"

"What?"

"That I'm so fuckin' wrapped around your little finger," he says in a low, dark tone, his eyes flashing, "that I come runnin' every time you call me. Every time you scream my name, I bust down doors. I tear through woods. I beat a man half to death just so I can get to you."

I bite my lip. "I don't… I didn't mean to make you worry."

A puff of breath escapes him, and his fingers tighten even further in my hair. "Then you should've stayed in your bed tonight."

"My bed?"

"Yeah. You should've been sleepin' in it when I came to the room."

At this, my movements stop. "You came…you came to the room tonight?"

"Thought you'd run away." He licks his lips as his eyes rove over my features. "Thought I scared you after last night. Fucked you too hard maybe. Made you bleed too much, left too many marks on your ripe little body. Trashed that pussy so bad and now you don't want my filthy cowboy hands on it."

I dig my nails into his hard thighs and shake my head. "No, you didn't. You… I'd never run from you, Arsen. I—"

"Then I thought," he keeps going, his thighs tensing around me, "they took you."

My heart drops at what that means. "The Turners?"

"Thought they came for you," he says. "They did once, didn't they? They took everything from me. So they could do it again. They could and I thought this time around I'd fuckin' burn them to the ground. I'd kill every single Turner on that ranch until I found you."

My hands fly over to his face and clutch it like it's the most precious thing in my life. And it is. He's my husband, even if only for a little while. He's the love of my life. I don't want him to suffer. I *never* want him to suffer.

"Look, Arsen," I say, trying to get his attention because he looks lost in his own world. "I'm here, okay? I'm *with* you. You saved me. You—"

"Was almost out the door when Rad found me. Said we could look for you on the cameras. We've got cameras all over the ranch. Said I needed to slow down. I needed to think." Another puff of air that makes his entire frame shudder. "But I couldn't think. I didn't think there was time for me to *think*. Thought I was goin' to be too late like last time. Then I saw you on the screen, walkin' through the woods, headin' to fuck knows where, and I took off. I rode like I've never ridden before and just as we were comin' up the path, I heard you scream my name and I…"

"Arsen," I say, trying again to get his attention.

But he still doesn't give it to me, and his next words tell me why: "She died because of it."

"Because of what?"

"Rawhide Redemption."

"What?"

"They were lookin' into it. Back then. They were hell-bent on finding evidence against us. So they could use it and have our land seized. And when they couldn't find somethin'"—he pauses to take in a broken breath that swells his chest out so much that it must be painful—"they took her instead."

Oh God. Oh my fucking God. Of course he looked like he was stuck in the past. *Of course* he looked haunted. She died because of it, because of what we were looking into tonight, and I…

I give in to the urge to kiss him and lean forward. I'm this close to putting my mouth on his when his focus comes back and his fingers flex in my hair. When something brutal flashes through his eyes and he says roughly, "You're not her."

And I flinch, a sharp pain piercing my chest. But oblivious, he keeps going, his voice all grunts and growls, "But somehow it doesn't matter. Somehow, never been able to think straight when it comes to you. Not even in the beginning. Not since the first letter."

"What about the first letter?"

He watches me a beat before saying, "I did it."

"You did what?"

"Kept them away," he explains, his eyes flicking back and forth between mine. "All the other inmates."

My heart skips a beat. "From writing back to me?"

He licks his lips. "Wanted you to be mine."

"I *am* yours," I say, my fingers trembling on his face.

"And then I did the other thing too."

"What thing?"

"Sent that professor away."

I'm shaking now. Shaking and shivering and sweating with how *heated* he's making me with his confessions. "The one… The one who made a pass at me?"

His eyes narrow for a second. "The one I asked you to stay away from. But you didn't listen."

"*You* sent him away?"

"Got a cop to do it. To run him out of town."

"I don't… I didn't… You never said anything."

"Didn't want anyone comin' between you and me."

"Arsen," I whisper because I don't know what else to say. I don't know how to *handle* all the things he's saying to me. I joked about it, yes, but I never, not in a million years, could've imagined him actually doing something like that.

For me.

"Woulda pissed a circle around you, if I could," he goes on, his eyes flashing. "To keep all the motherfuckin' dogs away."

"You don't have to. There's no one except—"

"It don't make sense though, do it? You were a Turner," he accuses in almost an unhinged way.

"I wasn't a Turner," I insist. "I'm *not* a Turner. You know that. I'm—"

His eyes bore into mine then. "And somehow you turned out to be more dangerous than one."

I'm so confused. I don't know what he's saying. And he doesn't give me time to understand, either, because he goes, "You thought it was over, huh. This mornin'."

I swallow. "But I didn't want it to be."

He clenches his jaw. "You will."

"What?"

"By the time tonight ends, you'll wish it was over."

Fear pierces my chest, and I lose my breath. "What—"

He licks his lips again, and squeezing my throat, he commands, "Take me out."

"I-I'm sorry?"

Letting go of me, he sits back and for a few seconds, I feel so unmoored without his brutal hands on me. Without his fingers pulling my hair and holding my breaths captive. I watch him widen his thighs, sliding down on the chair so he looks as if he's draped on it like a king of some sort.

No, a cowboy who owns this ranch. This dark cabin with its dark secrets.

"Unzip me and take my dick out."

My thighs clench, and I feel another drop of cream sliding out of my pussy. It's so twisted, everything he makes me feel. Before I met him, I never knew fear could be a turn-on too. Or that discomfort and adrenaline, apprehension, could make your heart race so much that it feels like you're flying. You're riding like the wind. You're riding with *him* as you watch the world go by in the periphery.

When all I do is stare at him wordlessly, he growls, "Do it or fuck off."

My hands fly to do his bidding then, all eagerly but haphazardly. And he notices. Even though I'm focused on getting his jeans undone, which I'll admit I'm totally screwing up, I know he's watching me. And I know he's doing it with a challenge in his stare. Arrogance dripping from every inch of his burly cowboy frame.

"Little miss eager, aren't you," he taunts, his voice rough.

Blush paints my cheeks. It paints my entire body, and I'm thankful for the meager lighting. Or he'd be able to see me all red and hot and bothered. As it is, I think he can hear it in my breathless voice: "No, just your sweet little wife doing as you say."

His chest shakes with a gusty breath. "The kind of mood I'm in, it's gonna serve you well either way."

"W-what mood?" I ask, finally getting his button undone and moving on to the zipper.

"The kind where my *sweet little wife* pisses me off and I make her choke on my cock."

My hands stumble and I look up. "Ch-choke?"

His features are so tight in this moment, tight and brutal. "Choke."

"But I—"

"And trust me when I say, you wanna choke on it, darlin'."

I shake my head, fear winning out in this moment. "I don't."

"Yeah, you do," he insists, his eyes flashing. "You want me to choke you. You want me to make you gag."

"No."

"Because the more you gag on my big fat dick, the better it'll be for you."

"It won't be."

"Later."

My heart thuds. "Later?"

"When I put it in your ass."

"What?"

His eyes rove over my features, and he leans forward as he says, "You didn't think I'd make you blow me in a dark cabin and we'd call it a day, did you?"

"I didn't—"

He keeps studying me like I'm some novel object, his eyes almost fond. "You know, I should be used to it by now."

"Used to what?"

"How young you are. How innocent. All shiny and bright like the sun, sweet like a flower." Then, as if to himself, he mutters, "My sweet little wife."

"Arsen, stop."

He comes back to me. "Makes me almost wanna leave you alone."

"No, don't. I—"

"But I won't," he says, putting me at ease. "And blowin' me right next to the man I almost killed for you is only the beginning."

Once again, I forgot that there is a man next to us, lying unconscious because Arsen beat him up for me. And *again*, I don't find it as revolting as I should. I'm more concerned with what Arsen has planned for me. Which he tells me in very graphic detail.

"First, I'm gonna slide my dick in your mouth," he begins, as if we're in a class and he's teaching me "how to please your husband after you piss him off and make him almost kill someone." "And fuck your tight little throat. I'm gonna fuck it so long and so hard that you'll be lubing it up not only with your spit but also with your tears. You'll gag and drip on my cock. You'll make a mess. It'll be hard to breathe for a while but then, you should've thought of that when you went lookin' for trouble tonight, yeah? Anyhow, I know it sounds brutal and mean but as I said, it'll be good for you. So I want you to gag, all right, I want you to fuckin' choke and drown my big fat dick in your spit and tears. Because then, I'm gonna turn you around and put you on your hands and knees. Do you know what position that is?"

I jerk out a nod, my breaths already choppy in this moment, already hard to come by, and he hasn't even done anything yet.

"Tell it to me," he orders.

"D-doggie style," I whisper and then blush like crazy.

His lips stretch up in a lopsided smile as he praises, "Good girl."

God, he shouldn't say things like this when I'm so scared. Because then I become even more turned on and I don't know what to do with myself.

"You read that in a book?" he asks next.

"Yes," I reply, clenching and unclenching my thighs.

His smile widens and so does the fondness in his eyes, in his tone. "Yeah, you did. 'Cause my sweet wife is a college girl, ain't she? Straight-A student, no less. Except sociology though. That's how she got stuck with a no-good ex-con like me."

"Arsen, you—"

"And the reason it's called that is 'cause that's how dogs fuck," he says, making me flinch and somehow even hornier. "That's how all animals fuck, by the way. Don't know if they taught you that in your big, fancy college but you grow up on a ranch, you know these things. But the point is I'm gonna fuck you like that. Gonna mount you like a goddamn bull you reduce me to, all horny and randy and lookin' to get his nut off. But I ain't fuckin' that pussy, I'm fuckin' your ass." His jaw clenches for a second, but he isn't done scaring me because he goes on, "And if my dick felt *so* big last night, sliding into that tight little college girl snatch, it's gonna feel fuckin' monstrous goin' into that tiny little asshole. So do you understand what I'm sayin' to you? You wanna choke on my cock, darlin', so it goes easy for you when I fuck you in your ass later."

"But it's going to hurt," I blurt out.

At my words, his dick under my hands jumps. "It is."

"What if… What if I can't sit right for a while?"

"You won't be able to walk right for a while too."

My eyes pop wide. "No."

"Fuck yes," he counters. "But then again, I can't think straight from all the pain *you* put in my ass so it's only fair, isn't it?"

I squeeze his dick with my hands, but I don't think it hurts him like I want it to. "I don't even think it's…*made* for that."

"Oh, it's made for that," he disagrees, his nostrils flaring. "If you don't believe anything I say, baby, you better believe your asshole's made for my dick. You better fuckin' believe *every* hole in your juicy little body is made for my dick. And before this night's over, I'm gonna bang every single one of them."

My thighs clench again, and I know I'm wetter than ever before. It's just that I'm also more scared than I've ever been before. "Will you p-please be gentle?"

His eyes rove over my features, something intense and heavy in his gaze. "Yeah. I'm gonna have to. Because for some reason, the thought of hurtin' you makes me sick to my stomach. For some goddamn reason, I can't stop myself from comin' to your rescue. And I don't get why."

I do, though. I know, and despite all the fear and apprehension, I tell him: "Because we're branded, you and me. Because eight years ago, when your life burned down, you saved mine from the fire. So now every time something bad happens, I can't help but think of you. When he was…" I trail off and his thighs tighten around me as if hugging me; and his fingers around my throat hold me firmly as if lending me strength to go on. "When he was on me, all I could think about was you. Calling out to you, screaming your name. No one else. I knew you were the only one who could save me. Because you always do. Somehow, *someway* you always find a way to come to my rescue. And I know you don't like to talk about it and maybe you don't even believe it but I'm the girl who was never saved by anyone. No one has ever chosen me. Except you. So eight years ago, you branded yourself on my soul and maybe somewhere along the way, I branded myself on you too."

Our bond is forged in fire. It's forged in tragedy and violence. It's stronger than a piece of paper and all the laws of the world. It's stronger than even him and me, and maybe he feels the same way because as soon as I finish, he puts his mouth on mine and steals my breath away. We use each other to breathe. We use each other to stay alive in this moment, in this dark cabin.

This time, I'm the one to break the kiss off so I can finally finish what I started, unzipping him and pulling him out. And as soon as he's out, all hard and throbbing, wet like he was last night, I fall on him. I have to. I've been dying to suck him off, probably the moment I felt it in the small of my back when we rode on the horse together for the first time, so it's not really a surprise that I take to it like a fish to water.

He's all salty and musky, sweet, too, somehow, and the more I suck on his head, the more pre-cum he makes and the tastier he becomes. So I spend some time there, licking it, paying all my love and attention to it.

I'm not going to lie, though; another reason I don't go any further is because I'm afraid. Not of choking on him and gagging. It's good for me like he said. It's good to lube up his big fat monster cock before it goes into my tiny little asshole. I'm hesitating because his skin is so soft. God, it's like velvet. It's as soft as his cock is hard, and I'm afraid I'll damage it somehow. I'll nick it with my teeth or scratch it with my nails, so I'm careful. I'm gentle when I wrap both my hands around his root, and I watch my teeth when I lick his head.

But then, he puts his big palm on the back of my head and pushes me down, growling, "Deeper. Need...deeper."

So then I have to obey him. I take him in deeper. And when he curses and practically jumps off the chair, his hand fisting in my hair and his abdomen tightening, I don't think it's such a bad thing. Maybe I can scrape him with my teeth a little, too, and I can hold him tighter. And when I do those things, he curses louder and shoves his dick into my mouth even more.

I shed all my shyness and carefulness then. I should've expected that, though. When has my careful, cautious life worked out for me anyway? So I suck like I want to suck him. Like I should suck him, with abandon and freedom. And soon, I'm choking on his cock. I'm taking him deeper and deeper, ever deeper, and gagging on him.

I feel my saliva dripping on my chest, making my tits sticky, my nipples even harder. My pussy isn't a slouch either; she's dripping, too, making a mess of my thighs, making a puddle on the floor. Plus, his cock in my mouth is pulsing, throbbing, dripping as well. It's like the very air is swollen and heavy and liquid.

Dripping lust like rain.

And if he doesn't get inside me soon, I'm going to pass out. It's like he heard my thoughts, because the moment I feel I can't take it anymore, he pulls me away from his cock. I mourn its loss, but I know what's coming so I console myself.

Like he said, he turns me around and puts me on my hands and knees. And then he mounts me like the bull he is and sticks his dick into my ass. I know I'm saying it like it was quick, but it doesn't just happen right away.

He has to make it fit.

He has to make sure I'm okay. That's his main priority here. When he said he'd be gentle, he *really* meant it. He's even gentler and slower than last night. Although I *will* say that I ruined his plans by pushing myself onto his cock, but still. And what a stupid thing it was to do, because tonight I get to see, get to *witness*, how he breaks in a virgin.

How skilled he is at this.

He wants to break horses for a living, doesn't he, and he totally should because holy God, he's good. He's fucking fantastic at it.

He grabs me by the hip with one hand to keep me stable and then uses his other hand to guide his cock inside half an inch at a time. Every time he gains an inch, he pulls back to let me breathe. He shushes me and tells me I'm doing good. He tells me to push back and when I do, he calls me his good girl. He tells me that I'm amazing. That I'm so sweet to listen to him. To let him do this to me. And on a floor, no less, streaked with dirt and blood and cracks. He says my ass feels like heaven, all tight and soft, and that I'm slowly killing him.

I want to tell him he's slowly killing me, too, but all I can do is moan. And whimper and hiss when the pain becomes too much and breathe when he gives me sweet relief.

I don't know how long it takes for him to fit his entire length inside of me, but when he's done, we're both slick with sweat. The cabin is sweltering and I'm a mess of pain and pleasure. My pussy is throbbing, *aching*, and there's a fist inside my tummy, waiting to unfurl. Which is probably why it takes me a second to realize that there's another presence in the room.

I open my eyes and there he is. The man who attacked me and almost got killed for it. His eyes are open, or rather his one good eye that's also swollen, and he's staring directly at us. I tense, and of course Arsen notices because he's so in tune with me. He also notices why because I hear him growl, both his hands on my hips going tight with aggression. But before he can say anything, I surprise him: "It's okay. Let him watch."

I feel his fingers flex and I look back at him.

God, he's magnificent.

All broad and bare-chested. He unbuttoned his shirt at some point so now it hangs open, and every muscle on his torso is on display. It's bathed by sweat and the meager moonlight, and I don't think he's ever been more beautiful than he is now.

I look into his glittering eyes as I breathe out, my chest heaving, "He tried to touch me with his filthy hands. So he should know. He should see. How *you* touch me. How you make me go to pieces for you. How no one can do what you do because you're my everything. My husband, my savior. My daddy. If he hears me screaming out my daddy's name, he'll know not to touch me."

His features are all tight, his jaw pulsing for a few seconds. "You wanna save his life, baby?"

I swallow. "I wanna s-save *you*."

He slides his hand up my spine, bending down, his dick in my ass moving painfully, before grabbing the back of my neck and growling, "So you better scream your daddy's name loud enough to bring down this motherfuckin' roof and shatter his goddamn eardrums because if he forgets that you belong to me, even for a single second of his godforsaken life you're askin' me to spare, I'll end him." He squeezes my neck, smashing his thumb into my pulse. "You wanna save me, darlin', you put on a hell of a show and show him what a whore you are for your daddy. Lettin' me ass fuck you inches away from the man who thought he could touch what's mine, yeah? That's the only way I'm gonna be able to hold it together and not crush this little cockroach under my boots."

So I do that. I scream and moan and put on a show for him. I show him what my husband does to me. If I reduce him to a bull, an animal who only knows how to mate, then he turns me into his whore who lets him fuck her ass inches away from a dying man who watches the whole thing. I don't even think about what my body looks like in this moment. How my tits jiggle; how he *makes* them jiggle with his thrusts. How he grabs hold of my ass and makes it shake, and how every part of me is curvy and thick and awkward, because I don't feel awkward. In this moment, I feel beautiful.

I feel *his*.

Because he's losing it behind me. His hands are shaking. He's breathing hard. His thrusts are haphazard. No to mention, he *tells* me. He says I'm beautiful. That I'm the most beautiful thing he's ever seen. He calls me gorgeous, stunning, breathtaking.

He calls me his wife.

Somehow, it makes him go first. Calling me his wife or maybe it's the fact that my ass is just that tight. Whatever it is, he's the first to come and growl, "Mother*fuck*."

His dick throbs inside of me, lashing out cum, all hot and thick. Which is what makes me go over, and I come. I come so much, writhing and twisting, shaking, that my arms give out. But he catches me. He gently detaches himself from me and cradles me in his arms. He places soft kisses on my face before shedding his shirt and draping it over me.

I'm thankful for it because once the heat of the moment is over, I don't want anyone to see me but my husband. So when he kicks that asshole in his stomach hard enough to make him grunt before he carries me out of the cabin, I don't mind. I nuzzle my nose in his sweet-smelling throat and smile.

He takes me to Rebel and puts me up on the saddle before climbing on himself. I'm settled against him as we take off at a slow gait when I remember something. "I saw you."

His bare chest moves up and down with his breaths as he grunts, "Saw me where?"

I look up. "Through the kitchen window. With that cop."

The moonlight hits him just then, revealing his clenched jaw. "You don't need to worry about it."

"It was the Turners, right? They sent him."

"Told you, you don't need to worry about it."

"But Arsen, they're not going to stop. Especially now that they know what you're planning and—"

"They don't know what I'm plannin'."

My heart clenches in fear. He's right. They don't know. No one else does; only him. He has been lying to everyone except me.

Although that's not much consolation given he won't tell me anything more. And for the hundredth time since yesterday when he told Peyton and me about what he wants us to do, I think about finding a way to make him stop. Only I can't even imagine a way where he'll give up taking revenge for the death of his ex-girlfriend.

"I think we need new rules," I blurt out.

"Rules."

"About the whole marriage thing."

He at last looks down at me. "You mean where you don't think it's over just because I don't show up all day."

I frown. "Hey, it was a valid concern. It's not as if you tell me things."

His arm around my belly flexes. "What are the new rules?"

"We need to have at least one meal together during the day."

"Dinner," he suggests immediately, as if it was sitting on the tip of his tongue.

And I melt a little. "Where we *talk*."

His chest moves with another breath, which I think is his way of agreeing to it. "What else?"

I breathe out, too, feeling slightly better. "And you'll…keep me informed."

His brow furrows. "Of what?"

"Of things. Of your day. Like if you're okay. If you can't make it to lunch, things like that."

"Why?"

"So I don't worry about you." Before he can say anything, I go, "And don't you dare not tell me to worry about you because I will and also because I will punch you in the face."

His eyes circle around my features before he asks, "Is that a wife thing?"

"Worrying about her husband? Yes. You wanted a wife, didn't you? Well, you got one."

"Yeah," he rasps, his gaze still studying my features, his arm flexing around my belly. "I got one."

I refuse to let my heart race at his warm tone. "So? You'll do it?"

"How do I do it?"

"Um, use a phone."

"Don't got a phone."

"What?"

"Threw it away the moment we came back to the ranch."

"You threw away your cell phone? Why?"

"Don't need it."

I look at him like he's lost his mind. "You do need it. Everyone needs a cell phone." Then, "People had cell phones eight years ago too, Arsen. You know that, right?"

His chest moves with a sharp, short breath. "Didn't like it back then. Like it even less now."

"But—"

"Makes the world feel more crowded." He swallows. "Suffocatin'."

My heart clenches then. It's his PTSD, isn't it. God, why won't he just listen to me and do everything I tell him to do? His life would be so much easier. Then I wonder if all wives think that about their husbands.

I shake all these thoughts away and reach up to cup his jaw. "Okay, this is what we're going to do: You're going to get another cell phone but you'll only use it to call either Haven or Axton to let them know that you're okay. So they can let *me* know that you're okay. Just those two numbers. And the rest of the time, you'll keep your phone switched off so no one can bother you. Does that make sense? Can we do that at least?"

"We," he murmurs mysteriously.

"What?"

"You said *we*."

"Um, okay. So?"

He looks at me a beat longer before replying, "Nothin'."

I press my fingers to his jaw to get back his attention. "The world won't feel so crowded then, right? With just you and me."

His eyes bore into mine. "No."

"So you'll do it?"

"Yeah."

Smiling, I reach up and kiss him. My intention is a small peck, but he grabs the side of my face and prolongs it, and it turns into long moments of bliss, all my worries and angst forgotten. At least for now.

Once we break, he growls against my mouth, "Same bed."

I blink up at him, all dazed-like. "What?"

"We sleep in the same bed," he declares. "Every night."

I smile again and tuck my face in his neck, closing my eyes. "Okay."

Several moments pass with us riding at a sedate pace when I blurt out, "Oh and I want two letters. Tomorrow. Because you forgot to write me one today."

His response is to squeeze his arm around my belly and let me sleep. Which I don't wonder about. Not until he's putting me down in his bed and I blink my eyes open do I realize he's brought me to that barn again. The one we had sex in the first time. I'm watching him go around the space, close windows, and divest himself of his clothes when I spy something on the pillow. A piece of paper.

My heart jumps in my chest when I realize what it could be. I reach out for it, and I'm right. It's a letter. With one true thing. That he didn't forget to write me this morning.

To my wife,

Last night was the first time since I got out that I was able to sleep without nightmares. And when I woke up the first light of the sun spun your skin into gold and I remembered why dawn used to be my favorite part of the day.

Your husband

PS: I know you wanted me to start and end the letter differently but nothing felt right or true except calling you my wife and me your husband.

CHAPTER THIRTY

I SEE HIM from afar.

His skin shines under the afternoon sun, all bronzed and slick with sweat as he wields the hammer and knocks the boards off along the fence. Apparently cattle ran into it while grazing yesterday and damaged the already-damaged wood. So they're replacing the whole railing, and it's going to be a long day.

As I get closer to where he's working with a bunch of ranch hands, I notice other details. Such as how his back twitches and flutters when he raises and lowers his arm, and how his shoulders are all tensed with muscles standing in stark relief. How his brand that I traced with my fingers and my mouth last night looks so pale against the backdrop of his honeyed skin.

How every inch of him drips strength and power.

But how every night when I touch him, his skin shivers and his chest shakes. His breathing falters and his moans echo deep in my belly. I love his moans. All thick and low, rough like the caress of his scraped hands, and I've become quite an expert at eliciting them from him. For a girl who was a virgin until last week, I've taken to sex quite well and quite fast. Well, I always was a straight-A student, so maybe it makes sense that I'll learn all the tricks about how to make my husband weak in the knees fast.

I also know how to make him angry. Because I know he's going to be as soon as he sees me. And I'm right because the moment he hears the rumble of the ATV coming up the path, he turns around. Even though his hat is perched low on his head, I know when his eyes lock on me because he straightens up and I see his stubbled jaw clench. It's not as wildly stubbled or bordering on a beard like it was when we first arrived at the ranch a week ago, but it's still thick enough that it scrapes my thighs when he eats my pussy and gives me burns around the column of my neck when he kisses me there.

In fact, the marks he left on me just this morning—more like, at the crack of dawn—before he went off to work on the fence tingle at the thought. I should stop thinking about these things or I'll start blushing. Maybe I already am, and there's company all around. Besides, he's not really happy about my arrival, so I should probably think about that.

The ATV stops and I hop off. I paste a cheery smile on my face and wave *Hi*. Not only to him but to all the other men too. After only a week, I think I know most of them by their faces, if not by their names. I'm not going to lie, I do think they were criminals who were in the Rawhide Redemption program or whatever that thing is that I still don't understand. But I try not to judge them for a variety of reasons, including the fact that they've not once been disrespectful to me. Even now, as I'm coming up the path, they tip their hats or jerk up their chins before getting back to work, all polite-like.

My husband, though, walks toward me with a frown. Or rather he prowls with long, confident steps. Masculine and dominating. Everything about him is that way, isn't it.

Even the simple act of him taking his work gloves off and tucking them into the back of his washed-out jeans, where his black T-shirt is tucked as well, seems full of authority. Not to mention those hard slabs of his chest and the ridges of his eight-packs. That dusting of dark hair that I still haven't gotten over even after a week. How it thickens around his belly button and keeps getting thicker as it moves lower. Everything about him is just so sexy and erotic and…

"Eyes up here," he commands as he comes to a stop a few feet away from me.

I snap my gaze up and, as always, lie when I get caught: "I wasn't staring."

He takes my blushing cheeks in and rumbles, "Somethin' down there calls you a liar."

I blush harder and accuse without much steam, "You were staring too."

"I was," he admits unabashedly, his eyes flashing and dropping to my chest.

My nipples bead under the dress. "I—"

"Just don't like how other men are too."

I glance at the other men before saying, "No one is."

And they truly aren't; they're all back to working. I feel him move closer and I look back at him. He does it in a way that hides me away from them. He's always doing things like that, tucking me against his body, standing so close to me that I disappear in the breadth of his chest, the width of his shoulders.

Two days ago, there was another bonfire—something I'm coming to realize these people have frequently; a way for all the weary cowboys to relax and mingle at the end of a long day—and I was standing in a group with Haven, Axton, and Peyton, and he was standing on his own in a lonely corner, away from the crowd because he hates them. I was about to go to him because I didn't want him to be alone when he suddenly appeared beside me just because he didn't like the way Axton was staring at me. Something he told me later when we were in the barn, up in his makeshift bedroom, about to go to sleep.

In the *same* bed. Like the rule he made.

For the record, Axton was not staring at me. I mean he does stare, but it's gotten way better now.

"That's because they know I'll beat the shit outta them if they do," he replies back before jerking his chin at something over my shoulder. "It's the other asshole I'm talkin' about."

I sigh. "He isn't staring."

He glances at said asshole and his jaw hardens. "He is but he won't be for long after I'm done with him."

I move closer to him then and crane my neck up. "He's your brother."

And given that we're talking about Axton, I can totally picture him smirking at his older brother right now while Arsen glares at him. "And that's how I know he needs a big ass whoopin'."

"He does not," I say, putting my hand on his side. "He's just a kid."

He finally looks at me. Well, first he looks at my hand on his body, all pale-looking and small. So feminine that a current rushes through my body and I have to bite my lip. Then he stares at my mouth for a few seconds until I let my lip go before, at last, making his way up to my eyes. At which point, he growls, "He's your age."

"He's a year younger," I remind him. Axton is eighteen—although he does not look it at all—and I'm nineteen.

"Same thing."

"Well, age is just a number and good for you, because I'm more interested in his grumpy and *old* older brother," I say, going up on my tiptoes. "In fact, I'm married to him."

His eyes flash under his hat and he inches even closer, giving me a whiff of his musky scent. "What the fuck are you doin' here?"

"You know, you should be a little nicer to me."

"Yeah?"

"Yes. In fact, I think we should make it a rule. Be nice to your wife."

He hums. "I would, except I think she likes me mean."

"She does not."

"Well, depends on who you ask."

"And who are you asking?"

"My wife's pussy."

I gasp, looking around, digging my nails into his sides. "That was... I can't believe you said that. In broad daylight, no less."

It's his turn to smirk, tipping his hat up with his stupid long and sexy index finger, and I can see where Ax gets all his cockiness. They're both cut from the same cloth.

"Done worse things than talkin' about my wife's pussy in broad daylight," he drawls.

He doesn't want me to breathe, does he? Because he keeps taking my breath away with the things he says. Not to mention the things he does, and he is right. Talking dirty when we aren't in bed or in the privacy of his barn isn't the worst thing he's ever done in the light of day. Like, for example, a few days back, he woke me up with his mouth between my thighs just as the dawn was breaking in the sky. He made me come that way before climbing up my body and fucking me into another orgasm, all the while making me look into his eyes, even though I wanted to close them out of shyness. And when I later berated him for it, he growled, "New rule: You keep your eyes on me when I'm fuckin' you."

Not to mention all the other mornings I wake up to him fucking me or sucking on my tits, jerking off to them, spilling his cum all over my body that he then feeds into my mouth with his. I especially like the times when he wakes me up by nudging my lips with his dick, making me blow him first thing in the morning like he did today.

I clear my throat. "I brought lunch."

"Lunch."

"You called saying you wouldn't be able to make it and so I thought I'd bring it to you."

He did call. Because he has a phone now. He bought it the very next day after I asked him to. And like I suggested, no one knows his number so no one can call him on it. *And* he keeps it switched off the whole time and turns it on only when *he* needs to. Although I know his family hates that they can't contact him—I overheard Haven grumbling about it on the phone the other day—but I'm just happy he's taking a step in the right direction.

And so proud.

Anyway, according to our rules, we don't have to have lunch together, only dinner, and that's not always possible, either, because he's usually busy working and eats at the bunkhouse with the men. But I didn't like that he'd have to skip doing even that today, so I thought I'd bring him and the other ranch hands their lunch. And Axton was around to drive me.

Because technically, he's still keeping an eye on me along with Haven. Although I think after spending all this time with them, we'd probably be hanging out together anyway. Not so much with Axton because Arsen wouldn't like it, but still.

In any case, I usually help Haven around the kitchen and the house. I work with her in her little vegetable garden and help out with the chicken coop and stuff like that. And I actually kinda like it. Even though I grew up at the Turner ranch, I never did things like that. Maybe because I was busy hiding and cowering and nursing my mother back to health, sometimes myself. But here at Rawhide, everything feels…so bright and positive. So *safe* that I can finally enjoy things. Live my life.

How ironic that I'm able to do that while being their captive.

"Anyway, it's in the ATV. So I'm just going to leave it for you guys and go," I finish, breaking my thoughts and taking a step back.

But that's the only step I get to take because he grabs my wrist and pulls me toward him. And he does it so hard that I go crashing against his chest, my curves molding themselves around his hard, bare torso so easily, without much resistance.

I push away from him, though. "Let me go."

He brings his arm around my waist at that, keeping me pinned to him. "No."

"Arsen, I—"

"You hurtin'?" he rasps, looking into my eyes.

My heart skips a beat, and I drop my eyes down to the triangle of his throat. "No."

He dips his face down, his hat casting a shadow on both of us, trying to snag back my gaze. "You sure?"

I shift on my feet, blushing. "Y-yes. Can you stop…*looking* at me when you talk about it?"

"Another one," he responds, letting my wrist go and using that hand to pull my head back and making me look into his eyes. "You don't need to look at anything else but me when I'm around."

"That's absurd."

"That's the rule."

I frown and bring us back to the topic. "It's almost over now anyway."

"Tomorrow, yeah?"

"I can't believe you *remember*."

"When you get off the rag." He completes the sentence that I wasn't trying to. "Yeah, I remember."

God, my cheeks are burning now, and I can't help but grumble, "Don't call it that. And it's not as if that kept you…away from me."

I know it sounds like I'm complaining, but I'm not. After my initial reluctance about having sex while on my period, I totally got on board with it. Probably because it involved having sex in the bathtub, which he specifically put in that barn for me. I actually saw him haul that thing up the stairs with the help of a couple of ranch hands the first day my period started and then, for the past four days, I've been watching him fill that tub with hot water that, again, he hauls up himself in a bucket.

All because I woke up with cramps one morning and told him my periods are brutal.

The only way I can operate is if I'm pumped full of drugs and I have a hot water bottle at all times. He got me both. While also becoming my personal heater that hugged me when we slept while massaging my lower tummy, telling me all the stories about how he grew up on the ranch, about the time when he broke his arm trying to ride a bronc, which was when his dad took him aside and told him he either needed to stay away from an unbroken horse or learn how to break one. He decided to learn.

Heaven.

His voice, his arms, his back and tummy massages. Even his orgasms because they help get the cramps out. Oh, and let's not forget all the junk food he stocked up on, candies and M&Ms and cupcakes. So again, I'm not complaining. It's just that does he really have to talk about it when everyone's so close and I'm already so turned on?

"Told you a little blood won't keep me off your pussy," he says, breaking into my thoughts.

I narrow my eyes at him. "Can I go now?"

"Not until you tell me how to fix it."

"Fix what?"

"Got you mad, didn't I? Tell me how to fix it."

I hold on to my ire, even if it's hard when he's looking at me like that, all molten eyes, lopsided smiles. "One of these days, you need to ditch this husband thing and come up with your own ideas on how to fix things."

"Yeah, one day. But until then, how about my wife teaches me. She's the straight-A student between the two of us."

I shake my head at him, my lips twitching. "First, compliment my dress and say it's pretty. You're the one who bought it."

I still can't believe that he did that. That he actually went shopping for me. In a mall. Where there were *other people*.

I honestly didn't breathe for several seconds when he dumped all his purchases on our bed in the barn the following day. And told me he was going to burn all the clothes Haven got for me because I was allowed to wear only these dresses. I couldn't stop thinking about how excruciating it must have been for him. To be around so many people when he can't bear to attend a bonfire on his own ranch.

So I tackled him. Literally. I sprang up from the bed, all naked and jiggling curves, and I launched myself at him. I kissed every inch of his face and then his bare chest before attack-worshipping his dick. I say attack-worshipping because that's exactly what I did. I didn't give him a chance to utter a single word before I put him in my mouth and proceeded to love on every inch of it.

"It's pretty," he rumbles. "But it ain't got nothin' on you."

I shake my head at him again. "Say thank you for bringing my delicious lunch."

"Thank you for bringing my lunch," he parrots, "but it won't be as delicious as dessert."

"What dessert?"

"The one I'll have after dinner tonight."

Okay, I give up. He's so freaking good at this. Making me melt and filling me with butterflies. "Are you trying to sweet-talk me into forgiving you?"

He smirks, his fingers flexing in my hair. "No, ma'am."

Damn it. Instant puddle.

"I want flowers," I tell him.

"Buttercups?"

"Will you take me to see them again?"

They're truly so beautiful, and when he took me to see them last time, I instantly fell in love.

"Tonight."

"And then can we go to the creek after?" I ask about another one of his favorite spots on the ranch. "We can have a picnic like we did before."

"Yeah."

"And… Will you do that thing where you…" I trail off on a blush.

"Where I what?"

I go up on my tiptoes and whisper, "Put it between my…you know."

He stares at me for a beat before pulling me farther up and squeezing his arm around my waist, leaving only my toes grazing the ground. "You askin' me to titty fuck you, darlin'?"

Well, yeah. I guess I can't really get mad at him for being so blunt and dirty when there are so many people around us, because it's not like I have any manners. But maybe I just like pretending I'm annoyed so he can be all sweet like this.

I bite my lip. "Will you?"

His eyes drop to my mouth before he says in a low voice, "Seein' as I dream about your milkmaid tits even with my eyes open and while nailin' these damn boards up, it ain't exactly a hardship."

My eyes are wide. "Arsen, you need to focus on this. You can't be distracted. It's dangerous."

He hums, his lips twitching. He thinks it's amusing the way I worry about him, but seriously, he could get hurt. Then he rumbles, totally ignoring me, "Well, what can I say, the only thing that can save me now is ridin' your juicy tits like I do your juicy pussy."

I clench my thighs tightly at his words. "The amount of obsession you have with my 'juicy pussy' is a little insane."

"Nah, the amount of obsession I have with your 'juicy pussy' is *a lot* insane." He lowers his voice. "But then again, they don't call me the Dark Stallion because I'm sane."

First, very cool nickname. Second, when he told me about it, I could absolutely see why. Again, I didn't know him eight years ago, but I could see how he used to be before he got put away. And the more time he spends with his family and at Rawhide, the more the "old" Arsen comes back. All wild and cocky, *happy*.

"Just for that, two letters, please," I say, trying to sound stern but totally failing.

Him giving me a letter is the best part of my day. It usually waits for me under my pillow when I wake up for the day. A little folded thing that contains his thoughts, his truths, little things about him that make me fall in love with him even more. I hoard them like candy, so getting two of them in one day is going to be wonderful.

"Fine."

"You know, you were right."

"Yeah? About what?"

"When you said cowboys may make bad boyfriends but they make the best husbands."

Chuckling, he comes in for a kiss, but I stop him. "Everyone's staring."

"Good. That's how they'll know not to go near your mouth, once I've fucked it with mine."

It's been a week since that night in the cabin, and I still can't believe I did what I did. That I let Arsen fuck me in the ass in front of that man. Which again, makes all my shyness and embarrassment moot because I've done worse, so I let my husband kiss me in front of everyone and stake his claim.

It's not as if they don't already know. If me bringing him lunch wasn't already a clue, they all know that once Arsen is done for the day, he rides over to the main house. He interrupts whatever it is I'm doing—probably helping Haven in the kitchen along with Peyton—and drags me out by the arm without a word. He puts me on the saddle and then takes me to his barn where we spend the night before he drops me back off at the main house for the day.

So I know they know.

I mean, Peyton knew the night we broke into the cabin, and I'm not going to lie, I was a little nervous to see her the following day. I thought she'd consider this a betrayal of our friendship or be totally fired up about destroying the Graysons. She was to some extent. She was hurt that I hid my feelings about Arsen from her, and then she was mad about him being such an asshole to me. And said that if he hurt me in any way, she'd cut his balls off. But I calmed her down and told her that I had it under control. She didn't like it, but she trusted my judgment. Also, as it turned out, she had other things on her mind.

Namely, Raddison.

"He saved us," she said, looking out the kitchen window as if in a trance.

"Yup."

"I'm, like, beholden to him."

"I've never heard you use that word before," I pointed out.

"I'm in his debt," she kept going. "And he's a Grayson."

"Well, technically he's a King. Radisson King. He's their cousin but I see what you mean."

She turned to me suddenly then. "Do you think it would make me a bad sister if I said I wanted to thank him?" Before I could answer, she continued, "I mean, I don't care about my father but my brother…" She bit her lip in thought. "I don't know. He's just so much like my father or that's what it seemed when we lived together. But sometimes I think maybe…he's not? I don't know. I just know that I can't trust Breck. So do you think if I thanked Radisson for, you know, saving me, it would be like a huge betrayal? Well, more than the whole going along with the Grayson revenge plan?"

"First, you're not betraying anyone. You *should* be wary of your brother because all men in our lives have failed us," I said, excluding Arsen from my list. "You need to look out for yourself." *Plus, I'm going to stop Arsen from exacting his revenge anyway*, I added silently before continuing, "And second, how are you going to thank him?"

She turned back to the window. "I don't know yet. But maybe…"

"Maybe what?"

"Maybe I can get him to talk."

"Talk?"

"Yeah. He doesn't talk. It's not healthy. He should be able to air his grievances, right?"

I frowned at her. "Are you planning on being his therapist?"

She frowned back at me. *"No*, I'm going to be his friend."

And that was that. I don't think she's been very successful at it. Because every time she comes around in a room, Radisson leaves it. At the bonfire two days ago, he kept avoiding her like the plague, and she seemed really frustrated about it. I feel bad for her because I think for the first time ever, Peyton genuinely likes a guy. She may even like him as much as I like Arsen, and if that's the case, then God help her.

All of this to say, people on the ranch know about Arsen and me. That's not the point. The point is that sometimes I catch them looking at me with pity.

Especially Haven.

Who I think knows that I've fallen in love with my forced-fake husband. And like I thought the first day I came here, she probably also knows everything about Arsen's past with Annie. About who she was, how they met, how long they were together before everything happened. How he was with her, the woman he loved. Did he laugh around her a lot? Did he share all his secrets with her, his dreams? They had all these plans for the future, didn't they? Buying land, setting up his own ranch and business. So maybe he did laugh and share things with her.

Sometimes I think I should just give in and ask Haven. Instead of torturing myself with curiosity. Because it's not as if he's open about his history with her.

Every time I broach the topic during one of our dinner conversations, he shuts down. He tells me he doesn't want to talk about it and that I shouldn't worry about it, either, because it's none of my concern. But it *is* my concern. The man I love is still in love with his ex-girlfriend. He spent eight years in prison for her. He's going to destroy his life, along with whatever peace he's managed to find now that he's back with his family, working on the ranch, and trying to get back his passion for breaking horses, all in the pursuit of vengeance for her—and I don't even know what she looks like.

Forget the past; he won't talk to me about his future, what he plans to do once all of this is over. We even had a big fight about it where he kept going on about all the wonderful things I'll do once I leave in one week and get far away from Black Rock and everything that's tainted in this town including him. But when I asked him about his plans, he shut me down. Fed me the same crap about it not being my business.

That freedom is for me but not for him.

I don't get it. How long is he going to punish himself for her death? What will be enough if eight years in prison and even revenge don't seem to be?

He even had the audacity to tell me I shouldn't feel guilty about my mother's death. But I do, even though rationally, I believe him—that I was just a child and I couldn't have done anything. He told me if I hadn't saved myself, we wouldn't be doing what we were doing right then. And then he proceeded to show me what that was: putting me on my tummy, arching my hips up, and sliding into my ass. All the while he fucked me, he made me say things; and if I refused, he'd smack my ass and make me say it anyway:

"My husband is right."

"My husband is so happy I'm alive."

"My husband is fucking ecstatic that he gets to fuck my juicy little asshole whenever he wants. And if I keep whining about things like that, he'll fuck my ass twice every single day until I get it through my head that I'm precious. And I should be protected at all costs."

God, he's so infuriating and sweet, and I just want to shake him. Anyway, the only reason I haven't yet gone to Haven is because I don't want to betray his trust.

Which is why a few days later, I do what I do.

I realize this is a breach of his trust as well. But it's been almost two weeks since we came to the ranch. Time's running out, and I'm no closer to finding a way to stop all this. I don't even know if what

I'm doing is going to help me in that regard, but if I don't do it, I *know* I will regret it.

"You know my brothers will kill me for this, yeah?" Axton grumbles, entering numbers on the safe keypad.

"You'll be fine," I tell him, looking toward the door of Marsden's office.

"Arsen's makin' me muck stalls every day of the week just 'cause I stared at you too long."

"So maybe don't stare at me then."

His eyes, almost as dark as those of his two brothers, fall to my chest for a second. "Hard to do with you lookin' like that."

"Hey." I smack his arm. "I'm your sister-in-law."

He looks up before smirking. "Yeah, you wish."

"Why are you such a cocky asshole?"

"I'm a cowboy, baby," he drawls, tipping his hat and finally getting the safe open. "It's my job to be a cocky asshole."

I roll my eyes at him.

"There," he goes. "Have at it. Just know you're enterin' sacred territory."

"You stole money from your sacred territory."

"Cash is different. Ain't never touched nothin' else in there except that."

I woke up with a mission this morning. Somehow I was going to do *something* toward my goal, and since I haven't been able to stop thinking about this safe I saw Axton break into days ago, I hunted him down and blackmailed him into helping me. I told him if he didn't help me break into the safe, I'd tell everyone about the money he stole.

Of course, Axton was less than graceful. So then I told him the truth. Everything. Including that I loved his brother and I wanted him to be safe.

It was a big risk, but I knew he'd cave. He may be an asshole, but Axton, like the rest of this family, loves Arsen. They all want him to be happy. They all want him to move on. So here we are, sneaking into Marsden's office when everyone else, including Peyton and Haven, are busy elsewhere. I root around the safe in desperation while Axton stands beside me. He asks me what it is I'm hoping to find in there, and I tell him I don't know yet. All I know is that I have to try. But so far it's all a bunch of useless crap.

Until I find a thick manila folder.

I'm expecting it to be more useless crap, but my heart stops the moment I see the letters written in bold with a photograph of a stunning brunette: Annie Cassidy.

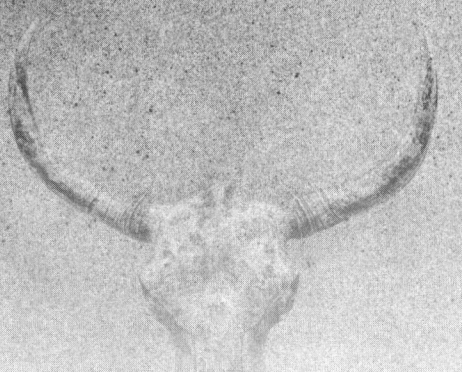

CHAPTER THIRTY-ONE

I HAVEN'T BEEN very brave in my life.

I'd always hide when my daddy came around. When he did catch me, I'd cower and crouch. I'd beg him to leave me alone. I'd beg him to leave my mother alone. I never just stood up and said enough. Granted, I was a child, but even when we left Wildfire and I became relatively safer, I still chose to hide behind things.

My clothes. My books. My insistence to never be like my mother, so I shut myself off from every experience and adventure. I even kept my dream, that I wanted to help women like my mother, a secret for the longest time. Because I kept telling myself if I couldn't stand up for my mother, how was I going to stand up for anyone else? He was the first person I told, and he was also the first person to tell me I'm brave.

So I want to be brave for him today.

Which is why I'm in the barn, up in our makeshift bedroom where I've spent every single night since I got here. Well, except the very first one, when he left me alone in his room because he misguidedly thought I should stay away from him. I'm glad I didn't. Because I never would've known this kind of love existed.

His thudding footsteps on the creaking stairs alert me that he's here. He's walking up and my heart starts racing. The moment he reaches the landing, his eyes lock with mine, and I lose my breath.

He's in his usual attire, a soft-looking dark T-shirt, a pair of washed-out jeans, and muddy boots, along with his brown Stetson. He usually also has leather chaps on when he's working with the horses, which he probably was. Given that he's been trying to break that bronc Axton was riding the first day we came in. He's made some progress with it, but the horse is still skittish and gets spooked easily. Anyway, my husband removes his chaps before coming to me. He also washes his mud-streaked hands and arms.

I asked him about that one day, and he said, "Can't put my filthy cowboy hands on your flower-soft skin now, can I?"

I swear I almost blurted it out then. That I love him, and he can put his hands on me any way he likes. Bloody, dirty, filthy. I'll take whatever he'll give me.

"You okay?" he asks, walking toward where I'm standing by the window, a frown creasing his brow.

I fist my dress and nod. "Yes."

He comes all the way over to me and frames my face with his hands. "Is it your period?"

I have to chuckle at this. "This is the first time you've used that term."

"What term?"

I grab his shirt at the sides. "Period. You usually just say 'on the rag' or something equally cowboy-ish." Then, "Actually, ever since we got here, you sound more like a cowboy than you ever did back when we were in the woods."

It's true. His drawl is more pronounced, and his words have a lazy pitch that wasn't there when I initially met him. Probably because this is his home, his place in the world.

His frown stays in place, telling me he doesn't find any of this amusing. "So is that it? You in pain?"

I shake my head, my heart clenching at his concern. "No. It's all over now. As of this afternoon."

The pads of his rough fingers dig into my cheek. "So then, what is it? Ax said he dropped you off here sometime before lunch."

After our little foray into Marsden's office and what I found in his safe, I told Axton to bring me to the barn. He didn't ask me what I read in that file, even though he was standing right there. He didn't even take a peek while I was reading it. I guess he really *was* serious when he said I was entering sacred territory. That he would steal money from the safe but not touch anything else. These three brothers are something else, aren't they?

"They're different," I say.

"What?"

"Your names," I explain. "Marsden, Arsenal, Axton."

His frown keeps deepening, and I don't blame him for that. I'm not making much sense to him. I'm not making much sense to myself either. All I know is that I want to find out everything about him. Every little thing. I want to get so close to him that nothing can ever tear us apart. Not even his thirst for revenge. Or his love for another woman.

"What the fuck are you talkin' about?" he growls.

"Was it your mom?" I ask instead. "Who named you all?"

He opens his mouth but closes it a second later. He searches my eyes, and I'm too overwhelmed right now to hide anything I'm feeling. I don't know what he sees in them—restlessness, heartbreak, panic, *love*—but whatever it is, it makes him pull me even closer, his palms splaying open on my cheeks, his fingers burying in my hair, his thumbs stroking the sides of my lips. Then with a low, rough voice, he replies, "Yeah. Off these books she used to read. All about cowboys and gunslingers."

"Your mom used to read books like me?"

"Clearly, I got my type from my ma."

Fisting his shirt, I swallow. "Your name's my favorite. Out of all your names. Out of all the names actually."

"Yeah?"

"It reminds me of fire. You know, like arson. A crime but I don't care."

His fingers flex on my face. "Darlin', you gotta tell me what's—"

"I know why you lied about it. In the beginning. But I wish you didn't need to."

I wish you didn't need to do what you're doing. I wish you were free.

"Baby, what's—"

"I love my name too," I say, cutting him off. "But I don't know where my mom got it from. She never told me."

He presses his fingers to my face, clearly getting impatient with me and my ramblings. "The only thing she did right in this life was makin' you and then givin' you that name, yeah? The *only fuckin'* thing. She didn't deserve your love when she was alive and she don't deserve it now when she's dead, you understand?"

I nod, my eyes stinging. "Yes."

I do. Along with being brave, he somehow taught me that too. That I'm worth protecting. I'm worth saving. I want him to know that he's worth protecting too. Worth *loving*. Because I already do.

"I'm leaving," I blurt out.

His frame tightens, his features going hard. "I know."

My fingers twist in his shirt. "In one week."

Something flickers through his features, quick like lightning, that I have no hope of understanding. "Yeah."

"I don't want—"

He squeezes my cheeks to shut me up. "No."

"But I'm going to m—"

"Fuck no."

I go up on my tiptoes and in his face. "You can't stop me from saying it."

He fists my hair. "I can."

I pull at his T-shirt. "You can't stop me from *feeling* it either."

His nostrils flare with anger and he snaps, "I can and I will. The only thing you need to *feel* right now is how you'll be free in a week. How you'll be goin' away, doin' this beautiful thing you wanted to do. How you'll help people. Save women from men like me and your daddy who make this world a shitty place." He fists my hair harder, pulling my head back. "The only thing you need to *remember* is that you're going to live your life. That nothin' they did to you, nothin' I did, mattered in the end. Because you're beautiful and brave and so fuckin' stunning you take my breath away. Do you understand?"

My breaths are all choppy now, my heart a mess. In fact, I'm worse than I've been before. All day, I've been crippled with a kind of restlessness I've never felt before, and now he's made it even worse with his *sweet, infuriating* words. So much so that I don't know what else to do but smack him. Scratch his neck and punch his chest. I don't know what else to do but rain my fists down on his mountain-like body and take my frustration out on him while screaming, "You make it so h-hard. God, you make everything so hard, Arsen. It's so h-hard to hate you but I should hate you. I *should*. You're the worst man I-I've ever met. You're bossy and controlling and dominating. And it's always your way or the highway and *God*, you make m-me so angry. You stupid, asshole cowboy. I wish—"

And just like that he's swallowing my words with his mouth.

He's kissing me so hard and so deep that it feels like my head is spinning. My entire body is spinning, and I have no choice but to hold on to him and kiss him back if I want to find my balance. I have no choice but to climb his body like the mountain he always feels like, strong and large and so steadfast, but also rocky and treacherous. I wrap my legs around his slim waist and wind my arms around his neck as I kiss, kiss, *kiss* him.

And as he kisses me back, he takes me to our bed.

The bed where I gave him my virginity, and as soft as that bed is—and it *is* soft—and as poetic as it would be to do this here, I still push him away with my hand on his shoulder. I still break our kiss and whisper against his mouth, "Not here."

Panting, he frowns too. "What?"

"M-mirror."

Our chests are clashing together as if fighting with each other. I bet our hearts are pounding in a way that could be called a war too. Drumming against our rib cages in a violent beat. Our blood could be kerosene, and this thing between us could be the match that lights everything on fire.

Him, me, this world.

"I want to see," I whisper when all he does is stare down at me with fiery eyes.

I've never asked this of him before.

He's the one who always initiates sex in front of the floor-length mirror that he put in himself just like the bathtub. The first time he insisted on having sex in front of it, I kept my eyes closed the whole time. I wasn't going to see all my thick curves jiggling and shaking with his deep, pounding thrusts. He let me, but then to punish me, he laid me down in front of it while pointing out all the places on my body that are his favorite.

My overflowing tits that are so heavy they sag to the side while I'm lying down. This little place on my waist that he said calls to him in a way that makes him want to sink his teeth into it. My soft tummy with a slight bulge that also makes him want to take a bite off, especially the area around my belly button. My hips, all cushiony and plump, that he said he loves to grab while taking me from behind. He called them handlebars that he could use to go to town on my college girl snatch. Before moving down to my thighs that he said make him dream of soft, fragile things full of sweet cream. Followed by my thick ass that he said makes him come just at the thought of it shaking. In fact, he deliberately fucks me hard so he can watch it shake and jiggle with the power of his thrusts.

"Your body's a fuckin' dreamland, darlin'," he growled before rolling over me once again and settling between my thighs. "It was made to fuck. To play with. To love on."

Then he proceeded to do just that. Love on my body while I watched him do it. I specifically remember him using that word, because like a beggar who's only ever been given scraps, I latched on to the L word. I let myself pretend that he meant what he said. That he really loved me and that was his way of showing me.

It wasn't; I know that.

But it could be mine.

If he won't let me say it to him, then I'll show him. By being brave.

So when he finally gets up and off the bed, I take charge. Without hesitation, I pull my dress up and off my body. I take off my bra and panties next, and I do that without blinking so much as an eye. When I'm all naked in front of him, I put my hands on his wildly breathing chest and walk him in front of the mirror. His eyes are on me the whole time I'm pushing him, his jaw clenched, his cheekbones high and taut.

When I've positioned him in front of it, I go for the hem of his T-shirt. I pull it up, and after a beat of staring down at me, he lets me continue. Good. I would've fought him otherwise. His hat was already knocked off in the battle of our mouths back there, so in one clean move, I take the garment off and drop it to the floor. Then I go down on my knees and unlace his boots. One by one, I take them off before moving up to his belt.

Which is when he stops me.

He grabs my hand and stares down at me. "You wanna run the show, darlin'?"

I look up at his muscular frame, his broad shoulders and sculpted torso. On my knees, he looks even bigger, larger than life. As large as the sky, as tough as the land he works. I could never move him, could I? But I have to try. I *have* to. Or at least die trying.

"I want to make you as crazy as you make me." Then, just to be defiant and bratty, I add, "Daddy."

His frame shudders and his stomach hollows out. "Yeah?"

I lift my chin, feeling the kind of determined I've never felt before. "Yes."

"By blowing him in front of the big, bad mirror."

"And fucking him in front of the big, bad mirror too."

He runs his eyes over my face for a moment or two before muttering to himself, "Yeah, don't think I'll ever get used to it."

"Get used to what?"

His grip on my hand flexes. "How young and naive you are."

"I'm not—"

"Have at it then, baby," he cuts me off. "Make me a goner but you should know somethin'."

"What?"

He leans down toward me, down and down, and brings our mouths together, whispering, "I'm already so far gone for my baby; more than she could ever be for me."

I open my mouth to protest. To tell him to stop lying because if he was so far gone, he wouldn't be sending me away, but he doesn't let me. He swallows down my words again with his mouth and kisses the hell out of me. I don't know how long it is before we come up for air, but when we do, he growls, "Now, suck your daddy off with your cock-sucking mouth like you mean it, and bring him to his knees, yeah?"

So I unbutton his jeans in a hurry and with a finesse that I could never have imagined possessing just last week when we were at the cabin and he was trying to punish me for worrying him. And when I get to his cock, all leaky and throbbing like it always is, and put it in my mouth, I could never have even dreamed of swallowing him down in one go.

But he changed all my dreams, didn't he?

I told him to give me dreams and take away my nightmares, and he did just that. He's made me suck his cock so much in the past week that I've become an expert at it. That my cocksucking mouth practically inhales his dick instead of struggling and me freaking out, and I can't help but preen under the growl he emits.

I can't help but hum around his length, making him go insane. A little trick I learned about my husband last week. He loves it when I make noises around his cock. He loves it when I scratch his thighs with my nails and use my tongue to lave the thick vein that goes up and down his hard dick.

He especially loves it when I gag on his cock. When I choke and my spit runs down his length.

He loves it when I drown him in my saliva and make a mess of my tits with it. And since I'm doing all of this in front of the big, bad mirror, I also put on a show for him. I know he loves it when my tits jiggle and curves shake. So I deliberately make them. I *deliberately*, exaggeratedly go up and down his length so that my big tits not only shake but also smack against each other. I even turn toward the mirror while still sucking his dick and pull at my nipples. I squeeze my tits. I heave them up in my hands and bring them together over and over, playing with them.

And I have to say, I get why he loves it. I get why he loves looking at me in the mirror because God, I *am* beautiful.

Out of shyness, I'd only look at myself in flashes before and mostly stare at *him* staring at *me*. But today, I keep my eyes on myself, and yeah, I understand why. I am a woman in love, sucking her man's cock. Of course I am beautiful. I have thick, gorgeous curves that my man goes crazy over. That he dreams about. How can I be anything but stunning, like he calls me?

How can my glistening thighs and spit-drenched tits be anything less than breathtaking? How can my wide hips and the soft rolls of my tummy that he holds on to so he can fuck me harder ever be anything less than glorious?

I could stare at myself forever.

But that's not what this is about. I need to focus on making *him* go crazy. And nothing makes him crazier than me locking eyes with him, so in the next breath I do that. I look at him in the mirror to find he's already been watching me. And God, he's almost in a trance.

His eyes glazed over, his chest gusting with breaths, and every muscle in his body clenched and standing in stark relief as he watches me suck his dick.

Plus, when he realizes that I'm looking into his eyes, his knees buckle and his thighs shake. His hands in my hair become painful and his face turns mean.

Before he yanks my mouth off his dick.

I'm not happy about it, but I like that trails of my spit connect my swollen lips to his dick. I like that even he can't sever our connection. He shakes my head with his fist and makes me look at him, not in the mirror, as he growls, all angry-like, "You wanted to make me crazy, didn't you"—another shake of my head—"well, you got it. You've got me so riled up that I'm *this* close to sayin' fuck it and goin' to town on your gorgeous porn-star body. So you wanna fuck your daddy, darlin', now's the time. Because pretty soon, playtime will be over and once your daddy gets goin', he won't let up until he's wrecked you and trashed that college girl pussy."

How is it that he can say the sweetest things in the scariest of ways. And how is it that I feel myself falling harder for him.

I attack him then. I push him down to the floor and get ready to take a ride. And again, if not for this past week, I would never have dreamed about being able to do it so easily. Being able to fit his fat cock into my tiny hole, let alone riding it on the top. And thank God, I can, because this is amazing.

It's fucking life-changing, having him so deep. It feels like he's almost touching my throat. It's transcendental, tunneling my fingers through his chest hair as I twist my hips on his cock, making him shudder and shake underneath me. All that power at my mercy. This is what he said riding a horse feels like, didn't he, and Jesus, I get it now too. I'm riding my dark stallion, and nothing could ever compare to this.

Not one thing could compare to bending over him, dangling my sticky tits over his mouth like ripe fruits, and watching him lean up to catch a nipple in his mouth, blindly almost. Because I'm making him lose his mind with my fucking. Not to mention that when I grind my clit on the base of his cock, he almost jackknifes up, growling in my tits. Not a single thing could compare to watching it all happen in the mirror. My ripe and flushed body riding my husband's cock.

But maybe what he says is true.

I'm so young and so naive that I can't handle riding him like some sort of a cowgirl because I'm coming within five seconds of doing this and watching ourselves in the mirror. My pussy is clenching on his cock, and I'm moaning from the ecstasy of it. From the sting of his teeth on my nipple. I'm so gone for him that I don't even protest when he sits up and takes charge.

I guess playtime is really over, and it's his turn now.

To wreck me and trash my pussy. He puts me on my back and enters me in one thrust, my core still coming and fluttering around his length. As he growls against my mouth, "Daddy's home."

And then he ruts inside of me. He fucks me so hard that I know I'll have bruises from his fingers on my hips, from the floor digging into the small of my back. I'll probably have bruises inside my pussy from his cock too. I'll be black and blue and so sore that I won't be able to walk for days.

But it's okay. I don't care.

I only care about him and being as close to him as possible. I only care about watching us fuck in the mirror. He's positioned us in a way so I have to tilt my head back to watch us upside down. I crane my neck up and watch his body all sweaty and strong moving over me, pumping into me, and I watch myself taking his thrusts, my body moving up and down the floor like a doll.

Like his sweet little wife. His college girl. His dream girl. His Reverie.

The girl who loves him.

And maybe he can see all of that reflected in my eyes because he seems to quicken his thrusts if that's possible. He makes them fast and dirty and mean and brutal. So much so that I want to close my eyes and lose myself in it. But I won't. This is for him.

I want him to see. How much I love him.

And it only makes him angrier. The lines on his face are tight and stark. His jaw is clenched so hard that it seems made of granite. It seems *painful*. So painful that I cup his jaw with my soft hand and whisper, all the while looking into his glittering eyes in the mirror, "Arsen."

Which is when he comes.

His body jerks and he growls. He pulls his cock out and spills his seed on my tummy. It comes out in thick and hot lashes, pooling in my belly button, while some of it slides down my sides. I wait for him to come down from his high so he can rub it into my skin like he always does. But even before he relaxes, I somehow know he isn't going to. He's going to get up and leave.

When what I predicted comes true, the accuracy of it hits me in the gut. It takes my breath away when he gets off my body and rises to his feet. He's still breathing harshly when he leaves me there, all battered and bruised, and goes in search of what I'm assuming to be his clothes. Somehow I make myself stand too.

Stand tall and bare.

Most of all, I stand bravely in front of the man who isn't technically my husband but feels like it because I'm in love with him.

"I love you," I call out to his back.

He's standing at the chest, opening and closing drawers, fishing for clothes. He finds his jeans, and without a word or any sign that he heard me, he proceeds to put them on.

I open and close my fists, my heart racing in my chest. "I've always loved you. Since the beginning. Ever since we were writing letters and I think it was because you made me feel alive for the first time in my life. I've spent my entire life trying to hide, trying to suppress things, trying to not feel any excitement or joy. But then I started writing to you and for the first time, I had no choice but to feel things and God, I… It's scary but also so thrilling."

I pause before saying, "I'm not going to lie to you and say that you've never hurt me or made me feel afraid. You have. You lied to me, threatened me, scared me. *Used* me. But somehow, you're the only man who's also protected me. You also made me feel safe, worthy, chosen. You're the one who made me realize that strong and powerful aren't bad things. That rough hands can have a soft touch and sharp teeth can feel so good when they bite. You're the one who made me realize that I could *take* both, rough and soft touch, and still flourish. Or that I'm beautiful both inside and out. You taught me I could kiss while riding a horse and wear clothes that won't hide me. But most of all, you taught me what love really is. It's not toxic like what my parents had and it's not careful like I wanted it to be. Love is an adventure. It has highs and lows. It scares you. It makes you feel safe. It's reckless and thoughtful. It's the biggest contradiction there is. Love is *you*. Because you're the biggest contradiction of my life."

At this, I do notice a slight tightening of his frame. I notice a twitch in his back, especially where his brand is. That fancy *R* that he burned onto himself. Or maybe I'm just imagining things right now. Whatever it is, I need to keep going. I need to be brave. For myself.

For him.

So I keep talking to his back. "I know you…love someone else. I know that. You don't talk about her. You don't talk about Annie but…" I watch his fists clench at his sides then and I swallow thickly. "I know you loved her so much that you tried to kill a man for her. You branded yourself for her, you spent eight years behind bars for her. Even now, you're ready to burn down the whole world for her. And the old Reverie wouldn't like that. She'd be afraid of the violence but now I get it. I get why you're doing this. I try to imagine it sometimes. How you feel. How you felt when you…heard the news, when you realized you were too late and I'm going to be honest with you, it scares me. It scares me so much that I don't *want* to imagine it. I don't want to imagine something happening to the man *I* love. And maybe it's selfish but I'm finding out love is selfish too. So I'm asking you, please, *please*, don't do it. I'm asking you as a girl in love with you, please don't put me through the pain that you've gone through, that you're going through.

"Because I know this revenge will kill something inside of you. You're not this man, Arsen. I know you don't want to believe me but it's the truth. I *know* you. You're a brother. Whose younger brother looks up to him and whose older brother wants you back for good. You're a cowboy in love with your land. You wake up with the dawn and work tirelessly on the ranch all day. Then you spend whatever hours you have left working with your horses, trying to break them. You rescue them, rehabilitate them. You *care* for them. You try to make them feel safe. But most of all, you're a man capable of love. I know you think you're like my father but you're not. My father pushed my mother down the stairs, but you're ready to destroy your life for the woman you loved. All because you think it's your fault that she died. It's not. It's theirs. You didn't kill her; you're trying to avenge her. So please, *please* don't do this. Please don't hurt yourself. You always tell me how I need to be free, don't you? How I need to live my life. And I will. I'll leave. I'll do all those beautiful things. I'll build my future. But please don't make me live in a world where you have none. Don't make me live in a world where you're suffering and in pain. Please, set yourself free for me. Just live, Arsen. *Please.*"

My cheeks are drenched with tears. I only realize that when I'm done talking and I taste salt on my lips. I also realize that I'm still naked, and somehow when I'm not talking and being brave, I'm more aware of it. I become *even* more aware, though, when he finally turns around.

His face a cool, stony mask. His eyes dark but dead.

It's not as if I thought this would be easy. I'm asking him to give up something he's been wanting for eight years now. And given how much he loves Annie still, I knew it would be a hard ask. But I had to do it. I *have* to do this. I'm not going to let him destroy his life for revenge.

I didn't want it before, and I want it even less now, after seeing that file.

So I have to make him understand. I open my mouth to say something. I don't know what, though, because I ran out of all my words just now, but he gets there first. "Put some clothes on and get out."

I fist my hands. "No."

His jaw clenches. "Don't make me drag you out of here."

"Do it," I dare him.

Only because I know he never will. He'll lose his mind first before dragging me out of here naked.

As I said, I *know* him.

And when his chest swells with a breath that seems resigned, I loosen my fingers. But I guess I did it too soon because he begins to walk then, heading to the stairs. I call out his name, but he doesn't stop. So in my desperation, I say the last thing I wanted to say: "I'll tell them."

He stops, again with his back to me, and I can't help but find this so tragically poetic. That all I can see is the brand he put on himself because of the woman he loved when I'm asking him to do the unthinkable.

"I'll tell them everything," I say and then immediately want to vomit because the words are repulsive. "I have leverage now. You gave it to me that night. So if you don't give up on your plan, I'll tell them what's happening on the ranch."

I press a hand to my belly and wait for him to turn around. Give me some reaction, anything to work with. But he resumes walking. He continues down the stairs, his back straight and made of steel, his brand standing pale and stark on his bronzed skin.

When he's almost at the bottom, I panic. I do it so hard that I say the only thing I have left in my arsenal. That it sounds exactly like his name is the irony I'm trying to ignore as I call out, "She was a mole."

That stops him. Dear Lord, that halts him in his tracks, and it also gets him to turn around. His eyes clash with mine and I grip the railing with trembling hands. I clench my eyes shut for a few seconds because I can't believe I'm doing this. I can't believe I'm telling him this, but I have no choice.

I open my eyes and my tears make his sight blurry as I say, "I-I broke into Marsden's office today. And his safe. The one that's in the wall behind your parents' portrait. I-I saw it the day Peyton and I went into the office where we got the map to the cabin. I blackmailed Axton to open the safe for me and I…" I clench my eyes shut again and this time, feel the tears fall down my cheeks as I continue, "There was a file. I-I think it was Marsden's. It had all this information about Annie. Her birth date, the city she was born in, those kinds of thing. And a PI report about how she came to Black Rock because she was working for the Turners. Hank Turner. There were bank receipts from him depositing money in her account every month. It said that it was most likely she was spying for them. She was…" A sob catches in my throat, but I keep going because now that I have started it, I need to finish it. "Arsen, I think… I think she was using you. I think the Turners were using *her* to get to you and your land. She wasn't… I know you loved her but she probably didn't…"

"She did," he says, his voice rough and low.

"But I saw—"

"Yeah, you don't know what you saw. You've got no clue about anything."

"Arsen—"

"In an hour when I come back, if you're still here, I'm draggin' you out, naked or not. Because you're not a Turner *or* a Grayson.

You're just some girl I made the mistake of puttin' through hell and then fuckin'. So get gone before I make you gone."

With that he leaves, and I fall down to my knees, sobbing as I crawl to our bed.

I don't know how long I stay there, crumpled in a ball, sobbing for my broken heart, for breaking his heart by telling him the truth. But at some point, shame becomes too much for me and I don't care about being brave. I put his discarded T-shirt on and wrap myself in his sheets.

The only way I know that an hour has passed   although it feels longer, *much longer* than that—is when I hear the creak of the stairs followed by a pair of arms wrapping around me. I'm about to hold on to them because he's back and he isn't dragging me out like he said when I realize it's not him at all.

It's a man in a mask, and before I scream, he's putting his hand on my mouth and I'm sliding into oblivion.

CHAPTER THIRTY-TWO

The Dark Stallion

THERE ARE THINGS about her she didn't know until I told her.

Secrets of her body. Like a mole on the small of her back that she didn't know existed until I traced it with my tongue one night and showed her in the mirror when she asked me what I was doing. Or that the back of her left knee is more ticklish than the right. She didn't know her belly button could be so sensitive that me playing with it would make her come until I did it twice in one night. She didn't know she frowns when she's rereading for the tenth time the little notes I leave for her. Or that every time she laughs, her nose crinkles a little. If she's trying to sass me but is turned on, the base of her neck will flush with heat as she glares at me.

There are a million other things I could list, and I do as I make the call and hear it ring. They come and go through me like flashes as I wait for him to pick up. Like how your life flashes before your eyes when you're about to die. Given that *she* is my life, it makes sense.

It makes sense that when he does pick up, I growl, my words low and vibrating, "Where is my wife?"

"She's safe," Brecken Turner tells me.

"*Where*," I ask again, as in my head I watch her giggle over something I said. "*Is. My. Wife.*"

"As I said, she's fine," he says in a calm voice. "And I'd like you to remember that you didn't afford me the same courtesy when I asked about my sister a couple of weeks ago."

I breathe in. I breathe out. Then I fist my palm around my open pocketknife, cutting my skin. I keep doing it, breathing and cutting my skin, until I can see clearly. Until it doesn't feel like my world is on fire. That my insides are split open and I'm coming apart.

It's important.

That's the first thing that came to mind when I went back to the barn after cooling off. After riding Rebel hard for hours. After mucking the stalls and wielding the axe to cut down enough timber to last for the next six months. After all of that, when I went back and found her gone, I knew I had to keep my cool.

At first, I thought she did it.

She did what I told her to, so I went to the main house. I went so I could apologize. For real. With words. By saying sorry. Like other men do. Normal men. Men who care about their wives, not motherfuckers like me who don't know what that word sounds like in their voice because they hardly ever use it. And then I was going to sit her down and tell her everything about Annie. I was going to tell her what she's been dying to know all this time. What I've been too afraid to say because then she'll really find out why she doesn't belong here.

Why she doesn't belong with me.

I know I've been acting like a big man, a big fucking noble man, these past couple of weeks, asking her to leave. Demanding that she run away from this ranch, this town. Me. But if I really was so noble, I would've told her about Annie. I would've told her the entire truth. But I didn't. And then when she confronted me with the truth, I flipped out on her.

So when I didn't find her in the main house, either, and she wasn't in any of the other barns and stables where Rad looked or other places that Ax and Haven and Peyton could think of to search, and after all the phone calls that Mars made, I knew that keeping my cool was what was going to save my life and quite possibly her life too. I couldn't lose it like I did that night in the cabin. I couldn't lose it like I did eight years ago either.

I needed to be smart. I needed to be levelheaded, because for the first time in my godforsaken life, I can't be selfish. I have a responsibility. She's *depending* on me. And I can live through anything, *any-fucking-thing*, any failure, all the broken promises, but letting her down is not something I'm willing to do. What that says about me in regard to Annie, I don't know. I'll let her be the judge of that when I tell her, but for now, I need her here. I need her safe.

I *need* her.

"What do you want?" I ask Brecken as calmly as I can.

"I think you know what I want," he says. "I want my sister back. Who by the way isn't really your wife."

"You—"

"One piece of advice: If you're going to leave your enemies alive, make sure they don't know your secrets," he says, cutting me off. "The man, the one you booted off your ranch last week, he ratted you out. He came to me and told me about how two Turner girls are living on the Grayson ranch, and how you were sweet on one of them. Not my sister though. The other girl. That you keep calling your wife. I was getting close to cracking it all open anyway but he made it easier. Not to mention, he had a lot to say about your little prison program."

The fire is threatening to overcome me, so once again, I wrap my hand around the knife and inject a dose of pain to keep myself sharp. "Let me talk to her."

"No," Brecken states, and I open my mouth to argue, but he keeps going. "Because you aren't making the rules anymore. Here is what's going to happen: If you want your *wife* back, you're going to bring my sister back to me and you're going to dissolve this sham of a marriage and your bullshit power of attorney. And then we're going to sit down and have a conversation about your dead girlfriend and this decades-old feud between our families. How if it ever comes up, I'm going to make sure you lose every bit of that land you stole from my forefathers. Is that clear?"

I feel the blood dripping down my palm and plopping onto the hardwood floor as I warn, "If you touch her, I—"

"I have no interest in touching her," Brecken says smoothly. "All I want is my sister back and this land business over with. You have twenty-four hours."

With that he ends the call, and I spring up from my seat. Twenty-four hours is too long. Too fucking long for her to be on that ranch. Where her daddy abused her, beat on her, fucking terrorized her.

She needs to come home right the fuck now.

And *this* is her home. With the Graysons. Who care about her. With Haven, who became her friend on day one and has been distraught ever since I showed up at the main house looking for her. With Ax even, who looks fucking traumatized by her disappearance and thinks it was somehow his fault because he was supposed to be watching. With Rad, who's been on her side since the beginning, since before I even brought her here.

"What do you need?" Rad asks me, reminding me that I'm in Mars's office.

But I focus on Marsden, who's sitting behind his desk. "Let me know when the lawyer calls back. I need to know when it's done." Before he can respond, I turn to Rad. "Peyton."

"Peyton."

"What about her?" he growls back.

If I tell him, he'll lose his shit. But he needs to know so I growl, clutching the knife, "Peyton's gonna help us get her back."

We're both at the door when Marsden's voice halts me in my tracks: "She loves you."

I turn around to face him. Sitting at his desk, he looks every inch the landowner he is. His shoulders straight, his eyes hard. "You know that, right? 'Cause if you don't, then you've gotta be the blindest fool to ever set foot in Black Rock. Everyone at Rawhide knows. She loves the Dark Stallion and he's been toyin' with her. Haven thinks you'll come around, but I know how stubborn you can be. How fuckin' hardheaded. And now there's a chance you're gonna lose her. You're gonna lose the girl who somehow, *some-goddamn-way* loves your fool, reckless ass, all because you can't let go of the girl you loved eight years ago."

He's right. I can be stubborn. I can be hardheaded. But I'm no fool, and I'm not blind. I know she loves me. I knew it before she told me tonight.

I didn't want her to love me, though.

So I kept reminding her, kept telling her she shouldn't. I'm not the man for her. I could never be the man for her. Her future is elsewhere. My sins are too big. My crimes are too harsh. I just wish now that instead of being a selfish motherfucker, I had told her the whole story. She would've known then.

To stay away. To keep her heart safe from the likes of me.

"I know you looked into Annie," I tell him. "I know you've got a file on her and I know you think I'm a fuckup. But if you don't butt out of my business, we're gonna have a big problem."

I'm going to tell her now, though. I'm going to tell her everything. Because she has a right to know everything about the man she loves. And because if I knew how to love, she'd be the one for me. But first, I need to get her back to where she belongs.

In her home.

Safe.

CHAPTER THIRTY-THREE

I KNOW WHERE I am. It smells like tobacco and mold. My old house. My old room. I also know I'm not alone. There's someone else here with me.

My father.

I should open my eyes now because I'm awake. I've been awake for some time, but I can't bring myself to. My heart is racing so hard, and my skin feels too tight for my body. I feel like a little girl again, pretending to be asleep so my daddy will pass me by instead of raining down his wrath on me. All panicky and terrified. My stomach is churning, and it feels like I'm going to throw up.

But I'm not a little girl anymore. I haven't been a little girl in years. The last time I was in this house, I was eleven. I was leaving for summer camp and so thrilled to be going just because I'd be away from my mom and dad. And then I got this unexpected, miraculous reprieve. I was saved by the man who wore a bull mask. He didn't know he was saving me, but that doesn't diminish what he did for me. He sprang me out of this prison and freed me from years of abuse.

So I can do this. I can open my eyes.

And as soon as I do, I see him, my father.

He's sitting at my desk by the wall with a beer bottle in his hand. He looks old, as expected. His dark hair has thinned, and his face that always looked too sharp and cruel has sagged. The last time I saw him was at my mother's funeral, which was six years ago. He wore a suit and a tie, and of course his black Stetson. He stood there all somber and serious, looking down at the casket and the woman he killed. And I stood beside him, the only person who knew he was a murderer. People came and went, paying their condolences to us, and he received them, though he had no right to.

And *I* received them without any right to. Back then, my guilt was too strong, and it still sometimes is despite what Arsen repeatedly told me.

My father pretty much abandoned me after my mother died, as if the only reason he put up with me was because of her; because I somehow came as a package deal and wasn't his own flesh and blood. It still doesn't mean that he's going to let me go unscathed. Not only because he's my father, but also because he works for the Turners.

And the Turners are the ones who brought me here.

I'm pretty sure it has something to do with what *he* has planned. Although why they would kidnap *me*, I don't know. I'm not a Turner or a Grayson. I'm just some girl who got caught up in all this.

So I push myself to sit up, and as soon as I do, my father's beady eyes take me in. He lowers his bottle and tips his hat up so he can look at me. He takes in my attire, which is just Arsen's T-shirt, and I feel naked. I force myself to sit up straight, though, folding my bare legs to the side. Before I can say anything, he goes, his voice scratchy and rough, "You look all grown up, girl."

He used to say that a lot: *girl*. Like I'm some nuisance and not his own daughter. It used to hurt me, but I don't have time to feel any hurt right now. I need to know what's going on so I can find a way to get out of this mess.

For good.

I grip the sheet and ask, "What... What am I doing here?"

"Brecken's men brought you," he tells me. "Told him I could take you off his hands until he does what needs gettin' done."

I swallow. "What does he need to do?"

"Some Grayson business. Wouldn't tell me what," he grumbles. "Except that you've taken up with a Grayson." He takes another look up and down my body, and I want to hide myself again. "And I can see that he was right."

"I don't understand what—"

He takes a pull of his beer. "Turned out to be a whore like your mama, didn't you." I flinch, but he keeps going: "Although even she wouldn't touch a Grayson."

"Graysons are ten times the men Turners will ever be," I snap, unable to stop myself. "Than *you* will ever be."

His dark eyes flash with anger. "See you get your mouth from your mama too."

"Don't talk about my mother."

"Is that right?" He chuckles, his beer belly shaking. "Wonder how you'd feel if you knew the truth about her."

"What truth?"

He shrugs then. "Maybe you already do. Who knows what she told you when you were both livin' in the big city."

My heart, which was already racing, starts beating in a different rhythm now. "What truth? What would she have told me that I didn't already know?"

He studies me for a beat, and I think he might be messing with me. My father was always fond of using his fists, but I can't remember him playing mind games. He was always too drunk to do things like that. But then he says, "You never wondered why you look so much like the Turner girl?"

And my heart drops down to my stomach.

Yes, I have wondered about that. How is it that we both look so similar, Peyton and I? How come we have the same shade of blond hair and blue eyes when both my parents have dark-colored hair and eyes?

"I see you figurin' things out," he drawls, taking another pull of his beer. "Told you your mama was a whore. All because I wouldn't pay her enough attention so she thought sleepin' with my boss would make me come around." He spits on the floor, making me flinch again. "Fuckin' crazy-ass woman. And then she tried to pass you off as mine like I'm some dumb asshole who can't tell his own fuckin' child…"

He says several other things after that, cursing my mother, but I don't hear them. I'm still reeling from the fact that I'm Hank Turner's daughter.

I *am* a Turner, after all.

Half Turner, but a Turner nonetheless.

I sit with it for a few seconds while my father rambles on about how my mother deserved every beating he gave her, how he was right to cheat on her, and how I deserved to be beaten as well because I mooched off him all my life even though I wasn't his daughter. I try to think how this news makes me feel, how it changes things. It does explain some things. Why my father never really treated me as his daughter. Why he was so abusive to both my mother and me. Maybe it also explains why Peyton and I are so close. Because we're sisters after all.

But other that that, I don't think it means anything. My mother is still the woman who fell for the wrong man and then got caught up in a twisted relationship and paid the ultimate price. And even if this man in front of me isn't my real father, my biological father is just as bad, if not worse, than him.

Most importantly, I still stand corrected about love. Love is not what my parents had, and I wish it hadn't taken me this long to figure that out. Maybe I would've lived my life more fully if I'd known.

"I know you killed her," I find myself saying.

And he stops talking, going on alert.

"I saw you," I tell him, staring at him through the space, the man whom I thought was my father but isn't really. "That night. I was there. I was hiding behind a couch like a coward. But I saw it happen. I *saw* you do it. You pushed her down the stairs. You killed my mother."

At this, he jerks up from his seat and throws his bottle at me. It crashes against the wall just a few inches away and shatters into loud and countless pieces. I wanted to bait him. I wanted to be brave, like I wasn't while I was growing up, and go head-to-head with the man who terrorized my entire childhood.

So when he comes for me, I'm ready.

I'm ready to scratch his face off. I'm ready to pull his hair. To smack him. To kick him. To scream and howl and take all my wrath out on him. All the times I hid and ran and cowered and took his beatings, I'm ready to make him pay for that. I'm ready for my revenge. And how ironic that I feel this way when only hours ago, I told the man I love to give up his quest.

Maybe we're not that different after all, he and I.

And maybe I shouldn't be thinking of him right now because this time around, it's really over. He told me in no uncertain terms that he wants me gone. So I should focus on other things, like that my father has a lot more strength than me. He can overpower my fists and my scratching nails. He can throw me to the floor and kick me in the stomach. That even if I manage to crawl away and find a shard of glass to stab his leg with, my father will still come after me.

But it's *Arsen's* thoughts that keep me going. It's *his* thoughts that keep me fighting. It was he who said I was brave. I'm beautiful and I'm a survivor. So I keep trying to survive.

Even when my father's body is pinning me down on the floor and his hands manage to find their way around my neck. He chokes me with them, squeezes my throat, blocks my airway, suffocating me. No matter how hard I struggle, I can't get his hands to budge. I can't shut his face out, his cruel eyes and clenched teeth, as he tries to kill me.

And as always, it's his name I whisper as I lay dying at the hands of my father: "Arsen."

I really hope he doesn't take this the wrong way. That he

couldn't protect me from my father. I know it's over between us, but I *know* him. He's going to think it's his fault. But it isn't. I baited my father myself. I knew what I was doing, and so this is not his crime. He doesn't need to suffer for it till the end of time.

Just as my vision is blanking and all thought is leaving my body, I see him.

I see a bull mask.

I see it descending upon me, and then, suddenly, I can breathe. I don't feel my father's hands around my throat. I don't feel his heavy, smelly body crushing my lungs. I don't know if it's a dream or if it's really happening. But I see my father being thrown across the room, grunting and groaning as he falls to the floor.

Then, the man in that mask is straddling my father's body and punching him over and over. He keeps smashing his face into the floor, and no matter what my father does, he can't get him off. No matter what my father does, he can't fight back, and soon he goes limp, just like that man in the cabin a couple of weeks ago.

I don't know how I do it, but somehow, I prop myself up on my trembling elbow and call out as loudly as I can, "Arsen, no. Please. Don't k-kill him. He's not…" I cough and struggle to get the words out, to stay propped up even. "He's not w-worth it. Not for me."

And then I go back down. The last thing I remember seeing is the man in the mask—Arsen, the love of my life, my husband—getting off my father's limp body and heading toward me.

———

It wasn't a dream.

That's my first thought as I come to. Immediately followed by: I know this room. I'd know it anywhere, even though I only spent one night in it. This is where I started when I came here for the first time. In his room at the Grayson ranch. I also know I'm not alone. There's someone else in the room with me. Someone who smells like the outdoors and tastes like lemonade.

Somehow, I'm more afraid to open my eyes than I was when I was stuck with my daddy. Or the man I thought was my daddy. Probably because I'm so eager to open them now and look at him when I should pace myself. I should err on the side of caution. This is the man I love who doesn't love me back.

A broken heart is a lot more painful than broken bones.

So I take my time and slowly blink my eyes open. While it took my father some time to realize I was awake, it isn't the case here. *He already knew* I was awake before I even opened my eyes because his own are locked on me and he's sitting at the edge of his seat, every line on his face, every muscle in his body tight and on edge. The moment our eyes meet, I see him go even more on edge, sliding down the chair, fisting his hands on his thighs, the frown on his face deepening.

I try to get up then and realize it's difficult. My elbows are shaking, and there's a distinct soreness in my spine and in my chest. My head too. But when I see him springing up from his seat to come help me, I have no choice but to thrust my hand out, asking him to stop so I can push myself up to sitting on my own, *without* his help.

I don't want him touching me.

He comes to an abrupt halt at my gesture, and I notice how his body strains with the effort. Like he has to physically stop himself from dashing over to me.

I lick my dry lips and ask, "Did you…"

I have to trail off because there's a sharp pain in my throat as I try to speak. Probably because my father tried to choke me to death. Tears threaten my eyes then, but I somehow hold them at bay.

Although it becomes really difficult to do that when, suddenly, a glass of water appears in front of me and I hear him say, "You're gonna have some soreness around your throat for a while. The doctor gave you a pain medication for that." His jaw clenches for a second before he adds, "And for other injuries."

I take the glass of water from him and take a sip. Even that is difficult. But water helps. At least my throat doesn't feel on fire like it did a second ago. Besides, I've seen and suffered worse than this. My father never tried to kill me before, but he did once dislocate my shoulder. Something I'd forgotten about up until now; so if I survived that, I guess I'll survive this too.

Although from the looks of it, Arsen might not.

Because after giving me the glass of water, he simply stands there, looking down at me, his hands fisted, his spine so straight that it must be painful, and his legs shoulder width apart. As if he's ready to go into battle and is just waiting for a sign from me.

Not to mention, his face. I've been trying not to study it too closely, but I can see how tired it looks. There are more lines around his eyes and his mouth than there were this morning. And his eyes are red-rimmed and look sunken. Plus, his clothes, his hair, even his boots, everything looks messy and wrinkled, like they've been through a wringer. Well, he did come to save me—God, for the thousandth time—so maybe he did go through the wringer, but still.

Most of all, though, he looks...lost.

Like he's determined to do something but doesn't know what that something is. So I help him out.

"Can you..." I have to massage my throat a bit, and he looks ready to lose his shit with how harshly he starts to breathe. So I swallow very gently and whisper, "Can you sit down? Please? You're...freaking me...out."

His brow wrinkles more, but he immediately obeys. Like a wooden puppet he drops down onto the chair, his jaw pulsing rhythmically. God, why does he have to look so tortured right now? All miserable and awkward.

Agonized.

I lick my lips again and ask, "Did you...kill him?"

I don't have to elaborate on who *he* is, because a violent expression passes through his face before he breathes out as if to calm himself. "No."

I breathe out, too, but mine is a breath of relief. "Thank you."

It only manages to make him angry. "He doesn't—"

"How did you...find me?" I ask, cutting him off.

Because I already know where he stands on this killing business. I already know he's hell-bent on revenge and righting all the wrongs, and he can do that. He can avenge this whole fucking world. As long as he doesn't do it for me, I'll make my peace with it.

The muscle on his cheek pulses for a few seconds before he replies, "Peyton. She gave us a list of possible places to look on the ranch. We combed through a couple before..." He has to pause to breathe in and out again. "I decided we needed to look elsewhere."

"My old house," I guess.

He gives me a curt nod.

I tighten my fingers around the glass as I ask, "You said *we*."

"Rad and I."

I swallow gently again before whispering, "You shouldn't have...done that. You shouldn't have come."

His nostrils flare then. And his chest swells up like a wave. But even his breathing exercises—and they seem to be that, strangely—don't calm him down, and his voice comes out a growl: "I should have."

"You're on parole," I remind him.

"Doesn't matter."

"You—"

"I wore a mask."

"The same one you wore that night."

"Doesn't fuckin' matter."

"Do you think...they won't put two and two together? If they haven't already, that is. You could go back to jail. You could—"

"Do you think I'd sit on my fuckin' ass," he thunders then, his spine snapping straight, his eyes shooting fire, "while they took my wife from me? While they took her away from her bed, from her goddamn home. Do you think I'd worry about my motherfuckin' parole, while you were in danger. While you were *put* in danger because of *me*. While you were back in that nightmare of a ranch where your father beat on you. While you lay on the floor with his hands…"

Instead of saying it, he breathes in and out. He visibly takes in a breath and then lets it out. He even grips his knees and sits straight as if doing a meditation exercise. Which is when I notice something. A bandage wrapped around his right palm.

"What… What is that?" I ask, motioning to his hand.

He doesn't look away from me as he responds, "Cut myself."

I open my mouth to ask him how. I mean, both of his hands look messed up, for sure. His knuckles are swollen and scraped, his skin red and bruised. But that's because of the beating he delivered to my father. This bandage thing looks different.

I shake it off, though. It's none of my business anymore, what happens to him. Instead, I put him at ease. Even though things aren't good between us, I still don't want him to suffer and blame himself for what I essentially did to myself.

"I'm fine," I tell him, holding the glass with both hands. "I know you have a habit of taking… blame for things but…" I swallow, drink a sip of water because it's becoming hard to talk once again. "I baited him. He wouldn't have attacked if I hadn't… So it's not your fault that I lay on the floor with his hands…"

I don't say it, either, because it felt like he was going to explode if I said the words "around my neck." So I let it go and just let it lie as I continue, "They'll know you took me back and attacked my father. Brecken is not stupid. He'll—"

"Again, don't fuckin' matter."

I lean forward then, even though my body is sore and aching and I just want to lie down. "What's going to happen to your revenge when you're behind bars?"

He opens his mouth but then closes it and breathes deep. Then, with a gravelly voice, he says, "It's not important right now so I want you to fuckin' drop it."

You know what, he's right. It's none of my business anymore. He can do whatever he wants. It's not as if he'll listen to me, right? He never has and he never will. I guess I should be thankful that he rescued me once again and leave it at that. Besides, it's not as if he's had a change of heart about the whole revenge thing. He's made it clear that nothing will stop him, not my useless confession of love. Not what I found in that file about Annie even.

"He's not my father," I blurt out, my fingers so tight around the glass that I might break it with bare hands.

"What?"

"My father, he…" I say this without knowing why I'm telling him after everything that's happened. "He isn't my biological father. Hank Turner is."

He straightens up then or rather straightens up more because he was already pulled tight like a string.

"So apparently, I'm a Turner after all," I half declare and half chuckle because the irony is fucking gut-wrenching. All this time he needed a Turner to get his revenge, but still, somehow I'm the wrong girl. Maybe I always *will be* the wrong girl.

"You're *not* a Turner."

As opposed to mine, his words are *all* declaration and even after so much time, they pierce me right in the chest. "My mom slept with Hank Turner at some point. To teach my dad a lesson but I guess it backfired, and she paid for it with her life." I shake my head, looking down at the glass of water. "It doesn't matter though because you're right, I'm not a Turner. I'm no one. Except some girl you were sleeping with."

Which is why they took me in the first place, I'm assuming. Because maybe they thought he cared about me enough to give up on his quest. He does care about me, but not enough to give up on ruining his life.

"A blowout," he says then.

I look up. "What?"

"An oil well blowout," he explains. "I was gonna rig their oil well, cause an explosion that'd destroy their land, their oil and every single thing on it. It'd make their land useless. And if there's no land, there is no war."

His revenge plan. This is it. I guess it makes sense, taking the land away, because they did it all for the land. Besides, Annie died in an explosion, so a retaliatory explosion would bring things full circle.

"So, you lied about letting them keep their business and sharing oil profits and all of that," I say pointlessly.

Of course he lied. He *told* me he was lying. Again, I need to take a step back. I need to stop worrying about him and his affairs. I need to come up with my own plan now. My plan of exiting, going back to my old life and somehow *living* it.

"You know what, you don't have to tell me anything," I say, shaking my head. "I don't—"

"I met her at the town fair," he says, cutting me off, his eyes full of something shiny and glittering, something I can't make sense of right now. "She was new in town. Never saw her before that day. Thought she was the most beautiful girl I'd ever seen." I flinch, and he catches it because he's watching me with an intensity that's making it hard for me to breathe. "I was a fool. Back then. Didn't know what I was talkin' about. I was young. I was horny, reckless. Girls would throw themselves at me because I was a cowboy, and I was a Grayson. So, I was a fuckin' rich cowboy whose family pretty much owned everything and everyone. When *she* threw herself at me, I didn't think it was anythin' different. All I was lookin' for was a good time, a one-night stand. Somethin' I was very good at back then. I was good at not gettin' tied down, no steady relationships. I thought I was some kind of a big shot, a stallion."

He shakes his head. "But all I was, was a goddamn asshole. So when she kept comin' back to me, I took her up on her offer. Told her it wasn't serious and she agreed. Even though after a while, I could see she was fallin' for me. I should've cut her loose then. But

I didn't." His jaw clenches here before he goes on, "She was on her own, takin' care of her sick mother and her younger brother. Had a job in town, on one of the ranches. She was bold, gutsy, adventurous. Everythin' I thought I liked in a girl. Because again, I didn't want any responsibilities, no one dependent on me.

"Anyway, somehow, we became steady. She'd come over to the ranch, spend time with my family. Haven, Ax. They both liked her. Not Mars though. Mars was suspicious. But then, Mars is always suspicious of everyone. Back then I was goin' through a phase where I loved him but hated his guts so if he wanted me to do one thing, I'd do another. When he told me I should be careful with Annie, that no one knew where she came from, who her people were, I told him to fuck off. I told Rad to fuck off too. He wasn't as bad as Mars but he was wary of her too. Sometimes I think that's why I kept her around, as a big fuck you to my family. To show them they couldn't control me. *Fuck*"—he scrubs his hands down his face, taking a deep breath—"I sound like a shithead. I *was* a shithead. Anyway, they all turned out to be right because one day a few months into our 'relationship,' she told me."

"Told you what?" I whisper, my eyes glued to him, his tortured face, his tight frame.

"That she was workin' for the Turners," he says, his liquid eyes boring into mine, and I freeze. "For Hank Turner. Said she met him at this strip club she worked at. She gave him a lap dance and he, drunk and horny, told her all his secrets. He promised that he'd pay her mother's medical bills and help out with her brother if she did this one thing for him. Find an in with the Graysons and find out about the Rawhide Redemption program so they could get our land. And she was desperate enough to say yes. Desperate enough to come up with a plan, seduce me, lure me out and use me. Mostly because being the reckless asshole I am, I was the easiest target. Mars would never have fallen for her and Ax was so young. So she found me, *targeted* me at the town fair, tryin' to establish a relationship with me. She said she was feedin' him information about our business, our bids on the livestock and other contracts, but she hadn't found anything about what he really wanted from her. And now she didn't want to either. She didn't want to do this anymore because she'd fallen for me and she…"

This time his breath is so big and large that I feel it all the way over where I'm sitting. I feel it waft over me, his scent, and I hold on to it, because for some reason I think the worst is yet to come. There's something life-changing that's coming, and I need to brace.

"She was pregnant," he says, and my heart drops. "Four months. She said it was mine, but she didn't have to because I knew. I could see the truth on her face. She was scared, terrified. She said she loved me. Again, she didn't have to either because I already knew. Said she didn't wanna betray me anymore. Didn't wanna betray my family that's been so good to her. She wanted to start fresh, get a clean slate. Wanted to have this baby with me, raise it together. And I…"

He takes a few deep breaths, pausing, and I find myself relating to Annie. In that she fell in love with him, fell in love with the Graysons. I could see how. When I leave, I realize I'm going to miss them too. Haven, even Ax, Rad. Maybe I'll miss Mars, too, just because he loves his brothers so much. I'm not sure, but I think that's why he did what he did, getting information on Annie. I understand that sentiment.

"I promised that I would. I would raise the baby with her. Even though I…" Again, he pauses as if he doesn't know what to say or rather *how* to say it. "I didn't love Annie, not even a little bit. I realized that as soon as she told me she loved me. But I loved her. The baby. It was going to be a girl." He swallows thickly. "Didn't even know you could tell the sex of a baby that early but apparently, you can. At ten weeks and as soon as she found out it was going to be a girl, she decided she had to tell me and God, I…I understood why she had to. Because the moment I heard *she* existed, somethin' shifted inside of me. Something big. Something that changed me. It wasn't anything I'd ever experienced. All I knew was that I wanted her. I wanted her so badly in my life. She was mine. I made her. Rose."

"Rose," I repeat, because I have to after how reverently he said that name.

"Her name," he says gutturally. "Knew it the moment I heard about her. Knew I was gonna name her after my ma. She always wanted a girl, see, but she got stuck with us three rowdy boys. So I thought I could...give her that. All my life, everyone told me that I was reckless. That I did things without thinkin' them through and they weren't wrong. But the moment Annie told me about *Rose* I knew I had to be smart. I had to think things through so I...bought a ranch. Away from Black Rock. I always wanted to do it but it was somethin' way into the future. Somethin' that I would do once my rowdy phase passed. But I knew I had to do it for Rosie. My baby girl wasn't gonna grow up on Rawhide. I had to keep her away from all the Grayson-Turner bullshit. All the bloody history, the feud, the war. I promised Annie I'd keep her safe until then. Until we were ready to move. Told her I'd take care of it all. Hank Turner, her family, everything. I promised to be there for her, throughout her pregnancy, love her, love Rosie. But I knew I was lyin'. I knew I'd never love Annie but for Rosie, I was gonna try. I was gonna try to give my baby girl everything but I..."

He swallows again, but I know his emotions don't go down as easily. I *know* that sheen in his eyes is tears because I'm already crying. "I was too late. They got to Annie before I could get her to a safe place and they... They killed her. They killed my baby girl. The 'R' on my back. It's for her. For Rosie. She was... There was no way to bury her. She wasn't... So I burned her name on my shoulder and made my body her tombstone. Couldn't keep her safe out in the world so I was gonna do it, keepin' her inside of me."

Even though it's hard and I'm too weak, I still reach up and wipe my tears so I can see him clearly. Because I won't let him be alone in this. In his pain, his misery, his *grief*. If his body is a tombstone for his baby girl, I want to see it, its tight lines and rigid muscles. I don't want to let him shoulder that burden alone.

Once again he takes a big breath, as if letting it all pass through him, burying her inside and keeping her safe like he wants. "So now you know. The whole truth. And it is that it was me. I ruined her life. Annie's. She might've started working for the Turners but it didn't end that way, because she fell for me. For a man who didn't love her, who didn't even know what love was. All I wanted was to have fun. I didn't even protect her from an accidental pregnancy. How much of a fuckup does a man have to be to do that? And then I lied to her. Told her we'd be together, that I'd keep her safe but I didn't. She's dead because of me, because she wouldn't betray me. If hadn't strung her along, maybe Hank Turner woulda found another way to get our land. Maybe he woulda spared her, let her go. But I didn't and so *he* didn't. And she died because of it. Her and my…"

He doesn't have the strength to say it, his baby girl's name, so he moves on, his jaw hard as granite. "So, see, I am like your father. He killed your mother and I killed the mother of my child. I killed my… I killed my baby girl too. And no amount of penance is ever gonna be enough for that. No brand, no jail time. I don't get a clean slate or a fresh start. I don't get to live. Because she didn't. It doesn't matter if I ruin my life or somethin' inside me goes dead because I deserve that. I deserve to die. To perish. To burn in this pain for eternity. But *you* don't."

A change comes over him at this. So far, he's been a man drowning in grief, but now, he's flooded with purpose. "You don't deserve this. You don't deserve to be in love with a man who's lied and broken promises, who's destroyed lives. I'm a Grayson. My family is forged in fire and blood. Once upon a time, I thought I was different. Thought I could break free but not anymore. This is my life. This is my destiny. I *want* this to be my destiny. Blood, war, pain. I want to die, do you understand? And you're too…pure for all that. You're too *alive* to be in love with a dying man like me."

I nod, my eyes stinging, tears wet on my cheeks. "When I was young and my mom would…use me to protect herself from my daddy, I'd think about my future. I'd think about how I'd never let it happen to *my* daughter. How I'd die for her, so I understand. I don't think I could ever imagine your pain, but on some level, I understand it. I applaud it because Lord knows, not every parent is like that. And it's a noble cause, dying for someone you love. There's already too much death and destruction in this world, too much hatred, so why not make it about love. But then… What about living? What about *living* for someone you love? And it's hard, isn't it, living. Sometimes so much harder than being dead. So how about instead of dying, you live for her? For Rose. She's inside of you, isn't she. You *made* her. You made your body her tombstone. So how about instead of killing yourself for her, you give her another life. You give her *your* life. You do all the things she didn't get to do. You live and breathe and dream and be… *free*."

His eyes are widened and his mouth is open. Not a lot, but since he hardly ever shows any reaction, it's big. That and the fact I can read him. I can see this has never occurred to him. To live for his baby girl. To give her a life because he has the power to. And for a second, my heart starts to beat with hope. I can feel life rushing through my tired limbs. Because maybe… Maybe *this* will make him stop. This will make him give up his quest and…

But I pace myself. I harden my limbs and take a painful breath. It still isn't any of my business, what he does with his life. I hope he sees the light, but it's not my job to *make* him see anymore. So I set my glass aside and fold my hands in my lap. "But you're right. You're not the man for me. I know that now." An emotion flashes over his features, but I look away quickly because I don't want to decipher it. I don't want to waste any more time on him than necessary. "And as soon as I'm able to, I'll leave. But for however long I'm here, can I ask you to do something for me?"

"Anything."

"Just stay away from me."

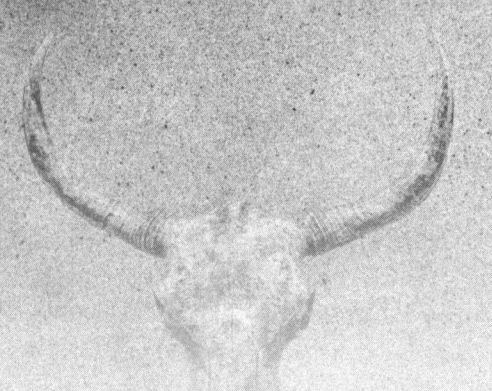

CHAPTER THIRTY-FOUR

"ARE YOU SURE you want to do this?" Peyton asks from beside me.

Sitting on the bed, I fold the last article of clothing, a dress, and put it in the little suitcase. I can't believe we're back to where we started this summer only a few weeks ago. This time, though, I'm packing my own suitcase rather than hers. Well, maybe not *my* suitcase because I borrowed it from Haven, but still.

I zip up my luggage and look at her. "Yes."

She's still not convinced. I didn't think she would be because this isn't the first time she's asked me this question. Even though I've given her the same answer all week.

"Because you know you could just stay here," she keeps insisting.

But I'm not going to stay here. I grab her hand and give it a squeeze. "Yes, I'm sure." She opens her mouth to protest, but I don't let her. "It's Bozeman, okay? I've lived there since I was eleven. And you should know that because you were there too. We lived together."

"But—"

"Not to mention, I'm going back to our apartment. So it's all good. I can handle it."

She keeps looking at me for a few seconds before sighing. "Fine. I just… I'm worried about you."

My heart squeezes in my chest because I love her. She's always been the one constant in my life, and I'm going to miss her. "I know. Because I'm worried about you too."

At this, she rolls her eyes. "I'll be fine. It's just Breck."

Now it's my turn to give her a look. Because it's not just Breck. It's the fact that her brother has asked her to live on the ranch for the summer. The ranch that we both left years ago because of all the violence and bloodshed. The ranch my friend never ever liked. I still had a few favorite spots on the property, but I know Peyton always felt trapped in that place. She always felt like she couldn't breathe. And now she's going back because that's her brother's condition. To forget what happened the night they kidnapped me a week ago.

As I predicted, Breck called the next day—as soon as he figured out my father was lying half-dead in our house—and he knew the part the Graysons had played to get me free. Not only that, but he knew exactly *who* came to my rescue; and when Breck threatened to call the cops on him, Peyton—my best friend, my constant—told Breck to cut it out or she'd never see him again. She also told him about her own part, not only in getting me rescued, because how dare he kidnap her best friend for his land, but also her part in the revenge plan.

I know she did it for me. Not only because she loves me and was so genuinely worried about me, but also because she knows how much I love... How much it meant to me that *he* didn't end up behind bars again. And it worked. Because her brother caved but on the condition that she spend the summer at Wildfire. Which she agreed to, but only after I'd recuperated from all the injuries that my father caused because of Breck.

Which means if I'm leaving for Bozeman today, she's leaving for Wildfire.

"I'm so worried, Pey," I tell her and not for the first time. "What if he uses you in some way? What if you need to get away from him and you can't? And your father, he... Now that we know about the will, about how it makes you a target, we need to be careful. I don't think you should go."

"And if I don't, what happens to him?"

This time when my heart squeezes, I have to take a second for the pain to pass. For the past week, people have been very careful around me. They walk on tiptoe and avoid any and all mention of him, even though I'm still living in his house. I'm still sleeping in his bedroom. I'm wearing the clothes he bought me. The latter is only because I have no other clothes to wear, and after everything that I've learned through all this, I can't go back to hiding. And well, I'm brave and strong but not so much that I can cut all ties with him right away. Which is why I'm also bringing these clothes with me to Bozeman.

He's the man I love, and you don't forget your love just like that. It's going to take time, but I'm not going to rush myself through it. I've already spent my entire life trying not to feel things. So if it's heartbreak I need to feel, then so be it.

Besides, what's important is that he's still keeping his promise of staying away from me. He never shows up for any of the meals. He's never in the corral where we saw Axton that first time. I never catch a passing glance of him through the kitchen window. In fact, I've seen more of Rebel, his horse, in the stables when I take my walks than I've seen of him.

Yes, I've started taking walks like I used to back at Wildfire. The doctor who came to check me out after my injuries said fresh air would do me good. Plus, I needed to keep myself busy or I'd lose my mind, waiting to get better and leave. So in addition to helping Haven around the house, I also decided to explore the ranch and its beautiful rolling meadows and blue skies. I make sure to steer clear of our barn, however. Too many memories, and I already have so many other things to contend with.

I've found a couple of reading spots for myself too. I will admit that every time I go for a walk, I hope to run into him. So much so that sometimes the back of my neck prickles and I feel him watching. I feel him following me, keeping an eye on me so I don't get lost on his land, and I have to turn back to check if I'm right.

I'm not.

Because as much as he wants to keep me safe and protect me from things, he's also very good at keeping his promises. I mean, he's keeping his promise to his baby girl, isn't he? He promised to keep her safe and he is.

Inside of him and not by seeking revenge.

God, okay. I need to take a breath here, because every time I think about it, I want to collapse on myself and sob. With joy. With victory. With all the emotions that he makes me feel. Turns out, after discovering my father's almost dead body in the middle of the day, Breck also got a call from his lawyer that Peyton's marriage and the power of attorney on her share of the land has been dissolved. Not that it was binding in any way, given that I'd signed the papers, and in my name, no less. While this was exactly what Breck wanted, or at least partially, Peyton was still trapped at Rawhide and he wanted her back. Which is why he'd called in the first place, to ask after Peyton. And when she made it clear that she hated her brother's guts for doing what he did to me, Breck had to resort to blackmail.

But the point is that Arsen gave it up.

He gave up on his quest for revenge, and no matter where things stand between us, I can't pretend I'm not affected by it. I can't pretend that I don't know he's doing it for Rose. He's finally, *finally*, going to live. He's finally going to move past it and let his baby girl live through him. As he should.

He deserves to live no matter what he thinks about himself.

So in the past week, while he was busy keeping his promise to stay away from me, I was also busy trying to not look for him and just…throw my arms around him and hold on to him. Just tell him how happy I am for him and how every night, I cry for him into my pillow.

At which point, I remind myself that even though he has a future now and *I* have a future, they're not the same. I don't *want* them to be the same. The truth is, I told him I loved him and he told me to leave. So I'm not going to beg someone for love. I'm not going to wonder why he doesn't love me. I've done all that before. So what I need to do now is forget I'm just some girl to him and move on with my *own* life.

Which brings me back to the moment and Peyton's question.

"Maybe there's another way," I tell her. "Besides, how do we know Breck's going to keep his promise? He could still call the cops when you're there."

Apparently, Breck has the camera footage from that night that shows Arsen and Rad entering the ranch, and he refuses to give it up or destroy it, calling it his insurance policy. Something no one in the Grayson family likes and for good reason. Except him. *He* doesn't care, and he said so. While the tape doesn't show Arsen's face, it does show a man wearing a bull mask, which can be traced back to the mask he wore eight years ago. Rad wore a mask, too, but there's less chance of him being made than of Arsen.

Marsden is extremely angry about it all, and both brothers had a huge problem with Arsen's recklessness. Also about the fact that Arsen didn't want Peyton to go, not for him. He didn't want anyone to risk their safety for him. While Marsden also doesn't like Breck's condition, he understood that they might not have a choice in the matter except delivering Peyton to them. Although none of them had anything on Rad's anger. That quiet man roared the loudest during the argument and said in no uncertain terms there was no way Peyton was going. Which pissed Peyton off because who the hell is he telling her what to do; and if she wanted to go, she would.

All in all, it was a big mess that involved a lot of shouting and cursing and big decisions. If I'd had the capacity to join in the shouting match, I would have. I didn't want Peyton to agree to Breck's condition either. But back then, I was still in a lot of pain, and all I could do was sit in Marsden's office when Breck called and let it all play out, while staring at my best friend with dread in my eyes.

"He won't if he knows what's good for him," Peyton says, lifting her chin.

"But—"

Now she grabs my hand and squeezes. "Look, I know you're worried about me but I promise you I can handle it. I know how to deal with my family. I'm more worried about you because you're going to be alone and…" She bites her lip. "Are you sure you can't work things out? I mean, with him."

Again, this isn't the first time she's asked me this—we've had plenty of conversations over the week, rehashing everything that happened that night, the possible future and my past—but the stab of pain I feel in my chest is just as fresh and new as it was when she asked me this earlier in the week. I have to break away from her grip and focus on fiddling with the zipper of my suitcase so I can answer: "He doesn't want anything to do with me."

"You're kidding, right?" Peyton raises her eyebrows. "He gave up his whole big plan of vengeance for you."

"He didn't do it for me."

He did it for Rose. He did it to keep her alive in his heart, and I'm so relieved about that, it doesn't even matter why. I'm so relieved there *was* something that could stop him; honestly, I don't even care why he stopped his plan, just that he did. Do I still love him? Of course I do. And do I wish he loved me back? Yes, I do wish that. But you can't always get what you want. I'm just thankful that I got one of my wishes at least.

While I told Peyton almost everything this past week, this is the one thing I can't share because it's not my place to do so. But if she knew the conversation we had just after he rescued me, she wouldn't be saying these things.

"You got kidnapped and he agreed to dissolve the stupid marriage the very next day," Peyton tells me like I don't know. "Who do you think he did that for?"

"It doesn't matter who he did it for," I tell her, shaking my head, trying not to let my heart soar; I do not need false hope. "All that matters is that he's going to be safe now. He's going to live and… That's the biggest thing I wanted for him. And yes, I love him and for a little while, I thought he was mine. He felt like mine. He felt like my safe space, my adventure. My husband. But it was fake. At least the husband part. It wasn't even my name on the certificate. It doesn't get faker than that. In any case, he didn't feel what I felt. He cared about me, yes, but…I was just some girl to him and I… All I want to do is move on."

Besides, it's not as if he's running after me. Granted, I told him to stay away. But if you want to be with someone, no one and nothing can hold you back, right? I've been living on this ranch for the past week, and if he wanted to, if he was dying to be with me like I was— *am*—dying to be with him, he could've found me, but he didn't.

I will admit that it makes me angry. It makes me furious that he hasn't yet come for me. I'm leaving in an hour, and I don't even know where he is. If he *knows* I'm leaving. But I don't want to do that. I don't want to color my memories of him with anger. I didn't want it before, and I definitely don't want it now when he's taught me so many things about myself. So I don't want to think about him anymore.

"Okay," Peyton agrees, albeit reluctantly.

"I'm going to miss you."

"I'm going to miss you too," she says, bumping our shoulders. "*Sister.*"

I chuckle. Out of all the misery and trauma of the last few weeks, finding out Peyton's my half sister has to be one of the highlights. We already knew we had a connection, but finding out how true it was makes me think everything is going to be okay.

So that's how I leave Rawhide with a smile on my face: because I have a sister. But I also have a broken heart in my chest because the man I love doesn't love me back. He isn't even there for the send-off. Only Haven and Marsden. I give Haven a tight hug and we decide to keep in touch. And even though Marsden isn't all that approachable,

I still end up giving him a hug and thanking him for giving me a place on his ranch. Axton is driving me back, so I guess our goodbye will happen when I reach the city.

In any case, I'm moving on and I'm going to live my life.

———

I'm crying.

No, I'm sobbing. I'm curled into a ball in my bed in the apartment in Bozeman and making a mess of my pillows. Which is fine; I don't care about my pillows *or* my sheets. They're the same ones from when I left weeks ago, so they are dirty. I don't have the strength to change them when my chest feels hollow. What I do care about is ruining the letters.

The ones he wrote from prison.

I've been reading them for hours now and crying. His letters didn't start my tears, though. It was Axton. It was what he said at the end, just before he left: "For what it's worth, I wanted you to be my sister-in-law too. I'd hug you but Arsen will tan my hide so—"

I already knew what he was going to say, so I just ignored it and hugged him anyway. I don't know when it happened, but he kind of grew on me these past weeks and that was a really sweet thing to say. Sweet and heartbreaking. As soon as I shut the door behind him, my tears started falling and I ran straight to my room. I went to my desk, opened the drawer where I keep his letters, and started reading them frantically.

Which only made things worse because now that I know the real him, every word he wrote as Bo screamed of the man I love. I could hear his voice while reading, all drawling and low. I could picture his expressions—whenever he lets them out—when he called me college girl for the first time. Or hinted about keeping the inmates away. His possessive voice when he told me to stay away from that professor or his angry one when I told him about my parents. I pictured him telling me about how he'd touch me if we ever met in real life, his eyes dark and his cheekbones flushed. How he thinks my body would be so soft and warm and how he'd want to leave his marks on me.

Then, to torture myself, I went on to read the little notes he'd written to me when we were at the ranch. No matter what, there was no way I was going to leave them back there. Even though I've read them all countless times and remember every word, I read them again. They'd range from his favorite color to any random thought he had during the day. A little tidbit about his childhood to what he wanted to do to me when he saw me later.

And hours later, here I am, sobbing and wheezing, hurting from all this pain in my chest, wondering where he is, what he's doing. Is he able to sleep? Where has he been this past week? How is it that we lived on the same ranch, and not once did we run into each other? It has to be deliberate, right, on his part. Because it wasn't as if *I* was trying to stay away from him.

When I'm tired and sick of myself for being a pathetic loser who can't get it through her head that it's over so I should stop wondering about such things, I force myself to get off the bed to go wash my face or something to shake it off. But I never make it past three steps to my destination because my eye catches a flash of something—a dark brown Stetson—through my bedroom window, and I freeze.

A dark figure stands right across the street, under a tree, a rocky mountain maple, looking up at my window.

For a few seconds, all I can do is stare. At the tree. At the figure—so familiar looking, so *achingly* familiar that I can't breathe. All I can think about is how I used to watch that tree every time I sat at the desk to write him a letter, and over the course of the last six months, it became my favorite. But I never in a thousand years imagined that he'd stand there in the flesh one day, and before I can give it much thought, I'm angrily wiping my tears away and running out of the bedroom.

I'm dashing to open my apartment door, in a hurry to get to him. I don't even check to make sure I've locked it behind me; I simply keep going, climbing down the stairs of the building faster than I ever have and bursting through the front entrance. At which point I stop, because he's still there, standing across the street where I saw him through the window.

It only occurs to me now, as I stand here watching him, that he may not have been real. I may have conjured him up from my imagination. That would've been better than him being real. Because I do *not* want him here. I absolutely do *not* want to see him. He doesn't get to just saunter back into my life.

I probably should've thought of that, though, before running out here barefoot and still in my travel-wrinkled dress. Because as soon as he sees me, he straightens up from the tree and starts walking toward me.

For some reason, I get so pissed at that. At his long steps and his Stetson sitting low, casting a shadow on the upper part of his face so I can't see his eyes and tell what he's thinking. Although, except for very rare occasions, when have I ever been able to tell what he's thinking. The thought makes me even angrier, and I fist my hands at my sides, ready for him.

"That's *my* tree," I blurt out just as he's within a few steps from me.

At my voice, he stops, and I finally get to see his face. Under a spotlight, no less, because of the streetlamp I'm standing by. Despite my anger at him, I can't help but devour his features with my eyes. I can't help but catalog every little detail of them because I didn't get to do that this past week. The last time I saw him was in Marsden's office during Breck's phone call. He stood on the other side of the room from me and in a corner that I thought Rad would've picked for himself. He kept his arms folded across his chest and head bent with his Stetson on so there was no chance of me getting to see anything. Marsden did all the talking on the phone, while the group consisting of Peyton, Rad, Haven, and Axton huddled around the desk. He spoke only when Breck mentioned his condition for

Peyton to visit him. Which quickly escalated into a heated argument that they had to cut the call to resolve.

Although now that I'm finally able to look at him, I don't know how it makes me feel. First, because everything about him is so contradictory in this moment. His clothes are severely rumpled, but his body seems snapped straight. His stubble-beard is back, which should make him also look rumpled, but it doesn't because of his clenched jaw. And while his eyes are red-rimmed and look utterly exhausted, I can see that they're alert and awake. He should look lost like he did the night he rescued me, but somehow, he looks recently found. Which is when it hits me.

I hope it's because of me. I still hope he *wants* me.

I hope it's because he's getting to look at me probably for the first time in the past week, too; and his eyes are frantically taking me in, devouring me like I've been devouring him. I hate that. I hate that my sight makes him look like he's found heaven after a long walk scouring the lands when I know it doesn't mean anything. I don't *want* it to mean anything.

"That's my tree," I repeat when all he does is stare at me.

"Your favorite," he tells me like I don't know. Like it wasn't me who told him about it in my letters in the first place. "The one you saved."

Along with telling him that it's my favorite, I also told him they were going to cut it down. And it was him who said I should get the neighborhood together and rally. Which I did and hence saved it. Somehow this piece of information makes me angrier still. Because what choice did I have but to fall in love with him when he was so… sweet? I hate that. I hate that he always does things like this. I hate that I'm curling my bare toes on the concrete at how nostalgic his voice sounds. It's ridiculous; I heard it six days ago. There hasn't been enough time to establish the stupid nostalgia that's running through my body.

That's why I say something completely childish: "You can't stand under it."

And yet he responds like it's the most riveting conversation of all time. "Didn't know where else to stand where I'd have a clear view of your window." Before I can say anything to that, he adds, "You shouldn't be out here."

"*You* shouldn't be out here," I accuse.

"Why aren't you sleepin'?"

"Why aren't *you* sleeping?" I keep accusing, but at this, I realize how ridiculous our exchange is. I know why he isn't sleeping. Because he can't. Because, apparently, he needs *me*. I'm his hypnotic. My scent is what lulls him to sleep; and I hate him, but I don't hate him enough to make light of something like this.

I go to apologize, but he doesn't seem to care as he searches my face with a frown. "You...you cryin'?"

This sends me back into the anger mode, and I fist my fingers tighter. "Yes, as a matter of fact, I was." He flinches and I feel a tiny bit bad for him but not enough to stop myself from continuing, "Because I miss Rawhide. I miss the people I met there. Haven, Ax, Rad. Even Mars. Why, does that bother you? That I *miss* them and I'm crying about them."

I know what I'm doing is petty. He didn't want me to tell him I was going to miss him when I left, so now, I'm bludgeoning him with the word. I also know I told myself to be dignified about all this. About how it's okay if he doesn't love me back. How I'm totally fine and I can handle things. But it all went poof the moment I saw him standing under my tree.

So fuck being dignified. Fuck *him* for ruining my plans of being dignified. He needs to suffer. Although it doesn't look like he's suffering. If anything, he seems to be coming awake and alive even more than before. With each passing second, the lines around his mouth are becoming slacker. And his eyes hold more fire and are glittering as he shakes his head slowly. "Missin' them, no. Cryin' over it, yeah."

"Well, you don't get a choice in the matter. If I want to cry, I'll cry. If I want to fill buckets with my tears, I'll do that too. You get no say in that."

His jaw clenches and regret clear as day passes through his features. "I know."

I harden myself against it. "So then, care to explain to me why you need a clear view of my window?"

"So I can see when you turn out the light."

"And why do you need to see *that*?"

He breathes in, his chest swelling. "So I know you're in bed."

"Okay but—"

"Safe," he adds, and I lose my breath.

Because I finally understand what he's doing, and even though it's hard, I show no emotion with my tone when I ask, "Is this because of what happened last week? Because they took…"

I don't complete the sentence and say "took *me*." Because just like the night he rescued me, he starts to breathe faster at the mention of my kidnapping. Like he still isn't over it. Like it happened only hours ago instead of a week. And while I can see why he'd feel this way, because I do get spooked from time to time myself, I know I'm safe. I know they won't come for me again. Not even my father, who's lying in a hospital bed right now, in a coma, because of this man standing in front of me. His rescue was absolute.

He gives his head a shake, which more or less is a jerk as he replies, "Can't get any peace if I don't know you are where you're supposed be. In your room or with Haven or Ax. Out takin' your walks, safe."

I notice how he said "peace" and not "sleep," because again, he doesn't get much of that when I'm away. I also notice the other things he mentioned, and before I can stop myself, I ask, or more like accuse, "You've been… You've been keeping tabs on me?"

His answer is immediate: "Yeah."

"How?"

"Just…askin' about you. To Haven, Ax, Peyton. Rad even." He

licks his lips, and I refuse to acknowledge to myself how shiny they look. "Followin' you when you'd take your walks. Standin' outside your door, waitin' to see the light go out from under the door."

"And here I thought I told you to keep your distance from me."

"I did." He nods. "Made sure to never let you know I was there or run into you."

So there's my answer. He *was* deliberately trying to not be seen. Although I do want to tell him that I knew. At least, when I was on my walks. I could feel him. Granted, I could never confirm it, but I knew. But that's not important. What's important is again, I don't know how it makes me feel. On one hand, I'm glad he honored my wishes; and on the other, I'm pissed that he gave me what I wanted. And since pissed is a bigger emotion for me in the moment, I keep accusing: "So basically, you've been stalking me all this time."

His breath puffs out as he says, "Stalkin' is more Rad's territory but if you wanna call it that, it's fine."

I clench my teeth. "Yes, I *do* want to call it that because that's what it is."

"I call it somethin' else."

"Yeah? What?"

His eyes flick back and forth between mine as he says in a rough voice, "Me keepin' tabs on you, watchin' you from a distance, finally leaving Rawhide to follow you to Bozeman, it's not stalkin'. I call it living."

My voice is high and my heart is sitting on the tip of my tongue when I ask, "You…you moved to Bozeman?"

He gives out a short nod. "Yeah."

"That's…" I shake my head, looking at him in disbelief. "Are you insane? Have you completely lost your mind?"

"Not yet."

"I can't…" I take in a sharp breath. "Do you realize how crazy this is? This is the city. Maybe it's not the busiest city or the biggest city in the world but it's crowded. It's *way* more crowded than Black

Rock, than your ranch. And you hate crowds. Not in the way where you find people annoying. Although, you do find them that but more in a real, symptomatic way."

His jaw is hard, and I expect him to wave it off or shut this down. But all he does is shrug—albeit extremely tightly—and reply, "A small price to pay for living."

This time when he uses that word, I can finally hear it, and it's not a good thing. Because I've been able to hold on to my ire all this time. I've been able to focus on distracting things instead of the most important fact of all: that he is *here* in the first place. But at this, my reprieve is over and I have to face facts.

And the fact is, he's here for me.

He can see it, too, that I've finally accepted the truth, because his chest swells again and he swallows thickly. "Pictured tellin' you this one day. Didn't know it'd be tonight though. It wasn't my intention when I came here. I just... I wanted to thank you."

"What?"

He swallows with difficulty again. "For savin' my life."

"I didn't—"

"For savin' *her* life. My... Rosie."

At this, I can't say anything. My words turn into pinpricks and get stuck in my throat, and all I can do is stare at him with stinging eyes. He shakes his head, looking over my shoulder. "It never occurred to me. To honor her in that way. Never thought I could... I knew nothin' would bring her back but I didn't think there was a way to still keep her alive. I thought I'd lost her and I know it sounds strange 'cause I never had her but... Just the idea of her was so...real. So vivid and visceral that I... I lost my head a little bit." He narrows his eyes as he keeps going as if he can see something in the distance that no one else can. "Can't say I've ever been really good at usin' my head. I was always this way, but I guess it got really bad when my parents passed. Ma was the only one I'd listen to, but when she was gone... All of us boys got real rowdy. I regret a lot of things in my life."

His eyes come back to mine then. "You already know that. But the biggest regret I've got is what I did to you. And I'm not talkin' about what I did before, when I lied to you and"—his jaw clenches—"kidnapped you. I do regret that still, but I… I'm talkin' about how I treated you when you told me. You told me your feelings. You were so brave that night, standin' there, bare body, bare soul and it… It was the most stunning you've ever been. Proud and vulnerable. Beautiful. So *strong* that it…"

He pauses to put his hand to his chest, rubbing it a bit. I don't even think he realizes he's doing it because his eyes once again have a faraway look, like he's actually picturing me from that night.

"It makes my chest hurt," he goes on, coming back to me again. "It makes my whole body hurt, *burn* that I… I sent you away. Instead of gatherin' you in my arms and giving you what you wanted: my truth. At the time, I told myself that I was doin' it for your own good. I was pushin' you away, tellin' you to run, breakin' your precious heart because that was the right thing to do. And maybe it was because God knows, I haven't really been a worthy man. Not even before I got put away. I was an asshole. I lied back then too. I used women. Never respected them enough to stick around. I was self-ish, had my fun and cut. But I've been doin' some soul-searchin' this past week and the *complete* truth is that you scare me. You scared me when I'd only read your words and you scared me even more when I saw you in that white dress I told you to wear. You *made* me feel too much. You make me feel too much. With you, I don't know what's right or what's wrong. I don't know up from down. I don't know if I should slow down or speed up. I push you away but I don't let go. I pull you closer but I'm afraid to hold on. Everything about you scares me. Your strength, your bravery when I've always been a coward when it comes to emotions. How you can be vulnerable when I don't know how. How you can fill all the empty spaces in my chest when I keep breakin' your heart. It scares me that you deserve so much more and so much better than me. Than a hardened ex-con with a million regrets who only started breathin' again when you made him. When you filled his lungs with your buttercup scent. When you filled his nightmares with dreams. When you got him to sleep."

His jaw clenches and his nostrils flare with a tough breath. "I've got nothin' to give you, only a bloody past and a prison record. I don't even know how to function in the outside world. I can't breathe with too many people around. I can't sleep without holdin' you in my arms. I'm barely a man so it terrifies me to be standin' here and tellin' you this but you deserve to know. You deserve to know that I love you. I'm in love with you. You're the only woman I've ever loved."

He shakes his head, his eyes molten. "I don't know anything about it, about this feeling. I don't know how to handle it. I don't know how to cope with it except when I think about my life, I think about you. I think about makin' you smile, makin' you laugh. Keepin' you safe, protectin' you, watchin' over you. I think about giving you your every wish, makin' you happy. Standin' outside of your window to make sure you got to sleep okay. Followin' you wherever you go and standin' guard so nothin' bad ever touches you. When I think about my life, I think about how you saved it. And how the only way I can ever repay you is by living it. Is by being alive, by keeping Rosie alive. So I moved to Bozeman because I wanted to live and the only place I want to live is where you are."

CHAPTER THIRTY-FIVE

IT'S BEEN A week, and he's still living his life.

If following me around is what you call life, and apparently, he does. He stands outside my window every night and doesn't leave until I turn out my lights. Every morning as I leave for work, I once again find him standing under my favorite tree, waiting for me. And then he walks me all the way to the abused-women's shelter where I'm volunteering for the summer. He disappears after that to God knows where and then comes back around when it's lunchtime. So he can follow me to a café nearby—not the one where we first met; I steer clear of that one on purpose—and watch me order my tea and my strawberry crumb muffin. I realize it's not really lunch, but that's all the appetite I have these days. Anyway, once I have my lunch, he walks me back—from a distance—to the shelter and comes back to do the same when the day's over and I need to go back.

Not once during this whole one-week period has he approached me or tried to talk to me. Well, except for the first day when he left a note at my door. I saw it when I came back from work. It said: *You need to eat lunch.* Because he must have seen me ordering my muffin and didn't like it. I'm not going to lie, it pissed me off a little bit. So much so that I took off the note taped to my door, unlocked it, and went to the window. As always, he was there under the tree, waiting for my lights to come on so he'd know I was home safe. As if some danger could befall me while climbing up two flights of stairs from the front door of the building to my apartment on the third floor.

I stared at him through the space, made a big show of holding the note up, and then crushed it in my hand and threw it into the trash can I held in my other hand. I will admit that my anger lasted for only about fifteen minutes. At which point I went back to the can, fished his note out, and stored it in the desk drawer with all his other letters and notes. And then wrote him a note and went outside to attach it to the tree.

I am eating lunch. PS: You need to stop following me. —R

To which he responded with:

Strawberry crumb muffin is not lunch. PS: I can't. —A

It is, if I want it to be. PS: Yes, you can. —R

If you don't start eating properly, I'm going to have to tell Haven. And she's already worried about you. PS: No. —A

Are you threatening to tell on me? PS: People at my work think you're a creep. —R

Yes, I am because again, you need to eat. PS: I don't care about other people. —A

You're an asshole. I'll eat what I want. PS: What if someone calls the cops? You're still on parole. —R

I called Haven today. She said she's going to send food with Ax. You can freeze it until you're ready to eat. PS: Again, I don't care about other people. —A

He did call Haven, and she called *me* the next day, worried. I told her I was fine and that I missed her. She said I should come visit soon. I agreed because I didn't want to seem rude, but we both knew I was lying. And then I cried for hours—I seem to do that every night, actually—because I can't believe he told on me and that my freezer is now overflowing with Haven's delicious cooking. I can't believe that for the past week, we've been passing notes like we're in grade school and he still won't leave.

So today, on day eight, I've decided to take the matter into my own hands. When I see him standing at the tree as I'm leaving for work, instead of ignoring him and going on my way, I head to him. I watch him stand up straight as he notices me crossing the street to him, and then I watch him watch me. Take in my pink-colored lacy dress—it's one of the dresses he bought me—and my Mary Janes. He looks at my braid hanging over my shoulder, and for a few seconds his eyes become glued to the swishing end, his fists clenching at his sides as if he's imagining touching it, my hair.

Just as I reach him, he looks up, and I say, "What happened to your hand?"

This wasn't the question I planned on asking him. So I'm surprised it came out, but it makes sense because there's a bandage around his right palm and it looks similar to the one he had the night he rescued me. And he's had it for two weeks now and shouldn't it be healed?

"Cut my hand," he says, his eyes never moving from mine.

"Again?"

"Yeah."

"At the same spot?"

"At the same spot."

"How's that…" I take a deep breath and let it go before asking, "Where do you live?"

He shifts on his feet. "In the bunkhouse."

"What bunkhouse?"

"The ranch where I work."

I frown. "You're *working* here?"

His lips twitch a little, and I swear to God, he looks like the Arsen back at Rawhide, all cocky and arrogant with his Stetson, his dark T-shirt and washed out jeans. His stubble-beard is back to being stubble, but his hair's growing longer; I can see the strands curling at the nape of his neck. The look is only for a moment, though, and then he's back to being a contradiction. Exhausted to the bone but oh so alive, like his life hasn't ever been better. "What else would I be doin'?"

"I don't know, going back to Black Rock? Working on *your* ranch. Breaking horses, thinking about your future. Any number of those things."

"Can't leave."

I curl and uncurl my fingers. "How long are you going to keep this up?"

"Keep what up?" he asks almost cheerfully, like sparring with me first thing in the morning is putting him in good spirits.

"This. Following me around, watching me, standing under my window, writing notes to me."

He pauses a beat to take me in. "You askin' when I'm gonna die, darlin'? Because it won't stop. Not until the last breath leaves my body."

"Don't call me that," I say, my chest tight, my belly fluttering.

For a second it looks like he's going to say something in retort, and God, I wait for it. Despite everything, I wait for him to give me a chance to sass him back. But a few seconds of scrutiny later, his chest swells with a breath. "You're gettin' late for work. And so am I."

He tips his chin at me, asking me without words to get going, but I don't move. Instead, I say, "You're torturing yourself."

He clenches his jaw then because he knows I'm right. "I'm fine."

"No, you're not," I insist, my tone urgent. "At first, I thought it was just the café but you live in a bunkhouse, Arsen. With God knows how many cowboys. You need to stop. You need to go back."

You need help.

I don't say it, but I know he gets my meaning. Because I'm right. He does need help, help with navigating on the outside. Especially navigating in crowded places, restaurants, bunkhouses. Every time I see him around lunch, his demeanor is different. He's on edge and intense, his frame tighter. To the outside world, he probably looks threatening and dangerous with his clenched jaw and pitch-black eyes, but to me, he appears to be struggling.

The first time he showed up during lunch, I finally connected the dots from the very beginning. When we met at that café. Why he looked so intense and alert. It was his PTSD, among other things. And now every time he comes around, I want to go to him and shake some sense into him.

"I can handle myself," he grunts, his jaw moving and back forth.

I don't know how I do it, but I manage to keep myself from punching him in the face for being such a stubborn asshole. All I do is glare and ask, "You want to watch me then?"

"Never wanna stop watchin' you."

His tone makes my heart race, but I focus only on my anger, as I have been this past week. "Fine. Go ahead and watch me."

This is diabolical, what I am doing, but it needs to be done.

He's given me no other choice. I've tried everything, glaring at him on my way to work, freezing him out on my way back, repeatedly writing notes that tell him to leave. But he won't listen. He won't leave, and I want him to *leave*.

I *need* him to.

He was right that night. I do not deserve a man like him. A man who breaks my heart over and over again. A man who strips me bare, also over and over again. Who lies and cheats and then comes all the way here to *thank* me for saving his life like I'm some kind of a hero instead of a pathetic girl in love who has trouble holding on to her justified anger at him. Oh, and then he proceeds to torture himself on a daily basis.

It doesn't matter if he loves me back, because it's too late. We have too much history and misery between us.

So this is the only way to send him away, even though I want to throw up. Especially when the guy sitting in front of me reaches out and grabs my hand on the table with a smile that makes my insides crawl. This wasn't what I had in mind when I pictured going on a date with another man.

He works at the shelter and has always been nice to me, smiling at me when I come in for work, waving good night to me at the end of the day. Most of all, he's *not* a cowboy. His parents do own a ranch, but he wasn't ever interested in things like that. His degree is in political science and psychology. So he seemed like a perfect candidate to ask out to dinner. Although I will say, I didn't tell him this was a date. All I said was I'd love to grab dinner with him tonight and catch up on things because I'm new here. So this is a date only for pretend purposes. For the purposes of my stalker who won't leave me alone. I figured if he wanted to watch, I should *give* him something to watch.

I also said to Colt—that's the guy's name—that we'd grab takeout and eat in the park instead of at the crowded and enclosed restaurant. I want Arsen to leave, not be further tortured. At least outside there's an option for him to move around or pick a lonely corner somewhere, which he sometimes likes to do when things get hard, especially during bonfires at the ranch.

I breathe in a sigh of relief when the food arrives and Colt has to let go of my hand to pick up the brown paper bag. As soon as we walk out the door, I know *he's* following me; he was there at the restaurant, too, at a table in a far corner. And he was across the street from the shelter to escort me back to the apartment at the end of my workday. I came out with Colt today, though, a first, so I don't know how that affected him. I also don't know what he thought about the detour we took to this restaurant.

But now that we're walking to the park, I can't ignore his heat. It's so thick that I can feel it grazing my back. It's brushing the nape of my neck, prickling the bare skin of my arms. And I just want to stop it. I want to tell Colt this was a mistake, that I'm not interested in him. I will never be interested in him or any other man because there's only one man I want and he's currently following us.

Just as I turn to Colt, he turns toward me and grabs my hand again. The shock makes me come to a halt. We're a block away from the park, on the sidewalk with an alley between two buildings. Seems like a good place to talk and get this awkward encounter over with. But he's the first to speak: "I never thought you'd be the one to ask a guy out."

Yikes. So he knew it was a date. It makes things even more awkward, but I have to forge ahead. "Um, yeah, about that. I think I—"

"You are the most beautiful girl I have ever seen," he says, his brown eyes sparkling.

"Oh, I... Thank you. But I just—"

"And truth be told," he keeps going, leaning toward me a little bit. "You're exactly my type." This is going downhill super fast, so once again, I take a breath to prepare to get my point across, but he doesn't let me. "I'm into heavier girls. With curves and all that..." He pauses to gesture with his hands and motions toward my chest and then my ass. "This is fucking amazing."

Embarrassed and quite frankly offended, I step back and finally speak: "I don't think this is going to work out."

But he either doesn't hear what I say or chooses to ignore me, because the moment I widen the gap between us, he closes it and obviously intends to put his mouth on mine. I can smell garlic on his breath from lunch. But before he can make contact, he's been pushed back.

He's been *dragged* back, because my stalker has decided to make his presence known.

He's got Colt by the collar as he slams his back into the brick wall. Colt groans and coughs, but Arsen doesn't give him a chance to catch his breath before he rears back and punches him in the face. And before Colt can recover from that, Arsen lays another one on him. Then he gets up in Colt's face, wrapping his fingers around his throat as he growls, "Stay the fuck away from her. You think you can touch her? You think you can touch what's mine?"

"Arsen!" I call out, his bearlike voice bringing me out of my shock. With my heart racing, I rush over to them. "Arsen, let him go."

He doesn't listen to me. Instead, I watch as his bicep bulges more and Colt's eyes bug out. "What if he calls the cops? You could go back to jail. Stop it, right now."

But of course he doesn't listen. If anything, his grip increases, and his expression turns even more mean. When has the threat of cops ever stopped this man? So I say the only thing that I know will get him to stop. "Arsen, if you don't stop, I'll... I'll never talk to you. I'll never write you another note and I'll—"

Just like that, he lets go. His fingers around Colt's throat loosen, and he steps back from him, turning toward me. Colt's body slumps, and he's coughing as he goes down to his knees on the pavement. But neither of us pays any attention to him. Arsen's focus is locked on me as my focus is on him.

I take in his wildly breathing chest, his fisted hands, his clenched jaw as I say, "I'm not yours."

He wipes his mouth with the back of one hand as he studies me back, my heaving chest, my flushed cheeks. "You did that on purpose."

My heart is pounding. "You could've killed him."

His nostrils flare with a big breath. "He would've deserved it for puttin' his hands on you."

I lift my trembling chin. "I wanted his hands on me."

His jaw tics. "No, you wanted to piss me off."

"I thought you wanted to watch," I taunt. "So I gave you something to watch."

"And put yourself in danger in the process."

I swallow as a small shiver of fear runs down my spine. Rationally, I know we were out in the open and so I probably could've gotten out of the kiss Colt was going to lay on me. But still, no girl wants to be kissed without her consent. So damn it, I'm grateful he came. But he doesn't need to know that so I lie, "It was fine. I was fine. You didn't need to barge in and save the day."

"When it comes to you, I'll always barge in and save the day. Or die tryin'."

"*God*," I growl, stomping my foot. "What about other guys, huh? Is that what you're going to do when I start dating other people? You'll come in and punch them and scare them away."

His chest shudders with a large breath and something violent passes through his features. "If they hurt you, yes."

"Oh, so, what, you're my bodyguard now? A guy has to pass your test to be deemed worthy of me?"

"*No one*," he growls, violence flickering through his features once again, "is worthy of you. No one will ever be worthy of you. No one will ever be fit to breathe in your direction, or share the same space as you. No one will ever come close." Then, with a large breath that seems designed to calm him down, "But I'll settle for someone who doesn't hurt you or make you cry. Or put his hands on you in an alley when you don't want it."

And you didn't want it.

He doesn't say that, but it's clear he means it; and Jesus, I'm so done with him. I'm done with his tortured expression, his anguish, his stubborn protectiveness. The fact is that I'm so fucking happy he put an end to this farce I started for reasons I can't remember right now. And I can't have that. I cannot have him melting me like this. What does it say about me if I keep forgiving him for all his crimes? If I keep giving him second chances.

"For the thousandth time, okay? Just leave. Leave, leave, *leave*. Go back to your ranch."

His eyes turn into angry slits and his chest vibrates with his next words: "And for the *thousandth* time, I'm not leavin'. I'm not goin' anywhere. I'm not wastin' my life livin' somewhere you are not. Somewhere I can't protect you, keep you safe, watch over you. Even if I have to do it from afar. And you can call me your bodyguard or whatever the fuck you want but you know who I am. You know I'm the man you saved. You know I'm the man you brought back from dead. I'm the man you taught how to dream again. I'm the man you let touch you with his filthy cowboy *criminal* hands. You gave me the *privilege* to touch you and I ain't forgettin' that.

"It doesn't matter if I have to watch you go with another man and if I have to cut myself every single minute of every single day just to stop myself from fuckin' him up because you smiled at him; I'll still do it. I'll walk through fire. I'll walk through land rigged with explosives. If it means I get to be able to look at you. So you wanna ignore me, you go ahead and ignore me. You don't wanna look at me, you go ahead and look somewhere else. You can walk by me and pretend I'm dead. You can go about your fuckin' day like I don't exist. It'll kill me but I'll take it. I'm not leavin', because I'm branded. You branded me when you saved my life. So I'm not leavin' and you need to get that through your head and stop actin' foolish."

You know what, fuck it. How dare he? How dare he throw my words back at me and call himself branded when he doesn't even know the meaning of it. When he doesn't even know how much it hurts me to ignore him and pretend he doesn't exist. So without thinking it through, I launch myself at him. I don't care that Colt is still coughing and wheezing somewhere close to us. I don't care that we're in the middle of a sidewalk and even though we were alone up until now, anyone could walk by and see a crazy girl in a pink dress beating on a huge cowboy who doesn't do anything to stop her.

He simply gives my foolhardy launch a safe place to land, his chest. He simply keeps me plastered to it with his arm around my waist as I keep punching him and smacking him and scratching his jaw and his face. And as I do it, I hear myself sob. I hear myself cry and chant how much I hate him. How he makes everything so hard. How he always, *always* does that. And if this is his way of protecting me and keeping me safe, then he's not really doing a good job of it, because he keeps hurting me himself.

I don't know how long I keep displaying my wrath, but at some point, I run out of steam and slump against his chest. I burrow my nose in his pecs and breathe him in, my lungs filling with his musky, outdoorsy smell, my tired body and battered heart resting in the cradle of his flexing arms. I realize we aren't on the sidewalk anymore but in the alley. I can see the brick wall he's leaning against as he rocks me back and forth.

Despite everything, my heart thinks it's poetic. It started in an alley when he grabbed me, so it should end in one too. Swallowing, I look up and our eyes tangle. "I hate you."

His chest shudders. "I know."

I look at the scratches on his face, especially a big one on his jaw. "I drew blood."

"I deserve more."

I clutch his T-shirt. "You're never going to leave, are you?"

He squeezes his arms around my waist and his voice sounds almost sad, as if he's delivering bad news. "No."

"Do you…" I twist his T-shirt, my heart racing in my chest. "Do you really love me?"

His eyes become liquid and shiny, and he squeezes me to his body again. "Yeah."

"You don't know what love is," I tell him.

Something like pain crosses his face and his breath hitches. "No."

I dig my knuckles into his chest and go up on my tiptoes. "So then how come you're the only one who knows how to love me?"

He watches me for a beat, his eyes going back and forth between mine. When he understands what he's looking at in my eyes, on my face, he brings his hand up to my face and shakes his head. "Oh, darlin', no. Don't you do it. Don't you forgive—"

"So you've been cutting yourself?" I speak over him.

He's cupping my jaw with the same hand and he swallows. "Pain helps me focus."

My heart drops to my stomach. "How often?"

His thumb rubs my cheek. "Only when I can't control the urge to see you. To bury my good intentions and bust down doors to go to you. To watch you sleep. To cut through a crowd and hunt you down to touch you." Then, after a pause and with his thumb still caressing my skin: "Bein' good don't come easy to me, darlin', but I'm tryin' and I'll be damned if I'll fail."

It takes me a few seconds to catch my breath, but when I do, I strain my legs to stand even taller. "You're going to stop."

He frowns. "What?"

"Cutting yourself," I order. "And you're going to go see someone about your PTSD." Before he can protest, I say, "I'm not going to argue with you about it. You've done it your way and now it's going to be *my* way."

He watches me a beat before giving out a very short nod, and I breathe out a sigh of relief. But it's not over yet because I have a couple more things to straighten out. "You're going back to your ranch tomorrow."

That gives him a pause and his frown comes back. "I thought we just—"

"There are shelters there too, right?" I keep going. "In Black Rock." He goes taut but I continue, "You said I could work there too, if I wanted. You wouldn't tie me to your bed or anything."

His features are firm when he says, "Reverie, no."

"Why?"

"Because you can't forgive me. I don't deserve to be forgiven. I—"

"It's not up to you, is it," I tell him, tightening my hold on his T-shirt. "Like it wasn't up to you that I fell in love with you. It wasn't *up to you* when I decided to be brave and tell you. I did what I did on my own. I knew I was taking a risk and yes, it backfired but again, it's not up to you to tell me how to handle that."

"But I—"

"You're always bossing me around, telling me to do things.

You're putting me in places I don't want to be. But again, it's not up to you. You can't tell me how to feel or what to do. I can decide for myself. I can decide whether I want to be with you or not. Whether I want to forgive you or not. All you can do"—I breathe deep—"is apologize."

We've had this discussion before, back when he brought me to the ranch and decided to end things between us because he thought that was what was good for me. I can see the memory of it flickering through his eyes. But I didn't let him decide for me back then, and I'm not going to let him do that now.

Still, though, he leans forward and argues, "But I can't promise that I'll never hurt you again."

"I'm not asking you to promise me that."

"I can't promise I won't make you cry."

"I'm not asking for that either."

He pauses a second to breathe through his nose, then brings his other hand up to my cheeks too. He cradles my face and drops his forehead over mine. "So what're you askin' for?"

I grab his wrists and crane my neck to whisper close to his mouth, "That you'll always love me in your way, the way I need. The way only you know how."

"Always."

"And you'll never forget to live."

"Never."

I close my eyes then as tears fall down my cheeks. Happy tears. Relieved tears. Tears for all that he's made me go through and all that he's gone through for me. And then there are tears for all that came before. All that happened eight years ago.

"Do you know," I begin, whispering against his mouth as he wipes my tears, "how brave you are? How beautiful and strong and I... I'm so... I know you call me brave. I know you call me beautiful but I couldn't have done what you did. I couldn't have... My chest hurts when I think about it, when I think about Rosie. I dream about her too. I see her at night and I think she looks like you. And every day, I carry that picture in my heart. Because I figure she needs all the hearts in the world where she can live, she can thrive. And because that's all I can do for you and it makes me feel so useless sometimes. So useless that I can't...I can't even imagine the pain correctly. I can't even wrap my head around it to give you what you need. And you... You did it. You gave it up. For Rosie. For—"

"For you."

"What?"

His eyes are wet. I can see water sitting on the rims and it breaks my heart further that he won't let them fall, his tears. That he will drink them down and absorb them inside instead of letting them out because he still thinks he deserves to live through hell for his failures. Then and there, I make a promise to change that. If I've given him life, then I can also teach him to live it in peace. He taught me to live mine, so this is only fair.

"I gave it up for you."

"M-me?"

He swallows thickly, his Adam's apple jerking. "When I found out you were gone. That they..." He has to breathe in and out again. "I knew what I had to do to get you back. I knew what they'd ask for. So I...I called the lawyer. I called him to dissolve everything. It didn't matter, the land, the revenge. None of it mattered when the price was too high. When the price was you." He rolls his forehead against mine, his fingers pressing into my cheeks. "I was still hell-bent on dyin' though. Still hell-bent on destroyin' myself. Thought I'd go away somewhere, live the rest of my godforsaken life away from all the people I've hurt. Away from *you*. So I didn't hurt you anymore, didn't make you cry. Didn't break your heart. But then you..." He keeps rolling his forehead against mine, his breaths choppy and sweet. "You showed me a better way. You showed me that Rosie could live and—"

I capture his words with my mouth. Because they're so precious, so fragile and spun from sugar, that they need to be protected at all costs. They need to be kept safe inside of me, on my tongue, in my bloodstream, so I can remember them forever. I can remember that he's the only one who's ever chosen me.

Over and over and *over again*.

I don't even know how I found him or how he found me, but I'm not letting him go. I'm never letting him go. And I tell him that with my kiss. I tell him when I fill his lungs with my air and he tells me back when he does the same. We kiss and kiss until the world stops and time loses all its meaning.

Until I whisper, "I love you."

"I love you too," he whispers.

"I'm not letting you go. No matter how much you argue. I'm coming with you to Black Rock."

"Yeah, you are," he rasps, followed by the sweetest words anyone has ever said in this world. "Till death do us part."

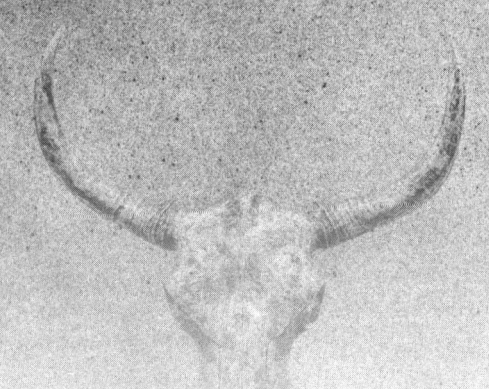

EPILOGUE

I AM RUNNING.

I am going as fast as my feet will take me, but it doesn't seem enough. It doesn't seem like I'll be able to get away. It's my dress. It's long and heavy, with a lacy trail and a tulle skirt, which keeps attracting brambles and foliage. It keeps getting caught, making me stumble, messing with my speed.

On my third stumble, I hear the footsteps and my heart jumps in my throat. They're thudding and powerful. They make the ground shake. They shift the gravity even, so it feels like my limbs are made of lead. I still try, though. I keep pushing, pumping my legs, rushing through the woods. But when my skirt catches on something again and I stumble, I know it's game over.

I'm going down.

And I'm proven correct when instead of meeting the ground, I meet a pair of corded arms that bind around me like ropes and break my fall. I'd be relieved that I don't hit the ground as viciously as I thought I would but I'm not because it's the very arms I have been running away from. So my first words are: "Please don't… please don't h-hurt me."

I'm on the ground now, on my belly, lying on those arms, and I feel him breathing against my back. I feel his chest sliding up and down, his weight heavy and suffocating. And then he says, directly into my ear, "Shh, not another word."

My fingers fist the dirt. "But I—"

I feel his head shaking slowly, deliberately, as he *tsks*. "If you keep breakin' the rules so soon, I'm gonna have to put a stop to this, and the fun is only beginning."

My heart is racing so fast that it's a wonder I can hear his voice. Let alone understand the implication of his words when those arms slide up from my belly and go to the bodice of my dress, pulling and tugging, causing me to break his rule again. "Please, not my—"

His impatient sigh halts my words, and fear skates down my spine. "Not your what?"

I'm panting, sweat pooling in the small of my back with his heat. "My d-dress. Don't…don't tear it."

"No?" he says in a silky soft voice.

"No, please, don't. Don't…"

"Why not?"

"It's my…my w-wedding dress."

He hums, his chest vibrating at my back, making me whimper. "Fuck yeah, it is, isn't it. Saw you walk down the aisle in it." He chuckles, all rough and almost angry. "Almost came in my pants, watchin' your titties bounce in that thing. You pick this out for your husband?"

I swallow. "Y-yes."

"Yeah, I bet you did. I bet he likes it, don't he. He likes to see 'em bounce too," he says roughly, his fingers grabbing one of my tits and giving it a squeeze.

A hard one that makes me arch up and moan, ashamed of myself at making these noises at such a violent grip. "Yes, h-he does."

"But I bet he doesn't like it when others watch, yeah?"

"No."

"Yeah, I knew it. He looks like a motherfucker, your new husband. He beat people up for you?" he asks next, squeezing my tit rhythmically.

It's so hard to keep my moans in check, but I do my best. I do my best to answer all his questions, too, play his game, but it's getting harder and harder to focus. With his weight, his mean fingers, his words. So dirty and God help me, so erotic.

"I don't… I don't want him to," I whisper.

"No? I bet that asshole doesn't listen to you though."

"S-sometimes he does when I…"

"When you what?"

Shame burns my cheeks as I reply, "I tell him if… if he lets it go, he can… he can put it in my ass."

His chest shudders with an amused chuckle. "Yeah, that'll get him to listen. You've got a bouncy ass too, don't you, baby, and I bet he's a sucker for it."

"He loves it."

"Don't blame him," he breathes in my ear. "I will say though that I'm awfully jealous of him. That he gets to tap it every night."

"Please just—"

"What else?" he cuts me off. "What else do you do to calm him down?"

Oh God, I can't say this, can I? It's not… exactly appropriate. It's not exactly what a good girl does to get her new husband to listen. But I have to or he won't let it go. "Sometimes I tell him to"—I swallow, my fingers digging into the earth—"fuck me in front of them. So they know… they know who I b-belong to."

He chuckles again, but this time it's strained, as if it's getting difficult to hold on to his composure. "Ah, what a sweet little whore."

His words are accompanied by a brutal squeeze of my tit and I arch up again. "*Please.*"

"I can see why that asshole wants to kill for you. Why he wants to burn down the world to keep you safe. He's still on parole, ain't he," he bites out. "Bet he don't care about that either. Bet he'll go to jail for you too, if it means he gets to kill whoever looks your way."

My heart twists in my chest and I struggle under him. "Stop… stop calling him an asshole. My husband is *not* an asshole."

His chest swells with a breath, and a second later, his weight disappears, and I'm being pulled off the ground. He flips me and puts me on my knees and I finally face my attacker. Just like any other guest at the wedding earlier, he's wearing a suit, black pants, black jacket. But other than his stature, which is larger than that of any other man at the wedding, the one thing that sets him apart and makes him so scary is the mask he has on.

The mask of a bull with horns.

My belly quivers at the sight of it, and I have to pace my breaths so as not to pass out with fear. And Lord, anticipation. He dips his face and I watch his lips move. "You're a mouthy one, aren't you?" He grips my hair and pulls at it, stretching my neck. "Let's see what else this pouty little mouth is good for. You made me watch you walk down the aisle in that dress with a fuckin' hard-on from hell, didn't you? So how about you put your mouth on my pissed-off cock and soothe it like your life depends on it. Like you were fuckin' born to do. Fuckin' take me out."

He jerks me forward, but I put my hands on his tree trunk thighs and stop him. I look up at him and whisper, "Please just… Don't come in my mouth."

I watch his stubbled jaw clench and I swear his pitch-black eyes narrow behind the mask. His grip in my hair turns even more brutal as he growls, "How about you let me give all the orders while you focus on followin' them? You wanna get out of here, don't you? You want your husband." I nod quickly. "So then, you do what God intended for you to do with your cocksucking mouth and fuckin' suck my cock and let *me* worry about where to put my cum."

With the way he's breathing, I don't think any more pleading will turn out well. His frame is jerking with his violent breaths, and I can see he keeps clenching his jaw, as if it's getting painful now to wait. It's better for me if I give him what he wants so I can finally meet my husband.

So I get to work. I unzip his pants and take him out. He's so big and thick. He's leaking, angry and ruddy. I can see why he'd be pissed off about it. I bet that thing is painful. So with my knees digging into the dirt, I lean forward and put my mouth on him. And then I suck like he said he wants me to. Like my life depends on it. Like God made me for this, and it's my job to be on my knees in front of him, servicing him, soothing him, sucking his cock.

Which means I don't give him a chance to force me to take him deeper because I get there first. I take him deeper and deeper with every suck until instead of my mouth, he's fucking my throat. And instead of standing there all tall and stoic, he's thrown his head back and he's shuddering with every pull of my mouth. When his thighs tense and it looks like he's going to come, he jerks me off his cock by my hair and flips me around. My knees and hands hit the ground again, the dirt and gravel somehow making me even dizzier than before.

Dizzier, more scared. More turned on. I shouldn't be, not at this, but I can't help it. I'm never ever able to help these things.

I feel him flip up my long skirt and get to my panties. He lowers them but doesn't take them off all the way. He leaves the elastic digging into my thighs as he lines up his cock, all lubed up with my spit and his own pre-cum, to my hole when he leans over my back, mounting me, and rasps, "You wanted me to come in your college girl snatch, didn't you?" I nod, clenching my eyes shut. "So then don't let it be said I never gave you nothin'."

With that, he slams inside of me, and I moan the loudest I've ever moaned. Even though he's so big like this, taking me from behind, it's still not a howl of pain. It's because of how turned on I am and how his pelvis bounces against my meaty ass.

In fact, the pain helps. The pain of his invasion, of his brutal thrusts and his grip on my hips makes everything even more glorious. The only downside is I can't pretend anymore. I can't keep up the game. His cock, like his voice, is like a truth serum, and I can't pretend I was running from him. And that I didn't want to be caught.

I wanted to be.

If he's the one catching me, I never ever want to get away.

"Oh God, you're so…" I whimper, all pretenses gone.

"Big," he finishes in my ear.

"Yes."

"That's 'cause of six months of fuckin' you and you're still so small."

I'm back to fisting the dirt again, feeling him throb inside of me. "I f-feel you…"

"In your belly, don't you?"

"I don't… It's too much. Like this."

"By the time I am done with you, darlin', you are gonna feel me in your throat, yeah? So quit your whining and take it like the sweet little wife you are," my husband says, and I moan.

He fucks me like the bull he is. So fast and hard, as if racing to the finish line. And I guess he is because I did make him watch me walk down the aisle in this dress. That I bought specifically for him. I knew it would drive him crazy and make him mad. And I wanted him to be mad so we could do this. So he could chase me through the woods in his mask. My savior from so long ago. A danger to others but a safe harbor for me. When he chases me through the woods, I feel so safe and free.

So alive.

Not as alive as I feel right now, however. With him pounding into me, fucking me, owning me, possessing every inch of who I am. When I'm close to coming, something he can feel, he pulls me up. He plasters my back to his chest, his hips still going, and I grab his horns and hold on.

"Tell me," he whispers in my ear again like he's taken to doing these days.

Not always, though. Just when things get hard for him. When he remembers how they took me from him and how he hurt me so badly that he almost lost me. So even though it's hard for me to focus with my channel pulsing over his length, I reply, "I am y-yours."

"And who am I?"

"Mine."

"Tell me your name."

"R-reverie."

"Like a daydream, yeah?"

"Your dream."

"And what's my name, darlin'?"

"Arsen," I moan out. "Like my f-fire."

That's all the answers I can give him because saying his name is like magic and I go over the edge. I come around his cock, my orgasm triggering his, and I feel him coming inside of me, his cock jerking and pulsing, shooting his cum. Not into a condom but into me, bare and raw. Because I wanted it.

I wanted it as my wedding present. Apart from this chase through the woods.

Five months ago, we moved back to Black Rock. I found a volunteer position at a local shelter, and when the fall came, I transferred to a college in town. Even though life has been good, living in the barn with the man I love, being accepted into a family that I found instead of the one I was born into, I wanted our life to start as soon as possible.

Which is why when one day he mentioned he'd marry me once his parole was over, I put my foot down. I told him I didn't want to wait that long. I'd already been waiting for him to ask me all proper-like and marry me for real this time for months now, so there was no way I was waiting for almost two years. So he gave in.

But then he said we had to at least wait until I finished college to start a family. By then, his new ranch—the one he bought for

Rosie way back when—and his horse-breaking business would be running smoothly too. I put my foot down harder.

So here we are, married and trying for a baby.

When we come down from the high, he gently lowers me onto the ground and turns me over. He covers me with his body, and taking his mask off, puts his mouth on mine. He gives me gentle kisses, as gentle as our lovemaking was hard.

"Hey," I whisper, opening my eyes.

His dark eyes are filled with concern. "You okay?"

"Uh-huh."

"That wasn't too rough?"

I throw him a blissful smile. "It was perfect."

He watches me smile for a moment before coming down for another lazy, cozy kiss. When that's over, it's my turn to ask, "Are *you* okay?"

His features tighten a bit, but then he says, "Yeah."

I cup his jaw. "The wedding wasn't too much for you?"

He swallows. "In the beginning."

"But then?"

He licks his lips, traces my face with his pitch-black eyes. "Then I saw you walk down the aisle, lookin' like a dream, and I forgot everythin' else. The world could be on fire and I wouldn't have noticed."

I smile again, relieved. Even though at my insistence he's seeing someone about his PTSD, I was worried about him in the crowd. When he proposed to me one night, by his favorite creek—he got me a ring and got down on his knee and everything—I told him that I didn't want a big wedding, just him and me with his family would work. But he said he'd already done that once. He'd already ruined my special day and colored it with blood so he was going to do this right. And if it meant learning more breathing exercises and suffering through a few hours of being in a crowd, he'd do it.

He's crazy that way, my husband.

But the ceremony was beautiful. All of his family was there, along with all the ranch hands. Rad was his best man, and obviously, Peyton was my maid of honor. But the most memorable part was my husband standing at the end of the aisle, wearing a suit that fit him like a glove and his brown Stetson. I don't think there's another man anywhere who's more handsome than Arsen.

I wind my arms around his neck and give him a peck on his jaw. "Are you trying to sweet-talk me?"

"Depends." He kisses me back. "Is it workin'?"

"Yeah. For a hardened cowboy with a record, you're a fast learner."

"What can I say, that's because for a naive little college girl, you're a good teacher."

"I love you."

"You're my life," he says, and I love that more than those three words because it's his way of declaring his love for me. And only he knows how to love me right.

"Happy wedding day, husband," I whisper, smiling.

He hums and kisses me again. Softly, gently. Until I run out of heartbeats and breath. But I'm still able to say, "Till death do us part."

He stares at me a beat before rasping, "Nah, not even then. Because even death can't tear me apart from my wife."

ACKNOWLEDGMENTS

I have so many people to thank who made this book possible. First and foremost, my agent, Josi Beck. She believed in me and found me at a time when I'd lost all faith in myself. Thank you for taking this book places. My editor, Sabrina Flemming, for her immense enthusiasm for my cowboys and her absolute faith in my ability to pull off something different. Thank you for giving my book a home with Forever. My husband, who is my heart and soul. Without him, I wouldn't be here at all. Thank you for all the plot twists and your unconditional love. My baby girl, Adora, who doesn't yet know how much I love her, but I hope when she looks back, these books will help her understand how immensely she impacted and changed my life. To my team, Christina Santos, Cass Thomasson, and Breanne Landers, for always having my back and getting me through difficult times. Thank you for not letting my ship sink when I'm in my deadline mode and forget everything else. And finally, my readers, for waiting for my books and showing up for me time and time again. Thank you for inviting me and my words into your life.

LETTER TO READERS

Dear Readers,

Thank you so much for reading Arsenal and Reverie's story. When I thought of Reverie, shy and bookish, struggling with body image issues but also so strong in her own way, I knew only a man like Arsenal would be a perfect fit for her. An ex-convict, he is hard and jaded but with so much love to give. He needs her quiet strength to calm the chaos in his soul. And Reverie deserves a man who's willing to do anything for the woman he loves.

It was such a fun experience writing this dark romance where boundaries are pushed and morally gray characters make you feel every range of emotion. That is always my wish with every book I write, and this book takes that to a whole next level. Plus, this is a brand-new series, and coming up with a whole new world of characters and their connections with one another is my favorite thing to do. I hope you found some of your favorites and are curious to know about their stories. But more than that, I hope you stick around for our stalker (and masked!) Radisson King and his obsession with Peyton Turner.

I also want to give a special thank-you to the fans in the list that follows, who have given their support for Branded.

Xoxo,
Saffron

Taylor Schuebel
Crystal Ingle
Laura Kavolius
Vanessa Miericke
Ashlie Barnes
Kirstin Garrison
Kamila Mykhailiuk
Kaitlyn Rider
Rabia Ali
Pamella Robinson
Emily Wilson
Jasmine Davey
Erin Mickey
Geniene Sadler
Diana Nguyen
Janessa England
Kenzy Rivers
Rosio Tapia
Yesaira Garcia
Joyce Watts
Rochelle Strzykalski
Emily Stellmar
Rachel Guzan
Mikayla Baca
Aleena Raja

Paola Matos-Labarca
Amy Lysne
Michelle Hughes
Rachel @rachellynnreadss
Briceida Rios
Eli Shah
Rabia Ali
april moreno
Stacy Castillo
Cathy Tighilt
Yaz Stone
Charlene Wilks
Kelly Amann
Elizabeth Eversen
Carolena Wilks
Amy Wendt
Ashley Moniz
Amanda Steckler
Rebecca Santos
Brittany Heller
Jillian Jamrozik
Cierra Hodge
Isha Nanda
Millie Benitez
Dawn Craycraft

ABOUT THE AUTHOR

Saffron A. Kent is a *USA Today* bestselling author of steamy, new adult romance, including *The Unrequited* and *Medicine Man*. She has an MFA in Creative Writing; and she lives in New York City with her nerdy and supportive husband, her daughter, and a million and one books.

Find out more at:

TheSaffronKent.com

TikTok @AuthorSaffronAKent

Instagram @TheSaffronKent

Facebook.com/TheSaffronKent

RAISING READERS
Books Build Bright Futures

Thank you for reading this book and for being a reader of books in general. As an author, I am so grateful to share being part of a community of readers with you, and I hope you will join me in passing our love of books on to the next generation of readers.

Did you know that reading for enjoyment is the single biggest predictor of a child's future happiness and success?

More than family circumstances, parents' educational background, or income, reading impacts a child's future academic performance, emotional well-being, communication skills, economic security, ambition, and happiness.

Studies show that kids reading for enjoyment in the US is in rapid decline:

- In 2012, 53% of 9-year-olds read almost every day. Just 10 years later, in 2022, the number had fallen to 39%.
- In 2012, 27% of 13-year-olds read for fun daily. By 2023, that number was just 14%.

Together, we can commit to **Raising Readers** and change this trend. How?

- Read to children in your life daily.
- Model reading as a fun activity.
- Reduce screen time.
- Start a family, school, or community book club.
- Visit bookstores and libraries regularly.
- Listen to audiobooks.
- Read the book before you see the movie.
- Encourage your child to read aloud to a pet or stuffed animal.
- Give books as gifts.
- Donate books to families and communities in need.

BOB1217

Books build bright futures, and **Raising Readers** is our shared responsibility.

For more information, visit **JoinRaisingReaders.com**

Sources: National Endowment for the Arts, National Assessment of Educational Progress, WorldBookDay.org, Nielsen BookData's 2023 "Understanding the Children's Book Consumer"